Dedalus Original Fi〔

MAPPAℕ

Christopher Harris was born i
ing school he studied art brieﬂy, ⸻
Later, he studied biology, and taught science for several years.
These jobs were interrupted by journeys to Italy, Greece and
Turkey, where he researched the background to the Byzan-
tine Trilogy: *Theodore*, (2000) *False Ambassador*, (2001) and
Memoirs of a Byzantine Eunuch (2002).

He now writes full-time and divides his time between his
homes in Birmingham and France. He is currently writing a
novel about Pelagius, a British heretic.

Christopher Harris

Mappamundi

Dedalus

Published in the UK by Dedalus Limited
24–26, St Judith's Lane, Sawtry, Cambs, PE28 5XE
email: info@dedalusbooks.com
www.dedalusbooks.com

ISBN 978 1 903517 77 2

Dedalus is distributed in the USA by SCB Distributors,
15608 South New Century Drive, Gardena, CA 90248
email: info@scbdistributors.com   web site: www.scbdistributors.com

Dedalus is distributed in Australia by Peribo Pty Ltd.
58, Beaumont Road, Mount Kuring-gai, N.S.W. 2080
email: info@peribo.com.au

Dedalus is distributed in Canada by Disticor Direct-Book Division
695, Westney Road South, Suite 14, Ajax, Ontario, LI6 6M9
email: ndalton@disticor.com   web site: www.disticordirect.com

First published by Dedalus in 2009
Mappamundi copyright © *Christopher Harris 2009*

Printed in Finland by WS. Bookwell
Typeset by RefineCatch Limited, Bungay, Suffolk

Part 1: Christendom

August 15th, 1464

It was a good thing that the pope died at Ancona. Not that I didn't like His Holiness. I counted him a friend, even though he made me serve him and never gave me the indulgence he promised. No doubt he would have freed and pardoned me eventually, had he lived. I liked the pope, and wished him no harm. It was the place of his dying that was a good thing, and the time, not the death itself. Had he died at Rome I might never have got away. Had he crossed the sea and begun his great venture we might all have been slaughtered by the Turks. And, having been nearly killed by the Turks already, that was something I was keen to avoid. So dying at Ancona was the best thing His Holiness could have done.

Even before Pope Pius died, his plans were falling apart. The rabble he called a crusade had mostly gone back to where they came from. As soon as they heard the sad news, the papal courtiers did the same, heading back to Rome before a new pope could be chosen. Pius's closest retainers stayed with his body, but only so that they could pilfer his belongings. How they must have wished he had died in the Vatican, where they could have looted his private apartments! In Ancona, in that bare room in a borrowed palace, there was little to steal. Even so, I knew I must take something to fund my escape.

The low-vaulted room was dimly lit. There was a lamp at the bedside, a few guttering candles elsewhere. A couple of servants attended to the pope's body, furtively searching him while they laid his limbs straight. Others were going through his baggage, turning out clothes and vestments, stripping them of embroidery or cloth of gold. I quickly looked around. On a table near the pope's deathbed was the book I had been reading to him, a new translation of Plato's *Timaeus*. In the rush to grab something of value it had been ignored by everyone. I was surprised that Patrizzi, the pope's secretary, had not taken it, as he resented the service I did for his friend and master. All the way to Ancona I had been reading bits of the book at the pope's bedside, so I knew it was as dull as anything of that sort could be. But it was neatly written in the fancy Italian style, and would bring me a good price from the right buyer. I have sold books before, and travelled far on the proceeds. It is just a matter of luck, of finding a wise fool who will pay well for what he cannot understand.

I picked the book up and slipped it under my tunic, and in doing so, saw something even more valuable. There, on the table, concealed by the book, was the Fisherman's Ring, the symbol of the pope's office, the seal Pius used on all his letters and pronouncements. His fingers were so bent and swollen that he could not wear the ring. It had been hung round his neck on a silken cord, but towards the end his skin was so inflamed that he could not bear the cord, and had begged his secretary to remove it. Even Patrizzi was not so haughty as to actually wear the pope's ring, so he must have put it down after sealing a letter, then forgotten about it.

Without thinking what I was doing, I slipped the ring onto my finger, turning it so that the seal of St Peter faced inwards. There are old tales about rings and their power. They can cure wounds, grant wishes, make a man invisible, let him assume the shape of any creature, render the speech of birds and beasts intelligible. Maybe it was the strangeness of the moment, with the Vicar of Christ dead in bed nearby, or the pleasure I got from taking those things before Patrizzi did: whatever the reason, I felt transformed by the ring, filled with confidence and power. I knew what to do and how to do it. The ring would help me to escape. It would get me to England, where I would settle, leave my past behind, and make something of myself.

There was a desk in the next room, with pens and parchment, and ink ready mixed, and letters half-written and laid out for finishing. Nearby was a leather bag for documents, stamped with the crossed keys and triple crown of the pope's crest. I chose an unfinished letter that began with a long preamble from His Holiness, then, as neatly as I could, wrote some lines telling all who read them to give assistance to one Tommaso d'Ancona, wherever he might pass, and whatever he might require. That is not my real name. I am Thomas Deerham, bastard son of an English soldier who caused no end of trouble with his lies and deceptions. I have tried to be more honest than he was, especially in this account of my adventures. If I have used false names or worn disguises, it was because someone made me, or because it was necessary. And my escape from Ancona was absolutely necessary. As I melted red wax onto a corner of the letter and pressed the ring into it, I felt rather pleased with myself, and with my new name.

I heard wailing from the next room. Others had arrived, more servants and hangers-on, competing in grief with those who had watched the pope die. Soon the bishop's palace would be full of scavengers. It was too late to return the Fisherman's Ring. I slipped it back on my finger, and looked around for something else to steal. All I could see was a silk cloth artfully painted to show the countries of the world. The pope had been studying it in his bed, looking at the lands lost to the Saracens, dreaming of leading an army to reconquer them. We all have our dreams, and if it would have taken a miracle to get the pope on his feet again and fit enough to lead an army, then who but a pope is most likely to be granted such a miracle? But there was no miracle. His illness took its course, and took his life. And I took the map. It folded up small and went into the leather messenger's bag, along with the book I had taken earlier.

So, there I was, with the book, the ring and the map, dressed in the fine livery of a papal servant, armed with a false name and passport, ready to make my escape into the warm Italian night. All the stories I've ever been told begin in such a way, with the hero setting off on some quest or other, about to make his way through the world, beset by troubles and difficulties. Well, I am no hero, and I intended no quest. All I wanted was to get back to England, to find me a good wife and a soft bed and a dry roof, to settle in some quiet corner and never venture out

9

of it. I'd been everywhere, or so I thought. The only place I wanted to go was home. I thought I had earned a few comforts, after the life I'd had. But philosophers tell us that the Wheel of Fortune never stops turning. It rolls onward, raising some men high, crushing others, dragging most of us behind it like dogs tied to a wagon. As for my luck, you can judge for yourself. This is no story. It is what really happened.

Turin

All through Italy my fake passport got me lodgings and horses, and I travelled faster than the news of the pope's death. I had not ridden for years, not since I took ship to Constantinople, to help defend that city against the Turks. We fought that great battle on foot, were defeated on foot, and fled on foot. Ever since then I had walked, trudged, crept and knelt, looking up at others, knowing my place by the weariness in my legs. It was good to feel a horse beneath me, to thunder over flat ground, the trees rushing past as though driven by a great wind. I felt like a man again, not like the fawning, grovelling creature I had been.

In Savoy, before going on, I took a good look at the mappamundi. England was an irregular shape on the northwest edge of the map. There was not much detail: a flag or two, a castle, some stippling. But I knew that home was there somewhere, and if I followed the mappamundi I would find it. Ahead of me the map showed mountains, marked in jagged brown. And beyond them was France, where I had fought as a boy soldier, where I learned to kill and rob. Since then, the French had risen up and driven the English out. My false name and passport would not protect me, as the French hated Pope Pius as much as they hated the English. They had defied his authority, and he had annoyed them by not supporting Duke René of Anjou as king of Naples. And the Cardinal of Arras, having fallen out with Pius in Rome, had gone back to his country to stir up more trouble. It could not be long before the remaining cardinals elected a new pope, but that would not help me. I folded the mappamundi away, knowing what I had to do.

In Turin, I found a quarter where old clothes hung from the eaves, festooned the windows, and were piled up on trestles in front of every shop. I wanted to exchange my papal livery for something plainer, but it was not easy. Old-clothes men, wearing half their stock, strolled the street like actors advertising their next performance. Others, from behind their trestles, eyed me up, pricing what I wore, wondering how much they could get out of me. The merchants were proud of their trade, and imagined me to be a man of substance. They offered me their most expensive garments, holding up fine doublets for dashing gentlemen, fancy hats to keep the sun out of my eyes, and long-toed shoes only fit for preening popinjays. When I declined them, they offered winter cloaks, sturdy boots, even clothes for women, all as good as new, or so their vendors claimed.

There is way of dealing with merchants, of getting what you want from them at a price you are willing to pay, but I am not practised in it. One of them, a dark man with a long beard, caught me like a fish and gently played me in.

"Every garment tells a story," he said, stepping into my path. He stroked the sprigged velvet gown he wore. "Your clothes tell me that you are servant of the pope. But your face tells me that you are not happy with your station. Perhaps you are trying to escape, to make your way to somewhere congenial. Am I right? I thought so. What can I do for you?"

His face was sad and wise, and I felt that I could trust him, though I knew that I could not. "I want to exchange these clothes," I said. "For something plainer."

"I might find you something," he said. "But a suit of clothes like yours . . ." He frowned at my tunic, which boldly bore the crest of Pope Pius, his four golden crescents on a blue cross, beneath the crossed keys and crown.

"The papal court wears nothing but the best," I said.

"Of course. Come into my shop and I'll see what I can do."

He examined my clothes, muttered to himself, rummaged through some chests and sacks, then held up a threadbare doublet and some much-patched hose. "For what you are wearing," he said, "I will give you these."

"But that's not a complete outfit. Surely you can give me more?"

"There's no market for clothes like yours. Maybe in Rome,

but not here. And further north it will be worse. They are no friends of your master in France."

"I know. That is why I want new clothes."

"Don't you have some money, or something you can sell?"

"No." In fact, I had a few gold coins hidden about me, but I meant to keep them.

"What about that ring?"

I clenched my fist, feeling the ring's big seal against my palm. It had proved useless. I had not dared show it to anyone, and it had brought me no advantage. There was no magic in it. What power it had could only be released by someone who knew how. I opened my hand so that the merchant could see the seal. Then I slipped the ring from my finger and held it out to him. Greed flashed for a moment in his eyes, then he mastered himself and looked at my offering with a mixture of gloom and contempt.

"I don't know," he said, taking the ring and weighing it in his palm. "I am no goldsmith, but there might be an ounce or so of gold in this ring."

"Is that all?"

"We will take it to my friend. He will tell us what the ring is worth, and I will pay you accordingly."

"You would weigh it? That's not just a lump of gold. Have you looked at the emblem on it?"

The merchant raised the ring to his face and peered at it.

"The ring of Saint Peter. The first of your popes. Now there was a man who was much misunderstood. A Jew, and the follower of a Jew, who sold the gentiles a new religion. He was the greatest merchant of them all. As I say, a Jew like me, but claimed by you Christians as one of yourselves."

"I claim nothing. I just want what the ring is worth."

"Who can say what a ring like this is worth? There are stories, but what do they tell us? Solomon, for all his wisdom, was nothing without his ring. That was a magic ring, stolen from him by a demon. Deprived of it, Solomon wandered the world like beggar, telling everyone how he had once been king. And do you know why he lost the ring?"

"How should I know?"

"God punished him. The king had sinned, grown too fond of worldly things, so God deprived him of them until he regained his wisdom and was worthy to be king again."

The merchant was playing with me. He had guessed my needs and knew he would supply them. "How much would you pay me?"

"That depends," he said. "What do we know of this ring? If I was as wise as Solomon, I might know its value. What powers does it have? Was it stolen? Are you, perhaps, a demon? Are there goats' feet hidden in your shoes, black wings folded tightly beneath that fine tunic of yours?"

"I am a man like you."

"Like me?" the merchant smiled sadly. "You concede that much? You do not despise me like others of your faith?"

"I have travelled in the East. I respect men of all faiths, if they treat me fairly. And that ring could be worth a fortune to someone who knew how to use it."

"A fortune!" The merchant shrugged. "If only I had such a fortune." He looked at the ring again. "For this ring I will fit you out like a gentleman, and not just with clothes. My friend the armourer will find you weapons . . ."

"I do not wish to dress as a gentleman, or bear arms like one. I need a modest costume and the money to continue my journey."

The old-clothes man kitted me out in underclothing of linen, a sombre grey doublet with dark red trim, and grey hose, none of them too musty. He found me some good boots that fitted me quite well, and I chose a grey cloak to cover myself. I did not need the cloak in the August heat, but the mountains were not far off, and the weather would be colder by the time I reached England. He tried to sell me a fancy hat with plumes and flounces, saying that a good merchant would wear something to show off his wealth, but I declined it and chose a beaver hat such as Englishmen had worn when I was young.

I wanted no signs or symbols in my clothing, no colours to show allegiance, or emblems to show my place of origin. I wanted to look like a merchant, a sober man of business who does not leave home without good reason. And, if the need arose I could wrap myself in my grey cloak and seem whatever I wanted to seem.

I have travelled as a merchant before: it is a safe guise, as long as you do not look too prosperous. Merchants pass everywhere without attracting much attention, unless they are carrying gold, or valuable goods. And if they are foreign, as merchants often are, no one expects them to abide by all the customs of the country.

In that guise I could not carry a sword, but I chose a good long knife that I could hide under my coat. With a blade like that, as I knew from bitter experience, I could kill a man as easily as with a two-handed sword.

Paris

Solitary travellers often despair. The road is hard. One place seems much like another. The company of inns and taverns is no company at all. No one can be trusted. Arriving at each place, it can be hard to make the simplest decision. I had the feeling that I was being followed. I often turned from my path and waited to see who passed. Sometimes I sat in tavern corners to see who came in after me. As it happened, I did have a pursuer, but he was not following me so closely. I was in more danger from the brigands: flayers, they were called. I knew their ways. I had been one of them. I shuddered at the things I had done in the cold winters of my youth. I had been forced into it, but could not deny to myself that I had robbed and pillaged with the worst of them. Did such things still happen now that the English had been driven from France? I feared to travel alone, yet dared not join a group. I regretted the Fisherman's Ring. What did I have without it? Old clothes, a dull book, a passport that brought me no benefits. Only the mappamundi gave me solace. After losing the pope's ring, I thought of that painted cloth as a sort of talisman. Its signs and marks had been laid out by a great scholar, who was skilled in astrology, as well as cosmography. I could not help feeling that the mappamundi was magical and had the power to guide me. Whenever I got the chance I spread it out, and looked at all the countries it showed, the oceans, forests, cities and wildernesses, glad that home, when I found it, would be safe on the world's edge.

By one means or another, using various names, speaking different languages, I went north, through Savoy, Burgundy and France, until I reached Paris.

It was evening, and the city rose all around me, its spires and turrets gilded by the setting sun, its alleys already in twilit gloom. The river stank, and so did the streets. On the other bank there was nothing but churches, and I was no pilgrim. I hesitated, brought low by the travellers' malaise. What should I do? Where should I go? I wanted to unfold the mappamundi and gaze at it. But, in that bustling city of strangers, I dared not open my bag.

I stood by the Petit-Pont, listening to passers-by, tuning my ear to their speech. The city grew dark while I waited. Old men dragged their chairs inside and shut their doors. Water-front hawkers stopped crying their wares. Boys ran home with loaves under their arms. The shops on the bridge closed, and linkmen lit braziers at each end. The crowds thinned. The curfew bells rang, but I had nowhere to go.

Nearby, a man was pacing back and forth by the stone wall that topped the riverbank. Several times, while I watched, he climbed onto the parapet, as though he intended to jump off. But each time he thought better of it and climbed down.

There is nothing like another's suffering to bring cheer to the miserable, and there was a poor fellow worse off than me. I was about to go over to him, to offer him a kind word, but before I could do so I felt a tugging at my cloak. I turned, but the heavy cloth was thrown over my head, rendering me blind. Then I felt a blow to my head, and I pitched forward helplessly.

I struggled with the cloak, trying to free myself, from its mud-soaked folds. I heard someone shouting in villainous French.

"You stinking dunghill dogs!" the voice called out. "You poxy sons of drunken whores! I'll shove you back up your mother's cunts if I ever catch you."

I got to my feet and looked around. The man I had been watching sat sprawled in the dirt, shaking his fist, flinging elaborate insults into the darkness. He was so eloquent that I forgot my plight. It was only when he fell silent that I realised that my bag, containing everything I owned, was gone. I must have said something, though I don't know what. Perhaps I gave myself away by cursing.

"You clumsy oaf," the man said, speaking my own lan-guage. He got to his feet and lurched towards me, brushing

17

himself down. "You fucking Goddam! I'm covered in shit now. What d'you mean, knocking me down like that?"

"Me? They knocked me down too. Look at the state of me." I held out my muddy cloak so he could see it in the light from the brazier. "And they robbed me too." He stepped nearer, and I saw that he wore the grey habit and cord belt of a Franciscan. Filthy in person and foul of tongue, he was a friar.

He must have seen my puzzlement. "I expect you are surprised," he said, "to hear one such as me speak like a scoundrel."

"Not me, brother. I know very well that monks and friars are just as likely to be scoundrels as the rest of us."

Pope Pius himself used to say that friars desire nothing so little as virtue. But they are usually careful to cover up their true natures. So what had this friar done, who had the ear of God, and could extort the aid of man, that might drive him to end his own life?

"I have my reasons," he said, "for speaking as I did."

"Anger is a sin." The chance to reproach a friar could not be missed.

"It is, and I am sorry for it."

"So is despair."

"It is not the worst sin."

"You were going to throw yourself into the water," I said.

"Was I?" The friar drew back. "Were you watching me?"

"I was," I said. "Why would a friar like you want to do that?"

"Why indeed? That's a good question. But why should I carry on living? Life has been unkind, throwing misfortunes at me like a fishwife clearing her stall at the end of a market day. Perhaps you are a fortunate man?"

"Me! Fortunate? I think not. I have just been robbed."

The friar peered at me, trying to make out my face in the firelight. He was a small man, thin and stooped, and the friar's habit was too big for him. Perhaps he was so old and useless that his brothers had thrown him out.

"What did they take?" he said.

"Everything I own."

"You're like me, then. A man with nothing."

Was the friar a decoy, a thief's accomplice? I felt inside my doublet. The knife was still there. I reached for it, making the gesture obvious. "I want my things back. And revenge, if I catch the thief."

He wasn't scared. "You're right," he said. "Revenge is good. What a fool I was to think of jumping! I haven't had a drink all day. When I leave this life, I certainly won't do it sober."

"Who robbed me?"

"I don't know," he said. "But I might be able to find out."

"How?"

"What we need," he said, "is some wine." He reached out, unsteadily, taking my arm. "Come with me."

I was reluctant. I wanted to chase the men who had stolen my bag. But what chance did I have in a strange city?

"You will have to pay," I said. "Everything I owned has been stolen."

"I am sure you must have a little something about you. The wise traveller always does."

I wasn't admitting anything. "Not me."

"Oh well. There are still one or two places where my credit is good."

Why would a man who could get drink on credit kill himself? And who would give credit, or anything, to a friar? He led me away from the bridge, along an alley to a door set deep in a high wall.

"Watch yourself," he said. "And if you say anything, speak French." He was careful to pull his hood round his face before we went in. I was wary too, as I did have some money hidden inside my doublet.

It was a low sort of place, hardly a tavern at all, more like a village alehouse where men drank until they dropped and were lucky not to be pissed on by the men who were still standing. The friar hailed a potboy, sent him for a pint of wine, and settled us in a corner, out of earshot of the few other drinkers. He sat with his back to the others, and looked down at the straw-strewn floor when the potboy came with the wine.

"The good wine of Gascony," he said, raising the jug. It was sour stuff, not much better than vinegar, but that is what you get when you drink wine in September, before the new vintage is in. We took our turns with it until our thirst was quenched, then the friar ordered another. "I haven't had enough of this lately," he said. "I suppose we'd be pushing our luck to try and get some food?"

"If your credit is good for it." Food was far from my thoughts, and I paid little attention to his question, though I ought to have been alerted to our true condition by his wheedling tone. "You said you'd help me," I reminded him. "I want my bag back, and everything in it. You said you could find the thieves. Or are there too many of them in Paris?"

"The French are a larcenous race, I'll grant you that. But the cause, I think, is the example set for us by the English. Your countrymen stole everything they could while they attempted to rule us. I take it you are English, despite those Italian clothes?"

"My father was English, my mother Gascon."

"I'm not sure which is worse."

"Neither am I." I have no reason to be grateful to my parents, and the friar must have heard that in my voice. He looked at me curiously, and I saw that he was not as old as I had thought. I guessed he was a score of years younger than my half-century, a young man, broken by ill-health or bad luck.

"Perhaps you Goddams are not all bad." He did not sound as though he believed it. "This bag," he said, "what did it look like?"

"It is about this big," I said, holding out my hands to show him, "of red leather, with a crest stamped on the flap."

"A crest? Whose?"

I hesitated. "The pope's."

"You must be an important fellow to carry a bag like that."

His tone was sly. I could tell he thought I had stolen the bag, that I was no better than the Frenchmen who had taken it from me. I was about to tell him that I had counted the pope as my friend, that I had served his Holiness loyally. Then I remembered that I had stolen the bag, and its contents.

"I'm just a merchant," I said, "on my way home. There are some documents in the bag, which I'd like to have back."

"Valuable ones?"

"Only to me."

He asked me questions, tried to find out my business, but I was careful not to say too much. Friars are as bad as priests. They pry your secrets out of you, then beg a coin or two for having heard your confession. If you don't pay they threaten you with eternal damnation, or with revealing your sins to all within earshot. After all, if you haven't paid, it's not a true confession, and the confessor isn't bound by the seal of secrecy. It is best to keep your sins to yourself, unless you really are confessing, and even then it's best to keep a few back.

"What about my bag?" I said. "Do you know who's stolen it?"

"I know who the thieves are in this quarter."

"Are they friends of yours?"

He sighed. "I have no friends. I am a dead man."

There was nothing ghostly about him. He stank. He might have been a walking corpse. I drew back. "You carry the plague?"

"No. I spoke metaphorically."

"Then talk straight, and take me to these thieves."

"Nothing can be done tonight," he said. "But in the morning, when the sun is shining, everything will look different." He looked around the room. "Now we must sleep."

"Where?"

"I know a place." He stood up and tottered towards the door. I followed him, no steadier.

"You there . . ." A big man in a leather apron was bearing down on us.

"Run!" the friar said. And I did, but the door was bolted. We both seized the bar together and tried to draw it. But men grabbed us from behind and threw us to the floor. I went for my knife but kicks stopped me, and more kicks hit my legs and arms, and would have hit my cod and yard if I hadn't curled up to protect myself. I could hear the friar wailing, but they were kicking me, not him. They shouted at us, and the friar whined and wheedled, and they kicked me again. The friar called out, threatening God's vengeance on men who were too mean to give alms to a mendicant. The men spat on him, then threw us out into the alley.

I heard the door slam, and fell forward into the foul ooze that fills all Paris as though the city was built on a dunghill. The friar was still wailing. I stood and reached out for him, dragging him by his cord belt until we were out of the alley and back at the riverside. We seemed to be alone. Were there no watchmen in Paris?

"Why did you do that?" I said, flinging him down by a brazier. The light from its coals made his face look devilish.

"It was my last chance," he said, half sitting up. "And I took it. No one will give me credit now. But at least we have had our wine."

"And paid for it in blows."

"Cheap at the price," he said. "I have often paid more."

"You didn't pay much tonight. You kept clear of the beating."

He shuffled backwards. "I can assure you I was hit too."

His tone angered me more than the beating I had just had. Everything they said about friars was true. I reached into my doublet and pulled out my knife. He saw the blade flash in the firelight. "A weapon!" he said. "A fine one, I am sure, for a man like you."

"It will do the job." But I was not sure what the job would be. Was the friar a drunken fool, a useless scrounger, a thief's decoy, or the only man in Paris who could help me?

While I hesitated he leapt to his feet and pulled out a blade of his own.

"Do friars carry knives, now?"

"I have to eat," he said, edging away from me. "To cut my bread, like anyone else."

It was no bread knife. It was the long, slim blade of a back-street brawler. I was sure of it: he was in league with whoever robbed me. "Stop!" I said. "Drop your knife."

He stopped, and held his hand out limply, allowing the

blade to droop. Then he lunged at me, aiming for my heart. I didn't think he would be so quick, but I was ready for him. I parried the blow, knocked the blade out his hand, grabbed his arm and pulled him forward, then tripped him, flinging him against the river wall. Old soldiers never forget. Fighting is in their blood, even when they have not fought for years.

The friar hung over the wall, the same wall he had tried to jump from not long before. I held onto his leg, letting his body dangle over the edge. Holding him took no effort: he hardly weighed anything. No wonder he had wanted food.

"Poor François!" he whined. "You won't let go, will you?"

"Won't I?" I held my blade over him, making sure he could see its glint.

"Don't kill me." His voice was feeble. There was no fight left in him.

"You wanted to die."

"But not to be killed."

"What's the difference?"

"I had lost hope. I wanted to slip away from this life, to leave my sins and my old self behind, not to have the life ripped out of me by an Englishman's blade."

His words touched me. They expressed my own half-formed desires. I too wished to leave my sins and old self behind. And I did not wish to commit another sin by harming someone as helpless as him. I hauled him in, and let him sit against the wall.

"I am Thomas," I said.

"I am François."

"What made you lose hope?"

"I'm not meant to be here," he said. "I've been exiled."

"By your order?" it was not unusual for fallen friars to be thrown out by their brothers.

"No. By the king and parliament. If the king's men catch me, they'll hang me. I don't want my corpse strung up for idlers to gawp at. Why should the scum of Paris look down on me while they gaze up at the gallows? I don't want the flesh torn off my bones by crows and kites. Why should birds feed well when I'm half-starved? Where's the justice in that? I want to choose for myself: life or death. And if death, what kind."

I put my knife away, and his, tucking both into my belt, where I could get at them easily. I didn't realise it then, but I had done something significant. Whether it was a mistake or not, you may judge when you have read the rest of this story. By sparing François I made myself his keeper, and from then on I was no more able to get rid of him than if he'd been chained to me.

François

The moon was up, and the river looked like silver. I walked like a man in a dream, following François along the waterfront, down the empty streets of a city I did not know, past narrow houses and stinking privies and fine gates and shuttered windows and bolted doors. He dashed down a side street and I followed him. It was pitch dark, and slippery underfoot, and I still feared trickery, even though I had taken his weapon. I heard him heaving at a door, then he called to me.

"In here! It's quite safe. There's no one here but me."

I went in. It might have been a thieves' den, the lair of the very men who robbed me, but what choice did I have?

The room was as dark as the alley outside.

"Upstairs," he said, from the other side of the room. Then he climbed up a ladder, leaving me alone. There was nothing for it but to climb up after him, which I did as well as I could, my legs being stiff from all the beating and brawling I had been through. The upstairs room was empty. Moonlight pouring through a broken shutter showed me François and a heap of straw, nothing else.

That night I fought with myself for longer than I had fought with François. I regretted having pulled a knife on him. When in Rome I had resolved to leave violence behind me. I had killed too many men, and feared that I would kill again when roused to anger. So why was I carrying a knife, if I did not intend violence? It would have been folly not too. No traveller goes unarmed. I had already been robbed, and stood a good chance of being swindled by the friar. What other dangers faced me? There were always thieves on the road, and tricksters in every town. To travel unarmed would be to make myself a victim. But I was a victim anyway, and my knife had not saved me.

So my thoughts went, turning in circles like a creaking

cartwheel, until I felt François shaking me, and heard him urging me out of bed.

He was carrying a dark lantern, its side slid up to let out a glow.

"It's still night," I said.

"The bells have struck three."

"Let me lie," I said. "My legs are as stiff as stockfish."

"I have been out and made enquiries."

"Do you know who the thieves are?"

"Yes."

I sat up and rubbed my eyes. "Then lead me to them."

He wrapped himself in his long Franciscan cloak and set off. I hobbled after him, down the stairs and out into the alley. Raising the lantern to show me the way, he darted through a doorless archway, into a maze of passages and yards. We skirted little squares and hidden courts, passed shuttered shops, emerged into patches of wasteland, reached dead ends and doubled back, cut through half-wrecked houses, clambering in one window and out of another. Was he trying to confuse me?

I tripped on rough cobbles, squelched through mud and filth, got caught on brambles, hit my head on low lintels. Once we went through a graveyard where whores lurked, their painted faces like death's-heads in the light of a dying bonfire. François slowed down, as though he was tempted to linger, then he twitched and shuddered like a man forced to watch something that disgusted him. He rushed on and I struggled to keep up with him. For a short-winded runt he moved fast, and I knew that if I lost sight of his lantern I would never find my way back to the river, or out of the city.

He stopped, at a doorway that looked no different from any other, and asked for his knife back. "I may need it," he said, "if I am to help you."

"I'll come in with you. And if anyone needs to use a knife, I will."

"You'll get nothing if you come in. You must leave it to me. Describe the bag again. Tell me exactly what was in it. Then I'll know what I'm looking for and whether or not I've found it."

"How do I know you won't trick me?"

"I give you my word."

I had a good idea how little his word was worth, but he had turned things his way, making me the beggar, not him, giving me no choice. I told him what to look for then stood watch while he silently prised open a shutter and climbed through the window. What kind of friar knows where thieves are to be found, and how to burgle a house without making a sound?

I paced the cobbles, looking this way and that for the men I was sure would come for me. Would they be watchmen, shop-guards, or thieving cutthroats? Had François guessed I still had some gold on me? And why did I want the bag so much? Its contents were of doubtful value. I knew I could sell the book, and maybe the map, if I was desperate, but the money I might get for them would be no use if I got killed in a Paris backstreet. Did I value my memories of Pope Pius so much that I was prepared to take that risk? I held on to my knife, ready to defend myself from anyone, or to rush after François if I heard a noise from the house. But I heard nothing, and feared the lying friar had slipped out of a window and made off into the night.

I could smell baking bread. Soon the city would wake, shutters would be thrown open, the streets would fill, and I would be a man in a crowd.

François climbed out of the window so silently that the first I knew of it was the slap of his feet on the cobbles. Then, as though he had been holding his breath the whole time, he took in a slow, wheezing chestful of air.

"Is this it?" he said, opening his dark lantern so I could see what he offered me. It was my bag, and I reached into it, feeling the book and a wad of silky cloth that must have been the map. There was no time to see what condition they were in.

"My passport," I said. "It was stamped with the pope's seal. It's not here."

"It wouldn't be much use. We won't be presenting ourselves at the gates. We'll slip out of Paris unseen."

"How?"

François led me back to the river by a much shorter route than the one we took earlier. Perhaps it was a different stretch. I couldn't tell. We climbed down some stone steps to a wharf where fishing boats and barges were moored, and he leapt from one vessel to another as nimbly as a goat. When I caught up with him he was untying a small boat.

"You'll have to row," he said, as I got in beside him. "I'd like to help, but I've not been well." He settled himself in the bows, wrapping his cloak around him like a blanket. "Keep to the centre," he said. "That's where the channel is."

I was no waterman, and after the drubbing they gave me in the tavern my arms were so stiff that I could hardly row. I managed a few clumsy strokes to get us out into the middle, then the current caught us, and I only used the oars when I had to, fending off obstacles, or guiding the boat round the river's curves. François pulled his hood over his eyes and slept.

Paris slipped past, lit by the hazy moon. Mist rose, and curled around us, lapping the boat until the water was invisible. It was good to sit, though I had to be careful not to fall asleep. Now and then having forgotten François' advice to keep to the centre, I had to punt through shallows until the current caught us again. Soon we were free of the city. Stone gave way to mud and reeds, and sheep lay huddled in fields. The sun rose, and gradually drove off the watery chill. Herons stood silent on the banks, flapped off as we approached, then circled round and landed again.

François woke with a start and began coughing. His thin chest heaved, and his face went red, and he leaned over the side, retching and spitting.

"If you are so ill," I said, "why don't you go back to your order? Surely your brothers would look after you."

He sat up and took deep, wheezing breaths. Old scars showed white on his blotchy face. "The truth is," he said, "I am not really a friar."

By then, I was not surprised.

"I never was one," he said. "I wear these clothes as a matter of convenience. I hate friars. Who doesn't? They are wandering parasites who profess poverty but live in luxury off whatever they can get from the pious. Well, that was what I thought. But I haven't got much from my imposture."

"What are you?"

"I was a scholar. I studied hard in my youth. And played hard. I fell in with wrong company, coquillards, we call them."

"Pilgrims?" I thought he meant travellers who wear the cockle shell of St James, on their way to Compostela.

He laughed. "They posed as such, when it suited them, just as I pose as a friar. But they were unruly men, older than me, veterans of the English wars, turned loose in peacetime, and devoted to all manner of crime and dishonesty. I found them interesting. I ran with them, and I drank with them. That was my downfall. I killed a priest when I was drunk. They locked me up for that. I was badly treated. Very badly. I would have died in a filthy dungeon, had not the king chanced to ride by."

"The king freed you?"

"We were all pardoned, turned out into the street, to honour the king's visit."

"You are a lucky man."

"You wouldn't say so if you had led my life. If I ever had any luck, it's run out. After they set me free, I committed another crime, a robbery, and now I am banished."

"From France?"

"From Paris."

"Is there a reward for your capture?" A reward would be worth having, if there was any way of claiming it.

"Only death."

"So why stay?"

"I left for a while, but I couldn't stand it. I hate the countryside. It's full of pigs and peasants. The people are too poor to beg from, and there's nothing worth stealing."

"There are other towns."

"They are too small, and I am too well known."

"You are well known?"

"In certain circles."

"So you risked death in Paris?"

"The city is life itself to me. I love the place: its sights and sounds, even its smells. But there is nothing for me in Paris now. All my friends are dead or turned traitor. Last night I thought I would rather die than leave the city again." François coughed again, his face wracked with pain. "I ought never to have gone back," he said. "Revisiting one's old haunts is seldom a good idea. I will have to move on. To England, perhaps. Do you think your countrymen would have me?"

"I don't know if they'll have me."

"Were your crimes that bad?"

"Who said I committed any?"

"I can guess."

I shoved an oar out to fend off a log, making more of a business of it than was necessary. "You won't get me to tell you," I said, when the log was safely behind us. "I wouldn't confess to you, even if you were a friar."

"I've been honest with you. If we are to be friends, you should, too."

"Are we to be friends?"

"I helped you," he said. "Now we are in the same boat."

"I'm rowing and you're lounging."

"You can see I'm ill, Thomas. I used up all my strength helping you. Please, humour a sick man. Tell me, what was your crime? Have you killed a man?"

"I was a soldier. I lost count of the men I killed."

He reached between my feet and picked up my bag. "How did you come by this?"

"I took it from the pope's bedside."

"What were you doing there?"

"I was in papal service," I said. "Until His Holiness died."

"Pope Pius? Is he dead? I had not heard."

"He died not long ago. I came straight from his deathbed."

"May God have mercy on his soul." François spoke so forcibly that he started coughing again. "Pope Pius was a good man," he wheezed. "And a friend of learning and literature."

I was surprised to hear a Frenchman say that, as Pius had

been no friend of France. It made me think François really was a scholar, as he claimed.

"Pope Pius was indeed a good man," I said, "though he never gave me the indulgence he promised."

"So, you wanted an indulgence! I was right. You are a sinner."

"I killed a man, and was locked up, like you. They let me go, in the end. But without my indulgence, I am still a sinner."

"If I really was a Franciscan," he said. "I might have given you an indulgence."

"Sold me one, more like." That was something I hadn't thought of before. If only I still had the pope's ring! With a false friar to do the talking, and the ring to do the sealing, I might have made a fortune by selling indulgences.

"You served the pope," he said. "How long for?"

"Three years."

François looked disappointed. Perhaps I should have exaggerated.

"I expect you served him well?"

"As well as I could."

"Well, who could ask for more? I am sure your sins were wiped out, even if His Holiness did not actually give you an indulgence."

"Do you really think so?"

"I am sure of it."

"If you, with your schoolman's learning, tell me that, then who am I to argue?"

"That settles it: you are absolved, and free to go home."

Of course, he said that because he wanted to go with me. But the words were still a comfort. I hadn't thought of my years at Rome counting for anything. Heaving on the oars, I took the boat round a great curve, taking care to keep away from the reed beds and shallows. Then, back on a long reach, I sat back and let the boat drift on the current. It was only a few hours since I had met François. Despite his crimes, he was a clever man, which is not always true of scholars. He knew more about me than I had told him. And he wanted to go to England. There was no need to give him an answer. He could go with me for a while. Then we would see.

"This is a good way to travel," I said. "Better then walking."

"We'll have to walk tomorrow."

"Why?"

"The river goes the wrong way. If we followed it we'd end up at Harfleur, and it's a long way to England from there."

It was indeed. My father had once walked it, slogging through the mud of Picardy, living off raw turnips, wading through the Somme, fighting the French at Agincourt before he got home. He never stopped talking about it, and I knew that route too well to want to walk it for myself.

"Will we be safe on the roads?"

"We will now. The king's men have rounded up all the flayers and cutpurses. I knew some of them, but they're all gone now. Hanged, mostly. Except for the ones who recanted. There's nothing worse than an old friend who's turned respectable. It's no good going to him and begging food and lodging for old time's sake. A man like that's likely to turn you in, to betray you to the watch, just to show how good he's become."

Was François really such a scoundrel? Or was he a man about town who fell in with low company and fancied himself as bad as his friends?

"Are you of good family?" I asked.

He laughed. "Oh yes! I come from the great family of de Montcorbier, or de Loges, as we were sometimes known."

He sounded very grand. "So those are your names?"

"Not exactly. My parents were so poor they couldn't feed me. I was taken in by a benefactor called Villon. It is his name I bear."

I didn't know what to think. The name hinted that he was a villain, or fancied himself to be one, but it gave me no idea of his true status. "Do you own any land?"

"Not a furrow."

"Have you ever been rich?"

"Once I had thirty nobles."

"How did you get it?"

32

"I stole it."

"How long did you keep it?"

"Not long."

We drifted on, talking of this and that, getting to know each other. François was not a well-made man. His face was narrow and scarred, and its usual expression was a frown. He was thin, bent, and weak, and he curled up in the boat's bow like a whipped dog. I didn't have to wonder what had made him like that. He told me, while he lay there, of the hardships of a scholar's life, of being sent to the university at twelve years old, of lectures at dawn, rising in the dark to escape a beating, of dull tutors, and learning everything by rote to escape more punishment. Though I had wanted to study as a youth, I did not envy that life of poverty, starvation and never-ending work.

François cheered up a bit when he told me about the larks they had had, the tricks and scams, drunken pranks, and the comic verses he wrote to annoy his enemies. He fancied himself a poet, and had written all sorts of verses, not just comic ones. But when he recounted his later ill luck, and the friends and patrons who had turned against him, he sank back into gloom, and seemed no livelier than a bundle of rags.

François wanted me to like him, to feel sorry for him, to be his friend. I once thought that His Holiness Pope Pius was my friend. How could that be true? The pope liked me well enough, but he liked his lapdog better, and when the dog died he mourned more than he would have done for any man. I was useful to the pope, like many others, and that was that.

François, it was clear, thought I might be useful to him. So why did I want to help him? Why was my heart filled with warm feelings towards him? Not long earlier, brawling on the riverfront, we would happily have killed each other. But I liked François, and I think he liked me. But liking was not the same as trusting. Even so, I told François about myself, describing my life as a soldier, and the places I had fought in. He forgave my trespasses in France, where I had served as a boy. I told him about the great battle to save Constantinople from the Turks, how the Christians were defeated, how I was captured and made a slave, and how I escaped. My adventures diverted him well enough, but what François really wanted to hear about was my time at Rome, where I served the pope. So I told him, making sure he knew I was no mere servant, that I knew the great and good men that gathered round the papal throne, and some of the bad men who did the same.

Pope Pius

There are fine rooms in the Vatican palace, bigger and grander than any you can imagine, paved with marble, held up by tree-like columns, decorated with pictures and carvings by the finest artists in the world. Anyone who has been there can describe them. I might have boasted to François, telling him I had lived in luxury, mixing with the great and good, enjoy ing their respect. But I spent my time in the pope's private chambers, at lamp-lit meetings held at night, among fawning courtiers, skulking conspirators, and the endless petitioners who pester every powerful man.

I was there because I had performed a service for His Holiness, exposing a fraud, saving him from expenditure and embarrassment. His reward was to keep me by him, in a sort of servitude. My duties were to serve the pope, in any way he commanded. I had fought the Turks, and Pope Pius wished to fight the Turks. I was one of the men who got away, the men who came back from Constantinople, having survived that great city's fall. We wandered Christendom, telling our stories to men who would not listen. The princes and nobles of the West did not care to be reminded of their neglect, of how they had failed to send aid to the emperor, and did nothing while the Turks took the city and enslaved its people. Only the pope listened, and he planned a last crusade to avenge the injury. While he prepared, I advised him, telling what I knew of the sultan's army, its ways of fighting, of Constantinople and its walls, of the enemies of the sultan and how they might be roused against him.

The other servants disliked me at first, as they disliked all tale-tellers returned from the East. Men like me diverted the pope from his proper task of making the Church powerful and its servants rich. Then the rumour spread that I had poisoned the pope's fool. In fact, the fool died after being bitten by the pope's lapdog. I would have put money on the dog dying first, but the wound festered and the fool died of a fever.

Perhaps the servants thought I had done it because it happened so soon after I arrived in Rome, and certainly, if I could have contrived such a thing, I would have done it, as the fool was no friend of mine.

Then the dog died, not from licking the fool's foul blood, but from falling out of a high window. Some of the servants blamed me for that too, and I did not protest. The dog was hated almost as much as the fool. When they were both gone the pope was sadder but easier to deal with, and I was respected, perhaps feared.

What was Pius like? Though not an old man, he was unlucky in his health, afflicted by a variety of ailments that made his work hard and shortened his life. Ceremony was torture to him, yet he endured it ceaselessly. Which makes me wonder whether God watches carefully over his servants, or whether He laughs at us from on high, showering curses and blessings randomly. You think me irreverent? A blasphemer, perhaps? Well, I've seen what I've seen, and I will tell it all. Don't judge me until you have heard my story.

Despite his high office and great learning, Pius enjoyed simple things, days in the countryside visiting monasteries and villages, or inspecting ancient ruins, followed by a picnic under a shady tree, a meal of fresh-caught trout from a nearby stream, freshly picked salads, a stew of eel and carp in local wine, ripe fruit straight from the tree, and cheeses made by humble villagers. Those things gave him more pleasure than a feast in a palace. Pius hated formal banquets, the kind where he dined in great pomp, sitting apart and looking down on everyone else, cardinals, ambassadors, even princes. Every mouthful had to be eaten in its own way, a way that was fitting with his status and with the nature of the food.

But what is the point of a meal if you can't talk to your friends? You can have a good conversation in any inn or tavern, so how are the rich and powerful better off than the poor and ordinary? The pope was a man once, a man who loved the pleasures of the flesh. Since his youth he had renounced excess, and even if he wished to indulge himself his ill health would not allow it. Towards the end he was too gouty to stroll in the open air, or to sit on damp grass, or do anything except lying in bed, sitting in a well-padded chair, or being carried in his litter. By then he could not eat much. It was sad to see him like that. He sniffed at fine dishes brought by Rome's best cooks, tasted the tiniest morsel, then sent them back. His guests were frustrated, but I did well on the leftovers, eating better than most of my countrymen have ever eaten. No knives were allowed to be brought near the pope, so all his food was cut up before serving, or cooked so soft you could cut it with a spoon. He feared poison, too, but not in his food. An intercepted letter had revealed a Florentine plot to rub poison on the pope's chair. Since Pius was so much in his chair he took the story seriously and had servants standing by to wipe and polish any furniture he had to touch, and he sometimes did without cushions, despite his ill health, in case the coverings had been infused with some deadly potion.

The pope's greatest pleasure was reading, and even that was difficult, as his sight was bad and he would not wear eyeglasses. He had several secretaries, including Agostino Patrizzi, a man who considered himself superior because he had known Pius when they were both students. Patrizzi wrote and read for his friend and master, but when he was busy or elsewhere, Pius liked me to read to him. That is another reason why he kept me near. Though I did not look like a scholar, he knew that I understood a good handful of languages, and that I would not gossip with the other servants.

"Read to me," he would say. "You are far too straight-forward a man to read anything but what is on the page."

It was true: when other men read to Pius, even Patrizzi, they often read more than was on the page, or less, or twisted the words to make them mean more than they did. I never did that. In truth, though I can speak well enough, I cannot read so well that I can give the words another meaning while I am reading them. At the pope's bedside I read to him from letters and reports sent from all over Christendom, and beyond. And there was a book he asked me to read, but only when no one else was about. It was a tale of two lovers, Lucretia and Euryalus, and their adventures in Siena, the pope's hometown. The tale was full of intrigue, deception and trickery, as well as lust, and longing, and fallen honour. The pope sighed and squirmed while I read it to him, and if I was amazed that he could enjoy such a book, I was astonished when he told me that he had written it himself. The book was a product of his youth, written before he was a priest, let alone pope, at a time when he loved worldly things and thought nothing of religion.

The pope was moved by what his young self had written. "I was Aeneas then, not Pius," he said. "And all men feel the pricks of love, even priests. If I were not so weak in my body, perhaps I too might feel those pangs again. After all, the Cardinal of Arras does not let his elevation distract him from his mistresses, as all Rome knows. So perhaps I am fortunate that I am less vigorous than him, that I can do my duty without distraction. But is it a sin, I wonder, to wish to be able to sin?"

Did Pius expect me to act as his confessor? "A soldier may wish for battle," I said, "without wishing for defeat."

"Well said, Thomas. Now read on. Let us get to end of the story, then we can put it away and not think of it again."

I read on, but was not moved by the story, even when the lovers finally met and lay together naked. Instead of getting on with what lovers do, Lucretia and Euryalus spouted poetry and compared themselves to ancient Greeks and Romans.

"Thank you Thomas," he said when I had finished. "I wanted to hear it one last time. Now I must put Aeneas behind me and become Pius again. The coming crusade will only be won by the pure."

"And by the well-informed, Holy Father."

"You are right. We will have nothing but the truth from now on. No more stories, nothing but intelligence from all parts of Christendom."

That suited me. I preferred the truth to poetry, and I read those reports and letters eagerly. Whether they were in

French, Greek or English, I turned them into the Tuscan tongue the pope knew best. Turkish was beyond me. I spoke the language well enough, but never learned the Saracen script they wrote it in.

I know those languages, and a few others, not because I have studied them like a scholar, but because I have a good ear. I am like a musician who can play a tune after hearing it once. I've picked up languages in all the places I've been to, though I could never make much of the savages' tongue. Rosenkreutz claimed to understand it, but he claimed to understand a lot of things. If he was right, that shows there was always a savagery in him, a wildness he kept well hidden until we were among the savages, when it turned into madness.

But that did not happen until later, and first I must explain who Rosenkreutz was, and how I met him.

Rosenkreutz

I was in a courtyard, resting on a stone bench, my eyes closed, face turned towards the warming sun. It was something I seldom did, as my duties usually required me to attend the pope at night, and I often slept in the daytime. I felt sleep creeping up on me then, and would happily have stretched out on the bench, but I sensed that someone was about.

My eyes opened when I heard a voice.

"Is this the way to the pope's private chambers?"

The speaker was tall and slightly stooping, with white hair that fell out of his hood and hung over his pale forehead. It was hard to guess how old he was. He might have been an old man who looked young, a young man who looked old, or man of my own middling years. The colour of his hair was no guide: it might have been white with age, but some men are born with white hair, especially in the North, and some go white when young, from worry or shock. His blue eyes hinted that his whiteness was natural, but they told me nothing of his age.

The robes he wore had a Saracen look, and were dusty from journeying. His question puzzled me. An official visitor would have been escorted, but he was alone. A courtier would have known where he was. Beggars and pilgrims were turned away at the gates. So how had he got so far into the palace if he did not know where he was going?

I stared at him, trying to guess his purpose. Should I call the guards, or take him where he wanted to go? He pulled his hood off and pushed back his pale fringe. At his throat hung a little emblem, a cross with a rose at its centre. Then I realised that I knew him, though we had met only once, briefly, at dusk, on the banks of the Golden Horn.

"I know you," I said. "I've seen you before. You are Christian Rosenkreutz."

"You may call me that." He smiled. "Or Gülhaç, if you prefer."

"I'll call you Rosenkreutz," As well as confirming that he was the man I took him for, he had scored a point by naming himself in Turkish. He knew that I spoke that tongue, that I had learned it in Constantinople, and must have guessed that I had been a slave.

"Why have you come after me?" I asked.

Rosenkreutz laughed. "Why would I come after you? What makes you so vain as to think that? You are not important."

"So you did not know you would find me here?"

"Don't presume to know what I don't know."

I did not like his manner. I thought again of calling the guards. But what if he had some business with the pope but had got lost in the palace? What if Rosenkreutz was important?

"What do you want here?" I asked.

"I must speak with His Holiness. It is most important. He will want to know what I have seen on my travels."

I knew then what Rosenkreutz was. He was a man like me, a returned wanderer with tales to tell and hopes of a reward.

"Where have you been?"

"I have been as far east as a man can go, " he said. "To the uttermost end of the earth."

I doubted it. I had seen him in Constantinople only a couple of years earlier. Could he have reached the ends of the earth and come back again in that time?

"And what did you see there?"

"You are a servant, are you not? Why should I tell someone as insignificant as you?"

His mistake was understandable. I wore the papal livery. "I am more than you think I am," I said. "I attend the pope and have his ear."

"Really? Perhaps you can be of use." He reached out and gripped my arm. "I helped you once, I seem to recall."

"You bought a book from me. I'm sure you did well out of it."

His blue eyes looked at me sadly. "I remember now. The author was not as wise as he thought he was, and the book was not worth as much as I paid you. Even so, I am glad to have bought it, if the money helped you."

"I got away, as you can see. Though the few coins you paid did not take me far. I got here by my own efforts, and stay because I am useful to Pope Pius."

"Yes." He let go of my arm. "You are clearly a resourceful man, one I would gladly have on my side. Perhaps you will join my scheme."

"What scheme?"

"I intend to return."

"You won't get me to go back to the East. I saw enough when I escaped from the Turks."

"I will go further than you did. I will reach Paradise."

"Is it a place?"

"The Earthly Paradise is a land in the East. Some say it is an island. Others that it only seems an island, because of the difficulty of travelling to it. Whatever the truth, Paradise lies beyond the Abode of Reasonable Men. It is bounded by a bottomless lake, on the far side of which is a great bank of earth, so steep as to be unclimbable. And even if you were as nimble as a goat, you would never reach Paradise, because on the far side of the earthen bank is a wall of fire. Anyone who passed through those barriers would cease to be a man. He would be cleansed by the elements, transformed into something beyond our understanding."

"And you think you can reach this place?"

"I believe it is possible."

"How?"

"The details must wait until later. First I must have an audience with the pope. A private one."

"And what will you say? That the King of Paradise will ride to the pope's aid with a horde of sinless horsemen? He has heard it all before. Wanderers are always telling him some such story. The king of this country, the prince of another, the sultan of somewhere else, all of them will fight for the pope, attacking the Saracens in the rear, sweeping the Turks from Christendom. But only if his Holiness will make a donation to the messenger, give him a little something to allow him to get back to the East with a message of encouragement. Is that what you will tell him?"

Rosenkreutz said nothing. He looked at me with a superior smile. And I wished I had kept quiet. I should have let him blunder into boasting to the pope, then watched his rejection. Instead, I had warned him off, and he was wise enough to take the hint.

I found myself confused by that visit, which reminded me of things I preferred to forget. Rosenkreutz himself disturbed me. He was the kind of man who has the knack of seeming saintly, but always gets exactly what he wants. Pope Pius, I was sure, would be intrigued by Rosenkreutz, should they ever meet. He would tell tales of the East that outdid any others. Pius would be impressed, and if that happened I would lose my place at the pope's bedside and become nothing but a servant. I made a vague promise to do what I could to arrange a meeting, then did nothing. Or rather, I did do one thing: I told the pope that a trickster called Rosenkreutz had tried to bribe me to arrange an audience. Pius smiled, and praised my honesty.

Rosenkreutz lingered in Rome for most of that year, and managed to get into the Vatican quite often. He was a persuasive man, and no doubt guessed that I would try to keep him away from Pius. He had stories from the East to tell, and information of all sorts, though he said nothing more about the Earthly Paradise. He was always proposing some scheme or other. Sometimes he had a rare old book to sell, or was seeking one to buy. Knowing that Pius was interested in antiquities, Rosenkreutz proposed digging up the tombs of the old Etruscans, to see what secrets they had left in them. After the alum mines were found, he claimed to have been their true discoverer, and offered to discover other mines yielding all kinds of minerals. It did not matter what he offered, as long as he had an excuse to visit the Vatican and mingle with courtiers and petitioners, scheming with the best of them.

Rosenkreutz might have been no more than a nuisance to me, but he became important. Why? Because of a supper he did not attend, and the things that were said there about the shape of the world. And because, as a consequence of that supper, I got hold of something he wanted.

Supper with Pius

The pope's suppers were the thing François liked to hear about most from my time in Rome. We were often hungry on our journey north, and it pleased us to think of the fine food we might have eaten had we been at one of those feasts. The suppers were for the pope's friends. So that the conversation could run free, there were no servants. The food was brought in and left on the table, or arranged on a sideboard so that the guests could help themselves. It was the same with the wine, which is why some of the guests drank too much of it. The nearest thing to a servant was me, and I did not serve the food or drink. I never did that. If Patrizzi did not serve at table, why should I?

The guests sat round the same table as their host, and shared the same dishes. They talked as they ate, and if they knew my master well, or if they had drunk unwisely of his wine, they argued with him. His Holiness did not mind. On the contrary, he was reminded of what he was before he became pope, of when he was Aeneas Sylvius Piccolomini, a worldly scholar with an appetite for the pleasures of the flesh. By gathering around him men who were still scholars, he was not betraying the trust put in him by the faithful. Nor was he shrugging off the burden of the Church. He was reminding himself that he was once a mere man, and that men must think as well as pray.

Even so, a papal supper was grander than most meals I have known. There were no trenchers for my master. He ate daintily off dishes of gold plate. The Vicar of Christ could not eat his food off soggy chunks of bread, even when surrounded by men he regarded as friends. The truth was that in his position he could have no real friends, as everyone had something they wanted, a privilege or promotion, a preferment for a relative, a sin they wanted forgotten. I was no better myself, and Pius was careful never to give me what I wanted.

There was one supper that I never forgot, because it had consequences that stayed with me for the rest of my life. Rosenkreutz was not there. I made sure he never got close to the pope. But he got his revenge, if you could call it that, in ways I could never have dreamt of.

"This evening," Pius said, "there will be something special." He was soaking in a bath of hot water, as prescribed by his doctor to ease the pain of his gout. While he soaked, a barber was tidying his hair, or what was left of it. "It will be something that will concentrate my guests' minds. Cardinal Arras has sent us a gift. I am not sure what he means by it, as nothing he does or says can be taken at face value. I daresay the gift is meant as a reproach of some sort, but, even so, it promises to be enjoyable."

"And what is the gift, Holy Father?"

"Music. He has sent some singers who will perform works by the Burgundian master Guillaume Dufay."

"Will that not divert the guests, rather than concentrating their minds?"

"No, Thomas. Not when they realise what they are hearing."

"And what will they hear?"

"Among other things, a motet on the Fall of Constantinople."

All the papal court hoped that Pius would eventually forget his dream of reconquering Constantinople. He thought of little but armies, and how they could be raised, equipped and sent to the East. But all the nations of Christendom were exhausted. France and England had fought each other for a century. Spain and Portugal were still campaigning against the Moors, Italy was divided against itself, the German empire battled with pagans and heretics. Where could an army come from?

"Do you think Arras is taunting me for not having launched my crusade yet?" Pius said. "Or is he encouraging me to set off soon, so as to get me out of the way? He would have a freer hand if I were not in Rome."

"I cannot say, Your Holiness."

The time for a crusade, as I had told Pius, was ten years earlier, before the Turks took the city. If they could have been stopped, that was the time to stop them. But it was hopeless. There were too many of them. They had defeated every army that stood in their way, had destroyed all foes and rebels, had made the city they had captured stronger than it was before, all in the name of what Pius called their filthy heresy.

"We will hear the music anyway," Pius said. "Whether meant as a taunt or encouragement, it will make my guests think of Constantinople, and then we will talk of what can be done."

Pius listened to me, sometimes, when he was in the mood. He could not argue with what I told him, but he still wanted a crusade, and he was convinced that there were ways round the Turks, tricks that might distract them, rebels who might be stirred up, Christians in the East who might march against the sultan. That was why he was so interested in cosmography, and why he began writing a book on the subject, though the work was mostly done by his secretaries. Scholars who had studied the antique philosophers, merchants who traded in Egypt or Muscovy, sailors who knew Africa, friars who had wandered Tartary, anyone, rich or poor, a rogue or an honest man, could be sure the pope would welcome him if he came back from the East with a few good stories. I never liked it when those dusty travellers told His Holiness what they had seen. So many marvels! What use were they? Why did Pius listen to men like that? Why did he give out indulgences to men who abandoned their faith to pass freely among the Moslems, though I, who fought the Turks, never got the indulgence His Holiness promised me?

Those were my thoughts as I escorted the pope to the reception room, and I did not cheer up when I saw the guests. There was Cardinal Bessarion, who had left Greece long ago, and Paolo Toscanelli, a Florentine scholar, and Patrizzi, the pope's secretary, and Alberti, a scholar who worked in the chancery and knew everything. I liked Alberti, a small, pink, bald man of about sixty, who never looked down on me like Patrizzi, but knew me for a man of experience, just as Pius did.

There were a few others who fancied themselves as scholars, but the grandest guest was the Despot Thomas Palaeologus, who had fled the Morea recently. He was the brother of the late emperor of Constantinople, whose other brother, Demetrius, had defected to the Turks. If anyone stood to gain from a reconquest of Constantinople, it was him. But the despot must have known how unlikely that was. Otherwise, why would he have abandoned his people and fled to Rome?

When all were settled and Pius was comfortable, he gave the signal. Two singers, one of them a piping eunuch, the other a fine tenor, intertwined their words while a lutenist strummed and a harpist plucked. First they sang about fate, and grief, and the leaving behind of worldly things. Master Dufay must have had a sad life, judging by his songs, and the sweetness of the singers' voices made every sorrow as sharp as a polished blade. When they sang the *Lamentatio sanctae matris ecclesiae constantinopolitanae* I almost cried. It was all about the great and holy city whose walls I had defended, the place where I was enslaved, from which I had only escaped by luck. The pope's guests look sad, but most of them could only imagine what I knew in my bones. Perhaps the two Greeks shared my feelings. The others enjoyed those sad songs, for there is a pleasure in melancholy, and in hearing of misfortune that is not your own. Not one of them was so sad that he actually lost his appetite. When the food was sent in they sniffed at the air, enjoying its savour. And when the dishes were laid out on the table they eyed them eagerly, then inspected the sideboard to see what lay in reserve.

Whatever Cardinal Arras may have intended, the music served the pope's purpose. While they ate, his guests talked about the crusade. They all had something to say, and something to gain. Pius still hoped that salvation might come from the East.

"The Turks can be outflanked," he said. "I'm sure of it. If only we can find allies in Tartary or the Indies. We must forge a grand alliance of Europe and Asia against Islam. Then the Saracens will be encircled and their foul faith extinguished."

Toscanelli, summoned specially from Florence, spoke at length, telling all he knew about the East and its peoples, and went on to describe the state of the heavens, hinting that the recent comets were portents.

"I have observed them most carefully," Toscanelli said. "I have noted their arrivals and departures, and measured their inclinations. And nothing could be clearer. The comets warn of great change."

"No one can know the future by looking at the stars," Pius said. "To guess the future we need only look east, where kingdoms and principalities have fallen to the Turks one after another. That will be our future if we don't find some way of stopping them."

"But that is what I am trying to tell you. The changes in the heavens clearly foretell . . ."

Pius raised his hand. "Let us hear nothing of this heathen nonsense. We weaken our case against the Moslems if we give in to superstition."

There was a silence, and Toscanelli looked embarrassed at having failed to please the pope. The other guests tried not to show their satisfaction, though the old Florentine's mistake was to their advantage.

Cosmography

"Give me enough men," the despot said, "and I'll chase the Turks to the ends of the Earth."

"The Earth doesn't have any ends," Pius said. "Does it?" He looked hopefully at Toscanelli. Pius was prepared to argue with the great scholar on matters of faith, but, despite his own learning, he would not risk asserting a fact that might be contradicted. He did not like to be in the wrong. Nor, in spite of his power, did he like to offend.

"No," Toscanelli said. "The earth has no ends, though it has plenty of obscure corners."

"It is truly round, then? Not pear-shaped, as some believe."

"I have heard it said that the world has a bulge at its northernmost point, which is why the northern latitudes are so cold. But others say that the bulge is in the Torrid Zone, and that Paradise lies on it, which is why Paradise is so hard to reach, and why its climate is perfect and equable in a zone that would otherwise be uninhabitable."

How glad I was that Rosenkreutz had not wormed his way into the pope's confidence.

"But you do not believe it?" Pius said.

"No. I think the world is sphere, which is after all a perfect shape."

"But it cannot be absolutely perfect," Pius said. "Mountains and valleys mar its smooth surface."

"No real thing is perfect. Perfection is in the mind of God. What we perceive is a pale shadow of what God conceives."

"Yes, of course," Bessarion said. "That is what Plato said."

"Plato was wise in many ways," Pius said. "But can we believe him on matters of that sort?"

"Of course!" Bessarion said. "Plato was almost a Christian, in his way. Do you know the *Timaeus*? It contains a most interesting account of the world's creation, which, apart from a few details, contains nothing offensive to men of faith. Plato

50

makes it clear that the world must be spherical, as must be the cosmos itself."

"I believe I may have read part of the *Timaeus*," Pius said. "But a long time ago."

"George of Trebizond has made a new translation. A full one. Has he not sent you a copy?"

"No."

"Perhaps it is just as well," Bessarion said. "Though George is an adequate translator, he is too much of an Aristotelian to do justice to Plato's ideas. And between ourselves, George is unsound on the Saracen question. He believes we should compromise with the Moslems, and look for common ground between the two faiths." Bessarion paused to enjoy the laughter his comments provoked. "I'll tell you what I'll do," he said. "I'll make a revised version of the *Timaeus* and have it copied for you. You will find it most interesting."

Pius smiled. "I would like that very much."

There was a pause while the guests considered the point Bessarion had scored.

"You scholars make a lot of fuss about nothing," the despot said. "To a practical man like me, the shape of the world is easy to understand." He looked around the table, hoping to see the faces of the pope's guests turned towards him, full of respect and eagerness. But the guests looked impatient. They thought the despot stupid, and despised him for having abandoned his people. They were also jealous of the priceless relic of Saint Andrew's head, which the despot had presented to Pius with great ceremony, in front of the entire population of Rome. None of them could vie with a gesture like that, though they all wanted to win the pope's favour.

The despot gestured at the painted ceiling. "The heavens are in the form of a dome," he said. "As anyone can see who has gazed up at the stars at night. And that is something that an old campaigner has often to do. A dome has to be supported on four columns, as any pious man who has stood beneath the dome of our great lost church of Hagia Sophia knows. So it follows that the dome of heaven must rest on four great pillars, each of which must stand on one of the corners of the earth. And the earth, it follows, must be square."

"So, you think the world is flat?"

"No. Everyone knows that the horizon is curved, and that ships drop beyond it. The world curves gently like an upturned bowl, and it has another bowl above it, the dome of the heavens, held up by pillars, just as I said."

There was a silence, and Pius gazed at an arrangement of fruit at the centre of the table. He may have condemned the Moslems as damnable heretics, but he had no scruples about eating fruits sent from their lands. There were early figs and grapes from Africa, oranges from Granada, and melons from Egypt, and some queer, curved, yellow things supposed by the Saracens to be the fruits of Paradise.

Pius reached out. "The world is round, just like this orange." He held up the fruit and turned it in his hand, but not with ease, as his fingers were hooked and stiff, struck by the same affliction that made it hard for him to walk. "And it has wrinkles on its surface, just like the skin of this fruit. As the learned cardinal has reminded us, the ancients knew the world was round long ago."

"They were benighted pagans," the despot said. "They knew nothing. Knowledge began when God sent his Son to redeem us."

"Moral knowledge began then," Pius said, "but not practical knowledge."

The despot was displeased. He considered himself both practical and moral. "If the world is shaped like that orange," he said, "then why don't we fall off it?"

"If the world was shaped like dish, as you seem to think, what would stop us falling off that?"

"It is obvious," the despot said. "On a dish, up is up and down is down. The matter requires no further explanation."

Alberti, the scholar who knew everything, decided to confuse matters. "Not all of the ancients thought the world was round," he said. Some of the other guests smiled. They knew his reputation as a joker. Alberti was adept at catching out other scholars by composing Latin verse and passing it off as antique, then revealing its true authorship. He was said to have invented several saints while compiling hagiographies for the papal library. Saint Expeditus, patron of those who get things done on time, was one of them. Various odd books circulated among the courtiers, supposedly written by Alberti, though no one was quite sure. He often poked fun at the ignorant by leading them into absurdity.

The despot, not knowing who Alberti was, looked hopeful. "Which of the ancients?" he asked.

Alberti composed his pink, round face into a sober expression. "Homer, if I have read him right, says that the world is rounder than a dish, more of a bowl or basin, and that its opening, the fiery rim of Tartarus, faces upwards. In which case, the habitable world lies on the underside of that bowl. What would prevent us from falling off that?"

"Some power, I suppose," the despot said. "Some love or attraction between the world God made and the creatures He populated it with."

"So why can birds fly?" Alberti said. "Do they love the world less than we do? Or does the world not love them?"

"I don't know! I am no theologian, just a simple man of faith."

Pius, seeing that his grandest guest was discomfited, held up a crooked hand. Alberti took the hint and sank back into his chair, looking around at the other guests to see what effect his mockery had had. They too had taken the hint, and were all trying to look wise and serious.

"It may be," Pius said, "that all of the ancients were right, insofar as they understood what they perceived. And that their knowledge does not contradict ours, or undermine our faith."

"How?"

"Thomas!" Pius said. I stepped from the shadows, into the warm glow of lamplight that bathed those priests, nobles and sages, and waited the pope's command. "Bring me a knife," he said.

"A knife, Your Holiness?" I was keen to say something, to be part of the pope's circle. "Are you sure?"

"Yes, Thomas," he said. "Get one from the servants."

That showed how much he trusted me, as no one else was ever allowed to bring a knife near his person. I did as he asked, and he smiled when brought the gleaming blade to the table.

"Agostino," Pius said. "Be a good fellow and choose a nice round piece of fruit and give it to Thomas."

The secretary inspected the fruit. Melons were the roundest, and he rolled one towards me, while Pius looked expectantly at his guests.

"Now, Thomas, take the knife and cut the melon across. Divide it, not into two halves, but into unequal portions, the one about three times the weight of the other."

Carefully, with all those wise men and dignitaries watching, I did as I was told, cutting the melon and laying the two portions before the pope.

"There!" Pius said, picking up the smaller portion. "This part is shallow and curved, just like a dish. The other part is rounded like a cauldron. This part," Pius raised the small portion, "is the world the ancients knew. And that," he pointed at the larger portion, "is the rest of the world. It is full, no doubt, of unknown lands, of cities, savages, monsters and treasures. But it may also be the source of our salvation. It is on this larger part that the great kingdoms and empires of the East lie. And it is only from them that we can expect help against the Turks."

"With respect, Your Holiness . . ." Alberti had resumed his serious expression. "According to many authorities, the other part of the world can never be reached."

"And why not?"

"Because of the ever-flowing Ocean that rushes around it. And because of the Torrid Zone of the South, in which any man who ventured would be roasted to a crisp like a sucking pig left too long in the oven."

"Nonsense!" Bessarion said.

"It is true! Solinus records it." Alberti looked around the table, defying the other guests to disagree with him.

Only Bessarion dared. "Solinus aped all Pliny's mistakes," he said, "then added some of his own. If we believed Solinus . . ."

"I do not know of this Solinus," the despot said. "But I am inclined to believe him. It is obvious that the climate is hotter in the south. The Torrid Zone will never be crossed."

"The Torrid Zone was crossed long ago," Bessarion said. "Herodotus reports it in his *Histories*."

"Herodotus? The father of lies!"

"He was no liar," Bessarion said. "He knew the world better than many who lived later. The ignorant disbelieve him, but a wise man knows how much he has to learn."

The guests all nodded wisely. All except for the despot, who may have suspected that he was being criticised by Bessarion, a man who had fled Greece while the despot was defending his homeland against the Turks. I knew how he felt: those of us who fought in the Morea and at Constantinople are used to being slighted and forgotten. It is best to win your wars if you want to be treated with respect.

"It was in the time of King Neco," Bessarion said, "who ruled over Egypt long before He who made the world sent His Son to save us. In order to make trade easier, this king cut a canal between the Nile and the Red Sea. But then, not satisfied with that, he sent Carthaginian ships out into the Red Sea with instructions to sail south to the end of Africa, then west and north until they got back through the Pillars of Hercules and into the Mediterranean."

"And they succeeded?" Pius said.

"They did. And others, Greeks and Persians, after them. But some, even Herodotus himself, have doubted the story because of what those Carthaginian sailors claimed to have seen. According to them, as they sailed west, along the south coast of Africa, the sun was on their right. In other words, at noon, the sun passed to the north of them."

"That proves it is nonsense," the despot said.

"No it doesn't," Toscanelli said. "It is exactly what one would expect, if the world is round. The sun passes to the south of us because we are in the northern hemisphere. If those Carthaginians sailed so far that they reached the southern hemisphere, then the sun would be to their north."

"If you ask me," the despot said, "they sailed to the nearest seaport and sat in a tavern making up stories."

"No! Let me show you." Toscanelli beckoned me. "Set that melon on its cut side, will you? And pick up that orange and hold it a little way from the melon. Then . . ."

Pius raised his hand before I had a chance to carry out any of Toscanelli's instructions. "What the ancients could do," he said, "we can emulate. Sailing round Africa! Is that not what Prince Henry of Portugal was attempting?"

"Indeed. But his ships did not get very far. They found some new islands in the Ocean, but were a long way from reaching their goal."

"But it is possible," Pius said. "A fleet sent round Africa might take the Turks in the rear."

"It is possible, though the Carthaginians took three years to sail right round the continent. They stopped and planted crops, and waited for a harvest before they continued. It might be done faster if enough food could be carried on board."

The despot picked up an orange and held it in his hand, looking at it scornfully. "Why stop at a little scheme like that?" he said. "If the world is round, as you claim it is, why not send a fleet west and sail right round it? That would take the Turks by surprise."

The pope's guests looked puzzled.

"You are right," Toscanelli said. "East and west are the same. Whichever way you sail you will reach the same place. Think of it! If you walk round the Colosseum, you will reach the Arch of Constantine whichever way you go. What you have proposed is an excellent idea. Prince Henry ought to have directed his ships to the west, rather than exploring a continent full of wild beasts and savages."

"I was joking," the despot said, rather wearily. "But even if you were right, even if it was possible to sail round Africa, or round the world, would it be worth the trouble? If we could assemble any kind of fleet it would be far simpler to send it down the Adriatic Sea to Constantinople. That's where the Turks are, and that's where we need to fight them. What we need is more men and more ships, not more mad ideas about what shape the world is."

There was a silence. The guests inspected their cups, reached for wine jugs, found something on a dish they had neglected to try. I backed away from the table and searched the sideboard for something to eat. A chicken leg did something to fill my belly, but most of the other dishes had been finished or ruined by the pope's guests.

"If the world is round," the despot said, "how can its kingdoms and continents be inscribed on a flat sheet of parchment? Answer me that."

"They cannot," Toscanelli said. "Not truly. But an approximation can be made, by one who has the necessary skill in such things."

"Do you have that skill?" Pius asked.

"I believe so. My friend Alberti has demonstrated a most interesting method for showing large things small and small things large. His mathematical technique is perfectly adapted for showing the shape of the world. Between the two of us . . ."

A huge grin spread across Alberti's pink face.

"Then make me a map," Pius said. "It must show all the nations of the world, Heathen as well as Christian, and all the lands, inhabited or not, and all the seas that surround those lands, and all the ways to and from them. There must be no monsters on it, or fabulous cities. Where we lack knowledge, the page should be left blank. A map like that would serve . . ."

"I will make you such a map that when you study it, you will know the world without getting out of your chair."

"That would be a mercy," Pius said. "Getting out of my chair is something I seldom achieve without help."

Toscanelli smiled. He knew that his map, if it could not outdo Despot Thomas's holy relic in the eyes of the faithful, might please the pope more than Bessarion's promised book. "With Alberti's help, I will draw it out," he said. "Then we will have it copied onto silk by the finest artist in Florence."

The alchemical wedding

It was not long before Rosenkreutz found another excuse to sneak into the Vatican, and when he had finished pestering all the other people he thought might be useful to him, he came to me and asked how soon he might expect to see the pope. I tried to divert him by describing the supper I had attended. I thought it might show that I was more important than he thought I was. But Rosenkreutz was unimpressed until I mentioned the map.

"I wonder how much Toscanelli knows," he said. "Has he been to the East like me?"

"He did not say he had travelled. Only that he had talked to those who have."

"If he means Nicolo da Conti, then the map will contain nothing new. Even so, I would like to see it, if the opportunity arises."

"Why? You have been everywhere, even to Paradise, you said."

"Not exactly. I reached a place where people talked of Paradise, saying it was not far off."

"And you think the pope's map will show where it is?"

"I doubt it. Not if Alberti has anything to do with it. He is clever. There is no doubt about that. But you cannot believe a word he says."

I could have said the same about Rosenkreutz, but he was probably right about Alberti.

"If I seek to know what other men know," Rosenkreutz said, "it is only so that I can see more clearly what they do not know."

"So Paradise will be a blank space on the map?"

Rosenkreutz frowned. He seemed to regret asking me about the map. "You have the wrong idea," he said. "Paradise is not truly a place. It is not what Christians expect. It is more of a state of mind, a Paradise of secret knowledge."

"You spoke of mountains, I think, and of lakes, and walls of fire."

"Such images are necessary for men like you."

"Like me?"

"Men with no imagination."

I did not argue. If I had any imagination I would have thought of a way of escaping from Rome by then. "If Paradise is not truly a place," I said, "why did you want to go there?"

"To reach the right state of mind, it is necessary to go to a place where men understand these things better. The Abode of Reasonable Men, as it is known. It is there that a man who is wise already can acquire the wisdom he needs to go further."

"How would you get there? Do you think this map would show you?"

"The way that can be spoken of is not the true way."

Rosenkreutz used to talk like that. Whatever language he spoke, and he knew as many as I did, he liked to sound mysterious.

"It is not so easy to get to the East," I said. "Not now that Constantinople is fallen. That is why Pius wants the map, so he can see who might help him against the Turks."

"His Holiness should listen to some of his cardinals. Nikolaus von Kues, for instance. He is a wise man, wise enough to call one of his books *The Wisdom of a Simpleton*, and another *On Learned Ignorance*. To him, all worship is worship of the same God. All faiths are one. And how can they not be, if God is infinite and indivisible? True philosophers know that. The Gymnosophists, the wise men of the East, have never doubted it. George of Trebizond is convinced of it. According to him, the sultan is almost a Christian, or could be made one with a little friendly persuasion."

"Pius intends unfriendly persuasion."

"Does he have an army?"

"Not yet."

"Then he would do better to contemplate what Christianity and Islam have in common. Spiritual union would be better by far than war."

"I don't know about that," I said. "But I've seen more than enough of war."

"Let me tell you a story about a spiritual union," Rosenkreutz said. "It may be that, in your ignorance, you see more in it than a learned man would."

He spoke of a wedding he had been to, and I listened at first, because I thought his story would tell me what kind of man he was, which had puzzled me until then. But it puzzled me still, as the wedding was no ordinary wedding, but a ceremony of some other kind, which I did not fully understand.

Rosenkreutz told how he was led by a mysterious old man to a castle full of wonders, where the guests included emperors, virgins, lions and unicorns. There was feasting and other merriment, which lasted seven days. Rosenkreutz was served by invisible attendants and obliged to undergo various tests and ordeals. There were lakes and ships, scales, weights, secret chambers, marvellous musicians, fountains of life-giving liquors, and alchemical transformations. Rosenkreutz spoke of a Virgin so often that it seemed that the wedding was a spiritual one, a union with Our Lady, with secret knowledge as its reward. But then he told me of a vision of the Lady Venus, which hinted at knowledge of quite another sort.

The rest of the story I did not understand. It was full of colours, beasts and symbols of all sorts. Rosenkreutz never mentioned gold, but he hinted at it. He raved about a trick that was played on him, that deprived him of some glory or other that he thought was rightfully his, as though there were men in the East who did not think him worthy of knowing what they knew. He spoke of an order, that he might or might not be a member of, and said he had written everything in a book, including things he had only guessed at, and hidden it in a place where it would be safe if anything happened to him.

Why he wasted the story on me, I do not know. I tried to interrupt him, to let him know that he need not tell me everything, but he would not stop, and wanted me to hear it all, as though it could be important to me, which it was not. He made it sound like a parable, such as Our Saviour told, though what he was trying to teach me from it, I cannot say. I never heard anything like it, even when I lived among the Greeks and Turks. If the wedding happened in the East, that might be why Rosenkreutz was so keen to get back there, though it may be that he imagined the whole thing after drinking some oriental draught.

I was sure of one thing though: the story of the wedding was full of heresy, if not of stark madness, and if Pius ever got to hear of it he would never think of meeting Rosenkreutz. I kept that fact to myself, in case it was ever needed.

Before I could leave, Rosenkreutz gripped my arm. "Perhaps I have not made myself clear," he said. "I told you I would like to see this mappamundi."

"If it arrives. It was only promised."

"Yes, of course. If it arrives. But there is something I would value more than merely seeing the map."

"What is that?"

"Owning it."

"You want me to take it for you, from the pope?"

Rosenkreutz let go of my arm. "It would not be theft," he said. "Knowledge belongs to the wise."

"I may not seem wise to you," I said. "But I know who my master is, and how best to serve him."

"Are you sure of that? The best master of a man is himself." Rosenkreutz looked at me, his blue eyes seeing right through me. "I could show you how to become your own master. You wish to escape from Rome, to leave the pope's service. You want to go home, don't you?"

I had said nothing to Rosenkreutz about that. Had he read my thoughts? Did he have that power? Or was it obvious that a man with no imagination would think of nothing but home?

"I would like to go back to England."

"Is that all you wish for?"

"It is."

"Then it should be easy to achieve. And I will help you. But first, you know what you must do."

I smiled at Rosenkreutz, and gave him some vague reassurance, but I knew that I would have to be in serious trouble before I asked for his help.

The Crusade

Pius had to wait nearly two years for his map of the world. He had to plan his crusade without it, and without the potentates of the East who he had hoped would form a grand alliance against the Turks. He had to rely on the princes of Christendom, and messages were sent out to all of them, asking what they would pledge for the great task. The kings and princes of the West were busy fighting each other, or trying to quell their rebellious nobles. The cities of Italy preferred squabbling among themselves, or trading with the Turks. Those who served the pope were kept busy trying to conceal from him that few of the messages were replied to, and that those who did reply were mostly apologetic or evasive. Turning the Turks out of Constantinople, which they had repaired, repopulated, and garrisoned with a huge army, was not an appealing task, and few volunteered to undertake it.

Most of the cardinals, who had watched the pope make his crusading vow, declared themselves too old or unwell to travel, and some whispered that it was unseemly for them to go to war. But Pius had devoted his reign to planning the crusade, and nothing would prevent him from leading it.

On the day we left there were heralds, banners, nobles in all their finery, liveried servants, uniformed guardsmen, priests and monks of all sorts, and a host of curious onlookers. The populace lined the Tiber, peering from every balcony and roof, knowing that any glimpse they got of the pope as he was carried away by barge would likely be their last. Indeed, the way they wept, it might have been his funeral barge.

It took us a month to reach Ancona, which we did in short stages, the pope travelling by litter when his barge would take him no further. Each night, when we stopped at some comfortable house or monastery, I read to Pius from the *Timaeus* of Plato that Bessarion had newly translated for him. Though Pius had sworn to read nothing but intelligence reports, he justified that nightly indulgence as a duty to a friend, and all were glad to see him distracted from the truth, which was that his crusade was doomed to come to nothing.

Even my bad Latin distracted him. I learned it long ago from a disgraced priest, who taught me some strange things, but not the language of the old philosophers. Pius interrupted me so often, to correct the way I said the words, or to argue with Plato's ideas, that he hardly noticed how hesitant I was. Often, the next day while he travelled in his litter, Pius would have Patrizzi, his secretary, walk beside him so they could discuss Plato's ideas, and I kept close to them so I could follow their talk, though I must confess the *Timaeus* did not interest me much. It was like that as we approached Ancona, when learned talk was interrupted by the noise of the papal guards turning a crowd of ragged men off the road.

"Who are these men?" Pius asked, barely able to rise from his pillows.

"Wanderers," Patrizzi said. "A rabble. Men like that are seen everywhere."

"Why do they not wander to Ancona and join my crusade?"

We could not tell him what we all knew, what he knew really, that they had been to Ancona, had found nothing ready and were returning home in despair. "We are better off without them," I said, edging Patrizzi aside. "Trust me. I have commanded men in war. I know the kind of men we need."

"And they will be waiting for us? With all the ships, stores, and everything else we need?"

"Undoubtedly." I tugged at his curtains, pulling them round him, shutting off his view of those men who were deserting before they had started. "The wind is cool," I said. "We must preserve your health."

We took him straight to the bishop's palace, which is by the cathedral, on a hill overlooking the sea. His spirits were lifted by the sight of some Venetian galleys moored below, but only briefly. He was put to bed and stayed there, barely able to receive visitors, which was just as well, as few came. One of those few was a messenger from Florence, who brought the map promised by Toscanelli. Patrizzi was all for concealing the map, claiming that it would over-excite his master. I suspected him of wanting it for himself, so I made sure Pius knew it had arrived, and he was indeed excited when it was unrolled for him and spread out on his bed. He sat up, propped by cushions, asking one minute for lamps to be brought forward, the next for them to be taken away in case they damaged Toscanelli's fine work.

"Lift it up, Thomas," he said, "Bring it nearer so that I may see the world."

I did so, and there, set out by the old Florentine, were all the lands that men know of, painted in different colours on strong silk, their names inscribed in the latest Tuscan style. Rivers, mountains, forests and deserts were all touched in with a fine brush, as were some of the creatures that lived in them. I could see all the places I had been to since leaving England as a boy. France and the Guyenne, the coasts of Spain and Portugal, Rome and Venice, the islands of the Middle Sea, all were marked, as was the Morea, where I spent several years, and the great City of Constantinople, which I nearly died defending when it was taken by the Turks. Further on were other places I had been to: the old cities of Anatolia, also conquered by the Turks, and Trebizond, where a Greek emperor still lived and ruled.

I thought I had travelled, had seen something of the world. But I had seen nothing. The places I knew were tiny, tucked into one corner of the map. Stretched out on the rest of the map were Muscovy, Persia, Arabia, Aethiopia, Cathay, the Realm of the Great Khan, Tartary, Cipangu, the Indies, the Islands of Spices, and the Terra Australis Incognita. All around them was the deep blue of the Ocean, dotted with little islands and pictures of ships, criss-crossed with lines to navigate by.

The mappamundi was a wonderful thing. I wish I could copy it, but I lack the skill.

Pius leaned forward and grasped that picture of the world in his crooked fingers. His hands trembled as he stared at the vast lands of the East over which the Church had no hold.

"Here is Cathay," he said, letting the map fall and jabbing a finger at it. "Look how big it is! How many cities there are!" He sank back onto his pillows. "How strong the kings of the East must be! Surely they will help us."

Was it possible that some kings of the East were Christian, that they would help the crusade by attacking the Turks in the rear? Seeing that wonderful map, I almost believed it.

"It is as well that I have this map," Pius said, "and not some worldly ruler or greedy merchant. Men like that would like nothing better than to know the exact shape of the world, to know where all its wealth is and how it could be transported across the Ocean from one place to another. Anyone who controlled the world's trade would be able to control the world itself. Such knowledge is dangerous, and best kept to philosophers and men of God."

But the more Pius studied the mappamundi the more he was gripped by a greed for power such as he condemned in princes and traders. The power he craved was the power to extend Christendom into every land depicted on the map. After his crusade had defeated the Turks and restored their old empire to the Greeks, Pius imagined the people of Persia, Egypt, India, Africa, Tartary and even Cathay, all abandoning their beliefs and flocking to join the Church he ruled. It was no use reminding Pius that Plato, in the book I had read to him, told of an ancient people whose empire was destroyed by God because of their lust for power. Pius was so excited by those dreams of dominion over the world that he grew feverish and began to babble.

Flanders

It was only a few days after Toscanneli's map arrived at Ancona that Pope Pius died. After that I escaped, taking with me the mappamundi, the book, and the ring, as I have already described. I sold the ring in Turin, and might have lost the other things in Paris but for François, as I have also described. François was not pleased when I first showed him the mappamundi.

"It's a filthy rag!" he said. "I wouldn't have risked my life for it if I'd known."

He was right. It looked as though the thieves had thrown it on the floor and trampled on it. "It wasn't filthy when I lost it. It was a thing of beauty, drawn up by a great scholar, painted by master craftsmen. I hoped it would guide me home."

He bent over the map and looked at it more closely. "Paris is a mere speck," he said. "France is tiny. So is England. A map like this is no use to travellers. Our wits should guide us, not maps."

He liked the *Timaeus* better, agreeing that it was nicely written in the fashionable Italian style, but he said it would have been better if it was by Aristotle, as there was a ready market for his books, but that pious scholars were suspicious of Plato. I knew by then that François grumbled about everything, and when he disparaged my treasures it was only to put me more in his debt.

Whether it was my map or François' wits that guided us, we reached the coast without mishap, and, having cleaned ourselves up, went to Calais. I looked like a merchant, and François seemed a mendicant friar. I thought it would be an easy matter to get home. But I was wrong.

It was a long walk along the bridge that crossed the moat. As we neared the city gates the men guarding them watched us like wolves.

"Show me your licence," the sergeant said.

"What licence?"

"Your king's licence. Your permit to travel."

"I have a permit from the pope." I reached into my bag, as though the passport was still there.

The sergeant raised his hand to stop me. "That's no good here. If you want to get into English territory you've got to show a licence saying you had permission to leave England in the first place."

"But I haven't got one. I was only a boy when I was sent to fight for my country in France."

"You ought to have got yourself a licence. How do I know you're not one of those Frenchmen the old queen is recruiting to put Henry back on the throne?"

"I am English. Surely you can hear it in my speech."

"I don't know. You could be foreign. And what about him?"

"He's a pilgrim," I said. "On his way to the tomb of St Thomas Becket at Canterbury."

"Where's his chains?"

"What chains? He's not my prisoner."

"If he was going to Canterbury he'd be wrapped in chains, and barefoot."

"Not yet. Not till he gets a bit closer. Then he'll put chains on, and take his shoes off. He'll probably do the last bit on his knees." François glared at me.

"He'll need a licence," the sergeant said.

"Why should a pilgrim need a licence?"

"It's the rules. I can't help that."

"Don't you recognise an old soldier when you see one?" I said. "I fought for the king." I did not add that I had quickly deserted and joined a gang of brigands.

"Which king?" The sergeant was smiling slyly, sure he had caught me out. Of course, I had fought for the old king, for mad King Henry who had been deposed and was running from Edward. But Edward had not been king for long, and the sergeant was a veteran.

"How many kings have you fought for?" I asked him.

His smile vanished. "I've only fought for the rightful king."

"Whoever he happened to be?"

"That's right."

"Well," I said. "We are the same. We have both fought for our king, and now I want to come back and live in my country."

"If you're an old soldier," the sergeant looked suspiciously at my foreign merchant's clothes, "then you'll know how things are for me. I've served my masters well, but have I had rightful reward?"

"It's a hard life, I know."

"I could tell you stories," he said.

I hoped he wouldn't. He reminded me of my father, who was always lamenting the wealth that would have been his if his companions in arms hadn't swindled him.

"What can I offer you?" I said, hoping he would not ask too much.

"I ask for nothing," the sergeant said. "Or not much. But my captain, he is a man who loves money . . ."

François tugged at my sleeve and drew me back, away from the wheedling sergeant. "Let us not waste money on these thieving Englishmen," he said. "If we bribe this guard, the next one will want more, and the one after that more still. They'll clean us out before we can set foot in a ship, and then where will we be?"

"Stuck in Calais. Or worse, outside its walls."

"There must be another way. A way that won't cost us anything."

"It is good of you," I said, "to be so concerned about *my* money."

"Let us go north," he said. "Further into Flanders. The English have no hold there."

"Nor the French."

"So it should suit us well. And I am sure we will find a passage without paying too much for it."

Along the coast, well beyond the English Pale, we found a marsh-bound inn and settled ourselves into it. I listened carefully while the innkeeper recited the long list of dishes we could choose from. It was a while since I had heard his language, and I struggled to understand him.

"What can we have?" François asked, keen to spend my money. The innkeeper, a squat, frog-mouthed, bow-legged fellow, stood waiting. "Eels," I said.

"Is that all? I thought he was listing a banquet."

"He was. He said we can have them fried, spiced, grilled, smoked, jellied, soused, stewed in red wine, baked in a pie, sauced with green herbs, baked with sweet onions, with mustard, or in almond sauce. There were some other ways, but I forget them. We could have had elvers, if the season was right."

"Is there nothing but eels?"

The innkeeper confirmed that there was nothing else.

"I don't want eel pies," François said. "I ate enough of them in Paris. I had to. They're easy to steal, and you can run with a pie in your hand. But there's no pleasure in what you have to wolf down in an alley before you have to run again." He thought for a moment. "Let us have our eels in green sauce. That's a dish to be eaten at leisure."

I gave the order, and the innkeeper demanded payment. He wasn't going to trust us, an Englishman and a French friar, and why should he?

"How is it that you understand Flemish?" François said.

"There were Flemings in the free company I served with."

"I suppose there would have been!" François spoke bitterly. "Men of all countries came to feast on the corpse of France."

I did not answer him. I had told François often enough that I was only a boy when they sent me to fight in France, and I knew better than to argue with him when he was in one of his black moods.

He cheered up when the food came, and so did I. The eels were sweet and tender and covered with a buttery sauce that was thick with egg-yolk and green with herbs. The wine was green too, sharp and fresh, the first of the season from a vineyard not far to the south. Despite his talk of eating at leisure, François ate like a dog that was afraid of being chased off, and I almost had to fight him to get my share, dipping in my fingers, scooping chunks of eel, wiping the bowl with bread until there was nothing left but bones.

"More wine?" the innkeeper asked. François understood that well enough, and gestured his agreement. When the wine came the innkeeper made me pay for it, then sat down with us to help drink it. He talked while he drank, telling us of the marshes and the men that lived in them, and the eels they caught, and all the ways to cook them.

"There's eels out there as fat as a man," he said. "They're as old as the Ocean, and wise with it. No one's ever caught one. The eels we eat are only the youngsters. But they're the best in all Christendom. Everyone says so. We even send them across the sea to the English."

"How do they get there?"

"By boat, of course. Do you think we make them swim?"

At first we could not find the eel boat, though we went where the innkeeper told us to. Among the reed clumps and muddy inlets there were boats of all sorts, some beached neatly, others upturned on halved logs, some holed or broken-backed, a few no more than skeletons of rotten timber. Most were no bigger than the boat I had rowed away from Paris.

"This can't be right," François said. "He must have been having us on. He'll be telling his other customers what fools we were to believe him."

"Maybe. But if you're right they'll all be waiting to have a good laugh at us. We might as well go on."

We came upon a fishermen bent over a bundle of withies which he was weaving into a trap, and I asked him about eel boats. He waved us on, further down the causeway to a clump of willows. In a creek beyond the trees lay the boat, bigger than the others, half sunk in the marshes.

"Fuck this for a lark!" François said, looking down at the mud that seeped between his toes. "It's a wreck. They're all in the same game, playing us foreigners for fools."

But it was the boat we were looking for, single-masted, broad and low, its hold stacked with baskets of wriggling eels. I talked to the skipper asking him about the crossing, how long it would take and where it would land, and whether there was a place for two landsmen who would do as they were told and be no trouble. There was a price to pay, of course, but not such a high price as we would have paid to the men who guarded Calais.

We settled ourselves aboard, finding what dry spots we could in that low-slung vessel, waiting until the crew hoisted the sail, and the hull lurched free of the mud, and our voyage began.

Out in the open, the crew slid up paddles that let seawater into the hold. After that the boat wallowed badly, and more water washed over the sides. François stared unbelievingly at the water swirling around the eel baskets and lapping at our feet. "It's a floating colander," he said. "Who'd go to sea in a vessel like this?"

"The eels are content. Why can't you be?"

"The ship will sink. We'll drown. I might as well have stayed in Paris and been hanged."

The crew laughed at our fears. They crossed to England often, and if they did it without sluicing the hold, the eels would be dead when they got there. Anyway, the hull was double, so the ship couldn't sink, or so they said. François refused to believe a word of it. Then it started to rain, and that deepened his gloom.

"On a Paris gibbet, the crows and kites would have torn my flesh. Here, the fish will eat me." He pulled his hood down over his face. "There's water all around us, in the sea, in the boat, pouring down on us from the sky. There are watery creatures in the hold, the crew are watery men from the marshes, the land we've just left was half water." He peeped out from under his hood. "You can't see the horizon," he said. "You can't tell sea from sky. If we get any wetter we might as well jump overboard and walk to England on the seabed."

We tried to sleep, as it was no quick dash across the narrow sea to Dover. The ship headed northwest to Essex, where the coast is pierced by creeks and bays, and eels were traded without the king's men interfering. It took a day and a night, and it was soon after dawn when the crew sighted land.

"Call that land?" François said. "It's as flat as Flanders. Are you sure they haven't taken us round in a circle?"

"It's flat all right. But it's England. I'm sure of it." I don't know how I knew. I hadn't set foot in England for many years. But something told me I was home, and even though my memories of England were not happy, my hopes were high and my heart beat a little faster as I looked at the grey streaks that marked the horizon. The ship wallowed into a creek barely wider than itself. On either side of us were mudbanks.

"This isn't Harwich," I said. "You said we'd land there."

"It's near enough."

"Couldn't you take us closer?"

"See those men?" The skipper pointed at some dark shapes that huddled on the low shore of a bigger island that lay astern, across a stretch of open water. "They're the men we're going to meet," he said "But not you. You don't want to meet them, any more than you want to meet the king's men. You and your friend are going ashore here, and if you've got any sense you'll head inland fast, and forget about Harwich."

There was no point in arguing with the skipper. On board his own ship he was all-powerful. I got him to change some money for me, and I thought I had done well until I found the English coins had been debased. Then we were dumped onshore and had to scramble from tussock to tussock until we got onto something like dry land. When we got a little way from the sea we looked back and saw that we were free of the ship's crew and the men they had gone to meet. I realised that we were safe at last in England, and felt more cheerful than I had for some time. Maybe that was why I listened to François and agreed to his scheme.

Essex

"The hero returns," François said. "Does Ulysses have a Penelope, patiently spinning and waiting?"

"What?"

"Do you have a wife, waiting by the fireside for your return?"

"I have no wife, no family, and no home. There's nothing I'd like better that to settle by the fireside and think of the past, to be fed well and waited on by a good woman. But everything my family owned was robbed and destroyed, leaving me with nothing."

"Oh well. At least we won't have to deal with any suitors."

We walked on for a while, but seemed to make no progress across that flat land.

"In France," François said, "you talked of going home."

"Home was what I hoped for, not what I had." I wanted to take out the mappamundi and consult it, but knew that François would scoff. As he had pointed out, there was not much detail on the map, and it couldn't show us the road to anywhere. I had thought of it as a talisman. It had power, certainly. Just looking at it brought on the fever that killed Pope Pius. But the power of the mappamundi was in its beauty, and that was lost when the thieves fouled it. Since then I had been led by chance, or by François. I thought of taking the cloth to a fuller to have the stains removed. Perhaps then it would lead me again, and I would find what I longed for most. There were sheep grazing nearby, and where there are sheep there are spinners, weavers, dyers and fullers. There is wealth, too, and that was something we wanted a share of.

"Is there no one here who would take us in?" François said.

"No one."

"Where are we going to go?"

"Wherever the Wheel of Fortune rolls us."

"In my experience," he said, "the Wheel of Fortune often needs a bit of a shove."

I took that for one of his poetic fancies, and didn't answer. We trudged on, getting no nearer the horizon. It was not cold, but the land's emptiness made me think all the more of warm hearths, comfortable beds and hot meals.

"Have you ever been married?" François asked.

"Not me. I've never stayed in one place for long enough."

"Have you been in love?"

"I loved a French girl once. And there was a woman I left behind in the Morea. It was all a long time ago."

"How old are you?" he asked.

"I am fifty years old, or thereabouts. And that is not an age when men think much of love."

"Marriage is worth thinking about, even at your age. If you found a rich woman and married her, you could live in comfort just as you wish."

"What sort of woman would marry me?"

"Widows are best," François said. "Especially young ones. They are full of lust, like a fire that has died down, but only wants new fuel to make it flare up again."

"And I would be the fuel?"

"Why not? A dry old stick burns better than a green shoot."

François talked on as we walked, and I listened. After a while I started to believe him. A rich young widow who would marry me would not be easy to find. But widows of any sort are usually in need of protection, and who could provide that better than a man with my experience of the world?

"Money is what we need," I said, "and if it can be got by marriage, then I'll try for it."

"We must play the game to win," François said. "Anything else would be folly."

I didn't doubt him. He knew all about folly, and so did I. "I'm with you there," I said. "Let's have no illusions about love and what it can lead to. Let's make comfort our goal, board and lodging, all free."

"Yes, we'll live at ease, if we can. Nothing is better than that."

"But how is it to be done?"

"I will help you," François said. "I will play the part of Cupid, summoning Venus to your Mars."

"Now you're talking nonsense. If you want to help me, you'll have to learn to talk plain English."

"French will have to do for the moment, until I get my ear tuned to the way your countrymen speak. But as for Venus and Mars, they are rightly linked, as Aristotle notes, for fighting men are much given to lust."

"I've put soldiering behind me. I am trying to seem a merchant."

"Perhaps you are right. Money and lust are also linked."

"Did Aristotle say that too?"

François pulled his hood tighter round his head.

"We'll find a widow," he said. "And you will woo her. To make you seem more mannerly, I'll write some verses for you to speak."

He wanted me to spout poetry like the lovers in the story Pius wrote. "Me, speak verse?"

"Why not? Women like it."

"Maybe. If it is spoken by a fine young blade. Or better, if it is sung. But not if it is croaked by an old soldier like me."

"Make your mind up," François said. "Are you an old soldier or not?"

"Yes, but . . ."

"Get your story right," François said. "That's the first rule of roguery. It's words that make us what we are."

"Not clothes?"

"Words make the clothes fit. Dress like a merchant and talk like a soldier, and people will wonder what you are. Deny being an old soldier, and their doubts will become certainties. Talk and dress like a merchant, and other men will think that's what you are."

François was good at that. He could talk like a scholar, a poet, or a scoundrel, and like a friar, when he was wheedling for charity.

"If I fashion some verses to fit your character," he said. "And if you speak them well, as I will school you to, then there is no reason why you should not win a woman over."

"These verses should be chaste. No tavern talk or rogues' jargon."

"Women like words to be well sauced."

"Frenchwomen, maybe. Englishwomen are more likely to think too much sauce covers rotten meat."

"Women are all the same, French or English, rich or poor. Surely you've learned that on your travels?"

I wasn't so sure, but I didn't argue with him. He'd have had more of my life out of me, and there were still things I didn't want him to know.

"First we must find our quarry," he said. "A tavern's the place."

"It always is."

"We'll make enquiries. For the price of a drink we'll find out what we want to know. But for the moment, let us rest a while."

François found a patch of soft dry grass and sat. He reached beneath his friar's habit and brought out a small loaf, then, after further rummaging, produced a lump of good yellow cheese.

"Where did you get those?" I asked, sitting beside him.

"I found them on the boat." He took out his knife and divided his spoils. "The sailors won't miss a little of their food. Let them eat eels, I say."

At Manningtree we found an alehouse and settled ourselves into it. I was glad to be in an English town drinking English ale, and hearing English talk, even if it was all about England's troubles, and what Warwick would do next, and which king would end up ruling us. Some were for Henry, and others preferred Edward, but none felt so strongly that they would fight for either of them. It made no difference to me. I just listened, and drank my ale, and counted myself happy to be home.

François would not forget his scheme. He talked to every-one in bad English, making them laugh, making them forget he was not only French but a friar and someone they should have been doubly suspicious of. He had the knack of making people like him, when he wanted to, by clowning, or by flattering. And if that didn't work he made people sorry for him. That night it was my money and the ale he bought with it that made people talk. And it cheered me to listen, as their Essex speech was not so different from the way men spoke in Norfolk where I grew up.

"There's no rich widows round here," an old man said. "Why would there be? With two kings fighting for one kingdom, and no one upholding the law, these are uncertain times. If a widow started out rich she'd soon have everything taken off her."

He was right. That happened to my mother. Neighbours pounced like wolves, taking everything she owned, even tearing down the timbers of her house. She blamed me, though my only fault was not being there. That memory made me feel bad about François' scheme. How could I prey on a widow?

"Unless," the old man said, "she married again quickly, and then she wouldn't be a widow, she'd be a wife."

"There must be some rich women in these parts," François said.

"Well, there's the abbess at Wix. They say she's got some money stashed away. But she's married to Christ, ain't she?"

"She is indeed," François said. "Surely there must be other rich women, who happen not to be married?"

"The only woman with money round here is the eelwife."

"I don't like the sound of her," I said.

"She's rich. She's made a fortune out of the eel trade, bringing them in from Flanders. Her men smoke them, and she sells them all over the kingdom. She's no widow, though. She never married."

"Perfect!" François said.

"Huh! If you're thinking of trying to get money out of her you'll have to be craftier than the bishop. He's been trying for years to get her to pay her taxes, but she hasn't paid a penny."

"All the richer," François grinned. "Where does she live?"

"On an island in Hamford Water."

"In a stinking smoke-shack?" I said. "Flooded by the tide twice a day?"

"No. In a fine house, raised up on posts, with a high tower built of Flemish brick. There's nothing quite like it round here. She lives well there in the marshes, kept dry by fires of Newcastle coal. You couldn't be warmer or drier than she is there. Or so people say. There's not many that go to or from the island, except them that work for her."

The Eelwife

The next morning, after a good night's sleep in a dry bed, we walked back to the coast. François was happy, and I was not, though my exile had ended and his had just begun. He skipped along beside me, laying out his plan, telling me what to say, spouting fragments of verse and getting me to repeat them. I did as he asked, but without much hope, repeating my lines as dully as a draper made to play Pontius Pilate in a mystery play. At least the draper would have had a fine costume, but all I had was the clothes I got in Turin, and they had worn badly and were still stained by the filth I had tumbled in at Paris. When I chose grey clothes, I chose more wisely than I knew.

"There are two ways to get money out of a woman such as this eelwife," François said. "One is the way we have already discussed, wooing her, marrying her, and winning all her wealth."

"And the other?"

"Convince her that we can make her rich. We'll offer to buy her eels. We'll dangle the chance of a fat deal in front of her. And then . . ."

"Then what?"

"There will be a setback. Some regrettable circumstance will prevent us from completing the deal, and we will lure her into giving us money to get it going again."

"What circumstance would that be? Apart from the fact that we don't have any money and don't want to buy any eels."

"Leave it to me. I'll think of something."

"How will we persuade her to believe in all this nonsense?"

"We'll pass you off as a rich merchant from overseas. A Fleming, since you speak the language."

"Why would a Fleming buy eels? Her stock comes from Flanders."

"You know nothing of trade."

"And you do?"

"I know that trade is not as simple as you think it is. If it was, why would she import eels when they must teem in English rivers? You have no answer to that, do you? Trade is a system of trickery, in which goods are bought cheap and sold dear, avoiding places where tax is levied."

"Did Aristotle teach you this?"

"Aristotle teaches that trade is little better than robbery. And robbery is something I do know about. Anyway, you can be a Tuscan merchant, if you think a Fleming implausible. You could pretend to want smoked eels, a great cargo of them."

"Why would a Tuscan come here to buy eels? There are plenty in Italy. Pope Pius liked few things better."

"Does she know that? You could tell her that the pope's dying wish was that his countrymen should eat nothing but eels, and she wouldn't know any better. You could tell her the pope's still alive, and longs for a dish of her eels. If you go to her offering to buy a great quantity of smoked eels, she'll welcome you with open arms. If not with open legs."

"You're hoping."

"Why not? If this woman likes you, there's no knowing what she might give you."

"I'm not pretending to be Tuscan. I'm finished with all that. I'll be the English agent of a foreigner, that's all."

"It will have to do, I suppose."

"It will. And what will you be? Why would a French friar travel with an English fish-broker? Or will you wait in the marshes and leave everything to me?"

"Have you no imagination? Monks and friars must eat more fish than other men. In fact, they eat more of everything than other men, and drink more, but that is another story. The monasteries of France consume vast quantities of fish, and the Hanseatic League ensures that stockfish is dear. What could be a better substitute than English smoked eel?"

I had to admire him. A lifetime of ducking and diving had given François a quick mind and ready tongue. But schemes made up on the spur of the moment are bound to fail. The eelwife would be a toothless ugly hag, stinking of fish. Her house would be a smoky hovel, her wealth no more than a few greasy pence hidden in a jar.

François talked on, telling me of tricks he had played when young, of women wooed by his friends, of cuckolded wives and swindled merchants. I ought not to have listened to him. In his mind, his schemes were marvellous things that always fell out exactly as he planned them. In reality they mostly ended with a drubbing, as I already knew. But I did listen, and he convinced me that there might be something to be got out of pretending to be merchants, even if it was only a night or two of board and lodging.

Hamford Water must have been five miles across, though it was hard to tell where the land ended and the water began. There were dozens of low islands, and shining mudflats dotted with reedy clumps and patches of samphire. In between were creeks and channels haunted by gulls, crabs and seals, and all the other creatures that live in such desolate spots. In places, the mud bubbled like soup, and nameless things stirred beneath its surface. We skirted the marshes, breathing the smell of stagnant water and rotting weeds, looking for the place we had been told about where poles in the mud marked a way across to the eelwife's island.

By the time we found the causeway the tide was well in, but even if it had been out I wouldn't have walked it, not even if Moses had appeared and led me across himself. We sat down on a dryish bank, and I thought it wouldn't be long before François started to think about ale, and about heading back to Manningtree. But before his thoughts turned that way a boat appeared. François stood and hailed it, and it rowed straight towards us, and before long we were explaining ourselves to four foul-smelling men. François sweet-talked them, telling them of the deal we hoped to make with their mistress, and how pleased she'd be if they helped us. I don't know how much they understood. His English was still half-French, though he was learning fast. The eelmen bundled us into their boat and rowed us across a stretch of water the same colour as the mud that lay all around it.

We soon saw the tower, rising out of the marshes, built of Flemish brick, just as they told us at Manningtree.

"It looks like the Tower of Babel," François said. "There is a picture just like it in a book of hours made for King René."

It was typical of François to talk of books at a time like that. He had to remind me he was a scholar. As the boat drew closer, I was looking out carefully to see what kind of place we were heading for. There were men at the top of the tower, labouring with hods and buckets, building it taller still. Around the tower, clinging to its base, was the house itself. It was a fine house, raised on piles above the highest tides. Great timbers taken from old ships leaned all around, forming the skeleton of the house, supporting its beams, crucks and rafters. It was well clad with tarred planks, and roofed with shingles. But its setting was dismal, on a swampy island, surrounded by sheds and shacks from which smoke billowed, mixing with the mist that already rose from foetid waters. As the boat drew closer we could see more. Between the sheds, hunched and filthy men scurried along walkways carrying burdens that dripped, wriggled or stank.

"What a terrible place," I said, speaking French so the eelmen would not understand.

"It is not so bad," François said. "Venice must have begun like this, a little hamlet of fishermen, building their shelters in the lagoon to escape the invading Huns. Perhaps in centuries to come a great city will arise here, a jewel on England's shore."

"Have you ever been to Venice?"

"No," he said.

"I have. There is no comparison."

But there was one comparison. After we had scrambled out of the boat onto a slippery jetty we were ushered into the eelwife's presence, and she was as comely as any whore of Venice, which is not the insult it might seem, as the women of that city, whether paid for their trouble or not, dress and paint themselves so well that they seem the most beautiful in the world. I could not tell if the eelwife was painted. Perhaps the chill air of the marshes gave her cheeks their red glow. She was a handsome woman, no more than forty years old, dressed in a russet gown that clung to her as though it was damp, which it may well have been. Wisps of brown hair escaped artfully from her kerchief. There was a softness about her body that would have made any man glad of the chance to curl up in bed with her. I began to think that François' first plan was not so bad. It might have been better to woo her than to trick her. Yet she must have been tough to live on that island and make her living from the marshes, trading with the Flemings and making a profit.

"So the pope wants to buy my eels?" she said, when François had told his story. "Ain't there no eels in Rome?" She gave a little smile, showing her gap teeth. "There's eels everywhere, if you know where to look for them. They're born from the mud, and there's mud everywhere. Just look around you if you don't believe me. Are you telling me there's no mud in Rome, and no eels?"

"You are right, mistress," François said. "There are eels in Italy, but inferior ones, born of inferior mud. As Aristotle tells us, there are qualities of mud . . ."

"What the learned friar means," I said, "is that His Holiness has heard that our English eels are the finest that can be had. And they say round here that your eels are the best, whether smoked or soused."

"And believe us," François said. "If His Holiness likes your eels, which he is sure to, judging by what we have been told, he will order great quantities."

"Great quantities?" she said, smiling again, though warily.

"Think of it!" he said. "The pope in his palace at Rome, surrounded by all his cardinals, and all the bishops and lesser clergy, not to mention the princes and ambassadors and other notables who visit him. Imagine the feasts they have, the quantities of food they eat! If His Holiness decides to feed his guests on your English eels, you will be sending off ships so laden with barrels that it will be a wonder they float!" He hesitated. "You do pack your eels in barrels?"

"I do," she said. "You can see them if you like. You can see everything, the sheds, the ponds, the smokehouse. If you've ready money to pay for my eels, you can see what you like."

At the mention of money François gave me an anxious look. He still hadn't told me what we were going to do about that.

The eelsheds

The eelwife did not come with us. No doubt she had business to attend to. As we walked away from the house I looked up at the tower and saw the builders toiling high above us.

"Why are they building the tower so high?" I asked.

"Don't ask me," our escort said. "They're Flemings, and I can't understand a word they say. They've got their own way of doing things, and they only answer to my mistress. She knows their speech, as her father was one of them. Maybe they're building it high so she can see Flanders from the top of it."

His tone told me that wasn't the truth, and that questions were unwelcome.

I cannot rightly remember all the sheds we were shown. When the first doors were flung open we were plunged into darkness, and never left it. Each shed was darker than the last, and while we were in them darkness settled over the island outside. The men did not stop working as night fell. They were half-naked from the heat, and as black as Moors from the smoke. Some of them carried baskets of eels, which they set down as gently as cradles. I looked into one of the baskets and saw foaming slime, writhing bodies and gaping, gulping mouths. Men with hatchets hooked out the eels and chopped them into twitching, shuddering chunks. Other men gutted whole eels with thin knives, spilling guts around their feet until they worked in inches of filth. Filleters slit the fish neatly with thin knives, fitting them for more dainty dishes. Slimy eel-chunks were skewered on huge spits, and thrust into blazing ovens. Those spits were as long as a man, and I could imagine them being put to other uses. Each time an oven opened, a blast of flames shot out, and the stink of burnt eel fat pierced our noses, driving out the smell of blood, slime and guts. Some of the men sang as they worked, but the sounds they made were more like the moanings of tortured souls.

"This place is like Hell," François muttered. "See how the mouths of those ovens gape! See how those smoke-black devils toil! Feel the slime and filth on your fingers! Breathe in the mephitic vapours!"

"You brought us here."

"No! Those boatmen did, rowing us like Charon across the Styx."

Our guide was watching us, puzzled by our words.

"We'll have to go on," I said. "And try to pay attention. We are supposed to be eel-brokers for the pope, and mustn't let Hell distract us."

We were led into the smoking shed where whole eels, long and black, hung like unsheathed swords from wooden racks above smouldering fires. Coughing and choking, we expressed our satisfaction with all we had seen. But there was more. Wielding a smoking torch the guide showed us the sousing shed, where fat morsels of roasted eel were dunked in barrels of spiced vinegar. He was keen to show us that the barrels were well packed, with good eels all the way down. In the salting shed, fillets of smoked eel were gently packed into beds of grey salt. Then there were the storehouses heaped with timber, empty barrels, salt and spices, and the holding ponds, and the fattening ponds, where the black water rippled in the light of the guide's torch. The only thing we didn't see was what we were most curious about: the eelwife's counting house.

"You'll be staying for supper," our guide said, when he had exhausted us with his tour of the island. "The mistress will want to talk again with valued customers like you."

His look told us that we had no choice. How would we have left without her permission?

"I wonder what she'll serve us," François said, drawing a glare from the guide. "Will there be no end of eels?"

"Speak English, sirs," the guide said. "It is our tongue, and a good one. Only the Flemings have leave to speak anything else."

The eelwife received us in a large room built against the

87

tower. The floor, of good planking, was strewn with fresh rushes and herbs, which helped drive the stink of eels from our noses. The brick wall had a fine fireplace in it, such as I had only seen in gentlemen's houses, and its grate was filled with sea coal, which glowed brighter than embers of wood. The other walls were hung with Arras tapestries, and there was a curtained alcove where she slept. In a corner were strong chests of carved wood that might have had money in them, and at the centre of the room was a table set out with bowls and trenchers.

The eelwife was a crafty woman. She wouldn't just let François tell her that we were pleased with all that we had seen. She questioned us, making sure that we understood what we were praising, and knew the business we claimed to be in. We had to hide behind his bad English to cover our ignorance, and pretend that things were done differently in Italy and France, which no doubt they were, for all we knew of the fish trade.

Eventually, tiring of questioning us, she invited us to sit, and called a servant to bring in some food.

I reached into the bowl and took out a morsel. It was a fat eelhead, complete with gaping gills and staring eyes. I looked at it, wondering how much meat there was on an eel's neck.

"They're good eating," the eelwife said, juice dripping down her dimpled chin.

I followed her example, sucking flesh from the cut neck, then laying the rest on my trencher.

"Are you leaving that?" she said. "What about the eyes? And the tongues? Those are the best bits."

François probed the bowl carefully, but drew nothing out. "Are there no eels' bodies in this dish?"

"No," she said. "Just the heads. They make a good dish for those that like them."

"Surely the bodies are better? After all, that is what you sell."

"That's why we eat the heads. You wouldn't expect me to eat what I can sell, would you?"

"No, of course not." François tried sucking at an eelhead, but it was obviously not to his taste.

"If we could eat the bones," she said, "we would. If my men could live on blood, guts and slime, all boiled up in a pudding, they would. But they can't, and every mouthful of food I'm obliged to give them, apart from these heads, eats away my profits."

I set to, and tried to look as enthusiastic as possible. She looked sadly at François. "There's some that don't like eels," she said. "They see the serpent in them that tempted Eve. But I say that God made the eel, just like He made all the other fishes. And He did a good job of it, too, giving the eel a fine flavour and firm flesh, making it fit to live everywhere and be easily caught and kept. So who are we to turn our noses up at God's good creatures when they are set in front of us?"

To our great relief, the eelheads were only a beginning. Perhaps they were a test, so she could see what we would do to please her. When we had done our best to separate eelflesh from jaws and gills, she nodded to her servants, who brought in a baked mullet, well sauced with mustard, then fried whitebait, and roasted ducks, and plenty of bread still hot from the ovens and smelling of scorched eelfat. We had pickled samphire, and seakale, and other green herbs, and there was good Laonais wine to drink, fresh and clear, with a prickle to it that cut through eelgrease. There were spiced egg puddings, too, but they had a fishy taste, as though the eggs came from waterfowl. The men who brought the food were cleaner than the men who toiled in the eelsheds, but they had the same dark look about them, as though they seldom went far from their ovens and cauldrons.

The eelwife lived well on her island, either from the waters around, or by trade. While we ate, she asked us about Rome, and the pope, and the ways of his court. François, cheered by the arrival of other dishes, began to make up answers. I could see that the eelwife didn't altogether believe us. She had a way of silently raising an eyebrow, or what would have been an eyebrow if she hadn't plucked them, that quite undid me.

François' plan looked nonsensical. How could we hope to fool her?

Even so, she softened a little by the end of the meal. "I won't send you back to the mainland tonight," she said. And I was glad to hear it. The thought of crossing the causeway in the dark made me shiver, despite the room's heat.

"I won't make you sleep with my gutters and smokers, either," she said. There was a glint in her eye like the sun catching a polished blade. Did the thin blades her men used ever catch the sun? "I can see you're too mannerly for that," she said, "having slept in palaces with the pope."

François and I glanced at each other. As he kept telling me, we had to stick to our story.

"It is true," he said. "The beds in Rome are all stuffed with finest swans' down."

"Men must be soft, too," she said, "if they've slept all their nights in feather beds."

I could see what she was getting at. "I've been everywhere," I said. "And done everything. I've lived rough as well as smooth . . ."

"But we like it better smooth," François said. "A soft bed would suit us best."

"I've a good soft bed," she said, glancing at her curtained alcove. "It might suit one of you."

François looked strangely alarmed, as though the thought of bedding a woman scared him. Yet he had boasted often enough of his amorous adventures. The eelwife gave him a haughty look. "I know friars are no chaster than other men, but I saw you picking at your supper. A man who fusses over good food is no use to me."

He glared at her. "I never fuss over good . . ."

I kicked him under the table. "It was a very good meal," I said. "I ate everything."

"I noticed. I like a man who eats well. He can usually do other things well. Can you?"

"I can do many things well. I know how to fight, and lead men. I speak a good handful of languages. I can read as well as any scholar." François scowled at me, but he had enough sense to keep quiet. I stood up and gave her my best smile, offering her my hand. "I know how to lead a woman to bed, and what to do when I get there."

"The friar thinks he is good with words," she said. "But you've talked your way into my bed. Take up a candle and follow me."

I did as she said, and was soon sat beside her in the alcove, the curtain drawn behind us, the candle flickering from a shelf. She didn't wait for any fine words or flattery, such as François had tried to fill my head with. That was just as well, as I had forgotten all his poetry. She tugged up her gown, showing me her round belly, and plump thighs, and what lay between them. Beneath my hose, my yard stirred. That was a good sign, as I hadn't had a woman for a while. Yet it was important not to rush. Her skin was smooth, and slightly oily. She smelled of eelgrease, but if I succeeded, that was something I would have to get used to. I reached between her legs and began to explore. The place I sought cannot be found on any map. I read about it in an old book of amatory secrets, shown to me by a disgraced priest. The book's descriptions were vague, and the priest could add little. But I was a young man, full of curiosity and quick to experiment. I soon found out where the place was, and how to touch it, and I never forgot that knowledge, taking it with me wherever I went, though I had no opportunity to use it in Rome.

The eelwife's sigh told me she was no different to other women. She sank back into her soft mattress and spread her legs, trembling beneath my touch. Out of the corner of my eye I could see that François had parted the curtains and was peeping through, but I didn't let that stop me. I turned my back to him and carried on, caressing the eelwife until her groans were so loud I feared the whole island would hear. She reached up and pulled me towards her. She was a strong woman, and knew what she wanted. I entered her, and she rocked beneath me like a boat, ploughing into the mattress, calling out in a muddle of tongues. I rode her roughly, pushing her down, plunging deep inside her. Just as François predicted, there was a smouldering fire of lust within her, and I

91

had stirred it up. Her delight was obvious, and if I could please her as much as that, what wouldn't she do for me? The flames of pleasure burned brightly for a moment, then with one last cry she sank down into the hollow we had dug in the mattress. I finished too, and slumped beside her.

I felt pleased with myself, and not just in the usual way. Everything had fallen out as we had hoped. The eelwife was rich, a queen on her little island, with an army of men to do whatever she told them. With luck, my travels were over. I would live beside her like a king, enjoying her fine house and all its comforts, commanding her army as if it was my own. I could see myself growing old and fat on that island. There was room for François, too, and I regretted doubting him earlier. Perhaps, in the morning, if he behaved himself, I would apologise.

I rolled over, ready to sleep soundly in her soft feather bed. But she jabbed me in the ribs and pushed me out.

"You can't stay here," she said.

"Why not?"

"It would never do. My men wouldn't stand for it. We'll talk business in the morning, but you must sleep with my Flemings tonight."

We bedded down with the Flemings, though we were so pestered by mosquitoes that we could hardly sleep. Every time I managed to doze off, François woke me by slapping at himself and muttering about fevers and agues, and cursing the marshes, calling them the Devil's privy, and their creatures the Devil's servants. Then the Flemings cursed him, and threatened to beat him with their shovels and throw him from the tower. François didn't understand them, but he got their gist and cursed them back in his rogue's French. Soon there was a slow quarrel going, simmering like stew, with gobbets of words bubbling up in the darkness, then sinking down again. I lay as still as I could, enduring bites and curses, wondering how things would turn out.

If the night was bad, the morning was worse. As soon as the

Flemings had gone out, a gang of eelmen came and roused us from our bed. I knew we weren't being summoned to see the eelwife. She wouldn't have sent her roughest, filthiest men for that. They dragged us out into the grey dawn and flung us down on the wet ground, and we lay there among brick chips and heaps of crushed shells, watched by the Flemings as they drank their morning ale.

The eelmen kicked at us, but only to wake us up. They slapped us, for the same reason. Then they held their slim blades at our throats.

"We know who you are," they said. "You are the king's men, sent here to find out our secrets."

"He is French," I said. "And I fought for the old king. How can we be the king's men?"

"The old king?" There was muttering among the eelmen. "Is mad Henry coming back? Does he want this island for a landing place? Is that why you are here?"

"Your mistress knows all about us. We came here to buy your good English eels. The pope sent us."

"Some of our men saw you the other day," an eelman said. "You came here on an eelboat, so you know our eels come from Flanders. Why didn't you stay there and buy your eels?"

I looked hopefully at François, but he hadn't thought out that part of our story.

The blades were pressed harder against our skin. We had seen those blades at work, and knew that a few deft strokes would fillet us nicely. "Tell us," they said. "If you're not the king's men, what are you doing here?"

"We came to woo your mistress," François said.

The eelmen's blades jerked, then slackened. "Who told you about her?"

"We were in an alehouse."

"In Manningtree?"

"It might have been."

The eelmen laughed. It was a wet, coughing, slippery sort of laugh. "And which of you was to wed her, brother? Do friars marry now, as well as lying and begging?"

"Him," François pointed at me. "He was to marry her."

"What a pair! Fancy believing what they say in Manningtree."

"He's talking nonsense," I said. "He's in a fever. The bad air of the marshes doesn't suit him. We are here to buy eels, as I said. Lead us to your mistress. She knows the truth."

The eelmen's leader bent over me and pointed his knife at my throat. "Here's the truth," he said. "You'll not be seeing our mistress again, whoever you say you are. There's nothing for you here. If you think you'll get your hands on her money you can think again. We're well set up in that house. We live well and eat well, and we'll not be turned out by a new master."

He kicked me hard, aiming at my belly. Then he kicked me again, and the others joined in, and I curled up to protect myself, so I couldn't see what they were doing to François, though I could hear his cries. I rolled this way and that, dodging what blows I could, knowing we would be lucky to avoid a filleting. Eventually the tide of kicks died down, and the air filled with the sound of panting and wheezing, and the eelmen stood steadying each other, their breath clouding the air. I tried to shuffle backwards, but the brick chips and shell heaps stopped me. When the eelmen had got their breath back they picked up sticks and drove us to the edge of the island, to a place where the land sloped down and poles showed the way across the glistening mud.

"Get out of here fast," their leader said. "Unless you want to find yourself tied up and dumped in an eelpond. And take that thieving Frenchman with you!"

The tide rose as we waded across. I stopped to take off my boots and hose. François kicked off his shoes and hoisted the skirts of his habit. The cold sea swirled against our ankles, then our shins. Soon the bruises we had from the eelmen's kicking were being bathed with cool water. We both finished the journey bare-arsed and mired to our thighs.

"It was a stupid idea," I said, as we tried to rub the mud off our legs with dry grass. "You came up with two plans, but

94

we didn't stick to either of them. A man can't ride two horses at once."

"Last night you sounded as though you were trying to ride a pair of sows. What a lot of sweating and fumbling. Two wrestlers at a Shrovetide fair couldn't have done better. No wonder she turned you out."

"I pleased her well. You must have seen that, looking through the curtains."

"I only peeped for a moment, to see if you were doing it right. There is an art to making love. The secret is in her *belle-chose*."

"I know all that! In my youth, I studied such things. And what I learned then I practised later, in France, in the Morea, and among the Turks. I'll tell you about it one day, if we ever find ourselves at our ease. Take it from me; I've pleasured many a woman."

That silenced him, for a while, at least. When he spoke again he was contrite.

"I am sorry," François said. "My scheme nearly worked. I just forgot that some of her men had seen us land."

I was sorry, too. The things I wanted, a house and a woman, had been dangled before me, then whisked away. I could have done without the marshes, and the eels, and the eelmen. But the eelwife herself was just the sort of woman I had dreamed of, and rich with it. We had nearly succeeded, and so soon after landing.

"We could try again," he said. "A new woman in a new town."

"Maybe. But let's get our story straight and stick to it."

Winter

I wasn't going back to Manningtree to be laughed at, so we stopped at Wix and begged hospitality from the nuns, telling them we had been set upon by robbers, showing them the message bag with its papal crest, hinting at a mission from Rome. The prioress let us sleep in an outhouse, and sent us a pot of balm for our injuries. The nuns fed us and cleaned our clothes, but that wasn't enough for François. While we lay at ease on clean straw he talked about wayward nuns and the pleasures that could be had with them. He had the idea of offering to hear the nuns' confessions, and some of them agreed, but he was disappointed by their sins. Those good women of Wix confessed to no more than murmuring when they ought to have been silent, or not sweeping their rooms thoroughly enough. While they knelt beside him, François whispered soft words to them, tempting them with sins worth confessing.

It was not long before their handyman came with a pitch-fork and saw us off.

"That's what happens when you act the serpent," I said, as we headed westwards. "You get driven out."

"It was Adam and Eve that were driven out of Eden," he said. "As far as we know, the serpent is still there."

"Crawling on its belly."

"I'll tell you one thing: I'll never eat another eel as long as I live."

We wandered for a while, but where we went, I cannot say. Every place looked the same, and no direction was worth following. We lived as well as we could on what François could beg and steal. Sometimes we got a night or two in a pilgrim's hostel, but they always made us move on. That was François' fault. He always said something, or did something, that turned people against us. We slept under hedges if we couldn't get indoors. François complained about that. In

France, he said, there were always empty barns and abandoned farmhouses where a traveller could spend a dry night. It wasn't like that when I was a youth. We always burned buildings after looting them.

Not long afterwards the north wind started to blow over that low, flat land. We were in winter's grip, and it was a grip harder than anyone could remember. It was no time to be wandering, but we had to keep moving if we weren't going to be hanged for thieving.

"I'm cold," François said, as we trudged along yet another road to nowhere. "And hungry. Where can we find shelter? This place must be the arsehole of England."

I was sick of his moaning. "A monastery might suit you. You'd be fed there, and looked after."

"Me, a monk?"

"It is what you pretend to be."

"You dress as a merchant, but can you make us any money? I'll go into a monastery on the day I see you sitting in a counting-house heaping gold coins by the dozen."

"Are you afraid of the vows?"

"No. Poverty would cause me no difficulties. I've always been poor, though I've tried not to be. Money never stays with me for long. You'd think the coins had sworn a vow of their own."

"And chastity?"

"It's the same with women as with money. I've no need to forswear them, as they've foresworn me."

"Obedience?"

"There you have me. I might promise obedience, but it is not in my nature. I am what the stars made me. I am base, and my needs are base, and they are all that I have obeyed."

"You're right," I said. "The true friars wouldn't have you."

"I'm happy enough as I am," François said. "I'll never starve, so long as I can talk my way to a meal or drink. I take things as they come. That's my philosophy."

I didn't bother to point out that he was contradicting himself. "You take things," I said. "That's certain. Like those boots you're wearing. Are friars allowed boots?"

"They are in my order."

"Which order is that?"

"The order of do as you will."

"This order lets you steal?"

"Didn't you steal, when you campaigned in France?"

"We took from the French. But we did it honestly, by force, not by stealth."

That was when we saw the armed men ahead of us. We had no chance to slip off the road, and even if we had it would have made no difference. The countryside was so flat, and the trees and hedges were so bare, that they could see us for miles. As they dropped their pikes to block our path I cursed myself for not keeping a lookout as an old soldier ought to.

The men spread out to surround us, and one of them, a sergeant, stepped forward.

"What's in the bag?" he said.

"Nothing of value." I held it up so he would see the papal crest. "Just documents. I am an envoy of the pope."

"The pope?" The sergeant looked round at his men. "Last time he sent anyone to England, it was to beg money to fight the Turks."

"I'm not asking for money."

François glared at me, as though asking for money might have been worth a try. "Thomas here is worthy of alms," he said. "He fought the Turks himself."

"Did you, old man?" The sergeant gave me a nasty smile. "You were a soldier once, like us?"

"I served in France," I said. "In the days when the English could still beat the French."

"He fought in the Morea, too," François said, trying not to sound French. "And at Constantinople. He stood firm against the sultan's finest troops. What were they called?"

"The Janissaries."

"That's right! The Janissaries." François held his hand up, admonishing the soldiers in a monkish manner. "And he fought the sultan's fearsome irregulars, as well. What were they called?"

"The Bashi-Bazouks."

"Bashi-Bazouks!" they shouted, mocking me. "Bashi-Bazouks!"

François was not abashed. "He was there when they took Constantinople," he said. "What a battle that was!"

"So why isn't he dead?"

"The sultan spared him," François said, "because of his great bravery."

The men laughed, and they'd have laughed louder if they'd known the truth. The story of my enslavement would win no sympathy from them. They were desperate men with knives and pikes, hoping to feed themselves by following one master one week and another the next. But they were armed, and that winter arms were all the law there was.

They took my bag and upturned it, emptying the book and the map onto the icy mud. Finding nothing of value to them, they turned to me, pulling off my coat and slitting its lining, poking their hands into my shirt and hose, making me open my mouth in case I had coins under my tongue. I knew all their tricks, having played them once myself, but they found nothing on me they wanted. They were luckier with François, who had an assortment of coins and small valuables concealed beneath his friar's habit.

The men I served with in my youth would have taken everything, stripped their victims, then turned them out into the cold to freeze or starve. But the fight must have gone out of my countrymen since then. The sergeant took François' haul, then the others objected, and soon they were all arguing. The sergeant tried to end it by ordering them to march on, and they did, leaving us by the roadside, angry but unharmed.

"You told me you had nothing," I said, picking up my coat from the ground.

"It's true now."

"Where did you get all that stuff?"

"I found it, here and there."

"What did you plan to do with it?"

"I thought it might be useful."

"When I'd spent all my money."

"That's right."

"Well, I spent it some time ago. Why didn't you tell me you had something? Why did you let us suffer when we could have lived off what you stole?"

"It's just my way," he said. "It is hard to change our ways."

"Well, now we've got nothing, and we're in the middle of nowhere, and if there was anything worth stealing round here, that rabble will have stolen it. We are lucky they didn't want clothes."

I put my coat and cloak back on, then gathered up the map and book. The mappamundi was filthier than before, but I looked at it anyway, hoping some vestige of its power might remain. It gave me no more guidance than any other old rag. Had it lost its power because François scorned it? Would it have guided me better if I had got it cleaned? I brushed the mud off it and put it in my bag.

François shivered as he pulled his habit around him. "We can't sink much lower," he said. But he was wrong.

We kept off the road after that, though the going was heavy. One night, just as it was getting dark, we smelled food, and as we were starving we followed the smell, determined to have some of whatever was cooking, whether we begged or stole it. The smell led us through hedge and thicket to a hovel built round the trunk of a tree. Bare branches rose above it, catching the last of the setting sun. There was a dog ahead of us, a big, heavy-jowled beast, that growled and waddled towards us. I have never been lucky with dogs, except for the pope's lap-dog, which died at just the right time. Dogs have always given me trouble, and I was ready to back off and try my luck somewhere else, only the smell of stew, wafting out of the hovel, was overpowering.

"Don't be afraid, old soldier," François said.

"Who said I was afraid?"

"I'll show you how to deal with dogs."

He got down on all fours, and hung his head, and made the sort of whimpering sounds that dogs make when they are getting to know each other. He shuffled forward, bent his back, thrust his arse in the air, kicked his legs. It was another of his performances, and it would have got us a jug or two of ale if he had done it in a tavern. It got the dog's attention, and when François spoke gently in French, coaxing and wheedling, the beast dropped its guard and let him pass.

"What a fine smelling stew!" he said, calling out so that whoever was in the hovel might hear. "Would there be a portion for a pair of hungry travellers?"

We could see firelight between the rough planks that formed the hovel's walls. We heard movement inside, then the door flap was flung open. A small, hunched figure stood before us, lit from behind by the fire.

"Good evening, mistress," François said. "What a fine hound you have. And what a good house. Built round a tree, I see. That must give it strength."

"You can cut out the sweet talk." It was a woman's voice, cracked and dry, but quite strong. "My hound keeps me in rabbits, and my house keeps out the wind and rain, for the most part. That's all that needs to be said about them."

"Your stew . . ."

"Is as good as it can be, flavoured with whatever I can gather. As for sharing it, I'll decide that when I've seen what kind of men you are. Step inside and sit by the fire so I can take a look at you."

We did as we were told, and soon we were staring at each other's faces in the firelight, though François looked mostly at the woman's cauldron, which was bubbling nicely over the fire. She was everything I feared the eelwife would be: old, dirty, ugly and poor. When she had looked at us for a while, she spoke.

"You can share my stew. But in return you'll have to do something for me."

"Anything!" François said.

Like me, he probably thought of chopping wood, or carrying water. Something of that sort would have been fair enough, for a good feed.

"I'm glad to find you so agreeable," she said, reaching for a bowl that lay nearby. She knelt by the cauldron and dipped the bowl in, then held it out, allowing us to see and smell the thick, meaty stew. My mouth watered and my belly rumbled. I wanted that stew inside me more than anything I could think of. I reached out, and so did François, but she plucked the bowl away. "You'll do anything?" she said. "Anything I ask?"

"Anything!" François said, and she gave him the bowl.

Of course, he shovelled as much of the stew down his throat as he could before handing any over to me. And while he wolfed it down, I thought. What if she asked for all our worldly goods, or made us forswear our freedom?

François' loose tongue licked the bowl clean. "Not bad," he said, giving it back to the old woman. "Though it would be improved by a pint or two of good red wine."

I feared she would be offended, but she laughed, and filled the bowl for me. "If I had a pint or two of good red wine," she said, "everything would be improved."

She watched me eat, then filled the bowl again for François. When she was sure we were both full, she smiled at us, showing us a mouthful of gaps and stumps. Her face was lined and blotched. Her hair stuck up like frosted straw. She was no beauty, but at that moment I thought her the kindest person we had met since landing in England. Then she spoke.

"You promised you would do anything I asked," she said. "Well, what I ask is this: one of you must bed me."

François belched loudly and thought quickly. "I yield to you, my master," he said, bowing his head to me. "The privilege is yours."

"Since when have you deferred to me?"

"Since Paris, when we met."

"Never! You've always looked after yourself before thinking of me."

François put on a sad face. "I am sorry, my master, if that is what you think. If I have failed in the past I make up for it now by yielding to you this fine and hospitable lady."

"Mistress," I said, "my friend and I must have words. You won't mind if we step outside?"

"Don't go too far," she said. "There's thorny thicket all around, and my dog is guarding the gap. He won't let anyone pass now that night has fallen."

"What's all this nonsense of calling me your master?" I said, when we had gone outside.

"That woman's stew put me in a good mood. I remembered the debt I owe you."

"No you didn't. You just don't want to bed her."

"Why should I?"

"You agreed to it," I said. "So you can clinch the bargain."

"I didn't know what I was agreeing to. No one should be held to a bargain like that."

"You have her. It's only fair. I had the eelwife, you have this one."

"I couldn't."

"You're younger than me," I said. "You'll please her more than I could."

"Why? You told me you could pleasure a woman. You said you knew all the secrets, though it didn't do much good with the eelwife. Her men threw us out anyway."

"They got rid of us because they feared I would please her too much, and become their master."

"Now is your chance to prove yourself."

"And yours," I said, "if you think you can do better."

"I yield to your age and experience."

I thought about creeping away into the night, but the dog was guarding the way, and I didn't fancy my chances of getting past it.

"She's a filthy old crone," I said. "How can I bed her?"

"Shut your eyes," he said. "And use your imagination. In your mind, her wrinkled dugs will be the pert breasts of a fragrant young girl. Her sagging belly will seem as smooth and white as marble, her slack buttocks as taut as a doe's rump. And if your imagination can't manage that, then there are advantages to age. Her hairy old quim will welcome your stiff yard more readily than the untried cleft of a virgin."

"You've really made her sound appetising now," I said. "It

sounds as though you've given the subject much thought. You should have her, not me."

"Don't you know the stories? The old tales of heroes who bed crones, and wake up to find them transformed into lovely damsels?"

I knew those stories: they were often retold. And in every one of them the hero learned a great secret in return for bedding the crone. All we had was a bellyful of stew. "I'm no hero," I said. "If you know those stories, then play the part yourself. Use your poetical fancy to make her seem a virgin. You told me that women had foresworn you, well here's one that's desperate for it. You can have her."

François' glib tongue failed him. He fell silent and stepped away, into the darkness. The dog growled. François snuffled and blubbed. When he turned back to the light, his face was wet with tears.

"I can't do it," he said. "There was no stopping me, once. Women led me into all sorts of trouble. But I paid the price. I was thrown into prison." He sobbed. "The things they did to me. The tortures. I'm no use to a woman now."

"So why do you talk about it so much?"

"I am a poet. It is my nature to talk of times past and things lost."

"Why did you stir up those nuns at Wix, filling their heads with sinful thoughts?"

"Talk and thoughts are all I have. Don't reproach me!"

He collapsed to the ground like a heap of rags, no use to anyone. Unless I could think of a way out, I would have to lie with the crone.

She stuck her head out of the doorway. "It's to be you, is it? I like an older man. Not too old, mind, but old enough to know what he's doing. Come to my bed and show me what you know."

Her bed was the same heap of straw we had sat on to eat. She lay on it and hoisted up her filthy skirts. She stank, but I daresay I did too. There was nothing for it but to go ahead.

I didn't bother with any fancy business. I had to think of myself, not her. I remembered my night with the eelwife, but I

104

couldn't forget the beating her men had given me, and my yard got no stiffer than a stunned eel. I thought of girls I had loved when young, women I had dallied with and left, a rose-scented woman in Constantinople. I thought hard until I was hard, then entered the old woman. She was soft and yielding, just like François said. When she sighed, I heard the sigh of a virgin, and was lost in my dreams until I finished.

I slept well that night. We had sunk so low that a hovel, a heap of straw and a hag by my side were the best I could hope for. In the morning I kicked François awake, ready to drag him away before the old woman could tempt us with more of her squalid delights. She was even uglier in daylight.

"I heard you last night," she said. "You two argue like man and wife. But I'll tell you this: no matter how much you bicker, you're stuck with each other. Nothing but death will part you."

Francois didn't comment on the old crone's prediction. He didn't thank me for earning his supper. He wouldn't tell me how he was unmanned in prison. He kept silent until we were well away from the hovel. "The countryside is killing me," he said. "We must go to a town. There's nothing else for it. The danger is greater, but the pickings are richer."

Colchester

At Colchester we lived in comfort for a few days, but when the innkeeper realised we could not pay he threw us out into the street, threatening to set the watchmen on us if we didn't come back with some money. To make things worse, François cursed him foully, mostly in French, but his meaning was clear. I dragged him off to the marketplace, where we could lose ourselves among the crowd.

"What shall we do?" I said, though I knew he could make no useful suggestion.

"We'd better have a drink."

"We can't pay."

"That didn't stop us before. Now, let us drink to forget that we cannot afford to drink."

"But where?"

You just can't drink anywhere. Alehouses are cheap, but strangers stand out, and François, speaking French, dressed as a friar, given to drunken versifying, was stranger than most. Some taverns welcome everyone, but you can't be there for long before someone wants to know all your business. The best places are in ports, by the waterside, where sailors and travellers gather. But you can't get credit, and we had no money.

"Anywhere will do," François said. "And as for money, you've been dragging that bag around with you, and its useless contents, ever since we left Paris. Why didn't you sell something when we had the chance?"

"I got those things from the pope."

"I risked my life to get that bag for you," he said. "If I'd known what was in it, I wouldn't have bothered."

"It's too late now. The bag's at the inn, and we won't get it back unless we can pay."

"Didn't you think of taking something out of it?"

I hesitated, knowing what he would say. "I've got the book. It's here, under my coat."

I don't know why I carried it on me. Perhaps it pleased me to keep a memory of my life in Rome, where I had lived in comfort and had the confidence of the pope. Though I had longed to leave that life, it seemed good to me when I had left it.

"The *Timaeus* of Plato?" François said. "You will have to sell it."

"Will I?" His tone annoyed me. "Why should I sell my book to please you?"

"Your book? You stole it from the pope."

"I took it from his deathbed. He had no further need of it."

"And neither do you. We can't eat or drink it, and it's not keeping us warm."

"Can you see a bookseller in this market? I can't. There's nothing but butchers, bakers, fishmongers, and men selling cloth and corn." One thing I could see was the pillory, standing there as a warning.

"There must be someone who would pay for a fine book, even here. The priests will know. Let us go and ask them. It won't take long in a little town like this."

We toured the churches of Colchester. Fine places they were, paid for by all the wealth that flowed through the market. But the priests were ignorant men, no better than sheep, or so François said. They were afraid of foreigners, jealous of friars, feared we had been sent to catch them out in error or heresy. I had to send François away, and he went angrily to an alehouse, saying that if I wouldn't pay, he could talk a drink out of anyone.

On my own, I got more out of the priests, learning that there was a scholar in the town who had a few books and might buy more. Pleased with myself, I went to the alehouse and looked for François. He had got himself a drink, and was telling a tall tale in bad English to some dyers who were laughing at him without understanding a word he said. Dyers are like that: driven half-mad by the dyes they use, they laugh at anything. I should have left him there, but I dragged him away, giving his new friends to understand that he was not right in the head, which they took as a taunt against them, so that our exit drew more attention than I would have liked.

"I have heard of someone who might buy the book."

"I will come with you." he said. "An English scholar would be a curiosity worth seeing."

"I will visit him alone," I said.

"So why did you interrupt my drinking?"

I couldn't think of an answer, except that he was attracting attention. "I'll go alone," I said. "He might be suspicious of you."

"And what about you? In your merchant's clothes you look fit to buy or sell wool, but a book?"

"I can speak to him in his own language."

"And I can speak to him in the language of scholars."

"You forget," I said. "I know Latin too."

"But not as well as I do."

I saw again the side of François that lost him friends and drove him into exile. If only he had been a little humbler, he might have been happier. "I will go alone," I said. "And you can wait nearby."

François looked up. "It's starting to snow again. This English climate is dreadful."

The marketplace was emptying, the traders closing their shops and stalls, their customers hurrying home before the snow settled. I pointed out an empty stall, told François to shelter in it, and set off to the scholar's house.

I had to knock long and loud before anyone opened the door. The scholar looked at my clothes, now dirty and threadbare, at my unshaven face, at my scarred and calloused hands, and at the cloth-wrapped object I held. It must have been hard for him to guess what my status or nature might be. "What do you want?"

"I have a book to sell."

"You? A book?"

He looked doubtful, and I feared that François was right. I have read a dozen books, perhaps more, but I am not a scholar.

I have not slaved for knowledge like François. Why should a man like me have a book to sell? And what could I say about Plato's *Timaeus* that would make anyone buy it?

"It is a very old book," I said. "Newly translated."

"I have recently bought a book." He spoke as though that settled the matter, and I looked at his thin face and musty robe, and noted that there appeared to be no servants in the house, and wondered whether he had enough money to buy the *Timaeus*. Then I remembered François, waiting in the market, ready to mock my failure.

"It is cold out here in the snow," I said. "Will you not let me in? I can show you my book."

The scholar forgot his suspicions and opened the door wider so I could step inside. His room was almost bare, furnished only with a stool, a small desk, and a couple of open book chests.

"Let us see what you know of books," he said, bending over a chest and pulling something out. He held a book up, showing me the title page, which was richly illustrated with birds and beasts and people dressed in exotic costumes.

"Le Divisament dou Monde," I said, reading the ornate letters that spelled out its title.

"You spoke the words like a Frenchman."

"Why not?" I said. "My mother was Gascon. I lived in France for years."

"I daresay you understand bills of lading, qualities of wool and wine, rates of exchange, and things of that sort."

"I am not a merchant," I said, "and I can read anything." It was an unwise boast, but I made it, and was obliged to prove myself.

"Really?" he said, pushing the book into my hands. "Read some more."

I began to read. The book's hero was called Marco Polo, but its author was a Pisan called Rustichello. Polo claimed to have travelled the East, and Rustichello wrote in a peculiar sort of French, full of high-flown words and touches of Italian, mentioning people and places I had never heard of. Perhaps François would have made more sense of it than I could, but I did my best, reading the book's introduction, which set out its subject and purpose.

"Enough!" the scholar said, when I had struggled through a few pages. He reached out for the book. "You are not as good as you think you are."

I knew that I was better than he thought me, but I was there to sell, and a good merchant knows better than to argue with a customer.

"My book," I said. "Would you like to see it?"

"What sort of a book is it? A romance?"

I reached beneath my cloak and pulled out the book. "It is by Plato. It is called the *Timaeus*. It is full of interesting things: the nature of man's soul, the creation of the world . . ."

"The Bible tells me all there is to know about the creation of the world."

"There is more," I said. "It tells of the world's soul, and how the elements were made . . ."

"Elements? Is it a manual of alchemy? I suppose you will tell me that if I buy the book it will make my fortune."

"No. It will make you wise."

He looked disappointed. Perhaps he was not a real scholar at all, but a reader of tall tales from abroad and stories of brave knights and courtly love. He took the book, frowning. "How do you know what it contains?"

"I have read it."

"You have read this?" He opened the book jabbed a delicate finger at one of its densely written pages. "It is in Latin."

"Newly translated from the Greek," I said.

"You look like a man who has lost all his money in business, yet you say you are not a merchant. What are you, a runaway priest?"

"I was a soldier, but I had some education when I was a young man."

"Prove that you can read this."

I did as he asked, reading some of the dialogue between Socrates and his friends that had consoled Pius on what turned out to be his deathbed. I had stumbled at first, when I read the book in Ancona, but Pius had guided me, and I was able to read well enough to that English scholar. I was sorry that François was not there to hear me, though no doubt he would have criticised my pronunciation, or found some other fault.

The scholar looked crestfallen.

"Do you know any other languages?"

"Tuscan, Turkish, Greek . . ."

"Greek? You speak the language of those schismatics and heretics? God has punished them by giving their kingdom to the Turks."

"I learned Greek in the Morea."

"You were there, among the heretics?"

"I was defending their kingdom against the Turks."

The scholar looked me over again, wondering what kind of man I was. I could tell that he was suspicious of anyone who had lived among heretics. Then a flicker of hope enlivened his face.

"You said you could read anything?"

"Yes," I said, confirming my foolish boast.

"I have something that I think may defeat you. A book that has puzzled me for years. If you are as clever as you think you are, you will understand it. If not, not."

The scholar knelt and rummaged beneath his desk. I looked around his room, noting its shabbiness. There was a smell of cat's piss, and of worse. He must have cared more for books than for his own comfort. I felt full of hope that I would impress him, and that he would give me a good price for the *Timaeus*. When he stood up he was holding a small chest, which he set down on the desk. He reached beneath his gown, produced the key, fiddled with it clumsily, then opened the lid and took out a book. I expected to see a precious volume, bound in finest leather, hinged and clasped with gold, panelled with ivory. But the book he showed me was nothing like that.

"What will you make of this?" he said, smiling oddly.

I held the book in my hands, and nothing that I saw or felt told me how important the book was, or what it would lead to. It was small, fat, and covered with soft leather. I looked at the scholar, and seeing encouragement in his face, dared to ask him a tactless question.

"How much did you pay for this book?"

"Pay? What makes you think I paid for it?"

"You buy books, don't you?"

"Not this one. It was left to me by my father, and he had it from a friend, who had it from another friend. So if you want to know how much I might pay for your book, you are out of luck."

"I was only . . ."

"Read from the book," he said. "Prove that you can read anything."

I opened the book. Each page was packed with words, all written in a tiny script, tightly looped and curled, as though a good scribe had tried to save space by fitting in as many words as he could. For the most part the words were written in neat lines running across the page, though sometimes they stopped short, like verse, or lists, or recipes. Some of the pages folded out to reveal charts or pictures. Other pictures interrupted the text, flowed down the pages, or filled the spaces round the edge. I saw, or thought I saw, a compass rose, homunculi, a coiled fern, queens and angels, a map, naked women, circles within circles, and other things, too strange to name. But the scholar had set me to read the text, and that is what I tried to do.

The writing was so small that I had to peer at the book closely. I looked for words I knew, but found none. The letters looked a little like Greek, and a little like Arabic, but were neither. I brought the book nearer to my eyes, then moved it back again. Meaning swam out of the pages, then dived back into obscurity. The thought struck me that it might have been written with a mirror, a trick some of the pope's spies used. I squinted, rubbed my eyes, tilted the book and turned my head, hoping to see the letters backwards or upside-down.

I could not understand a single word.

"I know it isn't Hebrew," the scholar said. "I have seen Hebrew books in Cambridge, and they look nothing like this."

I said nothing.

"It isn't Greek, is it?" he said. His tone was uncertain. If I had told him that it was Greek he would have believed me. But then he would have asked me to read it.

"No."

"You said you were in the East. Is it some Saracen tongue? Turkish, or Arabic?"

"No."

"You said you could read anything. What does it say?"

"I don't know."

"So what language is it written in?"

"I've never seen anything like it."

"I thought so," the scholar said. "You know nothing."

Kings and queens

François was still in the marketplace, but had moved to another stall, and was huddled over a dying brazier left by one of the traders.

"It is no use," I said. "He refused to buy the book."

"Why?" François wrapped his cloak around him.

"He was afraid of it." I took his place at the brazier, trying to warm my hands.

"Afraid of a book? What kind of scholar was he?"

"He called the Greeks heretics, and said that God had punished them."

"That's no reason for not studying their books. Was Aristotle a Christian? No. But every true scholar has read him."

"You would know."

"Perhaps your English scholar feared reading the *Timaeus* because he lacked the subtlety to understand it."

"It is a difficult book. Pope Pius said so."

"A true scholar would have bought the book and laboured till he understood it."

"He may be tired of that sort of labour," I said. "He showed me another book. A very strange one. He asked me to read it, but I couldn't."

"Why not?"

"Because it was written in a language I have never seen before."

"I thought you spoke every language known to man."

"I've never said that."

"You were the wrong person to sell the book. He would have bought it from me."

I was angry with François. Was it my fault that the scholar was not a true scholar, that he liked romances and feared philosophy, that he had defeated me with an impossible test? If I had known how difficult it would be, I would have sold the book in Italy, or in Paris, or some other place that was full of scholars and collectors.

"The curfew will sound soon," I said. "If we don't find somewhere to sleep, the watchmen will be along."

"The watch! Why should we fear them?"

"They'll throw us in jail as vagrants. That's if the innkeeper hasn't reported us as debtors. Didn't you see those prisoners chained up at the Moot Hall?"

"In Paris, the watchmen were my friends, for the most part. And the rest of them could be bribed."

"No one is your friend here. Or mine. And as for bribing, we have nothing to bribe with."

"Let me try," he said. "Give me the book. I will sell it."

"Do you think I'd trust you, a man who boasts of his thieving?"

"As I have already observed, you stole the book from the pope."

"Who are you to accuse me? You have scrounged off me ever since we first met. Now you expect me to sell everything I own to keep you in drink."

"You'd have nothing to sell if it wasn't for me."

"If I gave you the book, you'd run off with it, and I'd have nothing left at all."

"Have nothing then!" François said. "Be as you were when we met in Paris, friendless and penniless!"

At that, François shouted something else at me, then strode off into the darkness. I was glad to see him go. I had more than repaid him for the help he gave me in Paris. Had he forgotten that when I first saw him he was about to throw himself into the river? It was no wonder that an ingrate like him had run out of friends, that the rogues he drank with betrayed him, that he had been jailed and banished from France.

I pressed myself deeper into the wooden stall, trying to get out of the wind, looking at the last glow from the brazier, wondering what to do. I still had no money, but without François I stood more chance of finding food and lodging.

Or did I? It was his quick wits that had kept us in food and drink. I had lived so long as a slave and servant that I had forgotten how to fend for myself when the money runs short.

How had I managed before? I sat there, remembering my youth. I had fought in the king's army in France, then deserted and joined a gang of brigands. We had lived free, taking what we wanted, killing those who tried to stop us. I had been trying ever since to get my sins absolved. François was right. I was no better than he was.

I brooded on life's misfortunes, listening to the wind howling through thatched roofs. The snow was getting thicker. The country would be covered with drifts. Travel would be impossible. I was stuck in Colchester without money or friends.

I was not very surprised when François came back, his cloak thick with snow. I thought he might apologise or beg for help, but he spoke boldly, as though I was in the wrong and he was prepared to ignore it.

"I have thought of a plan," he said. "We must make our way to the queen."

"The queen?" Could he have got drunk in so short a time? Or had the cold brought on a fever that made him rave? I stood up and faced him. "Are you mad?"

"We must go to her," he said, shaking the snow from his cloak as though he meant to set off immediately. "Queen Margaret will help us. I knew her father, King René."

"Oh yes? You look like a man who consorts with royalty."

"If you were a friend of the pope, why should I not be a friend of kings? Kings need friends, just like everyone else."

"Yes, René was always begging favours from Pope Pius, always sending letters, always complaining."

"René has much to complain of, having many titles, but little land. He is Duke of Anjou, and of Bar and Lorraine. He is Marquis of Provence, King of Naples, and Sicily, Hungary, and Jerusalem." A stormy gust of wind blasted our faces with fine dry snow. François hardly noticed. "Or he would be if they let him."

"And Duke René was a friend of yours?"

"He liked people to call him king. You should have seen his castle, the things he had there, paintings, books, treasures. He encouraged the arts, welcomed poets and musicians."

"And he welcomed you?"

"He was more of a patron than a friend." François shivered. "The fires in his castle were hot. Always heaped with well-seasoned firewood. If you could get near them."

"We can't warm ourselves by thinking of fire."

"You're right," he said. "Isn't there something we could burn? Didn't you think of looking?"

"You were here for longer than me."

François stamped off to the other end of the marketplace, muttering to himself, bumping against barrels and stalls. He returned with an armful of straw mats, which he tipped into the brazier.

"The merchants won't be pleased," I said.

"Fuck them! They'll be in their nice warm houses, counting their takings. That's if they're not in bed, cuddled up with their well-fed wives."

The mats flared up, warming our hands and faces, lighting up the stall, making the world outside utterly black. If anyone saw the blaze we would be in trouble. But there was no danger. The fire died down as quickly as it started, leaving us colder than before.

"Come to think of it," François said, "King René wasn't a very generous patron. Not to me. In fact, I was sent on my way after only a few weeks at Angers. And I was never really admitted to the inner circle." François kicked angrily at the brazier. "But it might have been different! If I'd had the chance to show him what I could do, René might have found a place for me at his court, given me a pension."

"Even if he had, there'd be no point in paying our respects to Queen Margaret. She's on the run with King Henry, wherever he is. Scotland probably. Or France. So she's no use to us."

"How the mighty are fallen!"

Was François lamenting the queen's fate or his own?

"At Calais," he said, "didn't the guard say that Queen Margaret was recruiting men to fight for her husband? You fought for him before. You could take service with him again."

"I have done enough fighting. I came back to England to retire peacefully."

"And how will you do that, with no money?"

"I don't know."

"Fighting is where the money is. Whoever wins will reward his followers."

"Then volunteer yourself."

"I am, as you once pointed out, a backstreet brawler, not a soldier."

"And a thief, whose thieving has made it impossible to settle anywhere."

"Then let us move on. Let us look for the old king and his queen, and see whether we can get anything by serving them."

"Haven't you noticed the weather? By morning it will be impossible to go beyond the town walls."

"We could make a start."

"We'd have to go to Scotland, or back to France. We'd never find the queen. The way things are we can't even find ourselves a warm bed."

A pilgrim

A voice came out of the darkness. It spoke English, but roughly, like someone from the cold North. "Anything can be found," it said, "if you want to find it."

We looked out into the blizzard to see who had spoken. A man strode towards us, his shape emerging from the swirling whiteness that had filled the marketplace. He was a foot taller than either of us, cloaked and hooded and dusted with snow, a quarterstaff in his right hand. I did not recognise him at first. Instead of his Saracen clothes he was dressed as a pilgrim, his long tunic sewn with a red cross. His stance told me that the staff was not just a pilgrim's solace, that he was well able to use it, hitting hard at any man who stood in his way.

Christian Rosenkreutz was the last person I expected to see in England, and the last person I wished to meet again.

"Why have you come here?" I asked.

"You have something I want."

"How did you find me?"

"They talked of you in Rome. Patrizzi was not very complimentary. After that it was easy. You leave a trail behind you like a wounded boar. A trail of crimes, debts and insults. It is a wonder no one else has followed you. Or it would be, if I had not calmed things down by scattering a little gold."

"What is it you want?" François had heard him mention gold.

"I think Thomas knows." Rosenkreutz's voice was deep, calm, reproachful. "But first we need light. Find something to burn."

"There's nothing." François said. "If you want light, let's go to our inn. If there's something you want from us, you can pay our bill. Then we'll talk."

I thought Rosenkreutz would argue, but he did not. He allowed us to lead him to the inn, ignored the innkeeper's puzzlement, paid what he asked for, and some extra for a private room with a fire. François, not satisfied with luxury we had only dreamed of, demanded hippocras, and Rosenkreutz agreed to that, too.

The innkeeper was polite, but wary. Rosenkreutz, a tall blue-eyed foreigner who had befriended a pair of penniless scoundrels, might easily have been a spy, a man sent by the Hanseatic League to find out England's secrets. Such men were found in every seaport, and reporting them to the harbourmaster might well bring a small reward. And the coins Rosenkreutz paid with would have attracted attention anywhere.

"Now, Thomas," Rosenkreutz said, when we were settled into the room, and the fire was burning nicely, and we each had our hands round a cup of hot spiced wine. "Will you show me what I came for?"

"What is that?"

"You know very well."

"The book?" I reached beneath my doublet and brought out the *Timaeus*. If he was willing to pay me for it I would regard him as a friend. Even if he wasn't, we had won ourselves a night of warmth and comfort. François didn't care. He had the jug, and was busy pouring himself another cup of wine.

Rosenkreutz looked briefly at the book and handed it back. "I think not. Books like that are two a penny in Constantinople. I didn't come all the way here for that."

"Then what do you want from me?"

"The mappamundi, of course. I know you have it."

I had last seen Rosenkreutz in Rome. The mappamundi had not arrived until we reached Ancona. Patrizzi must have guessed I had it, and told Rosenkreutz.

"How did you get here?" I said. "Didn't the king's men stop you?"

Rosenkreutz laughed. "Does England have a king?" He sipped a little of his hippocras. "A boy and a madman both call themselves king. But can either of them rule?"

"The king's men turned us back in Calais."

"No one stops me," he said. "Why should they? I am a pious pilgrim on his way to Walsingham."

"Who is he?" François asked, looking up from his wine at last, wondering who he was scrounging from.

"He is Christian Rosenkreutz."

Rosenkreutz turned to François and bowed his head slightly. There was no humility in the gesture.

"Please allow me to introduce myself," he said. "I am a traveller, a man dedicated to the acquiring of wisdom."

"And you have come to England for that?" François laughed and returned to his wine.

"I have come for what Thomas has. But England is not entirely devoid of wisdom. I have been here before. It was when they starved King Richard to death."

"That's an old story," I said. "The king's sad end was a tale my father used to tell. It happened before we were born. Long before. You can't have been there."

"Can't I? I've been around for a long time. I lived through the great plague. It did not kill me, but made me strong. I've seen war, too, and survived that. I was at Nicopolis when Sultan Bayezit crushed the Last Crusade. So many dead! Ten thousand men beheaded. But not me. I kept my head and went east. I was at Ankara when Tamburlaine routed the Turks. Afterwards, I saw Sultan Bayezit in his golden cage, driven mad by Tamburlaine's taunts. He wasn't the only one: half the world's mad, and has been for a hundred years. I was there at Rouen when they burned Joan the Virgin at the stake. What visions she must have had!"

"I saw Joan," I said. "It was at Orléans. She fought well, and so did her followers."

Rosenkreutz put down his wine cup. "Her battles hold no interest for me. The only true victory is the triumph of one nature over another, the transformation that is in us all, if we are strong enough."

Could I believe a word Rosenkreutz said? I looked at his face, trying to guess how old he was. If his tales were true, he would have been a hundred years old, yet he was no more wrinkled than I was. If anything, François looked older, and he was not much more than thirty. François' short, hard life was all there in his raddled face, but Rosenkreutz's face told me nothing.

François had been listening with increasing interest. The hippocras had warmed and revived him. "And what of Julius Caesar?" he said. "And Alexander? Or Xerxes, Achilles, and Helen of Troy? Did you know them, too? Did you watch them brought down by fate?"

"I have seen what I have seen," Rosenkreutz said.

"If you have been to all those places," François said, "and seen all those things. Why have I never heard of you?"

"In the days of my youth, I was not fully myself. The journeys I made then were little more than idle wanderings. My true voyage began later, and is not yet over." He gave us a disdainful look, giving us to understand that his voyaging was more of the spirit than the body. "Besides," he said. "I use other names when it suits me, just as you do."

François seemed about to protest.

"I know who you are," Rosenkreutz said. "I have even read some of your immoral verses."

"Don't you mean immortal?"

"Immortality is something I cannot judge," Rosenkreutz said. "Not yet. But I know about your crimes and follies," he said. "You were lucky they didn't hang you. And so is Thomas. What a pair you are!" Rosenkreutz paused to admire us. "Yet you did the job."

"What job?" I said.

"You got the mappamundi away from Ancona, brought it here, where no one knows what it is or what to do with it."

"You knew we would do that?"

"Don't be surprised at what I know." Rosenkreutz said. "I have seen such things, the likes of which you can never dream of."

"I did no job for you," François said. "I came here of my own free will, to help Thomas."

"Free will? Does a creature like you presume to have such a thing? What choice did you have? It was England or the gallows, for you."

François had no answer to that, except to stare angrily into his empty cup. Rosenkreutz reached out his hand. "Show me the mappamundi."

We had to summon the innkeeper and pay him again before he would hand over my bag. When he had gone, I took out the folded silk map and gave it to Rosenkreutz. His hands trembled slightly as he set it down on the bedcover and spread it out. Then he frowned. "It's filthy!" he said.

"It was stolen in Paris."

"I got it back," François said. "But the thieves had fouled it."

Rosenkreutz tugged at the map's frayed corners, trying to stretch it flat. "You have been careless. Do you not realise how valuable this map is?"

François glanced at me, and I saw what he was thinking. If Rosenkreutz wanted the map, we might get more than just a night or two's lodging out of him.

"It is well drawn," I said. "Master Toscanelli knew his work."

"Yes!" Rosenkreutz said, bending over the map. "Everything is set out clearly, despite the tears and smudges. Christendom is here, the lost empire of the Greeks is there, and Aethiopia, Arabia, the lands of the Great Khan, the frozen North, Cathay, India, Cipangu, the two Javas, the Spice Islands, are all in their proper places." He looked up at us and smiled. "When I wandered the East, I had no map. As a result I did not find everything I looked for. With this to guide me, I can resume my search."

"It is my map," I said. "I need it. I was following it." I wasn't just trying to get the price up. I didn't want to lose the map. In fact, I wanted it more than before, as Rosenkreutz had reawakened its power. As he smoothed it out and brushed at the stains with his bony fingers the colours glowed brighter, the shapes of land and sea showed clearer, the magic of a cloth that held the world felt stronger.

Rosenkreutz smiled. "Well, Thomas, you were right to try following it, but . . ."

"I hoped it would lead me home."

"It can lead you nowhere if you lack the wisdom to

understand it. I have that wisdom, and with me to interpret it, the map will lead us wherever we want to go."

"How much will you pay for it?" François said.

"Pay?" Rosenkreutz raised his hand and waved it, gesturing at the room, the fire, the empty wine jug. "You want more?"

"We need money," François said. "We've nothing left."

"Then sell something," Rosenkreutz said. "That book Thomas showed me. The *Timaeus*."

"I tried selling it to a scholar in the town," I said. "But he wouldn't buy it. He said it was heretical."

"He wouldn't have understood it. Few Englishmen could."

Though I had not much liked the scholar, I felt obliged to defend English scholarship. "He had other books. Lots of them. He showed me one called *Le Divisament dou Monde*."

"Everyone knows that book," François said. "Though some say it is full of lies."

"They are right," Rosenkreutz said. "I don't believe Marco Polo went to Cathay. He made up his stories. I have seen much more than him!"

"The scholar had other books," I said. "There was one that was like nothing I've ever seen." I tried to tell Rosenkreutz about the strange script that I could not read, but he soon held up his hand to stop me.

"Was this book illustrated?"

"Yes."

"Tell me about the pictures," he said. "Describe them to me."

I did my best, and Rosenkreutz grew strangely agitated, allowing the map to fall, standing and pacing the room.

"I can hardly believe it," he said. "It sounds like one of the Seven Tomes."

"What are they?" François said.

"Your ignorance does not surprise me. The Tomes are books of secret knowledge written by great Sages, each of them ciphered so that only the wisest will understand."

"And there are seven of them?"

"Seven originals. There may be copies. I have heard rumours." Rosenkreutz turned to me. "How is it that you can stumble across such a thing when the world's greatest scholars have spent lifetimes searching?" He looked down at me with his cold blue eyes. "You are lucky," he said. "I knew it. Anyone who can escape Constantinople as you did must be very lucky indeed. That is why I entrusted you with the map-pamundi. I must keep you about me to aid my own luck."

"Lucky?" I said, remembering François' way with a sad story. "Constant sorrow, that's been my life. Nothing's gone right for me. I've lived for fifty years and suffered a century's worth of misfortunes."

"Yet you are alive. That proves your good luck."

"I'm penniless. What sort of luck is that?"

"Luck has nothing to do with money," Rosenkreutz said. "We must test yours again."

"How?"

"You must get me this book you saw."

"I don't think the owner will sell it."

"Neither do I. Not if it is what you say it is. You will have to take it."

"Are you asking me to break into the scholar's house?"

"What is rightly ours will come our way."

I didn't know what he meant by that. "I am no burglar," I said.

"No," François said. "You were a soldier. You might blunder in with a blade in your hand and demand the book. He'd hand it over all right, but unless you killed him he'd be straight off to the sergeant of the watch, or whatever you have in England, and we'd all be arrested."

"He is right," Rosenkreutz said. "We must not kill, and we do not want to be caught."

"I was a burglar," François said. "I went to prison for it. Remember how I got your bag back in Paris. I can get this book, too, if you tell me exactly where he keeps it. I will do it so cunningly that no one will know it has gone."

"What a fine fellow you are!" Rosenkreutz said. And he seemed to mean it.

"I'll need feeding," François said. "And a good night's sleep. I'll need my strength if I'm to do what you want."

The Tome

François stood by the fire, his cloak covered with snow, a pool of water seeping out of his boots. A big smile almost cut his thin face in half.

"Did you get it?" Rosenkreutz asked.

"Of course! It was a simple matter for a man with my skills. The shutters were half rotten, and the chest was just where Thomas said it was."

"You picked the lock?" I said.

"Easily. And better than that, when I closed the chest, I made sure the lock was damaged. Subtly, of course, so that the damage is invisible. He won't get it open with the key. He'll have to break the chest open. By the time he realises the book is gone, we will be gone too."

"Did you leave tracks?"

"I came through the marketplace on the way here. The snow is well trampled there. My footprints were lost among all the others."

"Never mind all that!" Rosenkreutz said. "Give me the book."

With a flourish, François reached beneath his cloak and pulled out his booty.

Outwardly, it was not a beautiful book. Its rough-cut vellum leaves were bound in a soft cover of plain leather. Some of the pages were folded over, making the book lumpy and irregular. Rosenkreutz held it tenderly in his hands, gazing at it like a mother with a newborn baby.

"I followed you for the map," he said. "I never dreamt you would lead me to one of the Tomes as well!" He gently turned the pages. "For years I have seen the Seven Tomes in my mind, imagined their occult texts, their illustrations . . ."

Had I really stumbled upon a book he wanted? Some men delude themselves when they are in love. They see a pretty face and convince themselves it belongs to the woman they have loved all their lives and were fated to meet. I daresay men who love books are the same. Love, in any case, is much the same as madness.

Perhaps such books are commonplace, spread all over Christendom, waiting to be found by anyone who searches for them. If so, that was his lookout. By his own admission, François and I had done him a great service. He was sure to be grateful, even generous.

"Who wrote the book?" François said.

"It is too early to say. It might have been any one of the Sages. I do not know which of the Tomes this is."

"Who were these Sages?"

"Opinions differ. Hermes Trismegistus was the first and greatest of them, but even you might have guessed that."

"And the others?"

"Proclus, Iamblichus, and Porphyry are all candidates. Al-Razi is another. Psellus is a possibility, though it is hard to tell how wise he was, as he tried to pass himself off as a pious and orthodox Christian."

"You don't know them all?"

"No one does, until all the Tomes have been read."

"How many have been found?"

"None, that I know of. This may be the first, unless there are others that have been found and kept secret. But I doubt it. There has been a gap in men's knowledge these last few centuries, and few have even searched for wisdom, still less the Tomes."

"Men still value learning in France. Nicholas Flamel searched for wisdom. He went as far as Spain to look for it."

"Spain! Do you call that far?" Rosenkreutz laughed. It was a cruel, barking laugh that exposed his teeth, and I was surprised to see he had a full set of them, sharp and white, despite the age he claimed. "Flamel was a charlatan."

"He had a secret book. All Paris knew it."

"It was not one of the Seven Tomes. Of that we may be sure."

"You won't admit a Frenchman might be wise?"

"I have no prejudice against Frenchmen. Or Englishmen,

for that matter. One of the wisest men in Christendom was English. Roger Bacon knew everything: great and small, near and far, past and present. He even looked into the future and saw things that are yet to be."

"Bacon studied in Paris," François said. "It was there that he learned everything he knew."

"It was from there that he was banished, and sent to prison."

"There's no need to rub it in," François said. "We all know I was in prison and then banished."

"For crimes, not for excess wisdom, like Bacon. And wisdom is the only thing worth suffering for."

"I've suffered enough," François said.

"Then you ought to be wiser." Rosenkreutz gazed at the book again. "It may be that the wisdom of the Seven Sages is a mere shadow of the true wisdom of the East," he said. "If only I had had this book in Rome. Pius would have listened to me then. He would have backed me, and sent me to Cathay as his ambassador."

He was probably right. Pius would have been impressed by the Tome. I looked at the words on the page, the script that had defeated me at the scholar's house. "Do you understand this writing?"

Rosenkreutz paused before answering. That was as near as he ever got to admitting ignorance. "I am sure it will not be long before I understand what this book contains."

François had taken off his cloak and was drier after standing by the fire. "What might that be?" he said.

"Everything."

"A book that tells us everything," François said, "is a book that tells us nothing."

Rosenkreutz turned on him. "That is what I would expect," he said, "from your narrow schoolman's mind. Your sort has been poisoned by the pedantry of Aristotle. Following him, you divide knowledge into little compartments, each too small to contain anything of use."

"Roger Bacon was as much a follower of Aristotle as any man who studied at Paris."

"He may have followed for a while, but he soon went beyond what the old Greeks knew. And he was wise enough to know that new knowledge is best kept secret."

"That is not what the humanists believe."

"Humanists? Do you think a pathetic creature like man is fit to be put at the centre of things? The main task of man is to transform himself into something better. Though you," Rosenkreutz said, "seem to have struggled for most of your short life not to become something worse."

"Fortune has broken better men than me," François said.

"That is why you must take hold of Fortune and make it do your will. This book is my Fortune. It will help me transform myself."

"How?" François jabbed a finger at the book. "It's all gibberish. Only a fool would value such a thing."

I wished that François would keep quiet. Was he calling Rosenkreutz a fool, or the man he stole the book from? If we wanted money out of Rosenkreutz it would be best not to say the book was gibberish.

Rosenkreutz snatched the book away from François' grubby finger and stared closely at the page to make sure it was not stained. "Look!" he said. "If you cannot read the words, look at the illustrations. Look at the wonders revealed here!"

He showed us pages covered with entwined plants, their leaves inked a brilliant green, their stems and roots delicately drawn. There were many of them, and those pictures were not like monks' work, done to show men God's Creation. They were sketchy, incomplete, sometimes filled with colour and detail, and at other times left half-blank, as though the illustrator meant to go back one day and finish his work. Some of the plants looked familiar. I might have seen them growing by the wayside, or in a garden. Others were like nothing I had ever seen. They had huge leaves, writhing, serpentine tendrils, monstrous fruits and flowers, roots shaped like entwined limbs. Some clustered together in inky thickets, their stems crawling with miniature men or devils. Such plants could never have grown in any real field or garden. The slightest wind would have blown them over. Their own weight would have dragged them to the ground.

"Maybe it is a herbal," François said. "Such books are commonplace."

"Is that all you can see?" Rosenkreutz turned more pages, revealing pictures of women bathing in green liquid that trickled down the page. Other pages, in the spaces around the text, were decorated with coiling pipes and tubes, mysterious vessels filled with coloured liquid, charts and symbols such as astrologers use.

"It is a manual for alchemists," François said. "I have seen books like this before. It is not unusual for them to be written in a cipher of some sort. That conceals their secrets, or the lack of them."

"Really?" Rosenkreutz turned the pages again, ignoring the text, pausing at lists and tables, at circles crossed and looped and marked with signs, animalcules, dwarfs and hunchbacks, goats, alembics, faces, miniature maidens, maps of unknown lands set with rivers and castles. Then he stopped, holding out a page filled with one big picture, a mass of little stars, and blue disks, and black dots, all enveloped by a frilly fringe, overlaid with pen marks like the spokes of a spinning wagon wheel.

"What do you make of that?" Rosenkreutz said.

François peered at the picture, turning his head this way and that. "Nothing," he admitted. "It looks like the sort of thing an idiot child might draw."

"It is a whirlpool of stars." Rosenkreutz said. "A skyful of stars, swirling round like pondweed in a millrace, turning in the heavens like a great wheel."

"Stars are bright," François said. "And those dots are black."

"Light and dark are easily reversed."

"Perhaps. By those who confuse good and evil."

"You think there is something demonic in this book?" Rosenkreutz closed the book and gave François a chilling stare. "You look like a man who might have dabbled in what your countrymen call diabolism."

"Why would I seek out the Devil?" François said. "He has had me in his grip too often."

"I can believe that." Rosenkreutz thought for a moment, then held out the book to François. "I have a challenge for you," he said. "Study this book. Look at it for as long as you like. See if you can extract any meaning from it, any wisdom. If you can, I will be very keen to hear of it. If not, perhaps you will listen to me when I tell you what it means."

Because of the snow that lay all around we could not move on to another town. And because of the theft we had committed, we dared not go out into the streets. We stayed at the inn, keeping warm by the fire, eating and drinking as often as we liked, sleeping in a soft bed, all paid for by Rosenkreutz. He slept for hours at a time, lying stiff and straight with his arms folded across his chest. With his white hair, pale face and grey clothes, he looked like a marble effigy, and I wondered whether it was sleep he slipped into or death. You may think that a mad fancy, but if Rosenkreutz died sometimes instead of sleeping, that might explain why he looked so much younger than he said he was. Perhaps he had crept into some mountain cave and spent years in a living death, not aging until he woke. I had heard of such things from the Slavs and Albanians in the Morea. They also told of lycanthropes, and the unclean dead, and of men that wake only at night and drink the blood of good Christians. Who is to say those stories are not true?

I slept, too, but fitfully, for being shut up indoors troubled me, and I wanted to get away from the scene of our crime.

François was proud enough to spend a day or so going through the book, but no more than that.

"What do you make of it?" Rosenkreutz asked, when he judged that enough time had passed.

"Very little, I must confess."

"I thought so." Rosenkreutz turned to me. "Did you study it too?"

"I looked at it," I said. "But it meant nothing to me either."

"And you have been carrying the *Timaeus* around with you for weeks. Did you understand nothing of that book?"

"Parts of it. But the Latin is difficult. Pius said so himself. If the *Timaeus* had been written in English, I might have understood it all."

"Perhaps. But even then you would only have had a glimpse of the truths it contains. Books are for studying, not just for buying and selling."

"Or stealing," François said.

"Don't reproach me with that!" Rosenkreutz said. "Or yourself. It is no crime to take a book from a fool and give it to a wise man." He reached out to François and took back the book, careful not to look too eager. "Perhaps you think I have been sleeping, these last few days. In fact, I have been contemplating. And I have come to a conclusion. Since we found this book in England, it must be by an English sage, and that can only be Roger Bacon."

"How can you know that?" François said.

"I told you the book could tell us everything," he said. "You doubted me, but I was right. In these words and pictures a careful observer will find our ultimate origin and our end. The whole universe is here, spinning on its axis, just as Plato described in the *Timaeus*. Here is everything God created: man, beasts, plants, elements, stars and planets. There are things bigger than anyone but Friar Bacon has seen, and smaller, too. Look at these animalcules. They dwell within us. They are what we are!"

"Lice dwell on us," François said. "And worms dwell within us. But animalcules? Even if such things existed, how would anyone see them?"

"The same way that they would see the secrets of the universe, the stars, planets, moons, comets. By using mirrors and lenses, cunningly arranged to make distant things seem near, and tiny things seem big. That is what Friar Bacon did. He said as much in his *Opus maius*. And that is what he was condemned for, banished and kept in prison. No wonder he had to write this book in cipher. But I am no less a man than he was, and I believe I can understand what he wrote."

Rosenkreutz showed us the picture he had called a whirlpool of stars. "It shows the birth of the Universe," he said. "The moment of Creation, when Matter condensed out of

Chaos. It is the greatest transformation there has ever been. The book explains how each of us can make a similar transformation, becoming more than a man."

"Each of us?" François said. "Could I learn to read this language?"

"I doubt it. Your schoolman's ways hardly equip you for the task. The language of this book must be unlocked, not learned."

"I can pick locks, as I have proved."

Rosenkreutz made a sound that might have been a laugh.

"Do you have the key?" François said.

"I believe so."

"Then read to us. Share the book's wisdom."

Rosenkreutz looked uneasily at François. "I will not weary you with the words and what they mean," he said. "I doubt that you would believe me anyway. And what is eschatology to you, a man who has devoted years to Aristotle, toiling through a mass of facts so dense they prevent you from seeing the truth. But here . . ." He turned the book's pages until he found the one he wanted. "Here is a picture that shows you our goal."

It showed a plant with a monstrous, unbalanced bloom. The flower was huge, round, and yellow-petalled. "What do you see?"

"I see a badly-drawn dandelion."

"A dandelion!" Rosenkreutz glared at François. "How typical of the schoolman's mind. I show you an emblem of our destiny, and you see a weed, a plant so humble it is crushed by every foot. Friar Bacon set this picture here for a reason. And as a result of it I realise that I have been looking in the wrong place. For years I have wandered the East. Now I know that I must go to the West."

"This flower tells you that?"

"It is a flower like the sun. And it is the sun that I must follow. I must leave these islands and go west. I half-suspected it. Some of my researches hinted at it. Now I know it is true."

"We are in the West already," François said. "We can't go any farther."

"Yes we can," Rosenkreutz said. "We must voyage into the Ocean."

"Into the Ocean?" I echoed Rosenkreutz's words. The despot Thomas had proposed such a voyage as a joke, though Toscanelli, who drew the mappamundi, said it was possible.

"Think of the *Timaeus*! Do you not remember the tale Plato tells, of a great city that sank under the sea on account of its people's faults?"

"The city of Atlantis."

"So you have read it."

"I was reading it to His Holiness when he died."

"Then you will know that the city lies in the Ocean, west of the Pillars of Hercules."

"Pope Pius said the city was an allegory."

"No. It was a real place, and something of it may still exist."

"How?" François said. "If it sank beneath the sea."

"The book says there is nothing left of it but mudbanks."

"Allegorical mudbanks, I suppose."

"Thomas has only read the *Timaeus*," Rosenkreutz said. "And not much of that, by the sound of it. But there is another book, also by Plato, the *Critias*. The second book gives a much fuller account of Atlantis, which was not just a city, but a continent. Now, think of this: can a whole continent sink beneath the sea? I think not. You have sailed the sea to the Holy Land? You know the islands that dot the seas round Greece?"

I nodded. François tried to look wise.

"Then you have seen for yourself," Rosenkreutz said, "how mountains rise from the sea. We sail between them, high above what was once dry land, unaware of the dead cities beneath us. We see only what is on the surface."

François opened his mouth to speak, but changed his mind and said nothing. Rosenkreutz turned to me. "You English have what you call a university, not far from here."

"At Cambridge," I said. As a boy I had wanted to study there, but my father sent me instead to fight in France.

"Cambridge," Rosenkreutz said. "That would be the place."

"But hardly worthy of the name of university," François said. "Compared with Paris."

"Universities are all the same," Rosenkreutz said. "Except perhaps in the East. The Saracens have preserved much that is worth knowing. But in Christendom we have forgotten everything, and our colleges are no more than almshouses for page-turners and scribblers. Nothing worth knowing is to be learned in them. Kings and bishops bestow their wealth on fine colleges so that scholars can live like eunuchs, never knowing love, not loving knowledge, labouring all their lives to know everything there is to know about nothing at all."

"It's not as bad as that," François said. But he had already told me that it was.

Rosenkreutz did not trouble to argue. "However," he said. "There are times when a man who has laboured to learn everything about nothing is just what is needed. Even in Cambridge there must be a man of the type we need, a cosmographer who has looked westward. We will go and see if we can find him."

"We?" François said. "Why must *we* go and look for this mythical scholar in Cambridge? Why must we do anything? The countryside is deep in snow. Let us stay here and enjoy the comforts of this inn."

"You can stay," Rosenkreutz said, "if you can afford it. If you want me to pay, then you will have to travel with me."

"But the weather . . ."

"What is the matter with you? Ice and snow are easier to cross than mud. Where I come from we know about the cold."

Cambridge

At Cambridge Rosenkreutz got us lodgings, then sent me round the town with a list of questions. François came with me to speak Latin, but was not much use, as he insisted on quibbling, and correcting everyone we spoke to. Their Latin, he explained, was much inferior to what he had learned at Paris. It took a few days, but I found a scholar of the type Rosenkreutz wanted, a man called William of Tewksbury. I was glad of that as Tewksbury is a place I have never been to and where no one knows me. His room was bare, and little heat came from the brazier in the corner. There was no furniture but a desk and a couple of stools, and William had to send a boy for more stools before we could all sit down.

"Now let me see," William said, when Rosenkreutz had introduced us all. "You are travellers, men from across the sea, and you have come here to find out what I can tell you of the world?"

"Not exactly," Rosenkreutz said. "I have seen much of the world myself, or its eastern half. What I lack is knowledge of the West, of the Ocean, and the islands that lie in it. I am told that you know more of those islands than anyone."

"It is true," he said. "I have made a study of the subject. Even though my colleagues think I have wasted a lifetime." He smiled sadly, and pushed his eyeglasses more firmly onto his nose. "It was not like that in Paris."

"You studied there?" François said.

"At the College of Navarre."

"My old college," François said. His tone suggested a pride and regret that had not been evident when he told me of his student escapades.

"It was a long time ago," William said. "There were still men there who had studied under Pierre d'Ailly."

"A great man," François said.

That was not what Pope Pius thought. He had blamed d'Ailly for justifying priestly disobedience, stirring up French pride, undermining papal authority, and prolonging the schism that kept a rival papacy at Avignon.

"Great indeed," William said. "He was a philosopher and bishop, but above all a cosmographer. Thanks to him there were men at the college who knew about the world, who studied such questions as how much of it is known, what portions of it are inhabited, whether its extremities are too hot or cold to sustain life. Such were the matters that occupied my mind as a young man, and occupy it still."

"Have you travelled?" Rosenkreutz asked. "And seen anything of the world?"

"Travelled?" William looked horrified. "Paris was far enough away for me. I have lived in this college for thirty years, and hardly stepped outside its cloisters. Even so, you will not find many men who know more about the Ocean and its islands than I do. Except for those who have sailed to them. And they are either dead or sworn to secrecy." He gazed at us vaguely through his thumb-smeared lenses. "I daresay death is not far off for me. But I have sworn no oath, and can say what I like." He removed his eyeglasses and wiped them on the skirts of his mildewed black gown, then replaced them on his nose. "In fact, sirs, it will be a pleasure to share my knowledge with you."

"How far does your knowledge extend?"

"As far back as knowledge goes," William said. "It is worth recalling that in ancient times England was an unknown island in the Ocean. There was once a Greek called Pythias. He lived long ago, before the time of Our Redeemer. In those days these islands were inhabited by wild Britons, who were led into ignorance and error by the druids. Pythias sailed to Britain from Gaul, travelled round our coasts, endured dangers and saw many wonders. When he went back to Greece, no one believed him. It was impossible, they said, for men to live so far north, in a land covered with ice and shrouded permanently in fog. Strabo insisted on it. Yet we know that Britain exists, that men dwell here, that the cold is not too severe, this winter excepted."

William glanced anxiously at the fire, which was burning low. Rosenkreutz looked bored. He was not interested in England.

"The moral of my story is this," William said, wagging his finger as though addressing a class of boy scholars. "We know from our own experience that those ancient doubters were wrong. Pythias, the traveller, the teller of tall tales, was right. That is why I collect stories, old and new, and put them together in the hope of constructing a history of the Ocean."

"You are writing a history?" Rosenkreutz said.

"I have not begun the actual writing." William smiled regretfully. "But when I have the time . . ."

He rose from his stool, went out into the cloister and called for a servant. Shortly afterwards a boy came with a small basket of wood, which he tipped into the brazier. The dying flames took hold of the new wood, which spat and crackled, flaring up and giving us a little warmth. William, glad to find men who would listen patiently, resumed his story. He told us about men who had sailed the Ocean long ago, Egyptians, Greeks and Romans who had ventured beyond the Pillars of Hercules. Then he told us more recent tales, of Moors, wandering monks, Welsh outlaws, Biscay fishermen and exiled Norsemen.

He told us of great tempests, seas as high as houses, and easterly winds that blew relentlessly for a month. There were wrecks, becalmings, mutinies, drownings, whirlpools, ships crippled by storms, that limped back to port crewed by a handful of starving men. No one believed their stories, and no one tried to follow them. But the islands they told of lingered in men's memories. William told us about the Hesperides, Tir na nÓg, Hy-Brazil, the Isles of the Blessed, Saint Brendan's Isle and the voyage he made to it, the lost colony of Greenland and what lay beyond it, the Dog Islands, the Fortunate Isles, the Island of Wood, and so many other places that the Ocean seemed no more than a village duck pond dotted with stepping-stones.

Rosenkreutz leaned forward and asked a question. "Are there men in these islands?"

"Of course there are!" William said. "Men both wise and wild, as well as beasts and spirits." He told us more stories, about drowned savages washed up on the coast of Ireland, driftwood carved with strange runes, Indians cast ashore in Germany, leather boats hauled up by Icelandic fishermen, painted men found dead in the water by ships far from land, and fur-clad men who drove the Norsemen from icy islands in the North.

Those stories made me shiver. Who would willingly cross the Ocean, knowing that they would likely end up drowned or frozen, torn apart by sharks or gnawed by crabs? Not me. I was happy by the fire, like William. He had the right idea: go nowhere, but hold the whole world in your mind. Yet what kind of men had made those journeys? Sinners, murderers, outcasts. Men like me, and François.

As William talked on, it was as though he had just returned from Lisbon or Barcelona. He knew every detail of what the Spanish and Portuguese were up to, the lands they had claimed, the treasures and wonders they had found.

"What you have told us is very interesting," Rosenkreutz said. "It confirms what I already knew."

William looked disappointed. "What did you already know?"

"I know, as all wise men do, that there was once a great land in the Ocean called Atlantis. It was rich with cities and harbours, inhabited by powerful men. We were their slaves once. The whole world bowed to them, flinched beneath their whip. Everything that men produced flowed into their treasuries."

"But I have never heard of the place."

"Plato describes it."

"I have not read Plato," William said. "I prefer facts."

"Of course! You are a schoolman. I would expect nothing else. But Plato is full of facts, though they may not seem such to the uninitiated."

"So why do I know nothing of this Atlantis?"

"It no longer exists. The Atlantians grew proud, and God punished them by sending a great wave that inundated their land. Atlantis, or most of it, lies beneath the Ocean."

"A great land lost beneath the sea?" William said. "That is hard to believe."

"Why?" François said. "Islands have sunk before. There was the land of Lyonesse, though some say it is just a legend."

"Lyonesse is no legend." William said. "And it did not sink completely. The Scilly Islands are its remnants."

"Do you believe in Noah's flood?" Rosenkreutz said.

"Of course I do. Noah's flood is God's truth."

"Cities by the dozen must have sunk then. But Noah's flood receded, and life began again."

"That is true," William said. "Perhaps you are right. This Atlantis of Plato's may have existed."

"It certainly did," Rosenkreutz said. "But I do not believe that God meant to punish the Atlantians forever. Some traces of their land must remain, just like these Scilly Islands you mentioned. Perhaps the people of Atlantis live on, and remember something of their past glory, their ancient wisdom."

"Perhaps," William said, though he sounded doubtful.

Rosenkreutz talked on, telling William more about Plato's writings, describing the land of Atlantis, its size, climate and possible position. "In your opinion," he said. "Bearing in mind what I have told you, where might the remains of Atlantis be found?"

William thought for a while. He stood up and stared at the fire, kicking the brazier to stir the embers. Then he sat down again. "If I were going to look for this lost land, which, thank Heaven I am not, I would go to the island of Antillia. The name itself is suggestive of Atlantis, and it is quite a large island, or so I believe. Antillia is also known as the Island of Seven Cities, though whether the cities actually exist, I cannot tell you."

"And where is this island?"

"Beyond the Azores, which the Portuguese claim. But not far beyond. It may be that the Portuguese already hold Antillia, and are keeping their claim secret, in case the Spaniards drive them out."

"So it could be too late?"

"Possibly. Some say the Spaniards found Antillia long ago, when they were conquered by the Moors. But the seas are treacherous in those parts. Jago de Velasco, a navigator whose word can certainly be believed, was prevented from sailing on when his ship was caught by the keel in a great mat of floating seaweed. It went on for league after league, he said, and could not be crossed. Perhaps for that reason Antillia is also known as Satan's Isle."

"Can you show me where Antillia is?" Rosenkreutz said. "Do you have a map?"

William's face brightened with pride. "Yes," he said. "I have a very fine map, drawn up according to the most ancient principles of cosmography."

He lifted a chest onto the table, unlocked it, and took out the map, which he carefully unrolled. It showed the world as a circle divided into three, with Jerusalem at its centre, its edges bounded by a ring of ocean. There was one much like it in the mysterious Tome.

I am no better at drawing maps than I am at drawing anything else, but the map was so simple that anyone could copy it. It looked like this:

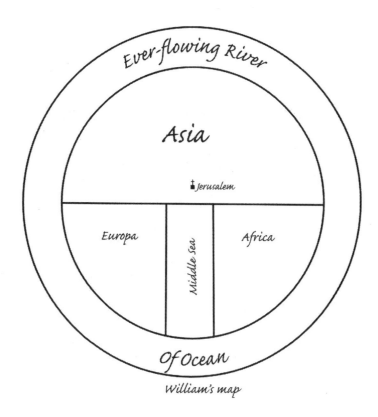

William's map

"Is that the best you have?" Rosenkreutz said.

"It shows the world as God made it."

"Yes, but not as navigators know it. Do you not have a map that shows these Ocean islands you have told us of?"

"I wish I did. Stories are cheap. You can hear them in any tavern. Books are dear, and I have gone without comforts to buy them. But maps of the type you ask for are impossible to obtain. Princes commission them, study them in secret, then lock them in their treasuries. Anyone who is shown such a map has to swear on his life not to reveal what he has seen. I have no maps of that sort, nor do I expect ever to see one."

"Couldn't you have drawn one, based on the knowledge you have collected?"

"I am a scholar, not a craftsman."

There was a pause while the two men stared at each other, their faces filled with different kinds of pride.

"We have a map," Rosenkreutz said. "A new one, drawn up by Master Paolo Toscanelli of Florence, showing everything he knows."

William's face was filled with yearning. "Would you show it to me?" he said.

"If you will help us."

I felt a stab of resentment. Why was Rosenkreutz making so free with my map? What right had he to show it to William? I knew what would happen if he did. William would be gripped by it like Pius. He would want to keep it, to own it, to hide it from everyone else, to be the only scholar who knew its secrets. His next words confirmed my fears.

"I would sell my soul to own a map like that."

"Your soul is safe," Rosenkreutz said. "The map is not for sale. I want information. I want you to show me on the map where the remnants of Atlantis might be, and what course a ship should sail to reach them."

Though the mappamundi had been eclipsed by the Tome for a while, it had not lost its power. When William saw it he went rigid, then trembled, then turned red and started muttering. His eyes opened so wide he might have been a boy peeping into a bathhouse and seeing a naked woman for the first time. His hands balled up into fists, and he waved them about wildly, skipping clumsily on the flagstones, as though fighting his own shadow. I feared we would have to fling a jug of cold water over him, but eventually he mastered himself, only his heavy breathing showing how excited he was.

"Well?" Rosenkreutz said.

William waved a finger over the map, not daring to touch it. "I cannot be sure," he said. "But Antillia must be somewhere round here."

We all bent over the mappamundi, our shoulders crowding and bumping. The part William indicated had been damaged by the Parisian thieves. The delicate lines drawn by Toscanelli had almost been rubbed out. The sea's blue had faded, and was smudged with brown.

"There is nothing there," François said.

Rosenkreutz edged him out of the way. "Of course there is something there. This map shows everything."

"It shows nothing," François insisted.

William ran an inky finger over the discoloured silk. "Yes it does. There is land marked here."

"That's not land," François said. "That's a shit stain."

William leaned carefully over the map, wrinkled his nose and sniffed. "It does not smell like ink," he said.

"That's because it is shit."

"Perhaps. But whoever fouled this map was wiser than he knew. There is a land in the West, and it lies just where this stain does. It is Antillia, I am sure."

"It's an island of shit."

Rosenkreutz ignored François. "And what lies beyond the map?" he said. "Beyond the western edge?"

"More islands."

"And beyond them?"

"Nothing but islands, dotting the Ocean."

"And beyond the Ocean itself?"

"How can there be anything beyond the ever-circling Ocean? It goes on forever."

A scheme

"He was a fool after all," Rosenkreutz said when we had left the college. "How can he have studied so much and understood so little?"

"Perhaps he should have stayed at Paris," François said.

"All universities are the same, full of fools who toil like spit-dogs on a treadmill. They sniff at the roast others will eat, then squabble over the bones."

"Yet he told you what you wanted to know. Didn't he?"

"Perhaps. But dealing with men like him is like eating an artichoke. You have to chew through a mountain of leaves to get a morsel of flesh."

"Enough!" François said. "You are making me hungry, and we can't fill our bellies with words."

"You would know. You failed to earn anything from all that verse you wrote. You had to turn to crime to fill your belly, and even that was unsuccessful. Didn't they catch you, throw you into jail, torture you?"

"Yes."

"Didn't they tie you up, shove a funnel down your throat, pour water into you until you couldn't piss it out fast enough? Your belly was full enough then, wasn't it?"

"Yes," François said. "How do you know so much about me?"

"Don't be surprised at what I know. You are notorious. You can never return to France, and you will never settle here in England. Not when you have to steal to pay for every meal. Your future lies elsewhere."

We walked silently back to the inn where we were staying. I daresay François was thinking about what Rosenkreutz had said, just as I was. It was frightening the way he knew everything. But he was paying for our food and lodging, and we had no choice but to keep in with him. He was never short of money. It was as though he could put his hand down

144

anywhere and bring it up filled with gold or silver. His coins were not English money, which had just been debased, causing much discontent among my countrymen. Nor could I tell you exactly where those coins came from. They were stamped with signs and symbols, and with cryptic abbreviated words. Pure gold or sterling silver, they weighed well, yet they were not so big that they could not easily be spent, and were accepted eagerly by all who saw them. So how could a wandering pilgrim, who appeared to carry nothing, pay constantly with coins better than the king's?

"We must go to a seaport," Rosenkreutz said, as we ate the food his coins had bought. "I have heard that Bristol is England's busiest port."

"Bristol?" I said. "It might not be best to go there."

"Why not?"

"It was Bristol I sailed from when I left England twenty years ago."

"So?"

"I have my reasons for not wanting to go back there."

"Some trouble you were in, I suppose?"

"Questions might be asked, if I was recognised."

"What about London? Ships sail from there to all over the place."

"I would rather not go to London."

"More roguery?"

I did not want to describe the crime I had committed there, or the time I spent in prison. Rosenkreutz probably knew already.

"Don't be hard on him," François said. "We've all done things we regret. As you reminded me, there are plenty of places I can't go back to."

"Then my scheme will suit you."

"What scheme?"

Rosenkreutz wiped his mouth with the back of his hand. Then he looked at me with his clear blue eyes, and I didn't feel at all comfortable, despite the good filling my belly had had. Maybe I had drunk too much wine, but I really thought that he could see deep into me, that I had become like one of those figures in a church window. I felt as though I had been filled with light, that light was streaming through me so that anyone could see that I was worthless. Then he turned to François and stared at him. I took another swig at the cup, and felt the strong Lisbon wine burn my throat and trickle down into my guts, and I knew that I was solid again, and that no one could see through me, though I was no less worthless than before.

Then Rosenkreutz looked at me again and spoke. "What do you want from life?"

François rolled his eyes, as though that was the most stupid question imaginable. I wondered that he was not cowed by Rosenkreutz's stare, and feared he would spout some verse or other that would show how clever he was. I decided to give a simple answer.

"I want a house," I said. "Like the one my father built, that was pulled down by his enemies. And I want a beautiful young wife, and good food on my table every day, and servants to cook it, and plenty of wood to warm me through the winter."

"Anything else?"

"A fine palfrey in the stable. Some hogsheads of Gascon wine in the cellar."

"A cellar! This house of yours will be a fine place, finer than any I have seen in England."

"You asked me what I wanted."

"I did." Rosenkreutz said. "And ask yourself, how will you get all these things?"

I didn't like to admit that I hoped the mappamundi would lead me to what I desired. "I don't know."

"Then let me tell you this: you won't gain anything by carrying on as you are. Not by stumbling from town to town trying to sell the things you stole in Rome. Not while François pilfers everything he sees. And not," Rosenkreutz leaned forward and lowered his voice, "while two kings fight each other for scraps like dunghill cocks. You would be better off out of this benighted country. Come with me. Sail the

Ocean to Antillia. See what Fortune brings, when it is assisted by Wisdom. Then come back when the little kings have finished their fight, when the country is at peace, and it is safe to be rich, and not even Frenchmen are resented."

"Will we make ourselves rich?" François asked.

Rosenkreutz looked at François as though he had forgotten he existed. "Rich? Yes. Didn't I say so? Material things do not interest me, but you may make yourselves rich. Travellers often return wealthier than when they left. But you will not return rich unless we actually set off. And for that, we need a seaport."

"What about Colchester?" I said. "There were plenty of ships calling there."

"We can't go back to Colchester," Rosenkreutz said.

"Why not?" François said. "We paid our bill. And I concealed my theft carefully. Even if the scholar has noticed that the book is missing, he cannot know who took it."

"I paid the bill," Rosenkreutz said. "But the coins I paid with have a tendency to turn into lead."

"I knew it!" François said. "You are a rogue, too. Your coins were lead all along."

"Are you philosopher enough to know the difference between appearance and reality?"

"I know how the world looks when you're drunk, and how it looks when you wake up sober. And if your lead coins will buy us another jug of wine, the world will assume an altogether better appearance."

We got some more wine and drank it. While we drank we talked of gems, gold and spices, imagining heaps of diamonds, amethysts, and carbuncles, sacks of peppers and cloves, and all the other things that might be found in the island of Antillia and its Seven Cities. Rosenkreutz said that all the things we wanted would probably be found there, though what interested him was rare books, and ancient wisdom, and traces of old Atlantis.

What he said made sense. I had made a mistake in going back to England. It was a bad place for someone like me, with no family to take me in, and no money left, and no chance of preferment. I had learned that the hard way, and François had learned it with me. We might have joined one of the gangs of cutthroats that roamed the country, or taken service with one of the noblemen who were jostling for power while the two kings fought. There was not much difference between them: they were all rogues. We both knew something of that way of life, and had no wish to go back to it.

Since Rosenkreutz had found us, the mappamundi's power had returned. He had the wisdom to understand it, and the Tome to help him. If his scheme was not fated in some way, how was it that I had the mappamundi and the *Timaeus*, and came across the Tome in Colchester? Those things had come into my hands as though for some purpose. And how was it that Rosenkreutz had found me, just at the right moment? I, worthless though I was, had been chosen, either by Rosenkreutz or fate. Yet I felt uneasy, like a man who has lost at cards, and thinks he's been cheated, but can't see how it was done.

After a while François winked at me.

"I need a piss," he said, getting up from the table.

"Me too," I said, following him.

Outside it was cold, and our piss steamed in the winter air.

"Rosenkreutz is mad," François said. "His Tome is mad. And his plan to sail to the island of Antillia is mad too."

"Do you think so?" I said. "I wasn't sure about the Tome, but the rest of it . . ."

"Believe me, it's all madness. Antillia is just a shit stain on the map."

"There might be something in it. William thought so."

"Do you really believe in islands full of gems and spices, and gold for the taking, where the wisdom of past ages is still preserved, where men like us may go and make our fortunes? It's all lies, just like the stories Marco Polo told."

Maybe François was right. But I still felt the power of the mappamundi, and was inclined to follow it, though not necessarily into the Ocean. Perhaps if we delayed, Rosenkreutz might come up with a new scheme, one that would bring us wealth and happiness without a risky voyage to the edge of the map. But my thoughts were far from clear. "So what are we going to do?"

"I don't know about you," François said, "but I'm not following him to the ends of the earth for a handful of fool's gold. Not when he's got real gold on him and he's paying it out freely."

"Made from lead, he said."

"That's a trick I'd like to learn."

"How?"

"We can watch him carefully, mark every move he makes."

"I've been doing that," I said. "And I don't even know where he gets his coins from. If he keeps them in a purse, it's one that doesn't clink. The coins seem to appear in his hand whenever he needs them."

"That's another trick I'd like to learn. If we both watch him, we can work it out. Where does he keep his coins? Do they turn to gold in his hand, or did he make them from lead earlier? How long do they last, before reverting to lead? How much does he carry on him? Those are all questions we can answer, if we set about it the right way."

"And then?"

"When we've found his secret, we kill him."

"Ever heard of the goose that laid golden eggs?"

"Of course. If Rosenkreutz shat gold out his arse, you'd have a point. But he makes it by a trick, and if we learn it, we can kill him, then work the trick on our own account."

"I've had enough of killing," I said. "Couldn't we just walk away and leave him?"

"He'd find us," François said. "He's good at that, like a bloodhound. If we want rid of him it will have to be a knife in his ribs while he sleeps."

"If he does sleep."

"You've wondered that, too?"

"It may be that the coin trick is one that only he can do, not something we can learn. We'd be better off humouring him, telling him we're in on his Antillia scheme, but not doing anything about it. That way he'll have to keep paying out, and we can live at our ease."

"He won't do that for ever. He's impatient now. Can't you see?"

"Let's string him along for the winter," I said. "When the weather warms we can think again. If we've learned his trick we'll work it for our own benefit. If not, we'll think of something else. In the meantime, let's take him to a seaport. When we're there we'll divert him. You can take an interest in his Tome."

"There's not much to be interested in."

"Pretend! Play the scholar. Say you want to learn the Tome's secrets. Get Rosenkreutz thinking of that, and he might forget about Antillia."

Ipswich

They told us at Cambridge that Ipswich was the place for us. There were no great lords there, as the town answered only to the king, and until the struggle between Henry and Edward was ended no one was sure who the rightful king was. In the meantime the townsfolk busied themselves with making money any way they could, trying to avoid paying tax to either king in case they ended up paying it to both.

It was a prosperous place, with goods of all sorts landed at the river and traded all over the town. Yet there were hulks in the river, and idle sailors everywhere, which suggested that all was not well. Ipswich had the advantage that we hadn't been there before, so no one knew about us. We lived away from the quays, in a comfortable inn used by the better sort of traveller. Rosenkreutz always said worldly things were unimportant, but he liked peace and quiet, and that meant a private room with a feather bed, and a fire to keep him warm while he sat and studied the Tome.

"Have you broken the cipher yet?" François said, when we had been there a few days.

"Cipher? Do you think it is as simple as that?"

"I am sure you said the Tome was written in a code that you would unlock."

"You mistook my meaning. If it was merely a cipher I could have read the whole text out to you as soon as I set my eyes on it. But the great Friar Bacon would not have used something so simple. For one thing, his enemies would have found him out. Even the Franciscans would have worked out a substitution cipher, eventually. Bacon was no scribbler of secret messages, like a spy or a diplomat. His purpose was more than just concealment. He meant the book to be understood, but only by the right person."

Rosenkreutz's talk of ciphers gave me an idea, a way of turning his thoughts away from Ocean voyages, perhaps even of sending him back to Rome.

"There is a man in Italy," I said, "who knows all about codes. He knows about everything. Pope Pius used him to conceal secrets, and to uncover them. He could unlock any kind of cipher, and would surely understand the Tome."

"I suppose you mean Alberti? He had a hand in drawing up the mappamundi, I believe. But you are wrong in thinking him clever enough to understand the Tome. As I am trying to explain, it is not written in a code or cipher."

"If it is not in cipher," François said, "then how will you read the book?"

"The Seven Tomes, as you will recall, were written by the Seven Sages, the greatest philosophers who ever lived." Rosenkreutz held up the book. "So it ought to be obvious that this one, like the others, is written in the Philosophical, or Original Tongue."

"And what is that, if it is not Latin?"

"That is just what I would expect from a Paris schoolman. Have you never wondered what language might be, if it was made anew? Or what language was, before mankind forgot and confused it? Language was once perfect, and will be again."

"I can't say I have wondered. Each language, imperfect though it is, has its charms. Much like the faces of old friends, in which character is revealed by imperfections."

"Perhaps I have misjudged you. You talk like a humanist, not a schoolman. But don't be misled, like those Italian amateurs who are so easily distracted from the truth by chance variations in the mere appearance of things. For them, the chipped surface of an old statue means more than what the statue once stood for. And the corruption of their ancient language helps hide their lack of meaning. Words should mean what we want them to mean, and nothing else."

"What use would a perfect language be? How could poets say anything if words meant only one thing?"

"Like Plato, I can see little use for poets. They tell lies."

"Only in order to tell a greater truth."

"If language was perfect, that would be impossible, and there would be no need for it. Language would be as precise and powerful as the al-jibr of the Arabs. In the Philosophical

Tongue there is no ambiguity or dishonesty. A word means what it means, and nothing else. Words summon to the mind the things they refer to as surely as if the word was the thing."

I was tired of their talk, though I would have paid more attention had I known what the quest to understand the Philosophical Tongue would lead to.

"Words can summon other things," I said. "They can summon us dinner, and some wine to go with it."

A boy brought a steaming bowl of stewed cockles, a loaf and a jug, and left us to dip in. Rosenkreutz hesitated, as though he had never seen a cockle before, then picked one out of the buttery sauce and popped it into his mouth. He must have liked the taste, as he leaned over the bowl and took another cockle, sucking the flesh, spitting the shell on the floor. Then he licked his fingers, which was unforgivable if he was thinking of putting them back in the bowl.

"Perhaps you'd like a little silver fork," François said. "Like King René ate with."

"And the pope," I said. "He was a dainty eater, too. He would never allow a knife to be brought near him, and all his food had to be cut up beforehand."

"In Cathay," Rosenkreutz said, "they eat with sticks."

"Sticks!" François laughed. "Is their food so filthy that they daren't touch it?"

"Their food is the finest imaginable," Rosenkreutz said. "And they are the most dexterous of men. They pick up their food with a pair of carved sticks. The poor use wood, and the rich use ivory."

He thrust his hand into the bowl and scooped out a few more cockles. Why was it that he knew how the men of the distant East ate, but not how ordinary men shared a dish? He licked his fingers again, and François frowned, and I feared that he would say something that would anger Rosenkreutz, who was paying for our meal, and for every meal we were likely to get, and for every bed we were likely to sleep in. If we were to argue, it would be best not to argue about our host's manners.

"Have you ever noticed," I said, "that cockles are always served with butter and pepper, yet they taste of butter and pepper already."

"Nonsense!" François said. "There are many ways to serve cockles. They can be cooked in white wine, with leeks or bacon, served in pies."

"Thomas is right," Rosenkreutz said. "The peppery, buttery essence of cockles is best brought out by adding a little butter and pepper. It is an alchemical principal. Everything contains within itself what is necessary for its own transformation."

"Everything?" François said, no doubt remembering some book he had read in Paris.

"Everything and everyone. We all have within us the essence of our own transformation. It is just a matter of discovering it, and applying whatever external agent is necessary."

As was his way, Rosenkreutz talked on, spouting about this and that in a way I could hardly understand. François argued with him, though not to much effect. Rosenkreutz picked up the *Timaeus*, and read out the bits about Atlantis, saying that we could all be transformed if we knew what those old Atlantians had known. We had it in us already, he said, it just needed bringing out. Then he got out the mappamundi and pointed at the shit stain he thought was Antillia, saying that if we could reach the Seven Cities that were supposed to be there, we could find that old wisdom and come back better men than we were. By the time the cookshop boy came back with a boiled fowl and a sugared quince pie, Rosenkreutz was saying that the three of us should bind ourselves together like brothers.

"A brotherhood?" François said, tearing a leg off the fowl.

"There have been orders and brotherhoods before. The Order of the Grail, for instance. Or the Templars. But they all failed. They revealed too much, allowed their knowledge to trickle out into the open like wine from a leaky barrel. And they grew too rich, tempting kings to topple them. We will succeed where they failed. Our Brotherhood of Three will go beyond the Ocean and find the remnants of Atlantis. Once there we will uncover the wisdom of the Ancients. And when we come back we will know more than anyone has ever known before."

I broke a chunk off the pie, trying to fill my belly with sweet pastry before François got to it. But I was listening, and I noticed what Rosenkreutz said about not getting too rich. I tried to catch François' eye, but he was too busy eating.

"Thomas!" Rosenkreutz said. "You are a quiet man. I like that. The greatest idiots always make the most noise."

"Thank you, I am sure."

"You will join me, will you not?"

When I fought in France the other soldiers used to say that we were a brotherhood. But that was just their way of getting my share of the loot off me. It was much the same with François, who had the friar's knack of getting other people to pay his way. I had no money by then, and neither did François. We had no interest in Antillia. He hoped to know the secret of Rosenkreutz's gold coins. I hoped the mappamundi would lead me to happiness, if not great wealth. Would joining in a brotherhood give us a better chance of success?

"When I left Rome," I said. "I promised myself that I would be my own man, that I would not take service with anyone. Is that what you are asking, for us to kneel and swear to follow you?"

"You misjudge me," Rosenkreutz said, "if you think I seek mastery over other men. I seek only mastery of myself, and over the elements and mysteries."

"Will we be free men if we join your brotherhood? A company of equals?"

"You will be as free as men ever are."

"And equal?"

"That too," he said. "As equal as men ever are."

Rosenkreutz wasn't giving much away. But he wasn't asking much, either. As long as there were no oaths or pledges, I was willing.

"Yes," I said. "I will join you."

"What about you, François?"

François dropped a chicken bone on the floor and wiped his hands on his sleeve. "I'll join too."

"Then it is agreed," Rosenkreutz said. "We are a Brotherhood of Three."

The great thing about the Brotherhood was that it was all in Rosenkreutz's mind. It made no difference to me or François. We carried on as before. François kept a watch on Rosenkreutz, and stuffed himself with food whenever he got the chance. I kept out of their way, giving them to understand that I was gathering information in the town. Sometimes I feared that when I returned to the inn I would find Rosenkreutz with a knife in his ribs and François gone, and my chance of getting rich gone with him. I needn't have worried. François forgot himself and became a scholar again, hunching over the Tome with Rosenkreutz, the two of them trying to find meaning in it, each in their own way. But François could not distract Rosenkreutz forever. One day, when the sun shone brightly but the air was still cold, Rosenkreutz noticed my lack of progress.

"Well, Thomas," he said. "Why do we have no ship?"

We had no ship because I had not looked for one. I was happy to postpone the voyage, to spend time in port rather than at sea. "It is winter," I said. "Not many ships are sailing."

"It will soon be spring."

"Trade is bad. That's what they're saying."

"In that case, someone will be glad to give us passage."

"Why? I can't just ask a shipman to carry us to Antillia. I need to find the right ship, and the right man, and think of a reason for the voyage. A reason that won't start rumours . . ."

"We can't wait here much longer."

"Why not?" I said. "You have plenty of money."

Rosenkreutz gave me one of his looks, the ones that made me feel like a figure in a church window with the light streaming through it. "Do I?"

"You're not running out of your fine gold coins?" François said.

"Do not take my gold coins for granted. It takes an effort to prevent them turning to lead. In each new coin I lose a little of myself. The longer we delay, the greater the effort." Rosenkreutz turned to me. "You must get on with it," he said. "Find us a ship."

"Why me? We are the Brotherhood of Three?"

"I would attract attention if I wandered the town asking questions. Foreigners like me are not always welcome in seaports. Not unless they are merchants or seamen. A man of my sort might easily be misunderstood."

"And François?"

"He is foreign, too. And he is helping me. You are the old soldier, the practical man. You must do it."

I saw nothing for it but to play along with Rosenkreutz's scheme. I went to the quays and spent much time there, hanging around in alehouses. So as to have something to report, I asked about ships, their comings and goings, what was being carried in them, and which merchants were flourishing. But I soon learned to be careful. Anyone who asked questions was likely to be a spy, for the Flemings, or the Hansa merchants, or for the king, old or new. I learned to listen, and heard a lot of tall stories, such as sailors are full of. Sometimes I added a few tales of my own, telling of my service in France, or the fighting I did in the Morea, or at the Great Siege of Constantinople. I don't suppose they believed me, any more than I believed them, but it passed the time. It was in a quayside tavern that I met Alison. She was no whore, though I had to pay her. She was a good woman fallen on hard times, and the money I gave her, small change from Rosenkreutz's gold, stopped her falling any further. As she had no fortune I could not think of marrying her. Even the bed we shared did not belong to her. But while we shared it I imagined myself living the life I dreamed of, and wondered whether it was necessary to follow the mappamundi into the Ocean to find it. I said nothing about my dalliance to the others. François would want to hear every detail, and Rosenkreutz would know I was wasting time. Nor did I say anything about the Brotherhood of Three to Alison.

I might have become an afternoon man, ploughing Alison into her soft bed, measuring out my life in jugs of ale. It is not a bad life, idling on another man's money. But it was not to last.

William

One afternoon, much like any other, I heard my name called. I turned and saw an old man standing there in cap and gown, his face twisted into a great grin, smeary glasses askew on his thin nose. It was William of Tewksbury, the scholar we had seen at Cambridge. "Thomas Deerham!" he said. "God led you to my college, and now He has led me here. You are not alone are you?" His grin collapsed into an anxious frown as he looked around the room. "The others are with you, aren't they?"

"They are not far off." My first thought was that he had followed me to try and take the mappamundi, though it was hardly mine any more. Rosenkreutz had claimed it, just as he claimed the Tome and the *Timaeus*. Even so, I was wary. "What are you doing here?" I said "I thought you never left your college."

"Let me buy us a drink." He hailed a pot-boy and ordered a jug, taking a couple of pence from a ragged purse as though they were a fortune. I suppose scholars don't have much need to spend their own money, living in colleges as they do.

"I want to go with you," he said, offering me first pull at the jug.

"What makes you think I am going anywhere?"

"Would you and your friends have come to me for information if you were not planning a voyage?"

"You said the Ocean cannot be crossed."

"It cannot. But the islands in it can be reached."

"You said you never wanted to travel, that you preferred books and stories."

I don't know why I argued with him. Perhaps I had caught the habit from François.

"I have changed my mind," he said. "I would like to see something of the world before I die."

By the look of him he didn't have long. A dried-up stick of a man like him wasn't my idea of a good travelling companion. But neither were François and Rosenkreutz. "If we were going anywhere, and I'm not saying we are, why should we take you with us?"

"Because I can find you a ship."

"How?"

"I know lots of shipmen. They come to me with their stories. Masters and owners, as well as pilots and navigators and ordinary sailors with minds quick enough to understand what they've seen."

"So?"

"I know the trades of the sea, the ways of merchants, and the conditions of the market."

"How will any of that help us?"

"Think of this: it is ten years or so since we lost Bordeaux. All the trade that flowed from that city to the English ports is lost. The ships that carried Gascon wine have nothing to carry. Their owners and masters are desperate. The wine ships are too big for what is wanted now. Some of them are trading with Iceland, but the German merchants are trying to keep them out. Some carriers have given up the trade, and left their ships to rot. Others are pressed by creditors, and are desperate for one last cargo to make them rich. There are men in these ports that will risk a ship in exchange for a fortune."

"We have no fortune." I wasn't going to tell him about Rosenkreutz's gold. We had not discovered his secret, and he had not denied that his coins might be running out.

"I guessed that," William said "The fortune must lie at the end of the voyage, not the beginning, otherwise no one would sail."

"I cannot see why anyone does."

"Have you never sailed?"

"Yes, to the Holy Land."

"And back?"

"No. I came back by other means. The ship that carried me sank."

"And you survived! You are a lucky man indeed. Any shipman would be happy to have you aboard."

"I was the only survivor."

"In that case, you had better not mention it. We don't want the sailors thinking you are a Jonah."

The memory of that shipwreck, which cut short an attempted pilgrimage and cast me ashore in the Morea, made me uneasy. I didn't want to go to sea again, whatever Rosenkreutz said about the Ocean and the islands in it. But as William talked on, telling me how we might use the wine trade to our advantage, I realised that he might be of use, though not in the way he claimed. He was an old scholar who had spent his life in colleges, knowing nothing but what he read in books or was told by travellers. I doubted that he could find a ship. He hadn't told me anything that I hadn't heard a dozen times from the men I had been drinking with. Merchants and shipmen moaned about lack of trade, but what did that prove? If William blundered about the town asking too many questions, he was likely to end up in the stocks or on the gibbet. That would show Rosenkreutz that his voyage was impossible. In the meantime, if Rosenkreutz had any more gold, William's scheme might flush some of it out, which would please François.

But if William succeeded, that would prove François wrong, and show that the mappamundi did have the power to guide us.

I went back to the inn happier than I had left it.

"I know how we can get a ship," I said.

"How?"

"By going into the wine trade."

"I have no interest in wine," Rosenkreutz said. "Or trade."

"It will be our pretext," I said.

François looked puzzled. "What made you think of wine?"

"A man I met suggested it."

"Who?"

"William of Tewksbury. He is waiting outside, and wants to join us."

"How can we be a Brotherhood of Three," François said, "if there are four of us?"

"He says he can find us a ship."

"He is a scholar. What does he know of ships?"

161

"More than us. He will find a ship and master willing to carry us anywhere."

"Then let him join us," Rosenkreutz said. "We three will still be a brotherhood."

"My idea is this," William said, when I brought him in. "There was a place called Wineland, or Vinland, as the Norsemen knew it. They voyaged there from Greenland, which, as everyone knows, is cold and icy. But Wineland, as the name suggests, was a green and fertile place where vines grew wild, without tending. Grapes might be had, just for the picking, and pressed into good wine. Since Bordeaux is lost to us, it would be a fine place to start a new wine trade."

"Is there no trade with Wineland now?"

"Not that I know of. It is a long time since the Norsemen went there, and they no longer go to Greenland. It may be that Wineland is merely a legend, or that it is the same as one of the islands newly found by the Portuguese. It may even be Antillia. Whatever the truth, it is the name that will serve us, not the actual place. Some seamen will have heard of it, if they've sailed the Northern seas. Others will like the sound of it. We will find a ship with no cargo, an owner in debt, a crew keen for one last venture, and propose to them a voyage to Wineland."

"But we will not actually go there?" Rosenkreutz said.

"Not unless, as I suggested, it turns out to be identical with Antillia."

"I like your plan," Rosenkreutz said. "The search for Wineland will be our pretext for the shipman. We will swear him to secrecy on that. Binding men with oaths is always a good thing, if men believe in them. Our shipman will be surer that Wineland is our true destination if he is sworn to secrecy."

"Exactly," William said. "But we will need permits to sail, and licences to trade. For that we will need another pretext. Something more commonplace will be best. Some of the wine ships are trading with Portugal, though most say the wine from there is not as good as Gascon wine. Even so, we might set up a voyage to Lisbon, then sail into the Ocean, just as you desire."

"Just as we all desire," Rosenkreutz said, looking at each of us to be sure.

"There is just one thing," William said. "Something I must do, to be sure our scheme is sound."

"What is that?" Rosenkreutz sounded wary, as though he feared that more of his gold coins were wanted.

"I must see the mappamundi again."

"You only want to look at it?"

"To study it, to make sure that all is as I think it is."

Rosenkreutz did not ask me. He took the cloth from the papal bag and unrolled it on the bed, as though it belonged to him, and always had. He forgot that I had saved the map from the pope's bedside and carried it safely away. He would have had no map if it wasn't for me, and no Tome either.

William grew agitated at the sight of the mappamundi, just as he had when he saw it the first time, ogling it as though a woman had spread herself over the bed. He took off his eyeglasses and rubbed them for a better look. "Yes," he said. "It is all there. All the lands of the world, set out just as they are. And the Ocean, with its islands. Not all of them, perhaps, but most that are known."

A little later, when we had eaten, and William was snoring in the great feather bed while Rosenkreutz read the *Timaeus* yet again, François beckoned me to follow him outside.

"What did you do that for?" he asked.

"What?"

"Why did you bring William here? Can't you see what he wants? He lusts after the mappamundi. That's all he cares about. It contains everything he's always wanted to know. He told us himself that only princes can afford maps like that, and that they are kept locked away, only shown to men who've sworn their loyalty. He'll take it if he gets the chance."

"That's it. The mappamundi drew him here. All winter, while we wasted time, it lay dormant. Now it is trying to guide us again."

163

François raised an eyebrow, making his face more crooked than usual. "And you accuse me of poetic fancies! It's greed, pure and simple, that's brought William here. The only good thing about his plan is that it is so complicated that it cannot possibly work. The scheme Rosenkreutz came up with, of sailing to Atlantis and finding the wisdom of the Ancients, is simple compared to what William's proposing. All those pretexts, permits, licences, crews and masters sworn to secrecy! Not to mention places that don't exist, which we wouldn't really be going to. We are quite safe. We won't be sailing anywhere."

Part 2: The Otherworld

Ice

The ice stretched as far as we could see. It was so bright that we had to shade our eyes, squinting and holding up gloved hands. Everywhere we looked, there were sheets and slabs of ice, gleaming and glimmering in the sun. There were no shadows, only patches where the blue was bluer. I have trudged through the deep snows of an endless English winter, sat frozen to stone floors in France, been cut to my bones by the bitter winds of Anatolia's high plains. Yet I could never have guessed that a place like that existed. It was a world of ice, a sea made solid by cold, then shattered, stirred and tilted. Only the waves beneath our hull still heaved, but for how much longer? Surely, if we stayed there, the ship and everything in it would freeze solid. The old philosophers were right: nothing could live that far north.

Yet we were not alone.

The creature scuttled across the ice, tripping sometimes, disappearing into holes and hollows, reappearing further away, scampering over heaps and shards. It was squat, hunched, short-limbed. Sometimes it seemed to look at us, slowing its pace for a moment and turning back. Did it have a head? Or was it one of those creatures that travellers tell of, manlike things with eyes on their chests or shoulders? If we reached dry land, would there be other beasts, giants, werewolves, man-eaters? Once, tales of such creatures had frightened me. Now I know that men are the most savage of beasts.

"There they go!" someone shouted, from high above us in the frozen rigging.

From the forecastle we could see what the creature could not. The ship's boat, rowed by eight of the strongest crewmen, was racing up an inlet in the ice. One man stood on a thwart, holding a crossbow, trying to balance as the boat bobbed and surged. Overhauling the creature, the men raised their oars, letting the boat drift on. The archer raised his crossbow, took aim, fired. The creature fell forward, sliding over the ice.

Rosenkreutz stood stiffly, gazing into the glare with his blue eyes. Though his hood was back and the wind tousled his pale hair, he did not notice the cold.

The men heaved the body onto the deck. It lay on the tarred boards, limp and bloodstained. It was not shaggy, as we had thought, but clothed in animal skins, all sewn together with sinews. They cut the coat off and showed us the body. We stood over it, gazing at the short, broad trunk, the bowed legs, and pale grimy skin. There was a smell of rancid fish.

He was a savage, a man who lived wild like a beast, eating whatever he could catch. Rosenkreutz looked sad. I thought he was full of sorrow to see a man killed.

"No," he said. "This is not the place. This is not Paradise."

He was right about that. The place we had come to was no Paradise. But who had thought it would be? I had no chance to ask what Rosenkreutz meant. While we were still looking at the dead savage more of his kind came out of the ice, rowing through it in skin boats, firing arrows at our ship.

"Sail off," Rosenkreutz shouted. He was not the ship's master, but the men obeyed him, running to the ropes, hoisting the boat aboard, unfurling sails, sending the ship out onto the grey sea, beyond reach of the savages archers.

"South!" Rosenkreutz said. "Head for the south."

Preparations

Things had happened quickly once William joined us. He rushed me round Ipswich, taking me everywhere that seamen and traders could be found. I was reluctant at first. I knew the taverns and alehouses well, and the drinkers knew me. My questions had already aroused suspicion. But there was something about William that disarmed people. With his mildewed scholar's gown, and smeared eyeglasses perched on his nose, he looked so harmless that his endless questions seemed no more than an old man's foible. Of course, I ought to have known he was good at getting people to talk: that was how he had gathered his tales of the Ocean. But getting away from his college had changed him, doubling his energy, filling him with enthusiasm. It was as Rosenkreutz said; we all have within us the means of our own transformation.

In William's company, Ipswich was a different place, full of hidden wealth, but hungry for more, its burghers, sailors and guildsmen linked by invisible webs of trade and intrigue. We followed those webs from place to place, gathering useful information as we went. William kept me so busy that I had no time for Alison, and I found that I was not as sorry as I might have been. Her bed was as soft as ever, but her heart had grown harder, and my visits gave more solace to her purse than they did to my weary body.

François did not stir from the inn. He stayed with Rosenkreutz, determined to learn his secrets. But every evening he catechised us, determined to know where we had been and what we had found out. He smiled and nodded when William spoke, but later, when the others were asleep, François poured out his overflowing doubts.

"William will fail," he said. "Who would carry a gang of rogues like the Brotherhood of Three?"

"We are four, now," I reminded him.

"Not for long. He'll get bored and go back to his college. Who would be stupid enough to risk a ship on a quest for

Wineland? If anyone was stupid enough to believe William's talk, nothing would come of it."

François was wrong. William found a man so much in debt that he was prepared to risk everything. Hugh the shipman was short and wide, well braced for life on a pitching ship. His clothes were all grey, and rimed by the sea. His face was as brown and wrinkled as an old glove. Only his beard, which was neatly forked, showed any sign that he cared for his appearance.

Hugh was brought to the inn, where Rosenkreutz swore him to secrecy as we had agreed, and told him of our plan to sail to Wineland.

"Can you take us there?" Rosenkreutz said.

"I don't see why not. There's some that might have said you shouldn't have started from here. Bristol's the place, for getting into the Ocean. But you can sail to anywhere from anywhere. That's the beauty of the seas: God made them so they all join together."

François said the ship would be a rotting hulk. There were plenty of them along the Orwell, some still floating, others beached, all falling to pieces while the men to mend and sail them drank and idled in the town, bemoaning the old days when England ruled half of France and trade was good. Hugh's ship proved to be a square-rigged carvel with a high forecastle and bigger castle at the stern. He said it was wea-therly, despite its small size, and just the thing for what we had in mind. It was moored down-river, away from the quays, where everything we needed was to be had. It was better that way, according to Hugh, as fewer men would know what we were up to. He already had a few men at work, caulking joints and seams, hammering dowels, scrubbing the hold with vinegar. The hold was empty, and we couldn't sail the Ocean without supplies, so William found a vintner who believed the story about Wineland and agreed to supply us. William made it sound such a certainty that some other merchants pitched in with supplies, and even sent trade goods to be sold in Wineland.

François still wasn't troubled. It was one thing to get

promises from merchants, quite another to crew a ship and sail it. Hugh had only a few loyal followers, not nearly enough to man his ship. He sent his mate and boatswain to scour the town's alehouses, and they found a score of idlers in need of employment. Some of them had sailed from Bristol in the past, and knew the Ocean, or said they did. Some were Irish, and also knew the western seas. One of them, called Jago, said he was a Spaniard, but he was so dark I knew him for a Moor. Hugh saw no harm in him, or in the others, who all agreed to join us when they saw a sample of Rosenkreutz's gold.

When he realised that we had a crew, François said that was the final blow to William's scheme. The men would see though all our pretexts, and would gossip in the taverns, and rumours would reach the harbourmaster, who would impound the ship and arrest us all in the hope of winning a reward from one or other of England's two kings. Having seen the crew, I was half inclined to agree with him. They were a rough-looking lot, just the sort to try and take Rosenkreutz's gold and dump us all over the side.

But Hugh worked them hard, and they caused no trouble. The hold filled up, and François muttered about running for it, and heading back to France. I didn't believe him. We had fought each other in Paris, then helped each other and travelled together. We had often argued, but, as the old hag said, we were stuck together like man and wife.

Rosenkreutz showed no interest in any of the preparations, but somehow he knew when everything was ready. He rose from his bed and demanded to be shown the ship, which he had not yet visited. Hugh sent a boat for us, and we were rowed down the Orwell, rocked and buffeted by the bitter wind, splashed by icy waves that broke over the bows. Our clothes were soaked by the time we climbed aboard.

"Would you like to see over the ship?" Hugh said. "My boatswain will show you everything."

"I think not," Rosenkreutz said. He was not shivering like the rest of us. He liked the cold. There was something icy in his character, despite what he told us later.

"Most landsmen find it very interesting."

"Not me," Rosenkreutz said.

Hugh frowned. Why were we wasting his time if not to look over the ship? "Are you sure you wouldn't like to view the spars, and climb up to the crow's-nest?"

"Mere mechanics, of no interest to me. The only thing I want to know is why we have not yet sailed."

Hugh looked at our wet clothes, and at the puddle that was spreading from our sodden feet, across his freshly scoured deck. "We have not yet sailed," he said, "because of the wind."

Rosenkreutz reached up and pushed his white hair out of his eyes. "The wind blows strongly enough."

"Too strongly," Hugh said. "And in the wrong direction. Surely you must have noticed how hard it was for my men to get you here. The wind is blowing straight up river, and has been for a fortnight. If we set sail in this we'd end up back at Ipswich quay."

"So we are imprisoned by the wind?"

"Until it turns. But it's not that simple. A westerly will get us down river and out to sea, but then we'll need easterlies to get us out of the English Channel and into the Ocean."

"I don't like it," Rosenkreutz said. "We should not be at the mercy of the elements."

"There's nothing to be done. Our departure is in God's hands. Only He can command the winds."

"On the contrary," Rosenkreutz said. "Men can control the elements, if they have the wisdom for it."

Hugh laughed. "You think you can turn the winds? That's a trick many a sailor would like to learn." Then he frowned. "But anything of that sort would be heresy, or worse. The only right way to get a good wind is to pray for it."

Elements

William stayed on board to help Hugh arrange everything in the hold. I went back to the inn with François and Rosenkreutz, who was as unquiet as the wind, refusing to rest or eat, but pacing the room, muttering.

"We have waited long enough," he said, when the first light showed through the chinks in the shutters. "We must depart as soon as possible."

"Could you raise a storm?" François said. "You hinted at it, but only a magician could do that." He winked at me, letting me know that this was our chance to learn something of Rosenkreutz's powers.

"We don't need a storm," Rosenkreutz said. "We just need the wind to turn for a day or two. That is what the shipman wants."

"Hugh told us it would be heresy," I said.

François glared at me, then turned to Rosenkreutz. "Could you do it?"

"Where is the heresy in it?" Rosenkreutz said. "We control water, digging channels for it, constraining it behind dams, releasing its force for our own use by sending it through pipes and conduits. We control earth too, heaping it high, and burrowing into it, extracting ores and metals from its depths. Fire is harder to control, but we can master it, concentrating it in furnaces, using its transforming power, extinguishing it with water. The meanest mechanic, the humblest peasant, can do these things. I do not see why a man like me should not master the winds."

"And men like us?" François said.

Rosenkreutz ignored him. "I have rested long enough. The fire in me rises." He touched the little emblem that hung at his neck, the rose and cross. "Each time I rest, the humours congeal and lie dormant. I am of the choleric type, and fire is my element. It burns in me always, though sometimes it is reduced to embers. When it revives, as it does now, it heats and incubates the other humours, releasing their essences, distilling them, setting them free to vie with each other. Yellow bile dominates my nature, driving me to do great things. I was born to lead, and I have chosen my followers well."

"You once told us," I said, "that you did not seek mastery over other men."

"I did, Thomas. You are quite right. But leadership is not the same as mastery. Have I compelled you to follow me? No. You follow me because it is in your interests to follow me. And because it is in your character. You, Thomas, are a phlegmatic type. You are dominated by water."

"That's true," I said. "I was shipwrecked once, and water has carried me here and there as though it had a will of its own."

Rosenkreutz looked down at me as though I had said something stupid. "I meant that your nature is dominated by the *element* of water, which predominates in the phlegmatic humour. Your season is winter, when it is always wet and cold, and it is your nature to be calm and dependable, which is why I chose you."

I used to think I was unlucky, but as Rosenkreutz once pointed out, I had survived all my bad luck, and I wasn't embittered by it like François.

"What about me?" François said.

"You are not such a good follower, but men of your sort cannot lead yourselves, so must follow someone. Like all poets, you are melancholy. Your nature is dominated by black bile, which fills your mind with poetic fancies, but makes you dissatisfied and unhappy. Your season is the autumn, which is the year's most melancholy time, and your element is earth."

"I suppose there is some truth in that," François said. "But I do not think . . ."

"I have not finished," Rosenkreutz said. "We are four. William is one of us, and his nature completes the scheme."

"What scheme?"

"The scheme of four. Just as there are four humours and four elements, so we are a Brotherhood of Four."

"So William is sanguine?" François said.

"Of course. He is dominated by blood, and his season is the spring, which we are just entering. His sanguine humour makes him optimistic and cheerful, though men like him are prone to whims. It was on a whim that he left his college to join us, though now that he is here he has worked tirelessly for our voyage." Rosenkreutz paused for a moment. "His element is air."

"So it is William we need," François said, "to master the winds."

"Nothing is that simple." Rosenkreutz ceased his pacing and eased himself down onto the bed. He shut his eyes and seemed about to sink into one of his deathly sleeps. François caught my eye, signalling that we were on to something, near to finding out Rosenkreutz's secrets.

"But you have not yet told us," François said. "How can we master the elements?"

Rosenkreutz opened his eyes, but did not sit up. "The same way that we can master men, by leading them where they want to go."

François winked at me again. He thought he was leading Rosenkreutz. "The elements do not have minds," he said. "Or desires. So how can they be led?"

"You are wrong, François, in thinking that the elements do not have desires. How else would a lodestone attract iron, except through mineral love? Why do flames rise so eagerly into the sky, if fire does not love air? And why does rain fall always downwards, if water does not love earth? If the elements lacked desires, each would keep to itself, and no compound matter would ever be formed. Wise men know this and exploit it."

"Does lead desire to be gold?"

"No. That is why the transformation takes so much effort."

François caught my eye, giving me a roguish, pleading look. "We can help you."

"You will have to," Rosenkreutz said. "Though in this case we will not be transforming metals."

"What must we do? If William's element is air, must he do something?"

175

"No. He is doing enough already. The three of us will suffice. Fire, earth and water will subjugate air."

"But how?" François was hopping up and down with excitement, just like William when he first saw the mappamundi.

"To calm the wind," Rosenkreutz said, "and perhaps to turn it, we must take an element and transform it into vapour."

"Which element?" François' agitated step was making the floorboards creak.

Rosenkreutz thought for a moment. "Wood."

"Is wood an element?"

"It is in the East, and men are wise there."

"If there are five elements," François said, "and wood is one of them, then what of the humours? Should there not be a fifth? And why are we a Brotherhood of Four? Should there not be a fifth brother, one whose nature is dominated by a dry, fibrous humour, making his character stiff and wooden? And why should there not be a sixth element, quicksilver, for instance? Or a seventh and eighth?"

It was François' turn to be stared at by Rosenkreutz as though he was stupid. "This schoolman's quibbling will get us nowhere. We must find some wood. Lots of it." He looked up at the rafters. "Where can we find some firewood?"

Burning down the inn did not seem to me a good way to end our stay in Ipswich.

"The hulks," François said.

"Where are these hulks?"

"We passed them," François said, "when we went down river. Those ships, dismasted and abandoned. The wreckage of England's dream of ruling France."

"Yes, I remember now. There is plenty of wood in them. They will burn well."

"You want to burn the hulks?" I said.

"We must turn the wood into vapour. How else can we do that, unless we burn it? Fire transforms everything."

"We can't burn the hulks," I said. "They belong to people, even if they are rotting. They'll see us doing it and send for the watch. We'll be arrested and chained up outside the jail as felons. Arson's as bad as murder. They'll hang us. And that's only if we're lucky. If they think we're heretics, like Hugh the shipman said, they'll burn us on our own bonfire."

François looked uneasy when I mentioned hanging, as I knew he would.

"There is no need to fear," Rosenkreutz said. "It will not take long. We will be gone very quickly. Let us send a message to the ship, then gather up what we need and go to the hulks." He reached beneath his pilgrim's robe and brought out a gold coin. "Here, Thomas. Pay off the innkeeper with this, and get a lantern from him."

"A lantern? It is almost day."

"Fire, Thomas! The element of transformation."

Of course, it wasn't as simple as setting a fire and leaving it to burn. François and I had to gather up what tinder we could find, mostly dry grass and frayed rope ends, bundling it with twigs and splinters beneath the smashed side of a beached hulk. While we worked, Rosenkreutz did a lot of pacing about with his staff, planting it in the earth, pointing it in various directions, stroking it and talking to it. And he breathed, too, sucking in air till his chest swelled, then blowing it out in great gusts as though he could tame the wind by the power of his own body.

None of that made any difference. The wind blew from the river, lashing the bank with waves, threatening to soak our tinder. Rosenkreutz shouted at the elements, daring them to defy us. Then he shouted at us, telling us to open the lantern and release the flame from its prison. We set our backs to the wind and carefully did what Rosenkreutz asked. As we slid up the lantern's side, the candle nearly died, but we touched it to the tinder and the wind caught it and whipped up a blaze.

"Air loves fire," Rosenkreutz said, pointing his staff at the flames. "They unite in transformation."

He turned his staff, describing a slow circle in the air.

The flames grew brighter, then found some tarred strakes

and leapt up the hulk's sides, turning it into a crackling, smoking beacon. Our faces seared, we leapt back, and only then noticed that there were people on the riverbank. I might have guessed it from Rosenkreutz's performance. He wouldn't have gone to all that trouble just to impress me and François. Yet witnesses were what we needed least.

A gang of ragged children stood watching us, their dirty faces lit by the mounting flames. The smoke rose so high it must have been visible from the town. Soon the watchmen would come, just as I had feared. I shuffled backwards, towards the river. The children looked at each other, guessing they would get rewards for catching us. But they were only children, and we were grown men. Rosenkreutz raised his staff and shook it, but that didn't stop them. Barefoot, their tattered clothes fluttering in the wind, they came towards us.

"Get back, you filthy vermin!" François shouted, waving his knife at them. "We are the Brotherhood of Three. Take one more step and it will be the worse for you!"

They only hesitated for a moment. I drew my knife and prepared to defend myself. If we did not stand our ground there was nowhere to go but the Orwell. Water is my element, or so Rosenkreutz said. I did not fancy my chances in the river, but it was that or a fight, or throwing myself into the fire to save the watchmen the trouble of hanging me.

The children charged at us, swarming like rats, nipping, biting and scratching. They screamed and shouted, summoning more of their kind from among the hulks. We fought them off as best we could, stabbing, kicking, hitting. As I had long suspected, Rosenkreutz knew how to use his staff. He swung it neatly, blocking and feinting, thrusting and parrying, fighting as well as any Englishman. But the children were too small, and too many. They ran under the staff, dodged our weapons, clung to our legs and weighed us down. We backed away until our feet were in the water, but the shrieking, ragged children did not let go. We waded in deeper, like dogs trying to rid ourselves of fleas, but some of the children still clung on, and others jeered at us and threw mud and burning brands at us from the bank.

That was what Rosenkreutz's attempt to master the elements amounted to: we nearly drowned in the water while being pelted with earth and fire. I was ready to give up the fight and swim for it, risking the icy water. Then I heard a shout, and looked round to see the ship's boat bearing down on us.

Rosenkreutz waited until we were safely aboard the ship, and the crew had found dry clothes for us, before he said anything. I thought he might apologise, or at least explain, but he did not.

"I turned the wind," he said. "I told you I could. What do you say now?"

Hugh's leathery mouth was pulled as tight as a miser's purse. "Do you claim that power?" he said. "Christ our Redeemer stilled a storm. He rebuked the sea, saying 'Peace, be still.' The wind ceased, and there was a great calm. Do you compare yourself to Him?"

"Can you not see?" Rosenkreutz pointed to the blazing hulk. "One element attracts another. Fire transforms all. I have mastered the wind with my knowledge."

"You may be a very clever man," Hugh said. "But you are not a very observant one. The meanest of my crew sees more than you do."

Rosenkreutz frowned. "What do you mean?"

"The wind turned in the night. It has been blowing from the west all morning. I prayed for a change, and the Lord sent it with the dawn. Whatever you did made no difference."

"You see only the surface. The fire, the things we did on the riverbank, are only the outward signs. My mastery of the winds began in the night. My thoughts began the transformation. Actions only completed it. Now I am exhausted by my efforts and must sleep. Show me my bed."

They took Rosenkreutz below and found a place for him to sleep. François and I stayed on deck and watched the land slipping past us, feeling the wind on our backs, wondering what had happened.

I don't know the truth of it. When we thought about it, we

saw that Hugh the shipman was right. The wind had already turned, only we were so busy with Rosenkreutz's rigmarole that we hadn't noticed. If you think that makes us look stupid, it was a mistake anyone might have made. The Orwell twists and turns as it leaves Ipswich, and the hulks were on a reach that runs south, so the direction of the wind was not so obvious. We were not sailors, anyway, and not skilled in such things. It may be that Rosenkreutz was right, and that he had begun to master the wind during the night, just as he said.

The voyage

One way or another we got the winds we needed, and they carried the ship round Essex and Kent, then along the whole of England's south coast until we got clear of Land's End. After that the ship pitched and wallowed so badly that we could get no rest, and it was hard to know whether to go below and be rolled about like a barrel, or sleep on deck and risk being tumbled overboard. The hold stank like a privy, but if we went on deck for fresh air the wind cut through to our bones, and the sea spray stung our faces and left us salted like hams. François moaned the most, as I had come to expect, but William suffered more, though he did it in silence.

After two weeks at sea we took refuge in Galway Bay. That was enough sailing for me, and I longed for respite, but only a few men went ashore to fill the casks. The rest of us gazed at Ireland's bleak and rocky shore as though it was the pleasantest country in the world, and we all knew what troubles afflicted the place. We did not have long to think of land. A gale blew us north and west, into the emptiness of the Ocean. It was so rough that only men who were used to the sea could bear to look at it. We landsmen wrapped ourselves up and hid where we could, sleeping or spewing as the sea commanded. The crew grumbled that the wind would blow us so far from home that we would never get back. If they were hinting to Rosenkreutz that he should change the wind again, they wasted their words, as he slept so deeply that he heard nothing.

"They call themselves sailors," William said. "But I, who have sat in my college for years, know better than they do. In the spring the winds always blow strongly from the east. Soon the easterlies will falter, and the winds will blow just as strongly from the west. The only danger is that the winds will change too soon, before we have reached Wineland." He winked, to remind me of our deception, though by then I wasn't sure who was deceiving who.

When the winds slackened they did not turn. Instead, we were becalmed, and surrounded by fog. It was thick, and white, and drenched everything it touched. We were ordered to keep silent so the crew could listen out for rocks or reefs. I don't know which was worse, being tossed by the wind and waves, or drifting silently through fog, not knowing what might be under the keel. Anyway, we couldn't keep quiet for long, as the bilges had to be pumped, so the silent drifting was interrupted by frantic squeaking and splashing. Those sounds were always accompanied by the singing of the pump men, the English and Irish trying to outdo each other, and one of the crew blowing on a trumpet, in case any other ships were near. It was enough to wake even Rosenkreutz.

"Why are so many crew necessary?" he asked. "Roger Bacon predicted that ships might be devised that could be crewed by one man, and which would sail safer than the ships of his day. He wrote two hundred years ago. Why have such ships not been built?"

"Did this Roger Bacon tell how it might be done?" Hugh said.

"Not in his known writings." Rosenkreutz clutched the papal bag to his chest. "But it may be written somewhere."

"Let us hope not. For if it could be done, and I doubt it, it would be heresy, just like turning the winds."

Rosenkreutz drank some broth and went back to sleep. I stayed on deck, wedging myself into a safe corner, gazing out into the fearful blankness, imagining nameless horrors beneath us. Eventually the westerlies arrived and cleared the fog. We found ourselves in a place where there was no night. That was when it got really cold, and we dressed ourselves in every garment we could find. It was a marvel to me that we could live like that, so far from land, so far from any sign of where land might be. The world was no longer solid. It might have been any shape, flat, round, like a bowl, rough or smooth. The philosophers could argue as much as they liked, but we floated on the world, feeling its watery power beneath us, driven by the wind. Would the world become solid again? Would there be land beyond the horizon?

A month after setting off, by which time I had lost all hope of seeing dry land again, we found the icy wilderness and the fur-clad savages. We guessed that there must have been land somewhere nearby, unless those savages spent their whole lives on the ice. Hugh said that might be true, as some seabirds spend their entire lives in the air. William was dragged from his sickbed to look at the savage's corpse, and the sight cheered him up no end. It proved the truth of all the stories he had told us about the Ocean and its islands. A handful of men could not live on their own, he said. There were bound to be women, children, and houses of some sort, perhaps made of skin, like their boats. Travellers had talked of such things, and now that William had seen them he could die happy.

We sailed south over a heaving grey sea, day after day of creaking ropes and slapping waves, with no sight of any islands, or of ships that might have sailed from them. Hugh would not kill the pig, or any of the chickens, so we had nothing to eat but salt meat and rotten biscuit, with sour ale to wash it down, and clean water only if it rained and the crew were quick enough with the canvas to catch the downpour and fill a few casks. On that southerly run the ship did not wallow much, and we got some rest, and as the weather warmed we took off some of the layers we had wrapped ourselves in. The men did their work well enough, as all our lives depended on it, but there was muttering among them, an uneasy mood I knew well from my time of commanding soldiers. Hugh tried to calm them, pointing out various signs that all sailors know, weed floating in the sea, birds that skimmed the waves, the smell of the breeze, clouds on the horizon, all of which showed that land was not far off. He said that fabled Wineland lay to the west, and the men were reassured, but Rosenkreutz said we had not gone far enough south. He unrolled the mappamundi and showed it to Hugh and his mate. They said it was a landsman's map, useless at sea. Rosenkreutz argued with them about mathematical navigation, and the three of them took an astrolabe and observed the sun. They looked at the stars when night fell, and studied the compass, and counted the hours by the sandglass. Then they stuck pegs in the traverse board and argued about how far we had sailed. Sometimes William joined in, especially when the mappamundi was consulted, as he could never resist taking another look at it. But none of them could agree on where we were, or how far we had come, or where we were going.

Talk of Wineland reminded me of our purpose, and the pretexts we had used to disguise it. It reminded me too of something Rosenkreutz said, weeks earlier, when we saw the fur-clad savages.

"Why did you say that icy place was not Paradise?" I said.

"Because it was not."

"That was obvious. So what made you think it might be?"

"I spoke rhetorically. That place was an icy Hell. I merely emphasised the point by contrasting it with Paradise."

"When you came to Rome you said you wanted to travel to Paradise. I remember now. You said you had almost reached it once. That was why you wanted a look at Toscanelli's map. That was why you followed me to England."

"Fate led me to you."

"You confused us with all that talk of Atlantis, just like we confused the shipman with the story about Wineland."

"That was William's idea, not mine."

William heard his name and looked up, but we were speaking French, in which, despite having studied in Paris, he was not fluent. It was impossible to be out of earshot on that ship, unless you climbed out onto the bowsprit where the wind would tear the words from your lips, so Rosenkreutz always chose his language well. He spoke French or Latin to keep the crew in the dark, and English when he wanted them to understand, though he was always wary when Jago was near. I think he suspected the Spaniard, as I did.

"You approved it," I said. "You were happy to pretend we were looking for Wineland."

"Thomas! It was you who brought the *Timaeus* from Rome. That was where the story of Atlantis came from."

"I didn't believe it. You persuaded me."

"He's right," François said. "You persuaded us to sail west to Atlantis, and now you speak of Paradise. Where are we? And where are you leading us."

"I am leading you nowhere," Rosenkreutz said. "We are following the mappamundi."

"Which you interpret, by using the Tome."

"We would be fools to reject such wisdom when it comes our way."

"So what does the Tome tell us?"

"I will reveal all. But first we must touch land again."

"What land?"

"If I am correct, the next land we see will be Antillia. Which, if my assumptions are correct, is a remnant of Atlantis."

"Is Atlantis our true goal?"

"If we can find it."

"And if not?"

"We will sail on."

"Where to?"

"If my calculations are correct," Rosenkreutz said. "We are three thousand miles west of Ireland. It cannot be far to Cathay."

There was such a silence among us that the crew noticed, and turned to see what we were being silent about.

François spoke first "Cathay's in the East," he whispered. "Everyone knows that. And we have sailed west."

"The world is round," Rosenkreutz said. "Cathay can be reached by sailing west!"

"Nonsense!"

"Are you as big a fool as William? You both went to the same college as Pierre D'Ailly, who affirmed what I say in his *Imago Mundi*."

"I have not read it."

"Did they teach you nothing in Paris? You must have read Macrobius!"

"Of course. But I recall nothing about sailing the Ocean."

"You call yourself a scholar!"

"I was one, and would be still, if it were not for my bad luck."

185

"Perhaps, in your youthful idleness, you read easier books. Books of travels, perhaps, like Mandeville's."

"I read that book," I said. "It scared me as boy. I had nightmares about monsters."

"Yes," François said. "There are too many monsters in Mandeville. Marco Polo told a more plausible story, though even he . . ."

"Marco Polo may be plausible to men with no imagination," Rosenkreutz said. "But if you had been to the East, like me . . ."

"Did you cross a sea of gravel?" François said. "Or a land of eternal darkness?"

"There are deserts in the East, but darkness is in the mind."

"Did you see monsters?" François said. "Any lycanthropes or anthropophagi? Any beasts with one eye, or one leg, or faces in their chests, or heads like dogs?"

"You mock, but miss the point. Some say that Marco Polo went no further than Persia. There are those who say that Mandeville travelled no further than his own library. Well, if so, at least he was curious enough to explore his books. Perhaps Mandeville borrowed some of his stories, but is that so bad? In any case, the true wonder in that book is an idea."

"Which is?"

"Mandeville tells of a man who travelled more than he did, an accidental traveller who wandered from one country to another, making his way by land and sea, all the while going east. Eventually, he was amazed to reach a country where they spoke his own language, and wondered how that could be. But the answer, as Mandeville knew, is obvious."

"Not to me."

"He went right round the world."

"It is impossible. Just like those tales of one-legged monsters."

"Mandeville knew more than you. He proved the world is round by citing the various stars and their declinations as viewed from places he went to."

"You can read about the stars in a library, just as you can read travellers' tales."

"Let me demonstrate." Rosenkreutz picked up the map-pamundi. With a solemn gesture, as though he was revealing a great mystery, he turned the sides back until they touched each other. Then he stood the loose roll of silk on the deck, holding it so that the join faced François. "There!" he said. "The ends of the Earth are not ends at all. They face each other. East and West are the same."

François laughed. "If ships sailed on cloth . . ."

There was cry from the crow's-nest. "Land ho!"

Antillia?

The crew rushed to their stations, and all around us sails flapped, ropes creaked and men shouted.

"Brother Francis," Hugh the shipman said. "Will you say a mass?"

"I am no priest," François said.

"You've been tonsured."

"As a scholar."

"Exactly," Hugh said. "You read Latin, and in England that makes you as good as a priest."

François smiled, his scarred lips twisting. "How good is that?"

"Good enough. Please can we have a mass? The crew would like it."

"One of the others can do it. Rosenkreutz? You wear the rosy cross."

"I cannot," Rosenkreutz said. "Not until I reach the end of my pilgrimage."

"William. You too are a scholar," François said. "According to the shipman, that makes you as good as a priest."

"Only in England," William said. "And we left England weeks ago."

"We have been godless since then," Hugh said. "That is why we need a mass."

I feared they might turn to me. I can read Latin, though not as well as the scholars. And I assisted a priest when I was young, so I know how masses go. But the honour went to François, and he took the stale ship's bread and sour wine the steward gave him, and went through the motions of celebrating a mass. Once he got going, enthusiasm seized hold of him, and he declaimed loud enough to fill a cathedral. He preached a sermon, too, all made up as he went along. François was never stuck for words. Even though I knew what kind of man he was, his words comforted me. Hugh and his officers were comforted too, though the rest of the men took no more notice of François than the tethered pig or the caged hens that cluttered the deck. The crew stuck to their tasks, which was just as well, as there is a lot that needs doing when a ship draws near to land. They heaved on ropes and took in the sails, swung the lead and tested the bottom, hung buckets over the side to sample the water. Only Jago, the Moor who called himself a Spaniard, stopped for a moment to listen to François' sermon. That, along with things I had seen on the voyage, made me think that there was more to Jago than there was to the rest of the crew. If he was a rogue like them, he was a clever one.

When François finished, we stood at the rail surveying the land we had reached. It was not much to look at, just low banks of sand or mud, with a bit of grass on the higher ground, but nothing bigger than a bush, and nothing built or touched by men.

"Where are we?" François said. "What fanciful theory do you have now?"

"Can you not see?" Rosenkreutz said. "Is it not obvious? We have crossed the Ocean."

"I am no more convinced than I was before."

"Neither am I," William said.

"You schoolmen are all the same," Rosenkreutz said. "Your noses always in books, your eyes bleary with reading, blind to what everyone else can see. Aristotle, who schoolmen revere, knew the world was round. So did Macrobius, and Ptolemy, and Pliny and all the Ancients."

"You are unjust," William said. "I have left my college to see the world. It is you who keeps citing old books."

"I don't dispute the shape of the world," François said. "It may well be round, though some say it is pear-shaped. I daresay you can find an authority for every opinion. But the world is a big place, and we have not sailed for long, so I doubt that we have crossed the Ocean, and am sure we have not sailed far enough to reach Cathay."

"He is right," William said, pulling his scholar's gown tightly around him, though the day was far from cold. "The

Ocean is a thing that cannot be crossed. That is its nature. We have merely ventured into the Ocean and found one of the islands in it. The question is, which island."

"This is surely Antillia," Rosenkreutz said. "Which is also Atlantis. The *Timaeus* is clear that mudbanks are all that was left of the place. Banks of impenetrable mud, Plato called them."

"There are mudbanks in the Seine," François said. "But if there are sunken cities beneath, no one has ever found them."

"Why won't you believe me? This is Atlantis!"

"This may be Antillia," William said. "Or it may be Hy-Brazil, or Wineland, or Saint Brendan's Isle, or any of the other islands that sailors tell of. But it is not Atlantis. It cannot be."

We all turned and stared at William, who, after lying sick for most of the voyage, was suddenly filled with a feverish energy.

"You speak with great certainty," Rosenkreutz said, "for someone who claimed to know nothing about Atlantis. Have you lied to us William?"

"I never said a word but the truth."

"But not the whole truth. I think you have concealed something from us. You knew about Atlantis all along."

"Not by name."

"But you knew of it."

"I knew what place it must be."

"Which is?"

"What your old book calls Atlantis can only be the lands of Albion that sank when the seas rose."

"Albion?" Rosenkreutz said. "Where is that?" It was the only time I can think of that he openly admitted ignorance of anything.

"Albion is old England. It was big once, bigger than France. And it was rich, too, with fine cities planted on its plains. It was a land of endless summer, and of eternal youth. Men were happy in those days, until the seas rose up and swallowed them. All the best land was lost then, and the cities, and the wealth. Not even King Arthur could revive its greatness, though some say he will when his long sleep ends."

Rosenkreutz fell silent, shocked to find that he had been deceived by the man he thought a dull-witted schoolman.

"If you knew all that," François said, "why did you send us across the Ocean to Antillia?"

"You enquired after islands in the Ocean," William said. "And Antillia is such an island. I gave you the advice you wanted."

"Why did you come with us?"

"It was a whim or fancy. I heard your talk, and saw your mappamundi."

"You wanted the map for yourself," François said. "I always knew it. That is why you came."

"No, it is not like that." William's face flushed, and he took off his spectacles and rubbed them. "After you left my room at Cambridge, I thought about all the places I had heard about but never seen. And I thought about my life as a scholar, and what thin pleasures I might expect in the years left to me. And I decided to go with you."

"To a place that doesn't exist."

"Antillia exists, I am sure of it. The tales of those old Spaniards were quite clear."

"What tales?"

"Centuries ago," William said, "when Spain was invaded by the Moors, some Christians, rather than submitting to the unbelievers, sailed to Antillia and settled there. The Seven Cities mentioned in the tales are supposed to have been built by seven bishops."

"How did those old Spaniards know about Antillia?" François said.

"I believe the Moors told them."

"And how did the Moors know?"

"That I cannot tell you."

"What a fine trick!" François said. "Those Moors were crafty, getting rid of Christians from their newly-conquered lands by telling them of some far-off, imaginary island."

"It was no trick. The island exists."

"So why do we know nothing of it? Why do ships not call at Spanish ports, laden with the wealth of Antillia?"

"Antillia was settled centuries ago," William said. "And ever since, the Spaniards and the Portuguese have been occupied with trying to drive the Moors from their country. Now that the reconquest is almost complete, they are sending out ships, and they have discovered much. But as far as I know, neither the Spanish nor the Portuguese have been able to find Antillia again. It may be concealed by the great sea of floating weed, which I believe I told you of."

"Perhaps it moved," François said. "Drifted off in the Ocean currents."

"It is not impossible," William said. "Men I trust well have told me of floating islands they saw with their own eyes."

"A floating island with seven cities on it! That would be something! But I see no cities here."

"Perhaps they sank, like the cities of old Albion."

"It seems to me," François said, "that you have tricked us as neatly as those Moors tricked the Spaniards. If there was ever anything here worth seeing or having, it is under the sea. If this is Antillia, then the men who fouled the map were right. This is an island of shit!"

Rosenkreutz roused himself from silence. "Wisdom is the thing most worth having," he said. "And that endures, whatever happens to seas and cities. We will press on. Look!" He pointed his staff westwards. "There is a gap in the sandbanks. They are not impenetrable. Surely there is more land beyond."

Hugh ordered the boat to be lowered, and some of the men got into it and went ahead of us, starting again with their lead-swinging and sounding. With much shouting and heaving they led the ship through a channel into the clear water that lay beyond the sandbars. Then we saw that Rosenkreutz was right. There was land ahead. It stretched to either side, as far as we could see, and was forested beyond a wide, sandy strand. The smell of it came wafting out to us: flowers of some sort that we could not recognise, pine trees, and the smell of the earth itself, of the soil we had not set foot on for weeks.

Land of the Rosy Cross

There are noises you don't notice until they have stopped. The shriek of an ungreased axle, the hammering of a distant blacksmith, the grinding of whetstones on steel before a battle. Sounds like that sink into the background, becoming almost like silence. Then they stop, and you realise with a jolt what real silence is like. So it was with the Ocean. All the time we had been at sea, tossed by the waves and driven by the winds, I had been anxious, but without quite knowing it. When the anchor bit into the seabed and the rope tightened, we were attached to land again. Even though we did not know what land it was or what dangers we might face, my fear and anxiety vanished.

It was the opposite for the crew. The sea was their element, and land made them uneasy. They rushed into action, reefing sails, coiling ropes, hauling up barrels from the hold. Some of them dragged the ship's guns out, mounting them in the forecastle, pointing them at the land. I hoped we would not have to fire them. What use were a couple of small swivel guns, when charged with damp powder and manned by sailors?

We were not quite done with the sea. We had to clamber down into the boat and be rowed ashore, the waves slopping over the sides and soaking us thoroughly. Then we had to climb out and get soaked again as we waded through the shallows. Rosenkreutz, taller than the rest of us, strode ashore, his pilgrim's tunic slapping wetly around his legs. As soon as he got above the strand line he planted his quarterstaff in the ground and spoke loudly. "I name this place the Land of the Rosy Cross."

"Not Antillia?" François said.

"A place must have a name in every language, and my choice will do well enough for us. Perhaps it will end your quibbling."

The crew were too busy to wonder where we were. Hugh sent some men to a creek, to wash out the barrels and fill them with sweet water. He sent others into the forest to see what food they could find, and to cut wood for cooking and repairs. For sailors, landfall is nothing more than a chance to get ready to sail again.

We were all filthy after those weeks at sea, so we stripped off our wet clothes and washed them in the creek, then washed ourselves. Then we got one of the crew to shave us, and to trim our hair, all except for Rosenkreutz, who washed, but would not submit to be shaved. He kept his beard, which was quite white, and never had it cut again as long as I knew him.

After our barbering we felt less like beasts and more like men. Our spirits rose, and we felt quite carefree as we lay in the sun to dry off.

While we lazed, the carpenter and his men cut wood.

"Those trees are so big," I said. "I've never seen a forest like that."

"I have," Rosenkreutz said. "In the East. Men there use elephants to drag the timber out."

"Elephants!" François laughed. "And did those men ride on ants the size of horses?"

Rosenkreutz did not reply.

"There's been no logging in these woods," I said. "Not judging by the size of those trees. In every forest I've seen men have cut the biggest trees to build ships and houses."

"There are no houses here," François said. "And there were no ships off the coast." He turned to Rosenkreutz. "Does the Great Khan have a navy?"

"He does," Rosenkreutz said.

"With wooden ships?"

"Bigger than any seen in Christendom."

I thought François was going to make a joke about ships that can fly through the air, or something of that sort. But he spoke soberly. "Then we cannot be in Cathay," he said. "This must be some other place."

"I said we were sailing to Cathay, and so we were. If those sandbars are Antillia, as William affirms . . ."

"I don't affirm anything," William said. "This place might be Antillia, or it might not."

"If this is not Antillia, then it is one of the islands that lie of Cathay's shores. There are many of them: Cipangu, the Spice Islands, the two Javas, as well as the Terra Australis Incognita, though we are not south enough for that. Those places are all marked on the mappamundi. My point, which you are all rather slow to take up, is that Antillia, as described by the Spaniards, is just another of those eastern islands. Do I have to roll up the mappamundi again and show you how east and west come together?"

"According to Marco Polo," François said, "the isles of the Indies are rich places, full of gold, jewels, and spices, wealthy people and great cities, like Cathay itself."

"Marco Polo told a million lies."

"He is not the only one. You told us we would find riches here."

Our clothes were dry, so we gathered them up and put them on, saying nothing while we did so. I was confused, and sick of all the scholars' squabbling. François and William were dead against the idea that we had reached the East, but as Rosenkreutz said, they were schoolmen, so full of book-learning that they couldn't see what was in front of them. I had heard talk of sailing round the world before. Toscanelli, who made the mappamundi, said it was possible, but he had shown the world as though it had two ends, each unreachable from the other. Perhaps, if he had painted the map on a wooden ball, he might have shown the world as it really is, and we might have known where we were.

By the time we were dressed, I was ready to say my piece.

"There are some things that need to be faced up to," I said. "There has been too much trickery on this voyage. We told the shipman we were looking for Wineland. He told the Ipswich harbourmaster we were headed for Lisbon. You told us that we were looking for Atlantis. William told us that Antillia was Atlantis, but now denies it. Now you tell us we're not far from Cathay, and might actually be there, but you called this place the Land of the Rosy Cross. One thing we're all agreed on is that wherever we are, there are no cities, spices, jewels or gold. How are we going to make ourselves rich, ready for when we go home? What did we come here for?"

Rosenkreutz looked at me doubtfully, then beckoned to us. "Gather round," he said. "I must speak quietly."

We did as he asked, and stood close to him.

"This land contains something that men desire above all other things. I am confident of it."

"And what is this thing?"

Rosenkreutz took out the Tome. He opened it to show us the picture of a flower that François had called a badly drawn dandelion. I thought it looked more like a marigold, but that just shows how badly drawn it was. "The key is here," he said. "I knew nothing until I saw this sign. Imagine! I devoted my life to a great quest, wandering for years, enduring privations, consulting the wisest of wise men. But all the time I was in ignorance of where my goal truly lay."

"What was your goal?" François said.

"My goal was Paradise. Everyone knows it lies in the East, beyond the Abode of Reasonable Men, as far east as you can go. I sought Paradise, and almost reached it. But, somehow, I lost my way and had to return. I understand now that I was not then wise enough. When I heard of Toscanelli's map, I thought it might guide me. But the mappamundi was not enough on its own." Rosenkreutz held the Tome up. "It was only when I saw this that I knew the truth." He pointed at the picture. "This flower revealed everything. It is like the sun. And it told me to follow the sun, that my true goal lay in the West."

"Atlantis?"

Rosenkreutz smiled. "That may have been a deception. Things are not always what they seem. But you were surely not fooled? You guessed it on the ship. Perhaps earlier?"

"Perhaps." François gave Rosenkreutz a cold look, but I couldn't tell whether he had guessed anything, or was as confused as me.

"Deceptions were necessary," Rosenkreutz said. "Otherwise the shipman and his crew would never have brought us here. But now, we four at least, can share the truth. Our goal, all along, was Paradise."

"Paradise?" François spoke loudly, and Rosenkreutz frowned. "You say we are in Paradise?"

The woodcutters stopped their work.

"Did you hear him?" the carpenter said. "He says we are in Paradise."

"No," Rosenkreutz turned angrily away from us and addressed the crewmen. "I did not say that!"

"What, sir, did you say then?" the carpenter spoke politely, but was carrying an axe.

"I said, or I meant to say, that Paradise is nearby. We are not there yet."

"How near is it?"

"For some of us," Rosenkreutz said, "it may be very close indeed. Perhaps only a few steps might take us there. For others it may be so distant that they will never reach it."

"Sir," another sailor said, taking his hat off and holding it humbly before him. "Will our sins be wiped out if we set foot in Paradise?"

"If we are in Paradise," the carpenter said, "then things will have to be different from what they were when we weren't."

The sailor looked puzzled. "What do you mean?"

"Remember the old verse?" the carpenter said. "When Adam delved and Eve span, who was then the gentleman?"

"No one," the sailor said. "That's who."

"Exactly."

"Listen to me!" Rosenkreutz raised his staff, and with his long beard and pilgrim's robe, he looked just like Moses in a church window. "We are not in Paradise yet."

"You said we were."

"No. I said it must be hereabouts."

The carpenter stepped forward, axe in hand, and confronted Rosenkreutz. "You've changed your tune now. But we heard you. Your French friend said it too. We're in Paradise, and that means we won't be taking orders any more. Not from you, nor from any of them that were gentlemen back in Christendom."

I have no idea whether Rosenkreutz counted as a gentleman in whichever country it was he came from. He used no titles, except his name, which was surely not the one he was born with. He bore no arms, except his staff. He despised universities so much that he had probably never been to one. But he despised wealth so much that his family was probably rich. In any case, he wasn't one for giving orders. He just argued until everyone was tired of it and did what he wanted. If the carpenter got above himself it was nothing to Rosenkreutz.

By then, Hugh the shipman had come over to see what the argument was about. He looked as sick as I felt when we were all at sea. "I don't like this talk," he said, pointing a finger at the carpenter. "I'm a better man than you'll ever be! You should not forget your place."

"Where are the priests and popes, the kings and princes who will tell us what to do? We are out of Christendom now."

"What do you mean by that?" Hugh said. "Do you think God would forsake us because we have crossed the Ocean? No! He watches over us, even here."

The carpenter stood his ground. "We have left our old lives behind," he said. "We're on the rough side of the Ocean now. This is another world, and things will be different here."

"Another world?" Hugh said. "The Creator only made one world, and we still are in it."

"Not necessarily," Rosenkreutz said. "Some of the ancients believed that beyond the Ocean lay another world, the Antipodes, put there by God to balance the world we know. But they thought the Antipodes unreachable, and we have reached this place, so it cannot be the Antipodes."

"You're trying to confuse us," the carpenter said. "We all heard you say this was Paradise. You can't unsay it now." He turned to the men, addressing them like a preacher. "All our sins will be wiped out in Paradise," he said. "We can do what we like."

It was then that the cook came out of the forest. Not noticing the dispute among his shipmates, he came forward and laid a basket at our feet.

"There's fruit in the woods," he said. "Just for the picking."

We looked in the basket. There were bright berries, green herbs, some fruit I could not recognise, and some tiny, unripe grapes.

"Wineland!" William said. "I knew it all along!"

"Paradise," the carpenter said. "This fruit proves it. Just for the picking, you say?"

"Fruit grows anywhere," Rosenkreutz said. "It proves nothing."

The cook was smiling, pleased with himself, more so than a small basket of unripe fruit warranted. "Wait till you see what else we found." He turned and whistled, and two men came out of the woods, each dragging a woman.

"Did someone mention Paradise?" the cook said.

The women were young, pretty, and naked, or nearly so, with only a sort of leather apron tied round their waists. Black hair, long and straight, hung over their shoulders, but did not cover their breasts, which were firm and round. The crew, who cared nothing for fresh fruit, gathered round to look at the women. Rosenkreutz raised his staff and tried to push through the crowd, uttering words in a dozen strange tongues.

"You old goat!" the carpenter said. "Want a good look at them, do you?"

"No," Rosenkreutz said. "I want to talk to them."

"You get back, old man. These girls are ours."

"I must question them. It is most important."

"Get back! See to it, boys!"

They grabbed his arms and frog-marched him away, throwing him down on the sand. There was nothing to be done, so we led Hugh and Rosenkreutz away, withdrawing along the strand to a point where we could watch the crew but were out of their way. They launched the boat again, and some of them went back to the ship, and we could see them going through the stores, taking whatever they wanted. We heard a squeal as they slaughtered the pig, and the clucking of the hens as they dragged them from the coop and trussed them. Hugh hopped up and down, shaking his fist and shouting. But he couldn't stop them. They were beyond our reach, and had the ship's guns. We had nothing but what we stood up in. And the mappamundi and the Tome, of course. Rosenkreutz kept them in the papal bag, which he had taken for himself and always had near him. The mappamundi wasn't much use to us when we could agree which end of it we were at. Neither was the Tome, not unless we found a passage in it in clear English, telling us where we were and what to do.

We watched as the crew filled the boat, rowed it back to the strand, and began to unload their haul. When Hugh saw them rolling a barrel over the side he couldn't keep still any longer.

"Stop!" he shouted, running towards the boat. "That's my wine, not yours."

"Not any more," The carpenter said. "Not now there's no gentlemen or commoners. We'll drink what we like."

"Not the hens. We need them for eggs. And that's my coat there. Put all those things back!"

"Lay not up for yourselves treasures upon earth," the carpenter quoted, "where moth and rust corrupt . . ."

". . . and where thieves do break in and steal." Hugh completed the verse. "We need those stores."

"What for?"

"The return voyage, of course."

"Who says we're going back? We're not going anywhere until we know if this is Paradise or not. Isn't that right?"

There was a cheer from the men.

"And if it is Paradise, then we'll see if we want to go back or not, won't we?"

There was another cheer, and men rolled the wine barrel up the strand and knocked the bung out. They caught the wine in jugs, which they shared around, toasting their good fortune. Then they piled up the wood they had cut and set a fire for roasting the pig.

Hugh gave up shouting at them and walked back to us. "What do they mean?" he said. "Quoting the Holy Scriptures against their masters. Have they all become Lollards? Have I sailed the Ocean with a crew of heretics?"

"That's the least of our problems," I said. "They've got the boat and the ship. How will we get back?"

"There is something in what they say," François said. "We are far from Christendom, with its mad kings, scheming nobles, grasping merchants, corrupt priests, and ignorant peasants."

"Are you on their side?" Hugh said.

"We're all on the same side," François said. "That's the point. We're on the rough side of the Ocean, one of them said. And who can say that we are worse off here?"

That was the only time I heard François say anything good about the place we had got to, which he usually cursed as the Island of Shit.

The Ocean was not far off, just the other side of the sandbars. We could hear the crashing of its waves. The forest was behind us, empty and silent. If there were birds and beasts in it, the crewmen's noise had scared them off. The strand was wide, but open. There was nowhere to hide, no way of escaping. Even Rosenkreutz was uneasy.

"Can you get to the ship?" he asked.

"Of course not," Hugh said. "They've got the boat."

"Can't you swim?"

"No. Can you?"

"I master the elements," Rosenkreutz said. "They do not master me."

"What do you mean by that?"

"You need not trouble yourself with what you do not understand. I asked about the ship because there is something aboard I would like to get hold of."

"I wouldn't count on it. They'll be nothing worth having on the ship now the crew have been at it."

"I doubt they will have taken the *Timaeus*."

"The what?"

"The *Timaeus* of Plato. A book that is necessary to my purpose."

"A book! You ask for a book when the crew have mutinied and cast us aside on an unknown shore."

"I should have thought to bring it with me."

Rosenkreutz sat silently for a while, then he suddenly started up. "The fire!" he said. "I must get to the fire."

"Sit down," I said, tugging at his cloak. "We'd all like to be warm, but you're safer here."

"It's light I need, not heat."

"Wait till the morning."

"I need to see the women."

François laughed. "I thought you were above all that."

"I am not in the least interested in those women for their own sakes," Rosenkreutz said. "I want to know who they are, and where we are."

"You said we are near Paradise."

"And so we are," Rosenkreutz said, sitting down again. "But how near? That is the question. Those women are the inhabitants of this region. If we know what race they are, we will know where we are."

"You spoke to them, but they didn't reply."

"The crew were confusing them. They should have understood me. They are the right colour, and have something of Cathay about the eyes."

"I don't know how much we can believe Marco Polo," William said. "But most authorities agree that the people of Cathay are civilised. These women are savages."

"They look like Gypsies to me," I said. "They have the same coppery skin and straight black hair.

"Perhaps," Rosenkreutz said. "Some claim the Gypsies are travellers from the East. I must talk to those women and find out who they are."

"They may not feel like talking," I said. "When the crew have finished with them."

Night

It grew darker, and the fire blazed bright. We could see the crew drinking, and hear them cheering and arguing, their faces lit by the flames. We couldn't see the women, or hear them. Had the men put them on the ship? Or were they still tied up? We sat in a huddle, staring longingly at the fire, driven mad by the smell of roasting pork. When they set to and started carving the beast, François was all for joining them. I would have gone with him, but Hugh was too proud, William had fallen asleep, and Rosenkreutz said that food was unimportant to men like him.

Then we saw someone coming towards us. That roused Hugh to anger, but I shut him up. One man was nothing to be afraid of, and there was no point in shouting orders at him. When he got closer, we saw that it was Jago, the Moor who said he was a Spaniard. He was in character, as he carried a jug of wine and a chunk of the roasted pig, both of which are forbidden to Moslems. He offered them to us, saying they were presents from the King of Paradise.

"Who's he then?" Hugh said.

"Him that was the carpenter before."

Hugh spluttered indignantly. "There's only one carpenter that will be King of Paradise. He promised it on the cross."

Jago went back to the mutineers, and we passed the jug round and divided up the meat. It was good to fill our bellies, but our prospects were no better than before.

"Why doesn't my mate join us?" Hugh said. "He has no place among the men. And my boatswain. He always seemed a sound fellow. Why do they stay with the crew?"

I had more hope of Jago, who never quite seemed one of the crew, even if he wasn't one of us. "Because they've got the ship and the stores," I said. "And we've got nothing. They'd be fools to join us."

"Sinners and heretics!" Hugh said.

"Men," François said. "That is all."

"Will they forget their madness in the morning?" William said.

"They'll soon tire of taking orders from the carpenter."

"He rewards his followers well."

"They'll all be kings before long," Hugh said, bitterly. "Or princes or earls. Perhaps they'll make you a bishop, eh, François?"

"Bishop of Paradise? That would be something!"

"Or you, Thomas. You're an old soldier. They might put you in charge of their army."

"I've commanded worse rabbles."

Hugh had no thoughts on how William or Rosenkreutz might be honoured by his crew, so he sat for a while and ate his share of the pork, gnawing thoughtfully at the charred skin.

"I knew a man who styled himself king," François said. "I don't know why. He had plenty of other titles. He was duke of one place, count of another, marquis of somewhere else. But he wasn't happy. He wanted to be king, and not just of one country, he claimed half a dozen crowns."

"King René," Rosenkreutz said, wiping his greasy mouth with the back of his hand.

"You knew him?"

"I have met him. And he is no fool, despite his love of titles. He is a scholar, of sorts, and knows something of the reality that lies beneath life's surface."

They were drifting off again, talking of trifles when our lives were in danger. The crew were getting steadily drunker on the shipman's wine. I tried to think how to get the better of them. Drunken men often turn violent, especially if there are women to be quarrelled over. If there was any sign of argument, that would be the moment to rush them and take the boat. Or they might fall into a stupor until noon. If so, the morning was the time to attack them.

But if the carpenter kept up his Lollard talk he might rouse the crew against us there and then. Whatever they did, we had to be ready for them. François and I were good with our knives. Rosenkreutz had his quarterstaff. Hugh looked strong, though I didn't know if he could fight. William was useless for anything but causing a distraction. Even so, we could probably put up a better fight than the crew would expect.

"We must sleep," I said. "So as to be ready for them."

"I'm all for sleeping," William said.

"Then sleep. But some of us must keep watch. François, you like the night. You take first watch. Wake me if anything happens. If not, wake me anyway, and I'll take a turn. At dawn, if they are quiet, we'll make our move."

I was dreaming of a warm bed in an English inn, with the prospect of a good breakfast and a pretty young woman to serve it to me, and to share my bed afterwards. Perhaps it was the sight of those naked savage women that set me thinking that way. I felt something jab me in the ribs, then a hand pressed against my mouth. I tried to sit up, but the hand stopped me. I opened my eyes and saw François looking down at me, his face all grey in the half-light. He touched a finger to his lips, then took his hand away from mine. Crouching down beside me, he pointed along the strand.

The fire still glowed, and around it the crew lay like logs. But they were not alone. Some men had come out of the woods and were watching them.

Of course! We should have been ready for them, but we were so busy thinking about our plight that we forgot that wherever there are savage women there must be savage men. Rosenkreutz sometimes spoke of Gymnosophists, or naked philosophers of the East. But if those men were philosophical they did not show it. Instead, they showed their savagery by slaughtering the crew where they lay. The men cannot have known what was happening to them. They were clubbed, stabbed, or pierced until all were dead. It did not take long. We heard the dull thud of wood against flesh, the crack of bones, a few faint groans, and the panting of the savages as they did their work. I knew those sounds well, having been in on a killing a few times myself. When they had finished, they stood over the corpses, poking at them, turning them this way and that, pulling at their clothes and hair. Then they saw us.

They ran towards us along the strand, no longer silent, but yelling and shouting, waving spears and clubs in the air. Our deaths were certain. Why should they spare us when they had just killed the crew? Time stands still when you are about to die. In the moments left to me I reflected on how stupid I had been to go on the voyage, how many sins I had committed in my life up till then, and the punishment I could expect when my soul was dragged before its Maker on Judgment Day. Eternal torment was a certainty. The others must have thought so too. Hugh cursed his crew as heretics, and begged God not to let him die the same way. William sobbed with fear, snivelling about his immortal soul, and François called on the Queen of Heaven to keep him safe from suffering. I hope I kept silent, but I cannot be sure of it.

It was Rosenkreutz who saved us, and he did it just by standing. The savages were of middling size, and Rosenkreutz was easily the tallest of us, and he had a way of standing with his staff in his hand, gazing into the distance, his white beard hanging down his chest, looking wise and noble. He was like one of those statues of antique philosophers you see in Constantinople, if the Turks haven't broken them all.

By the time the savages reached us the dawn had come up, and Rosenkreutz was lit by its golden glow so he looked even more like a statue. At the sight of him the savages faltered. One or two of them dropped to their knees, but their fellows kicked them and they rose up again. They came on more slowly, looking at us carefully to see what kind of men we were, just as we looked at them for the same reason. When they lowered their weapons I began to feel some hope.

The savages

They halted a few paces away from us. Like their women they were nearly naked, wearing only a belt, with a strip of something hanging before them to cover their private parts. Their skin was painted with black lines, circles and dots. Their hair was shaven, except for a strip that stood up like the crest on a boar's back. They were strong men, and would fight well. But in some ways they were like children, who take pleasure in trifles, such as the feathers and bits of shell they wore as adornment.

William was weeping with joy by then, and when he took off his glasses to wipe his eyes the savages howled with delight. They thought the lenses were his eyes, which he could remove at will, so the old scholar was a great wonder to them. While the savages pawed us, feeling our skin and clothes, Rosenkreutz ran through all his languages again, including Arabic, which he swore was spoken throughout the Great Khan's lands, and Hebrew, which would surely be understood in Paradise. He might as well have tried Flemish for all the good it did. There was no understanding between the savages and us, except what we could convey by signs and gestures.

Rosenkreutz tried the coin trick, which might have worked, had the savages known what coins were. One of them, who we took to be the chief, took the coin, looking briefly at its golden sheen and the moons and ciphers on it. Then he put it in his mouth and bit it. The coin was thin, as they all were, and when the savage took it out of his mouth it was bent. He frowned at it, then held up a disk of copper that hung round his neck. He smiled on showing us the copper, and frowned again at the gold. His meaning was clear, though puzzling: he preferred copper to gold.

After that they took us to their village, taking a long and winding path through the woods, so we were never sure afterwards how far we were from our landing place, or in which direction it lay. As soon as we got there, they showed us off to the rest of their people. Women, children and old men crowded round us, touched our pale skin, tugged at our clothes, looked at the things we carried with us. They were in some awe of Rosenkreutz, despite his being their captive. His beard impressed them most, as did ours when they grew back, and the hair on our bodies. Those savages were not a hairy race, and they looked on us as we might on a forest-caught woodwose.

But they were the wild men of the woods, not us. Despite our hairiness, we wore clothes, and spoke all the languages of Christendom, and a few others. We carried things they had never seen before, such as our knives, which they took from us and passed around, trying the blades and wondering at their sharpness. After that they searched us, and took all the iron we had, and much else. They left Rosenkreutz his staff, as wood was familiar to them, and his bag with the Tome and map in it, which they could see no value in. We could not stop them from robbing us, as they were so many, and armed. Their own weapons were made of wood tipped with shell or bone, but they were good enough in hands that knew nothing better. The only metal they had was copper, which some of them wore round their necks, or dangling from their ears, as if it was gold. The chief showed us a small knife with a blade of copper, but it was the only one we saw. That was why they were disappointed by Rosenkreutz's gold coin. They wanted hard metal not soft.

"We'll not find wealth here," François said. "Not if they prefer copper to gold."

"Who is to say," Rosenkreutz said, "that one metal has more intrinsic worth than another?"

"The example of men like you, who give everything to learn the trick of turning base metal into gold. That's what tells us the value of one metal compared to another."

"You confuse me with a mere alchemist," Rosenkreutz said. "Transmuting metals is nothing to me, a stepping stone on the path to true wisdom."

"If it's no trouble," François said, "why not make some copper? If these savages value it, we could exchange it for anything we fancied."

"It would be beneath me. We are here to gather wisdom, not to barter trinkets."

"We won't find much wisdom here. Not by the look of this lot." François gazed sadly at the savages who surrounded us. All were bigger and stronger than him, their skin the colour of the metal they craved, their bodies hardly covered by the little clothing they wore. "Come to think of it," he said, "there's nothing here worth bartering for. Save your transmutation for later, Rosenkreutz. When we find the fabled Seven Cities, that will be soon enough. I expect the sages of Antillia will be so impressed they will tell us everything we want to know, then heap us with riches and send us home in the flagship of their fleet. I daresay their ships are made of gold, as they have felled no timber from this forest. The sails will be of cloth of gold, the ropes of spun gold, the hold filled with gems. What a welcome we'll get, back in Christendom!"

That was the trouble with François. Nothing was good enough for him. He was always imagining some perfect world in which wine flowed like water, and rich patrons rewarded men like him. And when his flight of fancy was finished, he sank back into a state of melancholy.

"We will find the cities," Rosenkreutz said. "I am sure of it. But first we must learn something of this place and the people who live in it."

After showing us off and robbing us, the savages built us a hut, laying woven mats over a frame of laths and withies, as quickly and neatly as could be wished. It gave us shelter from the sun, and from the prying eyes of the villagers, who watched everything we did, noting the differences between us and them. They set guards outside, to keep the gawpers away, and us inside. And they began to make merry, singing and dancing, and cooking food.

Hugh groaned when he smelled roasting flesh, and fell to his knees praying.

"That mumbling won't save us," François said, though he prayed himself when he was scared enough.

"Those savages are less than men," Hugh said. "They are more like beasts."

"I've seen worse," I said.

"And where on your travels was this?"

"In France."

"They were English soldiers," François said, "no doubt, driven to savagery by greed and lust."

"They were Frenchmen, living wild in the woods."

"Ah yes! I know the type. Call them savages if you will. I call them poor wretches driven into the wilderness by the worse savagery of the English."

"Perhaps these people were driven here by the savagery of others."

"It makes no difference how they got here," Hugh said. "They are going to eat us."

"It is possible," Rosenkreutz said. "There are anthropophagi in the East. It will be interesting to find out whether these people are they. All travellers speak of anthropophagi."

"Liars, all of them," François said.

"This night will be a good test," Rosenkreutz said. "If the savages eat us, we may be sure that Marco Polo, Mandeville, Friar Odoric, and the rest, all reported their travels truly. If not, those authorities will be proved false, and we will be in a position to supplant them."

There was a long silence among us after that, during which it struck me, not for the first time, that scholars are utter fools. William, who believed every traveller's tale he had ever heard, had led us to that country, encouraged by Rosenkreutz. They had each tried to deceive the other as to where we were going, with the result that none of us had any idea where we were. And the test of the authorities they relied on was whether or not we would be eaten that night. I could see the flaw in their argument, even if they couldn't. If all those friars and merchants who ventured east had actually encountered anthropophagi they would have been eaten, and their stories would have remained unwritten. If anyone writes histories of their travels it should be men without imagination. I am one such, according to Rosenkreutz. I have never imagined anything, except in my dreams, which no honest man would confuse with reality.

The smells that reached our hut told me clearly that the savages were roasting venison, and why would they have done that if they intended eating us? They had slaughtered the crew a few hours earlier, and could have eaten them, if they had a taste for human flesh. I knew we were safe, but let the others stew, and enjoyed the fear on their faces when the savages took us out of the hut to join their feast.

The savages led us to a patch of trodden earth that served as their village green. They were standing all around as we came out, and greeted us with whoops and cheers. There were other noises, too, of stamping feet and drumming and shaking rattles, which scared my fellows, who still thought they were to be eaten. Some of the women had draped themselves with cloaks of painted deerskin, and they had decorated the place with hoops of bent branches hung with leaves, which we could see in the glow of the cooking fires. They plucked scorched meat from the flames and presented it to us. Hugh shied from the offering.

"They are going to fatten us up before eating us," he said.

"We are their honoured guests," I said. "And we'd better show our pleasure."

We made great show of putting the meat in our mouths and chewing it, then rubbing our bellies after swallowing it. We smiled, too, and found that smiling means the same everywhere. In fact, if there was such a thing as a Universal Tongue of the sort philosophers speak of, it is the language of signs and expressions. We Christians, stranded among savages that some of us feared were anthropophagi, spoke that language fluently, indicating with every feature of the face, and every movement of the body, how happy and honoured we were to be among them.

They were happy too, and brought us other food, which we ate greedily, not knowing what it was, filling our bellies while we had the chance. A fluent speaker of that wordless language would have known that we were scared, and that the savages were puzzled, and that neither side knew how the night would turn out. But they had their way of doing things, and we went along with it. When enough food had been eaten, steps danced, and drums beaten, we were led back to our hut and shown by gesture that we were to sleep.

There was no feasting the next day, though the savages did feed us. They brought us bowls of food and watched us eating as though we were menagerie beasts. After that we ceased to be curiosities and settled uneasily into the life of the village. It was a well ordered place, with huts and houses arranged round an open gathering place, with herb gardens and fruit trees nearby, all set within a spiked palisade. That ring of sharp stakes ought to have served as a warning, but we were so relieved at being saved, and so distracted by all the new things we saw, that we failed to notice its significance.

After we had rested for a few days, the savages led us out of the village, beyond the palisade to the forest. My companions were scared again, fearing that we were to be slaughtered, but the savages took us to their gardens, which were in glades among the trees. By gestures and actions, they made us understand that they expected us to work. They showed us what ground to till and how to till it, and how to sow the seeds they gave us, and how to heap the earth round each seed. They did not broadcast their seeds, nor did they have ploughs, or any beasts to draw them. The savages knew only a few crops, a kind of corn, beans, various herbs they use for medicine, and some fruit like melons, though not so sweet or juicy. The rest of their food they found in the woods and rivers.

Their corn is a remarkable plant. I hope you will not take me for a teller of tall tales, but I can only report what I have seen. Each stem of the savages' corn is as tall as a man, each ear is as long as a span, and each grain is the size of a pea. They grind it into coarse flour which they boil or use in other ways. It provides the savages' main food, and they look upon the plant as if it was some kind of god. Those who tended the corn were like servants of the god. Hugh hated that, saying that toiling in the savages' gardens was like idolatry. It didn't seem so bad to me, no more than being thankful for your daily bread. Rosenkreutz was excused much of the work, and spent his time reading the Tome, comparing its pictures to the things we saw around us. William was too weak to work. François and Hugh did as little as possible and bemoaned their lost dignity.

One morning, when it was particularly hot and we all ran with sweat, François flung his stick down. The rest of us stopped working too, and watched to see what whim had taken hold of him.

"I will not be a slave," he said, wiping his brow.

"We are not slaves," I said, scratching my stick in the soil so the savages would think I was working. "We are guests. The savages feed and shelter us. They toil in their gardens. Why should we not help?"

"It feels like slavery to me. We are made to work. What else would you call it?"

"I have been a slave," I said. "It was in Constantinople. I was shackled, chained and whipped by the Turks. I was half starved and worked till I dropped." I held out my hands to show the scars and calluses. "Your hands have never been marked by anything worse than ink stains."

In truth the work was not hard. We laboured for a few hours each morning in pleasant forest glades, ate a simple midday meal, then rested in the shade until evening.

Unlike the others, I did not complain. I remembered Pope Pius, and how he liked to escape from the Vatican into the countryside, eating informal meals provided by the peasantry. His Holiness would have liked the village, and admired the simple life of its people. He would have approved the food they ate, plenty of fish, freshly caught from the river, fruit gathered from wild trees, vegetables from well-tended little gardens, and game in abundance from the forests. It was what Pius liked to eat when he toured his realms in Italy. In many ways the savages were better off than simple folk in Christendom, as they had no lords or masters to tax them. Nor did they know anything of money, as all they needed was provided by nature.

The forest wasn't like the wild places I had known before. In Christendom a wilderness is a place God has turned his back on, where the Devil rules, where men and beasts do the Devil's work, or are slaves only to their lusts and appetites. In a wilderness, even the plants are bad, tangling the traveller in roots and tendrils, snagging him on thorns, tempting him with gaudy but deadly fruit.

The forests in Antillia, or the Land of the Rosy Cross, or wherever it was we had got to, were not like that. The savages lived in the forests just as we live in towns. To them, everything was edible or useful. The beasts, which they caught easily with their simple traps and weapons, gave skins for ropes and clothing, as well as meat. Deer gave sinews that strung the bows that shot them. Vines and bushes gave the savages everything they needed to make their traps. The trees gave fruit and nuts as well as timber for boats and huts. Even the poisonous plants were useful, giving fruits which the savages made into a liquor that stunned fish.

There was no wine that I could discover, but there were grapes, and beer might be brewed from their corn. In fact, all the skills the savages lacked might have been taught to them, and all comforts of England had in that far-off land.

Life there did not suit all of us. William was ill on the voyage, and, though he had revived somewhat on landing, sank back into sickness. He got it into his head that the food the savages gave us was unclean, and refused to eat it. I tried to persuade him, saying that fish, fowl and venison were much the same the world over, but he insisted that nothing the savages offered us was fit for Christian stomachs. I appealed to Rosenkreutz, and got him to agree that, as we were so close to Paradise, all the food was good. But Hugh reminded us of the Forbidden Fruit and its part in the Fall. Then, like the sailor he was, he changed course and said that all good Christians had a duty to keep body and soul together with whatever food came to hand. He told William that no foods were forbidden by the Scriptures, except in the book of Leviticus, which applied only to Jews and Moslems. In any case, nothing the savages offered us was forbidden to those peoples, as I knew from my time among the Turks. William lay in the hut, sweating and shaking in his scholar's gown, sometimes joining the debate, sometimes keeping silent.

"It is his whim not to eat," Rosenkreutz said. "And it is his nature to be whimsical. We will not change either."

The savages saw that William was ill, but did not understand the cause. They sent him meat, and broth, and infusions of herbs, all of which he refused. The woman who brought us all our food sat with William and spooned thin porridge into his mouth, but he always spewed it up and was left weaker than before. An old man waved burning leaves over him, and muttered savage prayers. Hugh said good Christian prayers. They made no difference. Within a fortnight of our landing William was dead, and we buried him in the forest, a little way from the village, but a long way from his college. Air was his element, and it blew us across the Ocean to a strange land full of savages. I hope he died happy after seeing it.

Soolia

William's death made me think. We had been led to that land by the mappamundi, and by Rosenkreutz's stories of treasure and wisdom. I was determined to do more than just die there. I wanted to make something of myself, which I had failed to do in England. I didn't believe in the Seven Cities of Antillia, and didn't care about the lost wisdom of Atlantis. Rosenkreutz studied, François grumbled, and Hugh prayed. But I saw that life in the forest was good, and might be made better.

I thought I could live among those savages, as I had once lived among Turks and Greeks, learning their ways, becoming one of them. Perhaps I might become their leader. I could see how it might be done. The woman who served us was called Soolia, or something like it. They have no writing, so I have set the name down as it sounded. Soolia was no maiden, but an older woman, though young enough for a greybeard like me. I kept a careful watch, and she served no one but us, so she was not a slave. And I never saw her with a man, which made me think she was a widow. She was well formed, with skin like polished copper, and hair as black as a raven's feather. Like all the savage women, her face was painted with black marks and spots, but she looked none the worse for it. She smiled at me when she brought us food, and always made sure I had plenty. I could not help thinking about her while I worked in the savages' gardens. Though François had talked a lot of nonsense when we trudged round England, he was right about one thing: a widow is always in want of a husband. That must be true all over the world, as widows are vulnerable to all life's misfortunes. Soolia was not rich, like the eelwife, nor did she command any men, but she had a place in the village, and if I married her I would no longer be an outsider, and might achieve honour and influence among the savages.

Before I could proceed, I would have to learn their tongue. François was also right when he said that women need to be sweet-talked, though I didn't want to spout poetry at Soolia. Young lovers might pour honeyed words over each other, but a mature man who woos a widow must deal with practical matters. By signs and gestures I made Soolia understand what I wanted, and by similar means she agreed to teach me. Our lessons were a good pretext for wooing. We sat together after she had brought our supper, and she pointed at various things and said their names, and I tried to repeat them. I did not tell the others what I was doing, but they quickly guessed.

"The effort to learn something is always worthwhile," Rosenkreutz said, when I returned to our hut after a session with Soolia. "Especially if it is a language. The question is, what language do they speak?"

"Antillian, surely?" François said. "Oh, but I forgot! There is no Antillia. What William took for an island is merely a shit stain on the map. Perhaps these savages are from Cathay? You said we were not far from there."

"I do not think these savages are men of Cathay," Rosenkreutz said. "If they were subjects of the Great Khan, they would speak Arabic, or at least recognise that language. Nor are they Tartars, though they resemble them in appearance."

"Their language is very difficult," I said. "Sometimes it sounds as strange as birdsong. When I think I have learned a few words, they slip away from me, and I find that I am as dumb as a beast."

"Perhaps you are not as good at languages as you think," François said. "Or is it that you are distracted by savage desires?"

I tried to think of an answer, but Rosenkreutz saved me the trouble. "It may be," he said, "that what Thomas is struggling to learn is the language of Paradise."

"You said we were not there."

"I have been giving the matter much thought. It seems to me that William was wrong. Atlantis must have lain to the west, as Plato said. I am convinced that this land is the remnant of it, and that what the Greeks called Atlantis is the same as what Christians call Paradise. The two stories, of happy lands destroyed by God's wrath, are essentially the same."

"You admitted that Atlantis was a deception," François said. "A trick to get us to sail west. You gave up that story as soon as we landed."

"No. I told you that things are not always what they seem."

"So where are the cities of Atlantis?" François said. "There ought to be ruins, at least. You told us there would be remnants of its past glories. All you've shown us is ignorant savages living in poverty in a forest. Why do we not search for the cities?"

"So that you can wallow in luxury?"

"Luxury? Do you see me consorting with savage women?"

Of course, I knew the reason why François kept away from women. So did Rosenkreutz. "What a state you have sunk to!" he said. "It was a city that dragged you down. Paris enslaved you to crime, drunkenness and sloth. Your torturers unmanned you, but a man is more than his *membrum virile*. A man is also his mind. Your mind was sharp, if wayward. Now it is dull. Why are you not curious about where we are, instead of complaining about where we are not?"

"I am curious. I want to find a city."

"You should be like Thomas," he said, "and embrace the simple life. He is more of a scholar than you are. Whether he beds the savage woman or learns her language, Thomas will be undertaking a most useful philosophical investigation, the results of which will help us understand who these savages are."

"How will bedding her help?" François said.

"He will learn whether she is made the same way as other women."

"We can see that," François said. "She goes stark naked."

"Not quite. The savages take care to conceal their organs of generation."

"Why should their cocks and cunts be any different to those of any other people?"

Rosenkreutz winced at François' crudity. "Because those are the organs by which Creation is perpetuated. If they are not like those of other races, then it may be that these savages are the result of a separate Creation. In which case, we may

218

never succeed in learning their language. That will be a grave setback. If, on the other hand, they resemble us in every way, then we may assume that they are of the race of Adam, and that their language will prove intelligible. In which case, the Tome will reveal its secrets, we will find our position on the mappamundi, and all knowledge will coalesce and become clear."

"You are wandering far from anything that might be called knowledge," François said.

"We have all wandered far. To make sense of our wanderings, our minds must travel further, if not our bodies. Thomas will be our pioneer, though in his case it will probably be his body which makes the most progress."

Rosenkreutz did not leave it there. In the small hours, I awoke to find him crouched over me, his face almost in mine. "She is the One," he whispered. "The Bride. The Savage Venus. Unite with her. East and West will return to each other and conjoin. Lost knowledge will be regained."

He went on, repeating things he had told me before, about a wedding he had been to, which may or may not have been real. I pretended to be asleep, but his words haunted me for the rest of the night. Despite François' doubts, I could not rid myself of the feeling that I had been chosen in some way, as the bearer of the mappamundi and the finder of the Tome. If meaning was to be found in those things, then it was right that I should help find it. And if I could do so by taking my pleasure with Soolia, so much the better.

In the morning I resolved to move quickly. While we worked in the gardens, François teased me, reciting verses about the whores of Paris and how they entertained their customers, while Hugh disapproved silently. Later, while the others rested, I kept a lookout until I saw that Soolia was alone. When I approached her, for all that she was nearly naked, she twirled her necklace as shyly as any maiden. I had not mastered much of her language, but I managed to make my meaning clear, and without causing her alarm or distress, which is easily done if you move clumsily in these matters.

She beckoned, and I followed her, beyond the palisade, into the forest, away from the village. Before long we reached a place where the river looped into the forest and formed a pool. There were smooth rocks, and soft sand, and shady trees arched over the water. It was as good as any bathhouse in Constantinople or Rome.

Soolia took my rough, scarred hands in hers and looked at them closely, trying to read their history. I thought that, if I ever learned her language, I would not tell her of my past. It would only scare her to learn of the wars, crimes and follies that plague the nations of Christendom. I hoped that Rosenkreutz was right, that the forest was a sort of paradise, a place where men might return to innocence, if not the actual garden Adam was expelled from. Soolia was without guile. She sat on a rock and untied her apron, letting it fall. I could see what scholars call the pudenda, and what François, when he was being polite, called the *belle-chose*. As far as I could tell, it was just like that of any other woman. So was the rest of her.

She reached out to me and tugged at my shirt. I unlaced the neck and pulled it over my head. In the heat of that country, it was all I wore. She had never seen me naked before, and stared at the hair on my body. To her, I must have looked as shaggy as a lycanthrope, yet she did not shy away. After a moment she took me by the arm and led me into the water. She made a game of it, ducking and splashing like a child, but I could tell that she wanted me to wash, so I got under and rubbed myself all over with cool water. After I had made a start, she joined in, cupping her hands and pouring water over my head and washing my hair. Was she setting herself to serve me like a good wife? Or did she think I was too dirty? I did not care, and it felt good to have a woman washing my body. Water is my element, or so Rosenkreutz said. I remembered the pictures in the Tome, of tiny women bathing in tubs and pools, laved with liquid spouting from outlandish vessels. Did he know Soolia would lead me to the river? Was my tryst no more than an alchemical experiment?

When I was clean enough she led me out of the pool to a

mossy hollow that was as soft as any feather bed. We lay on it and let the dappled sunlight fall on our naked skin. Braced by the water, flattered by Soolia's attentions, I felt young again, and ready for anything. Or almost ready. The cold water had shrunk my yard and shrivelled my cod. She saw my difficulty, and took my member in her hand. But her hands were cold, and brought little comfort. Seeing that it was not yet awakened, she crouched over me and took my member in her mouth, using her tongue to lick it back to life. I reached down, trying to touch her, and do the things that give a woman pleasure, but she pushed me back and carried on. Was it as Rosenkreutz suggested? Was she different to other women, made for men's pleasure and not her own? Did she lack the part that I had found and fondled in all the other women I had known?

I did not think long on that question. Soolia was taking me to the point of no return, when the match is lit and the piece will surely fire. A gunner should choose his target before then, and I had not chosen mine, but Soolia did it for me, lifting her head, sliding forward, easing herself onto my throbbing yard. I sank into her, feeling her moist readiness, and began to thrust. She writhed on top of me, doubling my motion, pressing me down on our mossy bed. I looked up at her painted face. Her dark eyes were wide open, her teeth were bared in a broad smile, her black hair hung down and whipped my brow. It did not take long after that. She quickened her pace, then held her breath, then let out a great moan. We shuddered, and gripped each other, and were transformed by pleasure. If that was alchemy, then I was willing to try the experiment as often as anyone desired.

She rolled off me, and we lay on the mossy bank, looking up at the trees and sky. I had never met a woman like Soolia before, yet I had no doubts that she was fully human, of the same race as me. When we had rested for a while, she insisted that we wash again. Afterwards, she pointed the way back to the village, and signalled that I was to go back alone. I ought to have been warned by that, but took her cautiousness as natural to one who has submitted to a new lover for the first time. I walked through the forest feeling half my age.

221

Back at the village, Rosenkreutz and François were waiting for me by the hut.

"What did you learn?" Rosenkreutz asked.

I hesitated. How did he know that I had learned anything?"

"Not much," François said. "He was too busy splashing in the water."

"You followed me!"

"I was strolling in the forest. I didn't know you were there."

"You didn't have to watch."

"I thought you were two savages, rutting like beasts."

"How much did you see?" I knew the answer. Though he could not perform the act himself, he liked to watch it, and would have spied on us until we were finished. Perhaps he hoped that the sight of another man's pleasure might arouse him, and cure the damage done by his torturers.

"Please!" Rosenkreutz said, touching the little emblem that hung at his neck. "We of the Brotherhood must not squabble. Tell us, Thomas, what did you learn?"

"I learned that Soolia is just like other women."

Rosenkreutz leaned forward eagerly. "In every detail?"

"Yes."

"That is wonderful news. It proves these savages are of the Race of Adam, in which case, they must speak the Tongue of Adam."

"Her quim tells us that?" François laughed.

"It tells us everything! She is of a branch of the human race that has not gone far from Paradise. We can be sure that her language is the Original Tongue, in which the Tome is written."

"Do you really believe that these savages speak the Original Tongue?" François said. "You told us that the Tome was written by Roger Bacon. How could they and he speak the same language?"

"The Original Tongue predates us all. Bacon discovered it, and the men of this land preserved it."

"I still don't believe it. How could an English friar discover the Original Tongue? Did they still speak it in England, in his time? Or did he travel here to learn it from these savages?" François laughed. "Is that what you want us to believe?"

"It is a certainty, I think, that the Original Tongue was revealed to Bacon, as a result of his experiences in Ancona, where he was imprisoned for a dozen years. Because his ideas were so dangerous, he was forbidden to speak or write. His jailors feared to talk to him in case they went to Hell. They were Franciscans, you know."

"Don't taunt me with that," François said. "I'm no friar."

"You have all the faults of a Franciscan: you resist new ideas, just as they do. However, with your sad history, you should not have much difficulty in picturing what it must have been like for Friar Bacon in prison. Silent for all those years! No thoughts but his own, no words at all, for all that time. It would have driven a lesser man mad."

François smiled. "We are nearer to the truth now. Bacon did go mad in prison, and wrote this mad book."

"No. Bacon's mind was too big for that. He sat in his cell, thinking of everything he knew. Cut off from the world, he created his own world. Deprived of language, he invented his own."

"Aha!" François said. "If he *invented* a language, then it cannot be the Original Tongue, which God taught to Adam. Not unless God visited Ancona and taught Bacon the language in his cell."

"You may scoff," Rosenkreutz said, holding up the Tome. "But the key to everything we desire is in this book. We must set to work immediately and learn the savages' language. François, you must help. Sharpen your mind and set to. And you, Thomas, must redouble your efforts. I daresay that will not be onerous."

Discord in Paradise

They were waiting for me in the forest, a dozen of the biggest, strongest savages, armed with sticks and clubs. There was no point in running. They threw me to the ground and kicked and pummelled me. They spat at me, yelled and shrieked. They beat me with their weapons. Knowing what they had done to the ship's crew, I curled up and hoped for the best, waiting for their blows to die down.

As they dragged me back to the village, bruised and bloody, I reflected on my fate, which was very different from what I had hoped for. It was like the eelmen, all over again, only I couldn't blame François. If anything, he had discouraged me. I might have blamed Rosenkreutz, but it was me, not him, who had dreamed of making myself king of the savages, and used Soolia to that end.

We had a miserable time of it after that. All of us, even Rosenkreutz, were set to work. The savages gave us no rest, watching us closely, goading us with their planting sticks. At night, guards stopped us from wandering. There was little food, only porridge, which was brought to us by a toothless hag. Soolia was kept well away from us. I only saw her once or twice, and she was careful to look at the ground, not at me.

François complained that he was starving, and that the hut was worse than the dungeons of Meung, where he had been kept and tortured for months.

"They should have hanged you," Hugh said. Being kept in the hut was worse for him. Though a ship is much like a prison, he had commanded his vessel, and was used to gazing at the horizon.

"François is unhangable," Rosenkreutz said.

"But not unstarveable." François groaned and rubbed his belly.

"You won't starve," Hugh said. "Better men than you have lived on worse food."

"William said it was the Devil's food, not fit for good Christians."

"All the better for you. If you want to forget the rumbling in your guts, then think of your sins."

"You're a real Job's comforter."

"I should have known better than to sail with men like you," Hugh said. "Thieves, rogues and heretics, the lot of you." He turned on Rosenkreutz. "You led me astray with your stories of islands in the Ocean. You told my crew they were in Paradise, then stirred them up to mutiny. That book of yours is ungodly. It is full of lines, circles, schemes, letters and characters. Yet you pore over it as though it was the holiest of scriptures. You even encouraged Thomas to sin with that naked whore of a savage. Slavery may be a fit punishment for your crimes, but why should I suffer?"

"We're all suffering," François said.

"The virtuous suffer more in captivity than the sinful. I am ruined! I have lost everything, my ship, my crew, my cargo, my good name. Why is God punishing me? How have I offended Him? William was right. I will not defile myself by eating the food of our captors."

"We should have dug William's grave deeper," François said. "You'll be dead soon, and the rest of us soon afterwards."

I doubted it. Hugh's fit of righteous anger would pass. He would eat the savages' food and slave for them, as we all would. It was a bitter end to all our dreams.

Slaves see no end to their bondage. Work drives away thoughts and hope. Even fear dies when your bones ache from ceaseless labour. If anything changed in the village I did not notice it, until, one night, everything changed.

We were fast asleep, tired out by a long day toiling under the sun. I felt something sharp in my ribs. In my dreams I was being goaded by copper-skinned devils with planting sticks. Then I woke and found François poking at me, his face lit by a red light from a fire burning somewhere outside.

"Something's happening," he said.

"What?" I sat up.

"Trouble."

I could hear shouting, the drumming of feet on dry earth, and another sound, one I had not heard for a while but knew well. It was the rush of arrows through the air.

"Have you looked outside?" I said.

"I've got more sense."

"You'd rather die in your bed?"

"If I have to die, then bed is the best place for it."

By then Rosenkreutz and Hugh had woken up. Gesturing to them to keep quiet, I carefully put my head out of the doorway. Our guards were gone. Some of the huts were burning. Savages were running from place to place, beating at the fires, leading women and children out of one hut and into another. With a great whoosh, a volley of arrows came in from the dark. Some of the savages fell. I could not see who was shooting, but they were making a good job of softening up their enemies before attacking.

It was war, and though war is a terrible thing, it is a thing I know about. My heart beat faster when I thought of the possibilities. A quick death or a slow one. Rape. Slavery. Or escape.

"This is our chance," I said. "While they are fighting, we can get away."

"Where to?" François said.

"Does it matter? You've been moaning the loudest at being kept here. Let's take our chance. If we get away we'll be no worse off than when we landed."

"Except for the weapons they stole from us."

François could always see the worst side of everything, but I had been following the example of the savages and stealing a few things from them. I felt under my bed, searching for what I had hidden among the corn husks. "Here," I said, handing François a stone knife.

"I can't fight with this," he said.

"You won't be fighting. You'll be running. We all will. It's our only hope, unless you want to be burnt to death in your bed."

I found a sharpened stick and gave it to Hugh, and kept a club-shaped bone for myself. A sword, a helmet and a mail-coat would have been better, but a club was all I had. "Rosenkreutz," I said. "You have your staff?"

"Yes." He rummaged through his bedding. "They have not taken it."

"If you want to live," I said, "you must do as I say." None of them spoke. "When I give the word, we will run."

"Where?" François said.

"You will follow me. Keep your weapons ready. But don't try to use them. This isn't a backstreet brawl. We will run while the savages fight."

I looked outside again. Lights flashed through the black sky. Burning arrows fell into the village, starting more fires, panicking the women and children. There was plenty of noise: flames crackled, huts crashed to the ground, women screamed, babies wailed. It was a good moment.

"Run!" I said, and we ran.

The village was ablaze all around us. The night was full of monsters, man-like creatures with hideous faces, all glowing white and red with firelight and anger. They ran between the blazing huts, yelping and whooping, striking at anything that came within their reach. It seemed that all the travellers' tales were true, that far off lands were full of satyrs, lycanthropes, troglodytes and cynocephalae.

"Fiends!" Hugh shouted. "Devils! Servants of Satan!" He ran towards them with his arms outstretched. "In the name of the Father, the Son, and the Holy Spirit, I command you to . . ."

His words were cut short by a spear through his chest. He fell forward, clutching at the shaft.

"Run!" I said. "There's no helping him."

The fires burned brightly, sparks rushing upwards. The villagers scurried from one place to another like rabbits flushed from a warren. Snarling beast-men caught women and trussed them like hogs. Burning wisps rained down from the sky, lighting our way. There were gaps in the palisade where the stakes had been smashed down. I made for one of them and dashed through it. The cool darkness was welcoming. I stopped, and turned to see if the others were following. Rosenkreutz came first, striding through the gap with the fire behind him, his staff held like a spear.

"Fire!" he said. "The element of transformation."

Then François came, scuttling out of the village like a thwarted thief.

"I'm wounded," he said.

"Where?"

"My shoulder," he whined.

"You can still run. Stay close and follow."

We blundered on, through the gardens we had tended, into the forest. Our faces were thrashed by branches, our ankles caught in vines. We stumbled through unseen undergrowth, fell on our faces, and picked ourselves up. François cursed every obstacle, anathemising the forest in his thieves' French, but Rosenkreutz kept silent, as though nothing was strange to him and a blind dash through a wilderness was no different to a stroll in a park.

After a while we saw a faint glow on our right hand. I feared it was another fire, that more villages were ablaze and that all the savages of that land were at war with each other. But the glow was something that, confined in our huts, secluded in the forest, we had not seen for some weeks. The dawn was breaking, the sun's red edge barely showing above the horizon. That told us that we were beyond the forest, in more open land, and that meant we could move faster.

"The sun!" Rosenkreutz said, raising his spear. "We must follow it."

He shouldered the papal bag and loped off. François complained about his wound, but I goaded him on. Whenever he faltered I reminded him of the beast-men behind us, telling him they were sure to be anthropophagi who would eat him first as he was the slowest. We didn't stop until the sun was well up and we had waded across a river. It was not deep enough to protect us, but it was wide, so we would know if we were being followed.

"I can't go on," François said, slumping down on the

riverbank. His face was the colour of tallow, and flecked with smuts from the fires we had run through. There was real anguish in his voice, not the false sorrow he used to get sympathy.

Rosenkreutz did not complain, but he too was covered with smuts and scratches.

"We'll rest," I said. "But not for long."

François had caught an arrow in his shoulder. The shaft had broken off, leaving the head stuck inside him. Cutting out an arrowhead was something I knew how to do, so I set to it, using the stone blade I had taken from the savages. I was ready for a stone arrowhead, and expected to pick out the chips, but I was wrong. The arrowhead was iron. It looked like a ship's nail, roughly sharpened and lashed to the shaft's stump with sinew.

"Interesting!" Rosenkreutz said. "Did those savages get it from our wreck? Or are there men nearby that know how to work iron?"

François didn't care what the arrowhead was made of, or where it had come from. He yelled when I pulled it out, and whimpered while I sewed him up with a bone needle. I washed the wound with river water, and hoped it wouldn't fester, as there was nothing clean to dress it with. François squirmed and grumbled the whole time, but Rosenkreutz sat on him, and didn't talk any of his usual nonsense, like saying that the wound was an illusion, or that François would get better when he found wellness within himself, or anything like that.

"I'm starving," François said, when we had finished with him. Back in England, I could have been sure that François would have stolen something, that he would have a cheese or a sausage hidden beneath his cloak. Among the savages he had lost his thieving habit, along with most of his clothes. We still had our shirts, which were filthy and ragged, and our boots, which were full of holes, and soaked from wading through the river. Rosenkreutz had some shreds of cloth draped round him that had once been his pilgrim's cloak. And he had kept hold of the bag with the Tome and mappamundi in it. Those things were all we had to set us apart from the naked savages of the forest.

"We'll find something to eat," I said.

"Where?"

"We'll live off the land," I said. "I've done it before."

"So have I," François said. "And I did it the same way that you did, by stealing from the peasants. Do you see any peasants round here? Any farms with pigs and chickens running around, ready for taking? Any barns full of hay to sleep on, or storehouses full of wine casks and pots of confit?"

"You must have done well for yourself in the countryside. It's a wonder you ever went back to Paris. When I served with my free company we had to rough the peasants up before they'd tell us where they'd buried everything, and even then there wasn't much to find."

"Free company! There's a fine name for a bunch of rogues and villains. Brigands, I'd call them."

"And what were you? A coquillard! If that doesn't mean a thief and a scoundrel, I don't know what does."

"Remember that we are a Brotherhood," Rosenkreutz said. "Can we not leave old arguments behind us? We must work together if we are to reach Paradise."

"Don't give us that again," François said. "How can Paradise be here? These savages are killers. The mark of Cain is on them. They killed the crew, and now we know that they kill their own kind. Is there war in Paradise?"

"This is not Paradise," Rosenkreutz said. "I have never said it was. Paradise is nearby. A river flows out of it, and that river divides as it flows, and feeds into all the great rivers of the world." He took out the mappamundi and spread it on the ground. "We have found a river," he said, pointing at the map. "Let us follow it. When we have found the source we will have found Paradise."

"The source?" I said. "You want us to go deeper inland?"

"Not me," François said. "All we'll find there is more savages and more forest."

"We were delayed among the savages because the others

230

were with us," Rosenkreutz said. "Hugh and William played their parts, but we do not need them now. We are three again, just as we were when we began this venture. We will follow the river to Paradise, and there we will find men who know no sin, who can teach us great wisdom. It is what we came for. We cannot give up now."

"And what will we eat on the way?" François said. "Milk and honey? Manna from Heaven?"

I looked at the mappamundi. It was crumpled and filthy, its colours dull. All the life had gone out of it, and I doubted it had the power to guide us. Then I had an idea. "Let us clean the mappamundi," I said. "The river sand is fine, just like fuller's earth. Let us scatter some on the cloth."

Rosenkreutz was reluctant, but I persuaded him, and soon gathered up some dry sand from the riverbank which I gently poured over the map, leaving it to warm up in the morning sun while François moaned and Rosenkreutz rambled. When I judged that enough time had passed, I shook the sand loose and spread out the cloth again. It was certainly cleaner. The colours glowed in the sun like a stained-glass window. The Ocean was blue again, and the mountains, forests, lakes, cities and beasts, all stood out in their natural colours. Many rivers were marked on the map. I had no idea which one was ours, but they all had one thing in common. They ran into the sea.

Rosenkreutz started up again, pointing at the painted East, with its cities and treasures, but I cut him short.

"We'll follow the river to the sea," I said, rolling the map up carefully and giving it to Rosenkreutz. "Let's start now. We've got a day ahead of us, and a good chance of getting away from the savages." I stood up, and took a step or two in the right direction.

François rose slowly, pulling faces to show the pain he was in. "Come on!" I said. "Let's go!"

François followed me, but Rosenkreutz did not. I turned and waited, and François caught up with me. "Leave him," he said. "He's a mad old fool and no good for anything. We'll save ourselves. Let him sit there and wait for a miracle."

I wasn't so sure. Rosenkreutz was stubborn, certainly, but not mad. Not yet. But François was proved right soon enough. In any case, I could not abandon Rosenkreutz, any more than I could kill him when François proposed it back in England. I went back to him, and held out my hand. "Come with us," I said. And I looked into his cold blue eyes and saw something I had never seen in him before. Weakness. For all his bluster and talk of secret wisdom, he was as lost as we were, and as scared. I took his hand and helped him to his feet. "Come on," I said. "As you told us, we are a Brotherhood of Three, and cannot be parted. The river will guide us and give us food. At the coast we will think again. Bring your staff, and the Tome. Help us find our way."

The Fountain

The river twisted and turned, sometimes heading towards our goal, sometimes away from it. It seemed as though that other-world we had stumbled upon was no more than one vast river, coiling around itself like an eel in a bucket. As we sweated along its banks, slipping in mud, clambering over stumps and branches, we saw no sign of Man or his work. It was a real wilderness, not like the tamed woods where the savages lived. Trees towered above us, their boughs hung with moss and creepers, blocking out the sun. Huge trunks lay rotting into the damp earth, blocking our path, sending us on detours through brushwood and undergrowth.

The damp air buzzed with biting, stinging insects. We heard frogs croaking, but never saw them. Larger beasts lurked in the deep shade, some of them strange and chimerical, one of them a spiky creature that François said was a porcupine.

"How do you know that?" I said. "Have you ever seen one?"

"Not in the flesh. But the beast is easily recognisable. It appears on King Rene's arms. I forget which of his many titles the porcupine stands for. Sicily, perhaps. Or Naples."

Having remembered King René, François could not resist telling us about the great feasts his followers had eaten, and that reminded me of the suppers Pope Pius had served to his friends. Those memories made our hunger worse, even though the forest teemed with beasts, and the river with fish, many of them good to eat. We had no real weapons to hunt with. François threw sticks and stones at any small beasts he saw, but he never hit anything. I tried to make snares from twigs and vines, but failed to catch anything. We were luckier at fishing. I sharpened a stick with my stone blade and managed to spear a few fish. They tasted good, grilled over glowing embers, and if we were lucky there was enough left over for another day. It was always me that made the fire, rubbing sticks like the savages. Rosenkreutz watched while I transformed one element into another. François grumbled until I had finished, but never helped.

My stone blade soon blunted, and I lacked the skill to make another. I realised, yet again, how much better the savages were than us at living in the forest. They knew what was good to eat, and how to catch or gather it, and how to cook it afterwards. They knew what was poisonous, or treacherous, and how to avoid it. And they knew how to make tools and cooking pots from anything that came to hand.

As we went downstream, the riverbank got so muddy that we could not follow it. We took detours, struggling deep into the forest, losing sight of the sun. Sometimes we came across what might once have been gardens, long abandoned. There were paths of a sort, though whether made by beasts or men we could not tell.

As the forest got darker, Rosenkreutz grew more cheerful. He did not notice the biting flies, the snagging thorns, the fallen branches that tripped us, or the swamps that threatened to swallow us. He talked of Nature and its wonders, telling us how lucky it was that the trees put forth such an abundance of fruits, even though we could find little to eat, and how fortunate we were to be shaded by the leaves and branches, even though by hiding the sun from us they led us into confusion. He quoted bits of verse about birds and beasts, about how each knew its place and was happy to do what the Creator ordained, even worms and vermin, however vile such creatures might seem to us. François laughed at the verse, saying it was the worst he had heard, and he had heard plenty of bad verse, composed to flatter lords and rich patrons. Every time he saw a forest bird or beast he told us whose emblem it was, as though he was the greatest herald in Christendom. That started him off again on how good life had been in France, where men like him were valued and rewarded, which I knew was nonsense as he had often told me the opposite. So what with Rosenkreutz imagining himself in Paradise, and François imagining himself among the lords of the Loire, it was only me that noticed where we actually were and kept an eye open for food or danger.

We saw a patch of light ahead, and made for it, hoping to observe the sun and find our direction again. It was a good-sized clearing, but when we reached it, Rosenkreutz forgot about the sun, and pointed his staff at the pond that lay ahead of us.

"Let us bathe," he said, tugging at the rags that draped his shoulders.

"If I wanted to bathe," François said, "I wouldn't bathe here. The water stinks."

"I knew you were blind to the truth," Rosenkreutz said. "Do all your senses deceive you? Do you not know what this place is?" He waved his arm at the pool. "It is a perfect circle, or nearly so." He reached into the bag and pulled out the Tome. "It is in here. The Fountain of Eternal Youth!"

"Fountain?" François said. "It's a stagnant pond in the middle of a dismal swamp."

Rosenkreutz was not listening. "Look!" he said. "Over there! A tube, communicating with the depths of the earth."

"It's a hollow log."

"No! It is the Source. It brings the healing waters from below."

"The water is green. I've seen cleaner flowing from a privy."

"Look in the Tome!" Rosenkreutz held it up, showing us one of the many illustrations of women bathing. His hands shook so much I could hardly see the picture. But I remembered it, the women round-bellied and eager, all facing left, up to their haunches in green liquid.

"There is no doubt about it," he said. "Men of all ages and nations have sought the secret of Eternal Youth. Scholars have trudged all over Christendom, and beyond. They have toiled in libraries, ransacked monasteries, endured fruitless lifetimes of study, worked long nights in fume-filled laboratories . . ."

"Sold their souls to the Devil," François said.

"Some may have imagined such a bargain. They aged and died nonetheless. But we, guided by the Tome, have found the source of Eternal Life. This is the place! Old men who bathe here will be made young, and young men will never grow old."

235

"Eternal life," François said. "Eternal misery! Who would willingly prolong life's sufferings?"

"These waters are full of virtue. They have the power to transform us, to release the power within. Bathe with me. Be purged of the melancholy that dooms you to misery. Leave sloth and accidie behind. Remake yourself!"

Rosenkreutz put the Tome back in the bag and hung it from a branch. He struggled out of what remained of his pilgrim's robes and stood before us naked. His beard hung down his chest, stuck with twigs and leaves. His skin was grey where it had been covered, and red where it was burned by the sun. His frail body shook with excitement.

"Be careful," I said, as he stepped forward.

"This is no time for care!" He slithered down the bank, fell to his knees, then crawled into the water. Bubbles rose from the mud, filling the air with a vile stink. Rosenkreutz plunged on, going in waist deep, then up to his shoulders. "Eternal Life!" he shouted, ducking down so that his head sank beneath the water. The green pond rippled like boiling soup. François and I watched from the bank. More bubbles rose, and the stink got worse, but Rosenkreutz stayed below.

"He'll drown," I said.

"Not now; he's immortal."

"Do you believe that?"

François stared calmly at the scummy water. "No," he said.

"Then we'd better save him." I stepped forward.

"Why? He's a useless burden. Let's leave him."

"He helped save you. I couldn't have treated your wound without him."

"He sat on me. That's all."

"I'm going in." I slid down the bank and floundered into the water. The stink bubbling up from the mud nearly choked me. I reached out to where Rosenkreutz had been, but touched nothing but water. I went in deeper, up to my chest, but still found nothing. Then I dragged my feet from the bottom and tried to swim. As I thrashed about in the filthy water my hand met something solid, but whether it was Rosenkreutz or a foul creature of the swamp, I could not tell. I

236

gripped it anyway, and gave it a great pull, and found that it was an arm. I heaved again, and pulled Rosenkreutz nearer to the bank, but he lay heavy in the water and I could not pull him out. I teetered in the shallows, stinking water pouring off me. Rosenkreutz lay face down, a dead weight.

"Help me!" I said, heaving again at the mud-slimed arm. "He'll drown."

I heard nothing from François. I could not see him, as I held on fast to Rosenkreutz and could not turn round. François might have wandered off into the forest and left us. Then I felt a hand on my arm and knew that François was beside me. Thrashing like mired pigs, the two of us hauled Rosenkreutz out. We bent him over and slapped his back, and held onto him until he had spewed up all the foul water he had swallowed. Then we led him onto dry land and leaned him against a tree until he got his breath back. His skin, hair and beard were all stained by the mud we had been wallowing in.

"You look like the Green Knight," François said.

"Of course!" Rosenkreutz raised his arms and stared down at them. "I am transformed," he said. "I was Christian Rosenkreutz. Now I am Al-Khidr."

"Who?"

"The one you call the Green Knight, or Green Man. He is older than the stories you know. Much older. The Saracens know him as Al-Khidr. He too drank from the Source and became immortal. He appears as a guide, and perhaps a tormenter. But torment can be guidance, as Job knew."

"You've led us into torment," François said. "That's true enough. But do you really expect us to believe that you have become this . . ."

"Al-Khidr. I have been known by other names. Why not a new one?"

Beneath the drying pond slime, his face was lit by a mad glow. I feared that he had taken a fever and would soon start raving.

"Should we call you by this new name?" I asked, thinking it best to humour him.

"Names are like clothes," he said. "They are not important.

The Turks called me Gülhaç, but they did not know what I would become. You could call me Pilgrim, if you wished. My search for wisdom is the one thing about me that has remained constant."

"I'll call you Rosenkreutz," François said. Silently, I agreed with him. Too much had changed, and names were something to hold onto.

"You've found what you wanted now," I said. "Put your clothes on and come away."

"This is only the start," he said. "I am renewed, and my task is renewed. All wisdom lies before me. Everything in the Tome will become clear." He looked around anxiously. "Where is it? Where is the bag? I must study it."

"Later," I said. "Let us get away from this place."

"Away? But this is the place we have been searching for."

"We must eat," I said. "And tell others of this wonderful place. You want that, don't you?"

Vaguely, like a drunkard answering an imaginary friend, he agreed.

Madness

Sometime after bathing in the pool Rosenkreutz lost his staff. When he realised, he begged us to go back and look for it, but we refused. I tried to cut him another, but my stone blade was as blunt as a pebble, and he had to make do with a ragged branch torn from a dead tree. He took it reluctantly, and whenever we stopped he tried to scratch marks on it to give it the power of his old staff.

It was no good. He could find nothing sharp enough to make an impression on the branch, and in his frustration he gnawed at it with his teeth. At that, fearing that he would break his teeth and be unable to eat, I flung the branch away. François and I led him through the forest, taking his hand to stop him wandering, supporting him between us when he weakened.

It was our privations that brought Rosenkreutz down. Slavery, starvation and ceaseless wandering exhausted him. He said he had travelled, but he hadn't roughed it like me and François. He pretended not to care about trifles such as good food and soft beds, though his tricks with gold coins meant he could always have them. In the wilderness, he was just like anyone else. His wisdom and philosophy were no use to him. There was no one to listen to his ideas, no one to impress, so he talked to himself.

"We are the New Men," Rosenkreutz babbled. "We are the Ones Who Know. We are the Three. We will endure, and be known forever. Whenever men ask where Knowledge comes from, the answer will be that we Three brought it back from Paradise."

"It's all in your mind, old man," François said. "We didn't get to Paradise. You said so yourself."

"Did we not?" Rosenkreutz's voice was weak. "Can you be sure?"

"This place is more like Hell than Paradise. The only good thing about it is that we have left those devils of savages behind."

It was after that that Rosenkreutz began reading to us from the Tome. Before, he had hinted that he understood it, or soon would, but after his dip in that stagnant pool he was able to speak out loud what his fingers touched on the pages. He read fluently, as though he not only knew the sounds those strange letters stood for, but understood the words. Of course, we urged him to translate, to tell us the secrets he had discovered, but he didn't seem to understand. He was reading from the Tome: why could we not follow what he read? It was simple: he had the key to everything!

We managed to find the river again, and followed it as best we could, for it was our only hope of reaching the sea, and the sea was our only hope of escaping the wilderness. But our hopes were dashed when we struggled out of a dense patch of forest to find ourselves on the end of a promontory. On our right we could see the opposite bank of the river we had been following. On our left we saw another bank, much further off. And ahead, where I judged the sea was, we could see more land, low and distant, half lost in mist.

"We have found it!" Rosenkreutz said, gazing out at the vast expanse that almost surrounded us. "The Ganges!" he said. "It flows out of Paradise, just as I told you. We would have got there, had we gone upstream."

"You told us once that Paradise was an island," I said. "A river this size can't flow from an island."

"Paradise is difficult to reach, certainly. Some say it is cut off by a bottomless lake, a wall of fire, and an unclimbable earthen bank, and that anyone who attempted to cross those obstacles would be blown back by an irresistible wind. It is protected by the four elements. To call it an island is a figure of speech."

"Another one!" François said. "When you call this river the Ganges, is that a figure of speech, too?"

"You claim to be a poet, François. You must know that language is always more powerful when it is indirect. A metaphor, an allusion, can say much more than a mere statement of fact. Until we all speak the Philosophers' Tongue, of course."

"So is this the Ganges?"

"The Ganges is the mightiest river in the world. The scriptures call it the River Physon, but travellers to the East know its true name. Its mouths are many, and so are its tributaries. The bay of the Ganges is huge. Look around you. Can you deny that we have found it?"

"Can you deny that we are stuck on the end of a miserable spit of land with nothing ahead of us but water and nothing behind us but swamp and forest?"

"We have reached the Ganges."

"If the Ganges is the greatest river in the world," I said, "would there not be great ports at its mouth?"

"Undoubtedly."

"And would there not be ships there, from all nations, one of which might carry us home?"

"We may be sure of it."

"I see no ports," François said. "Or ships."

"The river's true mouth is there." Rosenkreutz pointed to the East. "I always said we were near Cathay. The geography of this place has become clear to me."

He took out the mappamundi, draped it over a bush like a housewife setting washing to dry. Then he pointed at a part of the East that had many trees marked on it. "Behind us," he said, "beyond the Fountain of Eternal Life, is Paradise. It is a shame that we did not reach it, but that seems to be my fate." He pointed again, at a place where a great river divided into streams and flowed out into the painted Ocean. "Ahead of us is the mouth of the Ganges, which divides Cathay from the Indies. Which means that Cathay is to our north, and the Indies to our south. The wisdom of the East is within our grasp. And its wealth."

"Not the Seven Cities again!" François said.

"There are more than seven," Rosenkreutz said, gesturing vaguely at the map. "There are hundreds, each with its sultan or satrap, all subjects of the Great Khan. These rulers have palaces where treasure is heaped up high, and concubines recline on silk cushions as soft and plump as they are. Their barracks are manned by invincible hordes. Nearby are gilded temples, libraries full of ancient books, caravanserais with soft beds, and markets where unimaginable luxuries are bought and sold. Philosophers are to be found everywhere, living in monasteries, or on top of pillars. Anyone who is worthy can share their wisdom. What you would call magic is commonplace. The streets are thronged with men, eunuchs, and elephants. Beasts of many kinds draw carts laden with all the produce of the East. You who only know Paris or London cannot imagine the wealth of those places. Even Constantinople at its greatest was nothing to the cities of Cathay and the Indies."

"All we have to do is reach them," François said.

He looked south, to the other bank. It was much the same as the bank we were on, low and muddy, with tangled undergrowth and trees beyond it. But it did not end in a mud-spit. Instead, it stretched away in the far distance, perhaps to the coast. François turned to Rosenkreutz. "Can you walk on water, now that you are immortal?"

"If I were fully myself, anything might be possible."

"But you are not?"

"Transformation is exhausting."

"Tramping though swamps and forests is exhausting, especially when you're starving."

"It's more of the same," I said, "unless we can get across this river."

"Unless Rosenkreutz can master the elements," François said, "I don't see how."

Rosenkreutz could barely master himself. He was half-starved, almost naked, shaggy as the satyrs that live in the mountains of the Morea, plastered with stinking mud, and well on the way to stark madness. François and I were not much better, looking more like beasts than men. We might have sunk lower, killing and eating each other. I heard of such things when I campaigned in France, and not just among starving peasants. Gilles de Rais, marshal of France, companion in arms of Joan the Virgin, killed and ate babies, or so it was said.

What stopped us sinking that low was Rosenkreutz's talk.

Whether we believed him or not, his tales of great cities, wealth and wisdom gave François something to argue with, and reminded us that we were men and should live as such. That wilderness was no place for men, so we were determined to escape it. We could not wade or swim the river, and had no tools to make a boat, but we might float across, if we could find a log that would carry us. There were plenty of fallen trees, but most were too big to move, or still half-rooted in the soil. There was a tide in that stretch of river, and I reckoned that if we could find the right log it might float off when the water rose, and carry us with it. It was when trying to shift a smaller tree that we had a stroke of luck. In a pool beneath the trunk we found a great fish curled up in the mud. It was over a yard long, with a mouth like a frog's, and long whiskers hanging from either side. It was black and slimy and thrashed about like a wounded boar, but we killed it and roasted it, and ate our fill, with plenty left over for another day. There is nothing like a full belly to raise a man's spirits, and to give him strength. When we saw the tide turning, we set to and heaved on our tree, and soon had it afloat on the rising waters.

We ran into the river and climbed on. As nimbly as an old goat, Rosenkreutz scrambled into a fork and lodged himself there, clutching the bag with the precious Tome and map to his chest. François and I settled ourselves as best we could, gripping tightly like novice riders, fearing every movement as the trunk bucked and rolled beneath us.

"The current is strong," Rosenkreutz said, looking down at us from his perch as though he was master of our craft. "It will carry us to Cathay, if we are lucky."

"And if we're not lucky," François said, "it will carry us into the middle of this great confluence and drown us."

"You are lucky. And so is Thomas. That is why I chose you."

I clung on tighter when I heard that. If he was still relying on luck after all his talk of transformation then nothing much had changed. Then I remembered that, in our haste, we had left all our food behind. That fish was an ugly beast, but it tasted good, with white flesh fit to be dressed with sauce and sent to the table of any nobleman. The meal we had made of it seemed a feast as my belly rumbled with hunger. And if that wasn't enough, when I dipped a hand into the river and raised it to my mouth I found that the water was brackish, so we had nothing to drink. Then, further out, the tree got caught in a winding current and began to spin like a great cartwheel. Rosenkreutz only had to mention luck for luck to turn against us.

Although the tree turned, it did not move. We were stuck in the middle of the river, too far from either bank to do anything except sit and wait.

"Can't you do something," François said, looking up at Rosenkreutz.

"What?"

"You told us that wood is an element. Surely you can control this tree and command it to carry us to the other bank?"

"Wood is the stiffest of elements," Rosenkreutz said. "And the most stubborn. Trees die slowly, and there is life in this one yet. Like all trees, it retains an affinity for the place where it grew."

"You might have told us that before we climbed on."

"Would you have listened?"

"If you can't control this tree, then part the waters so we can wade ashore. Summon a wind to blow us towards the land. Anything!"

"The elements are strong." Rosenkreutz looked warily at François. "Do you see how much water surrounds us? Can you imagine the effort it would take to move it?"

"The air is light. Summon a wind."

"I am weak."

"You did it before, back in Ipswich. Or was the shipman right? Was it his prayers that shifted the wind?"

"I had fire in me then."

"Was it doused by the Fountain of Eternal Youth?"

"It is reduced to embers. The humours in me lie dormant."

"So, you were not rejuvenated?"

"Have you ever observed the growth of a caterpillar?"

François laughed. "Do you think I would waste my time studying vermin?"

"Why not? Aristotle though it worth his while."

"Aristotle! I suppose you knew him, in your youth. Did you not say he was a pedant?"

"It is scholars who read Aristotle without understanding who are the pedants. But you do not seem to have read him at all. If you had studied his *History of Animals*, you would know about the silkworm. It is not vermin, but a useful creature. When it has finished spinning, it becomes a butterfly. But the metamorphosis is not instant. First the worm forms a chrysalis. It lies inactive within its cloak of silk. Only after weeks of gradual change does it emerge." As he spoke, Rosenkreutz was looking down at the swirling water, edging himself away from it.

"Will you become a butterfly?" François said. "Then what? Will you flap your wings and fly away?"

"I am becoming something else, but in the meantime I am as helpless as a chrysalis."

"You always were," François said. "You can't do anything. You're a fraud, no better than the hucksters who sell love potions in country markets. I've seen it all: quack doctors peddling useless remedies, fortune tellers casting false horoscopes, pilgrims showing pigs' bones as holy relics, friars passing off stained sheets as Our Lord's Shroud."

"I have sold you nothing. On the contrary, I have paid your way ever since we met."

"With fake gold!"

"It was real, for a time."

"Tell us the secret. How did you work that trick?"

Rosenkreutz sat silently, looking down on us. François leaned forward, then twisted himself round so he was sitting upright on the tree trunk. "You lied and cheated," he said. "And led us on a fool's errand."

"I have offered you wisdom, which you failed to recognise."

François tried to crawl towards Rosenkreutz. "You're a mad old man spouting mad nonsense from a mad old book!"

"Sit down!" I said. "Or you'll end up in the river. I saved you from drowning once, but I won't do it again."

Rosenkreutz shuffled back up his fork. The tree tilted. François did not sit down.

"Both of you!" I said. "Keep still. You'll have us all in the water."

"Do you think I care?" François crawled forward a little. "You can't escape me, old man. You may hold on to that book, but I'll have it off you." François tried to stand, but could not keep his balance. He dropped to all fours, then sat down, his legs astride the trunk. "When I get that book," he said, "it's going in the river. That'll be the end of all this madness!"

Rosenkreutz held his bag with one hand, gripped a branch with the other, and managed to raise himself until he was almost upright. The tree bucked and rolled beneath us.

"Sit down!" I shouted.

Rosenkreutz let go of the bag, letting it hang from his neck. Reaching out with both arms, he got hold of two branches and, with a sudden lurch, stood up.

"I'm coming for you!" François said, hoisting himself forward like a child playing leapfrog. His feet dragged in the water, splashing his legs.

"Wait!" I said. I could not think what to say to them. I clung to the tree trunk as tightly as I could, hoping François would see sense, and that Rosenkreutz would sit down, and the tree would stop rolling beneath us.

Then I noticed that the air was no longer calm. "Stop!" I said. "Can you not feel it? A wind has sprung up."

François dipped his hand in the water and held it up. "Call that a wind," he said, after a moment. "I can hardly feel it."

But as soon as he spoke the wind strengthened, and the tree moved beneath us. Instead of spinning it was drifting, towards the far bank.

Rosenkreutz laughed, his thin body twisting as he hung on to the branches. His arms outstretched, his body slack, he looked like Our Lord on the Cross.

"You doubted me," he said. "But I found the power. It lay dormant within me."

The others

Our wanderings began again on the other side. The swamps, thickets and biting insects were all the same as we had encountered before, though we were luckier with food, as the year was advancing, and many of the trees were hung with fruit and nuts. With our hopes fading, we foraged like hogs, thinking more of our bellies than of getting to Cathay. Then we smelled scorched meat, and knew that there were men about, the first we had encountered for some time. We followed our noses, creeping through the undergrowth as stealthily as beasts, peering out of a covert to see what kind of men they were.

There were three of them, sitting round a fire, chewing silently at chunks of meat. Though as dark as savages they were as hirsute as we were, though rather better dressed, in good linen shirts. It is true that their clothes were dirty, but they were not ripped to shreds like ours. What struck me most was that they were carrying weapons. Each had a bow slung over his shoulder, like a savage. But one of them had an axe with a good iron blade, and the others long knives stuck in their belts. We had been in the wilderness for so long that those simple tools were a wonder to us.

"Christians!" François said. "We are saved."

He was all for running over to them and begging a share of their feast, but I caught his arm and stopped him. The night we spent in a hag's hovel in Essex, and our later troubles, had taught me to be careful who I supped with.

"We don't know who they are," I said. "I won't be enslaved again for the sake of a meal."

"They are not savages," he said. "They are wearing clothes."

"How do we know there aren't clothed savages round here?"

"The men of Cathay wear clothes," Rosenkreutz said.

"You told us that they were very clean in their ways. Those men look almost as filthy as we are."

"Perhaps they are dark skinned," Rosenkreutz said. "Like Indians."

"You said Indians went naked," I said. "You told me about them in Rome. Gymnosophists, you called them."

"Most Indians wear clothes."

"What sort? Do they dress like Christians? Or like Saracens?"

"How do they dress?" Rosenkreutz absent-mindedly picked a mossy twig from his beard and let it fall to the ground. "I cannot recall. These things are of no importance."

"Yes they are," I said. "When I was in the Morea we had to tell Turk from Christian. Our lives depended on it. And now we must know who those men are. Surely you can remember what kind of clothes they wear in Cathay and India?"

"My mind was on higher things."

"You can't expect him to have noticed," François said. "He spent all his time talking to naked philosophers."

"I did not say I had met a Gymnosophist, did I?"

"You implied it."

Rosenkreutz looked hurt. "You have misunderstood me," he said. "I know of the Gymnosophists from books, as all educated men do. Arrian described them in his life of Alexander. So did Plutarch. The sceptic philosophers were much influenced by them. Some would say that Christian ascetics have absorbed their influence, through the works of Dionysius the Areopagite, of course. The Gymnosophists were very important."

"But you have never met one?"

"My journey did not take me to the places where they are to be found."

"You did go to India?" François said.

"I have travelled all over the East."

"You told me you had got as far as Paradise," I said.

"Not quite that far," Rosenkreutz said. "Otherwise, why would I have led you here?"

"But India and Cathay!" François said. "You said you had been to those places."

"What traveller can tell exactly where he has been?"

"I know where I've been," I said. "We first met in Constantinople, so I know you got that far. From there, I went as far east as Trebizond. Did you travel as far?"

"Farther."

"Where, exactly?" François had been mocking before, but now he was angry.

"Where have you been?" Rosenkreutz said. "Before you met Thomas, Paris was your whole world. You would not know the places I went to. East of Anatolia all is confusion. Our maps show little. What seems a straight line may actually be a circle. Ask the natives where you are and they say, 'this is our town, our country.' Ask them who they are, and they say, 'we are ourselves, the people.' Ask them what lies beyond, and they say, 'another place, peopled by enemies.' A Babel of tongues clouds the truth."

"Your lies cloud the truth!" François jabbed a bony finger at Rosenkreutz. "It's just as I've always said! You're a fraud. You've been nowhere. Everything you've told us is nonsense."

Rosenkreutz opened his mouth, but said nothing. Then he teetered, and his legs buckled, and he slid down to the ground, lying as limply as a heap of rags and bones.

"We should never have trusted him," François said, prodding Rosenkreutz with a filthy foot. Rosenkreutz quivered slightly, but did not get up. "I'd rather put my trust in those men gorging themselves with roasted meat," he said. "They are Christians, like us. I am sure of it."

"Even if they are," I said. "They may not be our friends. Have you forgotten how it is in Christendom? Nation fights nation, and Christians are enemies to each other."

"You remind me of that?" he said. "You who despoiled my country!"

"Those men might be Spaniards," I said. "Or Portuguese. William told us that those nations claimed all new islands in the Ocean. They've been looking for Antillia, just like us."

"Is *that* what we are doing? I thought we were looking for a shit-stain on a painted cloth."

"We must be careful. We could be in danger if they think we know their secrets."

"What secrets?" François said. "We have found a wilderness full of savages. If we had found gold, or the fabled Seven Cities, you might have a point. But who could care about this place?"

"They may have found gold," I said. "The Seven Cities may not be far off. Just because we haven't found them, that doesn't mean they aren't there."

"You sound like Rosenkreutz."

At that, I knelt to tend the old man, hoping he was not about to sink into one of his deathly sleeps. "You'll have to help me," I said.

When I looked to François for a response there were two men beside him. "You'd better come with me," one of them said. "You look as though you could do with a good feed."

They were heavily bearded and burnt black by the sun, but I thought I knew their faces. It was only when they had carried Rosenkreutz to the campfire that I understood. They were Irish crewmen from our ship. The third man, still enjoying his meat, was Jago.

"We thought you were dead," I said, when our bellies were full.

"I knew you were not," Jago said.

"How did you survive the attack?"

"I wasn't there," he said. "I guessed what would happen. Men protect their women, even savages. I knew they would attack. I took these two and went away."

"Didn't the other crewmen stop you?"

"How? They were drunk."

"Why did you not come for us?"

"I heard you were happy in your village."

"You heard? Who from?"

"From the men who live in the woods. You are famous among them: the pale men who work as slaves."

"We were not slaves, exactly. Not at first. We earned our keep."

"You think so? Others think different."

"You understand them, speak their language?"

250

"I speak many languages. It is good for understanding. The people of the woods like me. I sell them things they like."

"What things?"

"From the ship. Cloth. Rope. Other things. We got a lot off before the hull broke up."

"What did you sell it for," Francois said. "Gold? Silver?"

"Food," Jago said. "They don't have any gold."

I remembered the iron arrowhead I had removed from François' shoulder. Had Jago traded it?

"You sold them ship's nails," I said. "They made them into arrowheads."

"We had to eat."

"Our village was attacked," I said. "Our savages were killed by men you armed."

"Why should we care about that? They enslaved you."

"I was shot by them," François said, turning to show his shoulder.

"I am sorry for that," Jago said, though he did not look at François' wound. "How could I have known these savages were so warlike?"

"Is that why you moved away from them?" I said.

"We moved on because we sold most of our things. But there was trouble among them. And sickness. It was not good to stay. Now we want to go home."

There was a little silence while we thought about what had been said, and where it left us, then Jago spoke again. "You had a map, didn't you? I saw it on the ship."

"It has guided us well," said Rosenkreutz, who had revived after a little food and water.

"Really?" Jago smiled. "It led you to us, but by the state of you, it led you the long way round."

"Where are we?" I asked.

"Not far from where we landed," Jago said. "Just far enough to be safe. If you still have the map, perhaps it will show us."

Rosenkreutz willingly unfolded the mappamundi, not thinking how valuable it might be to others. Jago bent over it, turning his head this way and that.

251

"On the ship," he said, "I saw you roll the map, putting the two ends together. You said the world was round."

"Since Eratosthenes, all wise men have known it."

"When we landed," he said, "you told us we were in Paradise, or Atlantis."

"Paradise lies here." Rosenkreutz pointed at well-wooded Tartary. "But we did not reach it."

Jago ran his finger over the eastern edge of the world. "Here are islands," he said. "And rivers."

"Rivers out of Paradise," Rosenkreutz said. "If we follow them we will get there."

"What I had in mind," Jago said, "was getting back across the Ocean."

The Irishmen nodded and smiled at that. So did François.

"Do you know where we are?" I asked.

Jago pointed at the painted coast. "My guess is here. The men of the woods say that forests run all the way to the north and west, just as the map shows. The coast turns east as it goes north. That, too, is what the men of the woods say. It goes as far as here, where the mapmaker has shown a rocky headland."

"That is Cape Cattigara," Rosenkreutz said. "Ptolemy named it long ago as Asia's furthest point."

"If you are right about the shape of the world, then it is the nearest point to Christendom. Cape Cattigara is where we must go."

"We cannot think of going back," Rosenkreutz said. "We have seen nothing of this land. We have not found the Seven Cities or the wealth and wisdom they contain, to say nothing of the actual land of Paradise. Would you return home with nothing?"

"I want to go home." I said. "I've had enough of wandering."

"You don't have a home," Rosenkreutz said. "And neither does François. I cannot speak for these others. But you two are still the vagabonds you always were, and will be nothing else until we discover a source of either wealth or wisdom."

"Perhaps we'll discover it on the way," François said.

"Who's to say those cities don't lie to the north, along the coast we will follow."

"We must not go that way!" Rosenkreutz reached into the bag and took out the Tome. "It is in here," he said, raising the book so that he looked like Moses with one of his tablets. His face was fiery with conviction, like a preaching prophet. "The Tome shows the flower of the sun. Its meaning is clear. We must follow the sun."

"We have already followed it," I said. "It led us here."

"If we follow it further it will take us home."

"Not me," François said. "If you mean to go west, I'll not take a step in that direction."

"Me neither," I said.

"Then you are fools!" Rosenkreutz scrabbled at the Tome's pages until he found the picture. We had all seen it before.

"Not the dandelion!" François said. "You'll see those anywhere."

"And marigolds," I said. "They are common too."

"Look! Look at the *planta solis*. It is just like the sun. So big and golden. It is the very emblem of gold. If we follow it, surely, gold is what we will find!"

"You've changed your tune," François said. "Before, you told us that gold was nothing and wisdom was everything."

"We will find both."

"Among these savages and forests?"

"We have not found much in the forest. I admit it. But now, thanks to Jago, we know where we are." He waved a hand over the mappamundi, as though an alchemical transformation could make the painted nations real. "West of here is Cathay with all its cities and wealth. Beyond Cathay is Tartary, with its trading posts and caravans. And look! West of Tartary is India, and Persia, and Turkey, all of them rich places. Tell them Thomas, you have been there."

"I'm not going back to the Turks," I said. "They enslaved me."

"Of course!" Rosenkreutz said, trying to look kind and reasonable. "I had forgotten. But there is no need to go by Turkey. We'll take the northern route. We'll go by Muscovy, and be in Christendom before you know it. You can't object to that, Thomas. Remember what the traveller Mandeville described? The one who went from country to country, getting further and further from home until he reached a place where they spoke his own language. We'll be like him!"

"No we won't," François said. "We'll be like men who are wise enough to know they've gone too far. We'll follow the coast and head for home."

"I agree," Jago said. "The men of the woods tell of no cities. There is nothing to the west but rivers and mountains, and lakes and trees, then more rivers and mountains. We will follow the coast."

Healing

We marched through the forest at Jago's pace. He was the leader, not me. He had flourished while we were enslaved. He knew how to build a shelter, where food was, and how to get it. With him, we ate well, slept dry, and set off fresh each morning. We did not get lost so often, and when we did it was not so bad. Where the forest was thick we had steel blades to clear our way. When we met savages he spoke to them, and they were friendly and helpful. How could I challenge him?

I tried to keep the Brotherhood together, so that we were still ourselves, not just Jago's crew. Rosenkreutz walked weakly, so I cut him a new staff, shaping it as much like the old one as possible. I offered to carry the papal bag, to relieve him of its burden. He was reluctant at first, but I insisted, and was glad to take charge of the things I had gathered on my travels.

We made good speed, but the year overtook us. The great heat of summer faded. The leaves turned red and gold. Monstrous toadstools sprouted from boles and leafdrifts. In the mornings, our woodland shelters were wrapped in mist. We had not prepared for winter. Perhaps, thinking ourselves close to Paradise, we imagined it would never come. But the cold nights, shortening days, and fresh wind on our faces, all told us that north was not a good way to be going. Yet it was the direction we had agreed on, except for Rosenkreutz, who still muttered about heading west for Muscovy. Had we made a mistake?

I took out the mappamundi and looked at it, remembering how I got it, hoping it would lead us in the right direction. François had no faith in the map's power, but it gave him an idea.

"If we ever get back to Christendom," he said, "you know what we ought to do? We should find a king who lacks land. A prince might be better. We should tell him about this place."

"This land of shit, as you called it?" I could see the way his mind was working. "This wilderness full of swamps and savages?"

"I'd make it sound better than that."

"A land flowing with milk and honey? An earthly Paradise?"

"You've got the idea. We'll sell the place to some prince or other, get him to send a fleet and an army to conquer the place."

"And then?"

"He'll reward us," François said. "With gold, pensions, and titles. We could be lords of Wineland."

"Or, if your prince is pious, the Land of the Rosy Cross."

"I prefer Wineland. It has a cheerful sound to it."

We reached a place where the forest thinned, and open land was visible beyond a thin screen of half-dead vines and leafless saplings. Jago said it would be a good place to find food. He set Rosenkreutz to gather firewood, then led his Irishmen into a thicket, where they made a lot of noise trying to flush out game. François and I foraged like savages, throwing sticks to bring down fruit, poking at the forest floor for nuts and mushrooms. After a while, Jago proudly flung down a brace of fine-looking birds, then looked at what we had found.

"If you eat those," he said, kicking contemptuously at our haul of mushrooms, "you'll be dead of a bloody flux before the night is out."

"Nonsense!" François said. "I have seen champignons like these served at the finest tables in France."

"You must have been peeping through the window," Jago said. He had listened carefully to our talk, and picked out the clues that told him what sort of man François was. "If they'd let you any closer," he said, "you'd have got a better look. Whatever the nobles of France eat, those ones are deadly."

François gazed down at the mushrooms, now scattered among the leaves. For a moment he looked ready to let fly with one of his ripe coquillard insults. But Jago had already turned away, and was demanding to know where Rosenkreutz had got to with the firewood.

When Rosenkreutz appeared, he was carrying nothing but his staff. "A city!" he said, waving towards the edge of the forest. "We have found the first of them. The Seven Cities of Antillia!"

Then he turned and loped away, his long legs raising flurries of dead leaves, his staff held high like a spear.

"Gold!" François said. "Silver! Untold wealth!"

"We must be careful," I said. "Whoever lives there might try to enslave us." No one listened. They all rushed after Rosenkreutz, and I had no choice but to follow them.

François, Jago, and the Irishmen had burst through the forest edge, and were scrambling down the slope. Ahead of them was a wide valley, with wooded hills beyond it. Rosenkreutz had reached the bottom, and was striding through long grass, heading towards the city. It was a city without walls, or towers, or fine buildings of any sort. There was no smoke. I set off after the others, wading through chest-high grass, clambering over the remains of a tumbled palisade, until I was among the houses.

Francois was nearby, gazing despondently around him. "This is no city," he said. "We'll find no gold among these hovels."

The houses were set in lines and circles, with spaces in between that were once gardens, neglected and overgrown. They were hump-backed, like upturned ships. Each was well made from logs and poles, covered with shingles and sheets of bark, all held down by laths and withies. Some were of a size that one or two men might live in, or a family. Others were big enough to hold a banquet. Whoever made those houses could have built a good Christian town if they had been shown how. But they had gone. We looked into some of the houses, and saw beds and benches, and racks and baskets where household goods were stored, all empty.

I looked at the abandoned houses and thought of the place we had left behind, and Soolia, who was probably dead, or slaving for the beast-men whose attack helped us flee.

Rosenkreutz appeared, smiling. "These houses look remarkably like barrels," he said. "Could this be a city of cynics, like old Diogenes?"

"Diogenes said that men should live like dogs," François said. "The savages live like dogs, so it may be that you are right. It makes no difference. The wretches have slunk off, leaving their kennels empty."

"I would like to question them. It would be most interesting to learn their philosophy. If we could trace their ideas back to Atlantis, much would be revealed about the Great River of Knowledge, and how it has diverged."

"I've had enough of rivers," François said. "And you'll find no philosophers here. This so-called city is no use to us."

"It could shelter us for the winter," I said.

"Let us consult the mappamundi, Thomas." Rosenkreutz held out his hand. "It will tell us which of the cities we have reached."

I did as I was asked, and we spread the map out. Rosenkreutz knelt over it, pointing at the cities of Cathay, which were far from the great forests of Tartary, where we most likely were. François wandered off, reciting some verses about Diogenes and his barrel, and what he said to Alexander. But he was soon back.

"The others have found something," he said, stopping Rosenkreutz's ramblings. We followed him to a big house set apart from the others. Jago and the Irishmen stood outside.

"I think there are people in there," Jago said.

"Have you looked?"

"Not me," Jago said. "It stinks."

Rosenkreutz pushed past him, opening the mat that served as a door, striding into the house. We gathered in the doorway and looked in. The house was dark. It certainly stank, but no worse than many other places I have known. Jago, having been a sailor, must have known worse too. But it was an odd smell, with something sickly and not quite human about it.

Rosenkreutz pulled a mat from the wall and let some light into the house. Savages were lying in a heap, half covered by skin cloaks, sunk into a deep layer of bracken.

"They are dead," Jago said. "Now we know why the others left."

"They are not dead," Rosenkreutz said, setting down his staff. "There is life in them, though not much."

"It's plague!" Jago said. "We can't stay here."

"We can overcome all sickness," Rosenkreutz said. "Now that we have found the power."

"What power?" Jago said.

François screwed his finger into his temple. "Ignore him," he said to Jago. "Rosenkreutz often talks that way. It signifies nothing."

"If he touches those bodies," Jago said, "then he can stay here with them. I'll not have him with us."

"He's always been a burden," François said. "Let's leave him with these sickly savages and find a better place to rest."

François had often suggested leaving Rosenkreutz behind, even killing him. I could not do that, any more than I could abandon François. The old hag I bedded in England said that François and I were bound together like man and wife. If so, by fawning on Jago he was being unfaithful. I had spared François' life in Paris, and that made me responsible for him, even though he showed little gratitude. What bound me to Rosenkreutz I cannot say, but I felt the bond, and could not break it.

Rosenkreutz knelt by one of the bodies.

"Don't touch them!" Jago shouted.

Rosenkreutz laid a hand on the savage.

Jago lifted his axe.

"Leave him," I said, reaching out to hold his arm back.

He shook off my hand. "I'll burn them all." He turned to the Irishmen. "Gather fuel," he said. "Pile it round the house."

"No," I said.

"Go in there with him if you like. Share his death."

Jago was so angry at the sight of those dying men, and at Rosenkreutz's willingness to help them, that I wondered what provoked him. What trouble had he been in that made him fear illness so much?

I stayed where I was, and so did the others. We were all watching Rosenkreutz. He held the Tome in one hand, laying the other on the savage's brow. Then he began to read, speaking words in the Philosophical Tongue, filling the house with the boom and echo of his voice. I couldn't tell you what those words meant, but they were full of power.

Jago let his axe fall. François and the Irishmen lowered their heads, as though at prayer. The savage began to stir, writhing beneath Rosenkreutz's hand, shaking his head, murmuring. Rosenkreutz stopped reading and gazed down at him. The savage opened his eyes and looked up at Rosenkreutz. He said a few words in his savage tongue. Rosenkreutz smiled at him. Light fell on him from the gap in the wall. Rosenkreutz looked like Our Lord raising Lazarus from the dead.

"It is no plague," he said, looking out at us. "I have seen this in the East. Simple people believe whatever they are told. If their sorcerers put a curse on them, they believe themselves to be cursed. They decline into illness, and eventually die."

The pious look that had filled François's face was replaced by his usual knowing expression. "So they are not really ill?" he said.

"Not in their bodies. In these cases it is the spirit that is sick."

After waking the first savage, Rosenkreutz turned to the others. He read to each of them, touched them on the brow or breast, watched them stirring into wakefulness. One by one they sat up, opened their eyes and spoke a few words. By the time he had finished, the first savage had struggled to his feet and was trying to walk.

"They are tired," Rosenkreutz said, as he emerged from the house. "And so am I. Each healing takes something from me."

"Just like the gold coin trick," François said.

"It is no trick. If it was, I could do it easily. But transforming base metal into gold, like transforming sickness into health, depletes my spirit. Men gripped by illness do not wish to become well, any more than lead wishes to become gold. The effort of curing them is like rolling a heavy stone uphill."

"You said they were not really sick."

"Not in their bodies. Their spirits were sick. You cannot

260

see the spirit. Nor can you weigh it in a balance. But the spirit is harder to move than any boulder." Rosenkreutz turned to Jago. "I must eat," he said. "Will you find me some food?"

Jago was still wary. He held back, and would not approach. I took Rosenkreutz's arm, led him away and found a bed for him in one of the empty houses. Afterwards I sat outside it, watching in case Jago tried to carry out his threat. But Jago was distracted by the savages, who came out of their house stumbling like drunkards, babbling with joy at having been saved. It was they who found us food, leading François and the Irishmen to a storehouse where there was dried meat and corn.

We ate well that night, and the next. In the days that followed, more savages came out of the forest to see their fellows, who they had given up for dead. Young men, pot-bellied elders, withered crones, women and children, all came to the house where Rosenkreutz rested and brought him gifts. The town came back to life, and savages set about gathering food and firewood, and putting the empty houses in order. They presented the biggest house to Rosenkreutz, who always said he did not mind where he lived, but moved into it on our urging, as it confirmed the honour they held him in. They offered everything to Rosenkreutz first. We were his friends, so we shared his tribute, and gave what we could not use to the savages, who were grateful for it and served us eagerly.

Jago was jealous. "The savages worship Rosenkreutz like a god," he said.

"Do they have any concept of God?" François said. "Can their savage minds comprehend such a noble idea? Or are they like the old pagans of Greece, who saw gods in trees and rivers?"

"I don't know about that," Jago said. "But the savages are calling him a 'man of power.' That kind of thing can turn a man's head."

"His head was turned long ago," François said. "And now he's stark mad. He bathed in a muddy pool and said he was immortal. He told us to call him Pilgrim, or by some Saracen name."

"What name was that?" Jago said.

"Al–something. What does it matter?"

"If it wasn't for Rosenkreutz," I said, "we might well be slaves again, not honoured guests."

"If he really has this power," François said, "why didn't he use it before? He might have saved us from being slaves in the first place. He might have saved the village from attack. We might have lived there as honoured guests. Imagine yourself, living in savage luxury, served and sated by Soolia. Why did Rosenkreutz deny you that?"

"He did not fully have the power until he bathed in the Fountain of Youth."

"We both bathed in it too," François said. "We had to, to pull him out. So why don't we have this power?"

"Perhaps we have it, but do not know it."

"Are you going mad, too, Thomas? Will you be calling yourself by some Saracen name and making the savages worship you?"

"You should know me better than that," I said. "We have wandered together for more than a year."

"Is it really that long?"

"It was the end of summer when we met in Paris. We endured a winter in England and a summer here. Now it is almost winter again."

"Then we have known Rosenkreutz for a year, without really knowing him at all."

"I thought him a trickster when I first met him in Rome," I said. "Since then he has done things I would not have thought possible."

"Turning lead into gold?"

"And turning the winds."

"If he did it. He might just have been lucky."

"We are lucky, not him. He told us so, and chose us for that reason."

"Why would he need luck, if he had power?"

"You can't deny that he healed the savages. We had nothing

to do with that. He can do things that no man can do. He knows more than anyone. He has lived longer than other men."

"If we believe his stories."

"When I lived in the Morea," I said, "the Greeks used to talk about their old gods. Some of them were, as you said, gods of trees and rivers. Others ruled the world, before the Saviour came and deposed them. Between those two were others, who wandered the world and had adventures. They were like men, yet more than human."

"Demigods, or heroes," François said. "Men who became gods through their deeds, like Hercules and Achilles."

"The Greeks still believe in their old gods," I said, "even though they are Christians. They say the best of them became saints, and the worst of them became demons."

"So which is Rosenkreutz?"

"I don't know. Perhaps he is a bit of both."

"In that case," François said, "he is exactly like the rest of us, a mere man."

Graven images

Winter is my season, or so Rosenkreutz said. And that winter was the nearest I ever got to living like a lord. When cold winds brought the first snows, the savages put on breeches and shirts of deerskin, fringed and painted cloaks, with greaves and shoes of soft leather. When they saw that we possessed nothing more than the rags we stood in, they clothed us too, giving us garments of the type they wore, and fur cloaks to keep us warm. We cast off our ragged clothes gladly, and from then on dressed like savages, almost forgetting we were Christians.

The real snows came later, and cold gripped the land for weeks on end. Without the savages we would have died. And without Rosenkreutz we would have had no savages to help us. When he read from the Tome they listened with awe, whether they understood him or not. They treated the rest of us with respect, whether we deserved it or not. We roamed the country as we pleased, treated the town as our own, grew fat on the food the savages gave us.

We hunted with the savages, though their skills made us look like bungling scavengers. We could track deer by their hoof prints, but the savages could follow a scent like St Hubert's hounds. We could see dung lying on the ground, but the savages could tell how old it was, whether it was from a buck or doe, and what the beast had eaten. From that they knew where deer were feeding, and where they would go to shelter. Most of all, they understood that rutting stags lose all caution, and may easily be caught, just as men who are driven mad by love or lust are easily gulled. Remembering my own follies, I felt almost sorry for the beasts we shot. And I kept clear of the savage women, though some of them were young and comely. I had had too many drubbings on account of women to risk another one.

When we killed a deer it was cut up on the spot with stone blades. The liver was torn out whole, cooked quickly on a stick fire, and offered to us half-raw. The savages believed that we would gain the strength and cunning of a stag. Perhaps they were right. Jago and I soon learned to shoot well with the savages' short bows. The Irish crewmen took to stalking as though they had done it all their lives, and were soon as stealthy as any savage. François was the exception. He complained all the time and scared off the prey. He was useless, even as a beater. Despite his faults, I insisted François always hunted with us. Otherwise he would have sat by the fire on his own, wrapped in furs, brooding. He grumbled, of course.

"What is the point of skulking after game like starved dogs?" he said. "Hawking is the thing for gentlemen, but do these savages know of it?"

I endured his moaning, knowing it was a sign that there was life and liveliness still in him. But, as it turned out, taking him hunting was a mistake. The trouble was caused by the savages' custom of offering a choice portion of the kill to a carved figure that hung from a post outside our house. They did it after every hunt, and I thought nothing of it, though I could imagine what Hugh the shipman would have said if he'd been there to see it. You'd think a sailor would understand that people do things differently abroad. But Hugh was such a narrow churchman that everything the savages did was heresy to him. And François too, was pious in his way, and despised the savages. One night, after a long hard hunt in the bitter midwinter cold, François' piety got the better of him.

"Do you realise what we have done?" he said, when we had eaten and retired to bed. "We have worshipped a graven image."

"The wooden figure? I didn't worship it. I bowed to it, to please the savages."

"We gave thanks to it for our supper," he said. "We should have thanked God." He sat up, throwing aside his fur blanket. I heard the savages stirring too, and muttering among themselves.

"I am a sinner," François said. "I have never denied it. But I never thought I would sink this low."

I knew his mood. Unless talked out of it he would disturb us all with a night of melancholy fitfulness. "It was only a savage idol," I said. "It means no more than a child's doll."

He sighed, and wrapped his cloak around his thin body. "Have you worshipped any other gods but God?"

"The Turks tried to get me to worship theirs," I said. "But some say their God is the same as ours."

"Have you taken His name in vain?"

"Often."

"Have you forgotten the Sabbath?"

"What day is it today?"

"I've no idea."

"Then we've both forgotten it," I said.

"We have forgotten God and our duty to him." François said. "I thought perhaps that I had become a better man, but I see now that if I have sinned less in this land it is because I am less able to sin. I am just as bad as I always was, perhaps worse." François groaned. "May God save my soul," he said. "I believe I may have broken every one of the Commandments."

"Not all of them, surely?"

"In your youth," he asked, "did you honour your father?"

"I obeyed him," I said. "When I had to. But I am not sure he really was my father. Anyway, he sent me away when I was still a boy, and I never saw him again."

"Mine died when I was young," François said. "I didn't have much chance to honour him. What about your mother?"

"The last time I saw her she cursed me and lied to me. Her lies led to . . ."

"I know you've killed," he said, "and made the usual soldier's excuses. But have you ever committed murder?"

"That was what my mother's lies led to. Among other sins."

"Have you ever committed adultery?"

"You know the answer to that. You spied on me while I did it."

"She was a savage, so it doesn't count."

I was thinking of the eelwife, but if François had forgotten

266

her, then so much the better. "I've never married," I said, "nor have I been chaste."

"But adultery . . ."

"I've had other men's wives."

"Have you stolen?" François sounded as grave as a confessing friar.

"How can *you* ask me that?"

"I ask merely to establish the fact."

"Yes, I have stolen."

"Have you borne false witness?"

For a moment I thought I might not be guilty of that, but then I remembered what the words meant, and the lies I had told, and silences that took the place of lies, and men who had suffered as a result. "Yes," I said.

"That leaves coveting your neighbour's house, or his oxen, or all those other things."

"I've never had a neighbour. Not since I was a child, and even then no one lived close to us. But as for coveting, yes, I've done a lot of that. I've wanted a home ever since I left Italy. You know that. It was what we were looking for in England, a place where we could live in comfort with all our needs met. If that's coveting, I'm guilty."

"Well, that's it then," François said. "We've both broken all the commandments. And now we've worshipped a graven image, we're as sinful as sinners can be. Eternal damnation is all we can expect."

"If God watches over us here."

"Do you think He does not?"

"It is what the ship's carpenter said, when he led the crew to mutiny."

"We're on the rough side of the Ocean, is what he said. But look what happened to him!"

"When we were in England Rosenkreutz said he would take us to another part of the world."

"He thought he was sailing to Paradise. And the sailors thought that would wipe out their sins. But we didn't get to Paradise, so we are still weighed down by our sins, to which we have added another."

"I am not so sure. The carpenter was right about one thing: we are out of Christendom now. So God may not be watching us."

"No," François said. "If God watches over the world, He must surely watch over the whole of it."

"If He did, surely the savages would know something of His laws, and would believe and act as we do."

"The world is full of heretics and unbelievers. God inspires good Christians to fight wars against them. The savages tempted me. Why did I not resist?"

The answer was obvious. François never resisted temptation.

"The French are great crusaders," he said. "Marshal Boucicaut was one of them, the bravest Frenchman of all. He fought the Moors, the Livonians, and the Turks."

"So did I!" Why did François always forget my part in defending Christendom? "I fought to defend Constantinople."

"You lost your battle, I seem to recall."

"So did Boucicaut. In the Morea, they tell stories about how he was captured and ransomed by the Turks. He lost at Agincourt, too. My father helped capture him."

"Your father preyed on France too! I might have guessed it."

He turned away from me, and we sat in silence for a while. The savages watched us, their faces lit by the faint flicker of a deer-fat lamp. No doubt they wondered what our hot words meant. It was not good to be seen arguing by them. We were the companions of Rosenkreutz, the man of power and wisdom. And it was stupid to argue about things that happened long ago and far away, in places we might never see again.

François spoke again, quietly. "The Greeks lost Constantinople because they are heretics."

"But the Turks are worse than heretics," I said "So God can't care too much what we think about Him. In fact, if the Turks flourish, and these savages go unpunished, I wonder whether God cares about us at all. Perhaps He made the world, causing men and beasts to be different in all its various places, then forgot about it."

François laughed, and I thought for a moment I had cheered him up.

"Like a capricious prince," he said, "who builds himself a great palace, lays out gardens, has lakes and rivers dug, stocks the grounds with game and fish and rare plants, then gets bored and never visits the place."

"You put it more poetically than me."

"If you are right," he said, "then it is not just this land of swamps and forests and savages that God has forgotten. He has forgotten all of Creation, including Christendom. We are alone, with no hope of Salvation."

He sank sadly back in his heap of fur blankets. My attempt to reassure him had failed. Despite that, it was François who soon got off to a deep, snoring sleep, and me who lay awake for most of the night thinking about what we had said.

You can't not believe in God. God is too mixed up in the world, and no one, not even Rosenkreutz, can explain anything of importance without mentioning Him. Even if you could pick God out of the world and discard Him, you couldn't admit it. Anyone who said he did not believe in God would be burned as a heretic. But you can say, like Rosenkreutz, that God is the same in all religions. If so, the details don't matter. Drinking wine is a sin for Moslems and a sacrament for us. Why should God care what meats we eat, when He created all the birds and beasts? The idle thought that struck me when trying to console François bore down on me more heavily: God created us, but has since lost interest in us.

François and I had both sinned. I had done it out of necessity, but he had wallowed in sin like a pig in shit. He sinned to make God take notice of him. If God would not pay François attention, who would? François probably thought there was a special place in Hell, kept ready for him alone. Only, when he got there, it wouldn't be good enough. The fires would be too cool, the brimstone not sulphurous enough, the pitchforks too blunt, the toadwives too beautiful, and, worst of all, the demons who tormented him would not appreciate the subtleties of his sins.

The witch

Just as the snows began to melt, three savages came to the town. People had drifted in from time to time, sometimes staying, sometimes moving on. But these three were different. Their leader was a woman, tall and slim, with a fine face, despite the lines and dots painted on it. Her voice was little more than a whisper, but the savages listened carefully. Her men deferred to her, which was a thing we had not seen before. The people of our town also treated her with respect, though there was a touch of fear in the way they hung back from her

Where she had been when the snows lay thickly, or how she had lived, we did not know. She and her followers were given one of the empty houses, and everything they needed to live in it. But the savages did not attend to her, as they did to us. Instead, they left food outside the house, and her followers took it inside, where they ate it privately. For a few days we saw nothing of her, and the savages gave us to understand that she slept all day and walked abroad at night. According to Jago, who was still trying to make himself the big man of the town, she did the opposite to the savages in all things, though what that meant we could not tell, as there was much we did not understand about the savages and their ways.

Then Jago told us that the savages were falling sick again. Several of them lay in one of the houses, where they waited to die, shunned by the other savages.

"Now we know why they feared her," he said. "She is a witch, and has cursed them."

"It may be," Rosenkreutz said, "that she brought a sickness from wherever it was she came from. What are the symptoms?"

Jago did not understand.

"Is it a fever?" Rosenkreutz said. "Are they marked by pustules or buboes? Has their skin changed colour?"

"Do you think I would go near them?" Jago looked horrified, and I remembered how he had threatened to burn the sick savages, and us with them. "They are lying in a house where the other savages left them."

"What if all the savages fall sick?" François said. "What if they die? Who will serve us then? Where will our food come from?"

Jago showed us the house, but would not go near it. We went to the doorway and saw immediately that we were too late. Inside, the sick savages lay heaped together in one bed, as was their way. The woman was crouched over the sweating body of one of the best huntsmen. She had thrown off her great cloak and was wearing a shift or tunic of soft leather, fringed and sewn with beads, such as the savage women wore in winter. Unlike any other such garment I had seen, it was boldly painted with moons and stars, and beasts with gaping mouths.

Her face, arms and legs were smeared with ash, so that she looked like a corpse. Round her neck, bunched together on strings, hung a collection of bones. There were ribs, finger bones, wolves' teeth, bits of deer horn, the skulls of black-billed crows, and of yellow-toothed rats. There were other bones, too, of creatures I did not know, as though she had combed a charnel house of beasts to adorn herself.

"She is a bringer of death," François whispered. "Jago was right."

She looked up at us, her grey face expressionless but threatening.

"Her face looks like a skull," François said. "What horrors has she seen?" He turned to Rosenkreutz. "Will you let the witch do her worst? She will kill that savage."

"Do not be deceived by symbols," Rosenkreutz said. "A skull has many meanings."

"True," François said. "But all of them remind us of death."

The witch turned back to the huntsman, leaned over him and began to murmur into his ear. He shook his head, feebly rolling it from one side to the other. She placed a hand on his chest and pushed it down. He was a strong man, or had been.

When I hunted with him he ran through the frozen forest for hours, never tiring before the prey did. But under the hand of that witch he was like a child's rag doll. His chest jerked upwards, then sank down. His legs twitched feebly. His arms flopped. The witch climbed on top of him, straddling him like a succubus. She pressed down hard on his chest with both hands. He groaned but did not resist. She gripped her right wrist with her left hand, made a fist and plunged it into his flesh. It seemed she would push right through him and reach the earth.

"I told you," François said. "She is killing him."

When she pulled her hand back it was covered in blood. She held it up, looking at us, displaying something she gripped in her fingers. It looked like a bone, but I could not be sure. She threw it onto the huntsman's chest, then stood up. The huntsman sat up a little, looked at the bloody bone, and muttered to himself. The witch stared at us, her skull-face full of triumph. One of her men came out of the house, raised his hands to his mouth and howled like a wolf.

Rosenkreutz backed away from the howling savage, and we followed him. "You were quite wrong, François," he said. "As I knew all along. She has not killed him, but effected a most interesting cure."

The savages were gathering, coming to the house to see the cured huntsman. They did not defer to Rosenkreutz as they pushed past us to look into the house. Inside, they helped the huntsman out into the light and eagerly inspected the bloodstained bone the witch had drawn from inside him.

François watched them with disgust. "Don't you see what this means?"

"Of course," Rosenkreutz said. "It confirms everything I have been telling you. It proves that we are indeed not far from Cathay."

"How?"

"Her method of healing is one that is practised in the East. Healers there secrete some object about their person, a bone, a pebble, a bloody cloth, then produce it with a flourish and announce that the cause of the sickness has been removed."

"If you knew that method," François said, "why did you not practise it?"

"I have the words of the Tome, and have bathed in the Fountain. I have the healing power within me."

"These savages don't know what a book is," François said. "They are like children. They cannot understand an idea unless it is embodied in an object. The witch knows that. Why can't you do what she does? She has shown them sickness in a handful of bone!"

Rosenkreutz gave François a puzzled look. "Why should I resort to trickery? I am not a charlatan."

François laughed. "You told us the savages were not really sick. So what you did was trickery too."

"I would not stoop so low."

"Your scruples may cost us everything," François said "You must go back in there and defeat the witch. If she supplants you, then we will be thrown out into the forest again."

"Defeat her? Would you have me dispute with a woman?"

"You must do more than that. You must drive her out."

"He's right," I said. "You can't let her take your place."

"Perhaps there is something in what you say," Rosenkreutz said. "It would be wrong to leave these people in ignorance."

"I don't care about the savages," François said. "They can be as ignorant as they like, and as stupid, as long as they respect you and feed us."

"Show her up," I said. "Reveal her fakery."

I think that was the only time on our voyage when François or I persuaded Rosenkreutz to do anything. There were times when he was too weak to argue, and when he had no choice but to follow us, but on that occasion François set him a challenge he could not refuse. As always, he reached into the bag to make sure that the Tome was still there, then he gripped his staff and strode into the house. The savages parted to let him through, but jostled us when we followed him. Inside, Rosenkreutz made for one of the sick savages, but the witch's helpers stopped him. He turned to us, silently imploring us to help him. But François and I could do nothing. The other savages had followed us into the house, and the press of their bodies prevented us from acting.

The witch had a staff of her own, a stick bound with cords and hung with feathers and little discs of copper. Slowly, she raised the stick and pointed it at Rosenkreutz, shaking it to make the discs rattle. The savages had a great reverence for metal, and when they heard the sound they fell back as though enchanted. Silently, they ranged themselves around the edge of the house, squatting on the floor, their backs to the bark walls. Having no choice, François and I followed them, leaving Rosenkreutz and the witch facing each other over a bedful of sick savages.

They stood before each other, as still as two carved figures on a cathedral porch. Rosenkreutz looked the saint, whatever his true nature. The witch looked like the sort of carving that spouts water when rain overruns the roof. While she stayed motionless, her helpers drew a leather curtain across the doorway, plunging the house into darkness. They flung wood into the firepit, our faces were lit by the blaze, and I saw that Jago and the crewmen had sneaked in after us. I knew that I could not rely on them, that they would not take our side if it came to a conflict. I knew also that I could never rely on François, that Rosenkreutz was not himself, and that our survival might depend on him.

The witch shook her stick at the heap of sick savages, speaking strange words in a hoarse croak. When one of the savages stirred, she leaned over him and stared at his face. His coppery skin was damp with sweat. He twitched when she touched him, but that was not enough for her. She tweaked his nose, poked fingers into his mouth, pinched his slack flesh. When she was satisfied that there was still some life in him she called her helpers, who hauled him out of the heap. They laid him on bare ground by the firepit, setting his limbs and body straight, while the witch chanted.

Rosenkreutz looked on, but did not know what to do. I

nudged François. "Come on," I said, getting to my feet. "She's got helpers. Let's help Rosenkreutz."

As I feared, François did not move. The savages watched us like drunkards waiting for an alehouse brawl.

"Do you want him to fail?" I said. "You know what will follow. The savages will throw us out into the snow. We will starve, freeze, and be eaten by wild beasts."

I knew that François had a horror of being eaten, even when dead. More than once he had described to me the kites and crows that peck at hanged men, and his fear of the gibbet. Slowly, he got up and followed me to Rosenkreutz. The three of us, a Brotherhood, as we had once named ourselves, stood together.

"What do we do now?" François said.

"We pick someone to heal." I pointed to a woman whose eyes were open. "She will do."

We pulled her from the heap and laid her out on the ground, just as the witch's helpers had done.

"Now what?" François said.

"They like the witch's mumblings," I said. "So give them what they want. You can do better than her. Chant a psalm, recite a poem. Anything, French or Latin, they won't know the difference."

He took a deep breath and began, declaiming something in his thieves' jargon. I didn't pay much attention to the words. Rosenkreutz was still hesitating, so I led him to the woman and made him kneel beside her. I slid the Tome from his bag, and opened it for him at one of the pages showing women bathing in green liquor. I still had no idea what the pages signified, but they looked as though they might have something to do with healing. Not that it mattered. Rosenkreutz had almost admitted that his cures were done by trickery, so it was all a matter of putting on a show. Anyway, it was too dark to read the words, even if Rosenkreutz did understand them.

He got the idea, and took the Tome in his hand, resting the other on the woman's brow. He began to speak, softly at first, then more boldly. François, too, had got louder, and was accompanying his recitation with gestures, which must have baffled the savages as much as they would have entertained a den of Paris coquillards. The savages looked from him to Rosenkreutz, and from Rosenkreutz to the witch, and back again. When François got to the end of a verse, I gestured to him to stop. His buffoonery had served its purpose. It had to be Rosenkreutz who won the savages over, not François.

Rosenkreutz hunched over the sick woman, his beard hanging so low that it tickled her breast. She squirmed at its touch, shuddering as though pleasured. Her eyes closed, then blinked open again. She raised a hand, trying feebly to push Rosenkreutz away. On the other side of the firepit the witch was holding up a bloodstained feather, and her helpers were dragging the patient to his feet. She called out, her voice rising above a whisper for the first time. The sound almost curdled my blood, as there was something deep and unwomanly about it, as though a spirit spoke through her. There were gasps from the other savages, who pressed forward to touch the healed man, running their hands over his chest, where the feather was supposed to have come from. While they led the man outside, I nodded to François.

"She is cured!" I said, kneeling and taking our patient's arm.

"Cured indeed!" François declaimed, looking round at the remaining savages. "No bones. No feathers. No blood. Just the healing power of the Tome, mediated through the Great Rosenkreutz, the wisest man the world has ever known."

Of course, the savages did not understand a word, but François, though small and ill-made, had a way of winning attention with his words, whether a rant or a recitation. He would have made a good fairground huckster or a wandering player. With his help I pulled the woman to her feet, and we gave her to the savages. She staggered as they took her outside, and I hoped she stayed cured for long enough.

François was already looking for the next patient, a man this time. We dragged him from the heap and laid him before Rosenkreutz, who bent over him and began the cure. The witch also had a new patient, and the savages were settling down to watch the next bout.

We worked hard, Rosenkreutz reading from the Tome and laying hands on sweating brows and breasts. As soon as we saw signs of revival, I dragged the patient away, and François announced a new miracle. But Rosenkreutz was slower than the witch. While he laboured to perform a few more cures, she rushed on, leaping from one sick savage to another, dancing, gesticulating, calling out in her unearthly voice, pummelling sweating bodies until they submitted to be cured, holding up bloodstained horrors as evidence of her craft. The other savages changed from an audience to a gang of helpers, confirming each cure and leading each patient away.

Jago and the crewmen might have helped us, but they did not. They sat and waited to see how things turned out. And when they saw that the sickbed was empty, and that the witch had done most of the cures, they went outside with the savages to join in the merriment. We could hear them, singing and dancing, shaking drums and rattles. Before long there would be a feast, but would we share it?

Only six of us were left. Once again, Rosenkreutz and the witch faced each other across the firepit. The savages had kept the fire well fed, and a huge heap of embers warmed the house. The witch's helpers picked up ashes from the edge of the pit and rubbed them onto their faces, leering and grimacing to make themselves look uglier. They danced a little, shuffling this way and that, raising their arms to their mistress, acknowledging her triumph. Then they brought a bundle of dried herbs and broke it up, scattering leafy fragments into the firepit. Dust from the herbs sparked and smouldered. Smoke rose up in tendrils, swirling around us, settling in a layer like river mist.

I thought the savages were trying to get us out of the house. I had done it myself when young, burning pitch and brimstone to drive some Frenchmen from their own castle. I was ready to run, to yield the house to the savages, but

Rosenkreutz stood his ground, and I could not abandon him. François showed no sign of fleeing. He had dropped to the floor, and sat cross-legged with his head hanging over his knees.

The herb fumes made us cough, but they soothed us, just as strong wine sears the throat while comforting the mind. The smoke wrapped us like a blanket, calming our raging humours. I was tired, and wanted to sleep. I could hardly move, and struggled to keep my eyes open. Despite the heat, my feet and hands felt cold. I longed for an English bed, thick-curtained, stuffed with feathers, heaped with well-warmed blankets. The sickbed, where all those savages had sweated, looked inviting. Shapes formed in the smoke, swirling ghostly forms that gathered around me like cats. I thought idly of spirits, and how they can get a grip on a man and steal his soul.

Like François, I slid to the ground.

Rosenkreutz was not affected by the fumes. He stood like a mountain ringed by cloud. The Tome was in his hand, and he said words in the Philosophers' Tongue, but he said them quietly, as though debating with a scholar. The witch listened at first, and looked at the Tome as though she had never seen such a thing before. When she raised her rattle stick and shook it at him, Rosenkreutz faltered. She began to speak, her voice deep and strong. Through the smoke, the skulls round her neck grinned at me. Her voice grew louder, her words more savage, her face more ugly and contorted. I was sure she was possessed, and hoped Rosenkreutz had the power to drive the demon from her. That would impress the savages. But if he failed, and was defeated by her, that would be the end of us.

She stepped forward, her eyes staring, her lips wet with foam. Her words meant nothing to me, but Rosenkreutz flinched as though whipped. His mouth fell open, his shoulders drooped and his face went slack. The helpers danced and jabbered. Were they possessed? Were they the witch's familiars, bound to obey her will? Rosenkreutz recoiled from them, holding up the Tome as a shield. He looked around as though he had lost something. I followed his gaze, and saw his staff lying on the ground. It was only the one I had cut for him, not the original, but it had some power in it, and Rosenkreutz needed it. I tried to get up, but my legs would not support me. I kicked feebly at François. He did not move, though I must have disturbed his sleep.

"The pelican!" he said, his head lolling back. "I see the pelican of Christ. She pricks her breast and feeds her young on blood. It is true! God does watch over us, even here."

I hoped he was right, though getting Rosenkreutz his staff would have been more use than holy visions. I tried again, and managed to stretch out my arm, but before I could reach the staff, one of the helpers stamped on my hand. I yelled and pulled my arm back. The savage kicked the staff into the firepit. It was good dry wood, and it quickly blazed up. Rosenkreutz gasped, and tried to reach for the staff's end, but the savages stopped him. They pulled him back by his arms, making him drop the Tome. Then they pushed him down, and he fell grovelling at the witch's feet.

We were supposed to be a Brotherhood of Three, but Rosenkreutz faced the witch on his own. François could do nothing but babble, and I could hardly move. The witch's words had robbed Rosenkreutz of his power. His staff was burning and the Tome lay useless on the ground. I had to do something.

I took a deep breath of the smoky air. I felt sick and dizzy. Fresh air and cold water were what I needed, but there was nothing but smoke. I took another breath, and tried to get up, but my head reeled and I fell back. I heard François muttering about Our Lady, and Rosenkreutz speaking in tongues, but could see nothing. I may have passed out for a moment.

When I came to myself again I felt something pressing against my hand. I moved my fingers and realised that they were touching the wall. It was made of bark sheets bent over withies. Just outside, if I could reach it, was the cool night air. I scrabbled at the rough bark. I grabbed at withies and shook them. I got to my knees and shuffled towards the wall, falling against it heavily. I punched the bark, but only grazed my knuckles. Angrily, I hoisted myself upright and kicked at the wall. The bark broke, and cold air poured in, but I no longer needed it. I had found my strength again.

When I turned to look at Rosenkreutz, I almost wished that I had not. His deerskin shirt had been hoisted over his head. The witch's helpers were holding him face down on the heap of corn husks and bracken that had been the sickbed. The witch was standing over him, looking down at his bare arse. She held something in her hand that no woman ought to possess.

She had a yard, just like a man. It was as stiff as a bone, as big as any I have seen. And it was quite clear what she was going to do with it.

"No!" I shouted, giving François a great kick.

"What?" he said, waking up.

"Look." I pointed at the witch, who was lowering herself onto Rosenkreutz.

"Holy Mother of God!" François said. "Save me, for this must be Hell."

"Let's save ourselves," I said, throwing myself at the witch.

I knocked her over, and we fell together in the dry bedding, rolling around like pigs in a cornfield. Her hands were at my face, and other hands grabbing my legs and pulling them apart. The witch held my arms and bent them back. I felt her yard pressing against me. Would she take me instead of Rosenkreutz?

I heard a great scream, and two of the hands that gripped me let go. I kicked my free leg, but the witch did not let go. There was another scream, more terrible than the first, then my other leg was free. I jerked my body round, and managed to throw off the witch. When I got free of her I saw that François was coming at her with a flaming brand. It was the staff I had cut for Rosenkreutz, or what was left of it. The two helpers were flapping blindly at their faces. I could smell scorched flesh.

While François held the witch at bay, I helped Rosenkreutz to his feet. He tugged his shirt down, covering himself. I picked up the Tome and gave it to him.

"Now!" I said. "See her off."

Rosenkreutz held the Tome in his hand, but did not know what to do with it. He had been defeated.

The witch, summoning her helpers, advanced. They were burnt and angry. François skipped to my side, still brandishing the staff. He was a backstreet brawler again, thrusting and feinting, leading the savages on, then driving them back. The three of us slowly retreated to the doorway. Then François flung the staff at the witch's feet. The dry bedding burst into flames. We stumbled out into the night.

We led Rosenkreutz slowly away from the town. The ground lay slushy underfoot. The burning house lit the sky behind us. The cold air cleared my mind, but I was confused. I was not sure whether the things I saw that night were real, or whether the herb smoke had made us see things that were not there.

We had not gone far when little groups of savages started to catch us up. They smiled when they saw us, and handed over gifts. Some gave us trinkets, others gave us useful things, such as food for our journey, cloaks to keep us warm at night, stone knives, and deerskin shoes. Some huntsmen gave us bows, with a bundle of arrows and spare strings. They gave me a pouch of stone arrowheads, with resin and sinews to bind them.

By the time the last of those savages left us we were as encumbered as peddlers. But we understood. They did not hate us. The witch had won the battle of the cures. She had proved stronger, so they were obliged to follow her. They could not resist her, any more than they could resist the turn of the year and its seasons. Jago understood that too. He and his crewmen stayed behind, and are there still, for all I know, ruling over those savages with the aid of the witch.

We walked on, silently, though the last of the night.

"I was wrong," Rosenkreutz said, gazing at the slip of sun that nudged above the horizon. "It is not the sunset we should have searched for. It is the dawn. The golden dawn."

It wasn't such a bad idea. The sunset had led us to that savage land. The dawn would lead us home, if we could find a way to follow it.

As Rosenkreutz had broken the silence, I felt able to ask about the things that had been troubling me.

"Did I dream it?" I said. "Or did the witch have a yard like a man?"

"It was no dream," Rosenkreutz said.

His answer raised a lot more questions, but I was reluctant to ask them. Rosenkreutz had been humiliated enough, and we knew how low he could sink when the spirit deserted him.

"I saw it too," François said. "And I saw what she did with it."

"You did?"

I felt Rosenkreutz sag, his bony arm pressing harder on my shoulder.

"Who'd have thought it?" François said. "Sodomites in a place like this! There are plenty of them in Paris, if you know where to look. Men who live as women, and dress like them too. But in a wilderness full of savages . . ."

"The witch is no sodomite. She is a hermaphrodite."

"A hermaphrodite! Strange then that we have seen no giants, pygmies, cyclopes, headless men, or any other monsters."

"We saw what we saw," Rosenkreutz said. "She is half man and half woman."

From what I saw, the witch was all man. I think François was right. The witch was a sodomite, if that is the right word to describe such people when they live among savages. We took him for a woman because of his dress and manner, but once he exposed his nether parts there was no doubt he was a man. Rosenkreutz must have known that as well as we did, but was consoling himself with travellers' tales.

"If the witch was half woman," François said, "why did she defeat you?"

"Because she was twice human."

"How can that be?"

"She is two spirits in one, both male and female. That makes her strong."

"Stronger than you?" François said. "You, who bathed in the Fountain of Eternal Life, and found the spirit within?"

Rosenkreutz did not notice he was being mocked, and I was glad of that, as it was not the time for mockery.

"There is another reason," Rosenkreutz said. "The witch fasted in a frozen wilderness. That made her spirit strong. I feasted and rested in the town, so my spirit is weak."

"Let us hope your strength returns," François said. "We are back in the wilderness now."

Part 3: Return

Aix en Provence

When we got back to Christendom the first thing François did was to get drunk. It was in Bilbao, where our rescuers dumped us. I got drunk too, but not as badly as François. Rosenkreutz sipped some wine and pronounced it good, but was not transformed by it. While we drank, François came up with the idea of seeking out King René and trying to win a place at his court. I think it was the best idea he ever had. Rosenkreutz agreed, and praised the king's wisdom. He had come to himself since his battle with the witch. He no longer raved, or spouted mad theories. And he no longer claimed to be able to read the Tome. If he had stayed mad, I doubt that we would have got home. During our long walk north he became a philosopher again, taking an interest in everything, looking at the Tome, but only to compare its pictures with the birds and beasts we saw. When we stumbled upon the Biscay men it was Rosenkreutz who spoke to them in their own tongue, and persuaded them to give us passage.

After listening to François recalling the good old days among the lords of the Loire, we took out the mappamundi and spread it on the tavern table, adding a few wine stains to its many colours. Sure enough, Aix en Provence, where René held his court, was marked on the map, though the name was a little hard to make out. I took that as a sign that the mappamundi was still leading us.

We set off the next day, with François moaning about the bad Biscay wine that soured his guts and gave him a headache. It was strange to pass through great towns full of well-built houses with churches towering above them, and to walk streets thronged with men and horses. Those streets stank, and were strewn with dung, which made me think that life among the savages, though simple, was not so bad. The same thought struck me when I saw the people, their bodies wrapped in thick encumbering clothes. We wore such clothes ourselves,

287

of course, and shoes. Though we were used to it, we could not go barefoot like savages.

Our journey was paid for by Rosenkreutz, who called at various houses on our way, which went from Navarre to Provence, coming out of each with a little money. How he knew of those houses, and who lived in them, I cannot say, as François and I were obliged to wait for him in some public place while he made his enquiries. Even after all our adventures he did not trust us fully. The coins he got were just like the ones he had spent in England, stamped with signs, symbols and cryptic words. By then I had guessed his secret. The secret was that there was no secret. His coins did not turn back to lead. Rosenkreutz told his story because he wanted to be thought of as a man to whom mere alchemy was a trifle. The coins he spent were the price he paid for his reputation, and in any case he showed more than he spent, and a little gold goes a long way when you live as we did. Even in Ipswich, it was the prospect of wealth, rather than actual gold that persuaded everyone to join our voyage. Rosenkreutz was a clever man, but not in the way we first thought. He had the power of making men do his will, and of transforming men's minds, which are softer than any metal.

At Aix we presented ourselves at King René's palace, and were allowed into his audience chamber, where he sat on a well-padded throne, plump and pink, dressed in bright brocade, as flat and stiff as a king painted on a playing card. The audience was almost over. Some of the petitioners were huddled by the doors, their faces telling us the results of their pleas. We were the last to be called forward, and King René looked bored.

François cut an odd figure in that gentle company. Short, ugly and crooked, his courtly gestures came out as clumsy capering. Yet he held the king's attention, making one of his prettiest, noblest speeches. He praised the king's learning and love of scholarship, and his hospitality, then he told something of our adventures, and the low state we had fallen into because of our pursuit of knowledge. Having studied the chamber's rich Arras hangings while we waited, he described Wineland as a Paradise, green and fertile, and full of heraldic beasts, all as tame as sheep. He did not forget to mention the king's own emblem, the porcupine. Then, pointing out that no other Christian princes knew of the place, he told the king that we had claimed Wineland for him, and that with a few ships and a small army he could make it his own.

"If this Wincland is so far away," King René said, "and so unfrequented by Christians, how did you get back?"

"Your Majesty, we walked for months through a great wilderness. It was not a land of plenty like Wineland. On the contrary, it was an immense wild wood, cast into eternal gloom by gigantic trees, inhabited only by fierce creatures and wretched people. We cured the sick, using strictly philosophical methods. We battled with wizards and wild beasts, but made good our escape. Some of our party wished to dally with savage women, but I led them from temptation. By then we had learned to live like savages. We knew something of their language, and were able to trade with them. We travelled like them, on foot, swiftly and silently through the great wilderness. We hunted like them, with bows and traps. And we slept like them, under shelters of leaves and boughs. Even so, despite our woodcraft, we often starved. We had to ford innumerable rivers, and cross endless swamps. Eventually, after unimaginable hardships, we reached Cape Cattigara, which, as Your Majesty will know, is the furthest point of Asia."

"Your return," King René said. "How did you manage it?"

"I will not try Your Majesty's patience by recounting how we travelled by skin boat, beyond the cape, from island to island. Our sufferings may easily be imagined by anyone who has gone to sea in a small boat. We hoped the islands might lead us back across the Ocean like stepping-stones across a shallow stream. Some cosmographers aver that such a thing is possible. But before we had got far, we discovered something remarkable. On one of the islands was a settlement of Christians."

"You said there were none," the king said.

"No Christians know of Wineland. Nor do they know of the great wilderness to the north of that green and gentle place. We only encountered Christians at the end of our travels, on a rocky island girt by treacherous tides."

I had to admire François. Throughout our long walk north, he did nothing but moan. He left all the hunting to others, but always ate more than his fair share. Only Rosenkreutz learned anything of the savages' tongue, and then not much. François could see no good in them, even when they gave us food or ferried us across rivers. When we reached the cape, he described it as the uttermost arsehole of nowhere, and the islands as stinking turds dangling out of it. Yet, telling of it to King René, François made our journey sound like something from an old romance, with him as the questing knight, and me and Rosenkreutz as his unreliable companions. All it needed was a scattering of anthropophagi, lycanthropes and cynocephalae, to make it as good as the tales of Marco Polo and Mandeville.

"This island," François said, "though barren, was a remarkable place. It stank so abominably of rotting fish, and was so badly infested with wheeling, mewing seabirds, that we supposed it enchanted, and feared another encounter with the forces of evil. The birds swarmed so thickly that they darkened the sky. They swooped like harpies, grabbing and befouling everything, but we mustered all our courage and struggled on. Imagine our surprise when we reached the other side and saw a great fleet of ships. Not only that! There were poles pitched all over the shore, ropes strung between them, with split cod hung from every rope, drying in the wind. And, working among all the ships and birds and fish, were men like us."

King René leaned forward, easing himself off his hard throne, looking interested. "What nation did they come from? And where, exactly, is this fishery?"

"Alas, Your Majesty, on those points we were sworn to secrecy. The fishermen were afraid that if anyone learned of their fishing grounds and sailing routes, the Hanseatic League would send a fleet and supplant them. If they did, their monopoly would be complete. I am sure Your Majesty would not wish the price of stockfish to rise any higher."

The king smiled very slightly.

"I can reveal one thing," François said. "The fishermen held a parliament and debated the virtues of helping us. Some said we should pay them, and demanded the treasures they said we must have gathered on our travels. We were able to show them that we had no gold or silver, and persuaded them that it was their Christian duty to carry us home. However, I must confess that we were not entirely honest with our rescuers. We did have a treasure, a very great one, which we have preserved and brought here as a gift to Your Majesty."

François beckoned me and I delved into the papal bag, drawing out the mappamundi with a flourish. Two of René's attendants stepped forward to receive the gift, but when they saw it they hesitated.

"It is a mappamundi, Your Majesty. Commissioned by the late Pope Pius, drawn up on mathematical principles by the great scholar Paolo Toscanelli, painted on fine silk by the best craftsmen in Florence."

The attendants looked more hopeful, and took the map and showed it to their king. His face fell. "It is a filthy rag," he said.

He was right. It was no longer the treasure I had once spread out before the pope, that had so gripped him that it brought on his final fever. The silk was creased, holed and ragged. The colours were dull. The seas, cities, rivers and mountains were obscured by nameless stains. All the power had gone out of it, as though, exhausted by guiding us, it had died.

François did not falter. "Oh no, Your Majesty. It may look like a filthy rag to the uninitiated. But to the wise, it is much more than that. His late Holiness would have used it to guide his crusade, had God spared him. But the wise Florentines who drew it up included far more than was needed for even that most noble of tasks. It shows each and every country of the world, laid out in its proper position, with lines of navigation set out most cunningly. With the knowledge contained in this map, Your Majesty will easily be able to make Wineland your own."

The king slumped slightly, so that his fat neck rolled over his fur collar.

"Perhaps the cloth is a little travel-stained." François sounded less confident. His wheedling tone returned. "It might be cleaned, restored . . ."

René waved away the attendants, who took the mappamundi, holding it gingerly by its corners. Then he looked around the room to see if there were any more petitioners. Seeing that there were none, he looked down at François and announced loftily that he would make good his claim on Jerusalem before declaring himself King of Wineland. I didn't know he had a claim on Jerusalem, but someone explained it to me afterwards, and the Holy City goes with Sicily and Naples, which René was king of but did not rule. It was not good news. We all know that Jerusalem is held by the Mamelukes, and the only person likely to take it away from them is the Sultan of Turkey.

François' scheme had failed.

Attendants advanced on us, ready to usher us out of the doors with the other petitioners.

We looked at each other. François had done his best. What could the rest of us offer?

Rosenkreutz fumbled in his sleeve, and for a moment I feared he would try the coin trick. He changed his mind and touched the emblem that hung at his neck, the little rosy cross. Then he gripped his staff as though he intended to summon the wind with it.

King René was running out of patience. His attendants were closing in.

I reached into the bag again and took out the Tome. Rosenkreutz looked dismayed, but I ignored him. I discovered the Tome, not him. I had as much right to give it away as he had to keep it.

"Your Majesty," I said, offering him the book. The attendants rushed forward to prevent any actual contact between king and petitioner. "It is a book, found in England, written by a great English scholar. It contains in it everything known to man."

King René no longer looked bored. His attendants took the Tome and showed it to him. On the outside, it was no more impressive than the mappamundi. It had travelled a long way since we took it, and the cover was as stained and battered as a pilgrim's prayer book. Some of the pages were ready to fall out, others were dog-eared, crumpled, smudged, or so badly rubbed that the writing was faint. The colour had ebbed from some of the pictures, dulling their mystery. Despite that, the king took the book in his own hands, and looked at the pages. He frowned at the pictures and peered doubtfully at the text. François and I looked at each other anxiously, remembering the doubts we had had, the times he had dismissed the book as the ravings of a madman.

Then Rosenkreutz, seeing the way things were going, decided to speak. He told King René that the Tome was written by the great sage Roger Bacon, and that he, Rosenkreutz, having made a few false starts, was well on the way to understanding it. He prattled on, dropping bits of Greek and Hebrew into his speech, and bits of what he said was the Philosophers' Tongue, in which the Tome was written. He promised the king that, if given a place at court, he would work ceaselessly to translate the Tome, write commentaries on it, and reveal its secret knowledge.

Eventually, when Rosenkreutz stopped talking, King René smiled.

"Welcome to my court," he said, looking not at us, but at the Tome. "A special place will be found for this book in my library. And you, Christian Rosenkreutz, will also have a place there."

The king nodded, and a liveried officer took Rosenkreutz's arm, and escorted him through a small doorway near the throne.

All the other petitioners had gone. François and I were left alone. Had we followed Rosenkreutz halfway round the world, then led him back again, only to be abandoned?

King René looked up from the Tome and saw us waiting. "You, too," he said. "I daresay you will be of some use, assisting Rosenkreutz, or something." Then he turned the Tome sideways and unfolded one of its double pages, staring silently at the strange things it showed.

Rosenkreutz pretends not to notice that we live in a palace. He has the run of René's library, which even he admits is full of well-chosen books. He labours at translating the Tome, which he now claims is written in a cipher which can be broken by mathematical means, but will not show anyone the results. He says that Paradise lies inside the world, which is a hollow shell. We would have found its entrance and descended into it, had we gone a little further west.

The trouble with Rosenkreutz is that his ideas do not fit together. He is like a mason trying to build a wall without first squaring up his stones. Fortunately, it does not matter how often his wall of ideas falls down. King René is patient, and I am in no hurry to move on.

François seldom speaks of the lands we went to, except to curse it as the Land of Shit. He spends his time making up poems, but not of his old sort. There's nothing of tarts and taverns or thieves and drunkards. His verse now is pious, and begs Our Lord for forgiveness and a place in Heaven.

Somewhere on my travels I left God behind. It might have been the night in Wineland when François reminded me that we had broken all the Commandments. The old-clothes man I dealt with in Turin told me that the Christians had been sold their faith by Saint Peter, who he called the greatest merchant of them all. Some say that the garment makes the man, so it may be that I lost my faith when I cast off my Christian clothes and dressed like a savage. Perhaps I saw through religion, and all its promises, when I lived in the Vatican. After that, I couldn't swallow it any more, just as François would not eat eels after seeing them killed and gutted, and smelling the blood and slime that fouled the eelsheds' floors. If so, it was not until I lived among the savages that I understood what I had learned. In truth, I never had much to do with God, though I used to fear being punished for my sins. Now I know that this world, with its wars and plagues, crimes and follies, filthiness and imperfection, is all we have. So we had better make the best of it, and not put everything off in the hope of some future reward. All of us, Christian and Moslem, schismatics and heretics, make the same mistake. Now that I know better, I intend to avoid it. I will live my life as well as I can, in the present, not the future.

Life is good here at Aix. King René provides the three of us with pensions. How things have changed! More than forty years ago I was in the English army besieging Orléans when René rode with the French army that broke the siege. I was only a boy then, and he was a young man bewitched by Joan the peasant girl. But René is old-fashioned and believes in chivalry, and in forgiving your enemies, even though that sort of thing ended in my father's day when they slaughtered the French nobles at Agincourt.

René has so much forgotten those times that he has made me a knight, which my father never was. There is no land with the title, but that is fitting, as there is no land with most of René's titles. None of his duchies and kingdoms is left to him. All are ruled by others, except for Provence.

The king of France grows stronger, and his vassals grow weaker. Impoverished lords from France and Italy, rebels from Naples and Aragon, and adventurers from all over Christendom, flock to Aix. Some of René's officers like to listen to my tales of voyages and strange lands. Their attention is flattering, even though I know that most of them don't really believe me. One of René's men, a young sailor from Genoa, takes my stories seriously. He is a handsome redheaded fellow called Cristoforo Colombo. He stays after the others, asks more questions, and even makes notes. I think he will go far.

Whether or not René really thinks he can win Jerusalem, he keeps up his campaign against the Aragonese who dispossessed him of Naples, and he sends his ships to battle the pirates of the Barbary Coast. For a dreamer, he is not powerless, but the men he gathers round him are no more reliable than those who promised to join the last crusade of Pope Pius. René buys help by giving men high titles, making them members of his various Orders. He has an Order of the Crescent, an Order of Faith, an Order of the Ship, and some others, founded on a whim and soon forgotten. Rosenkreutz suggested an Order of the Golden Dawn, which was to be reserved for seekers of secret knowledge, but René, though keen on such knowledge, was keener on military pomp, and could not see the point in lavishing robes and ceremonies on men whose work was done in private and could not be revealed. Rosenkreutz says the order exists anyway, that it was founded by his efforts and will flourish without ceremony wherever men seek the truth. He hints that François and I are members of it, but only of the lowest grade, like lay brothers in a monastery. He also says that he will seem to die in a few years time, and that what appears to be his body will be taken to a secret tomb already prepared for him in a mountain fastness. There he will sleep until his time comes again, and a new Order is ready to hear his wisdom.

I will believe it when I see it.

Thomas Deerham,
Aix-en-Provence, 1474

Recommended Reading

If you enjoyed reading *Mappamundi* there are three other historical novels by Christopher Harris which should appeal to you:

False Ambassador
Memoirs of a Byzantine Eunuch
Theodore

For further information about Christopher Harris please visit his website www.christopher-harris.co.uk

Other quirky and unusual historical novels on our list, which you might like to read, are:

The Man in Flames – Serge Filippini
The Arabian Nightmare – Robert Irwin
The Prayer-Cushions of the Flesh – Robert Irwin
The Father of Locks – Andrew Killeen
Memoirs of a Gnostic Dwarf – David Madsen
The Angel of the West Window – Gustav Meyrink

These can be bought from your local bookshop or online from amazon.co.uk or direct from Dedalus, either online or by post. Please write to **Cash Sales, Dedalus Limited, 24–26, St Judith's Lane, Sawtry, Cambs, PE28 5XE**. For further details of the Dedalus list please go to our website www.dedalusbooks.com or write to us for a catalogue.

Theodore – **Christopher Harris**

"Theodore of Tarsus – who became Archbishop of Canterbury in 668 – was a significant figure in ecclesiastical history, and his story is told in this well researched first-person novel what follows is an interesting account of the homosexual saint's life during strange and turbulent times."

Andrew Crumey in Scotland on Sunday

"It portrays the young Theodore as curious, sensual and very human, anxious to understand what exactly constitutes enlightenment, assailed by religious doubts and constantly at odds with the frequent irrational beliefs of the religious men surrounding him. The greatest strength of Harris' novel is the clear and simple presentation of its often complex moral ideas. Ultimately, this is a novel of curious decency, simply and movingly written by a first-time author of real promise."

Christopher Fowler in the Independent on Sunday

"At its heart, however, *Theodore* is a beautiful and poignant love story, examining the passion between twin souls – a love too intense to remain chaste. The author challenges us to consider that while Christianity owes a lot to such love, it will never acknowledge the debt."

Murrough O'Brien in The Daily Telegraph

£8.99   **ISBN 978 1 873982 49 5**   340p   **B. Format**

False Ambassador – **Christopher Harris**

"Beginning in 1428, this swashbuckling romp recreates a brutal medieval world on the cusp of civilisation. Despite his scholarly inclination, 15-year-old Thomas Deerham is sent by his father to be a soldier with the English Army. Our hero's adventures take us from savage encounters in France to Rome via Constantinople, with much murder, rape and pillaging along the way."

Lisa Allardice in The Independent on Sunday

"Set in Renaissance Europe, this entertaining novel tells the story of Thomas, a young soldier in the English army. After deciding to desert, he falls in with a gang of ruthless mercenaries, endures hideous privations, is enslaved and escapes the fall of Constantinople before ending up in Rome."

Angus Clarke in The Times

"Another fine historical tale from the author of *Theodore* . This time he takes us on a journey through the bloody savagery and the no-less-bloody nobility of fifteenth century Europe in a welter of mishap, mayhem and debauchery. An absorbing read that delights and disturbs in equal measure."

Sebastian Beaumont in Gay Times

£8.99   **ISBN 978 1 903517 00 0**   303p   **B. Format**

Memoirs of a Byzantine Eunuch – Christopher Harris

"Harris while writing a good yarn also treats us to the clear presentation of the ideas of Aristotle, Plato and long-forgotten philosophers combined with observations about the development of Christian orthodoxy and the exotic nature of the castrated, or eunuchs."

Ivan Willis in What's on in London

"Zeno, living in ninth-century Byzantium, has had a rough time of it. Taken from his native town and castrated by Norse pirates, he finds himself stranded by them in a tavern in the suburbs of Constantinople. Then, unsuspecting, he is swept off by the greatest missionary of the age to serve its greatest scholar, St Photius the Great. Though his social status rises, his problems multiply: he must help his new master in his ambitions, seek out depravities for Michael III, and guards his adopted sister Eudocia. He fails, of course, as he is dragged ever deeper into the eerie world of the palace eunuchs, the real rulers of the empire."

Murrough O'Brien in The Independent on Sunday

"If there is such a thing an archetypal Dedalus novel, the this is surely it. Here is a book that has the decadent ambience, well-researched historical background and racy literary style that this small (but perfectly formed) publishing house is getting a deserved name for. Harris paints a very convincing picture of a place and time not often portrayed in fiction and having Zeno as a narrator made it all seem more immediate. If you are looking for something a bit different, or just a jolly good read, I can recommend this one."

Rachel A. Hyde in The Historical Novel Review

£9.99   ISBN 1 903517 03 1   358p   B. Format